NEITHER FIVE NOR THREE

HELEN MACINNES, whom the *Sunday Express* calls 'the queen of spy writers', is the author of fifteen distinguished suspense novels.

Born in Scotland, she studied at the University of Glasgow and University College, London, then went to Oxford after her marriage to Gilbert Highet, the eminent critic and educator. In 1937 the Highets went to New York, and except during her husband's war service Helen MacInnes has lived there ever since.

Since her first novel *Above Suspicion* was published in 1941 to immediate success, all her novels have been bestsellers; *The Salzburg Connection* was also a major film. Her latest novel, *Prelude to Terror*, has been a top seller in both Britain and America.

HELEN MACINNES

Neither Five nor Three

To think that two and two are four
And neither five nor three
The heart of man has long been sore
And long 'tis like to be
A. E. HOUSMAN, *Last Poems*, XXXV

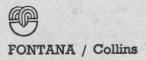

FONTANA / Collins

First published in 1951 by William Collins Sons and Co Ltd
First issued in Fontana Books 1969
Ninth Impression April 1979

© 1951 by Helen Highet

Made and printed in Great Britain by
William Collins Sons & Co Ltd Glasgow

To Naomi with love

All characters in this novel are entirely fictitious,
and no reference is intended to any actual person,
whether living or dead

The lines reprinted on the title page are from
"When first my way to fair I took" from *The
Collected Poems of A. E. Housman*, reprinted by
permission of The Society of Authors and
Jonathan Cape Ltd, London

I. Thesis

CHAPTER ONE

The dawn came slowly, cold and clear, thinning out the night sky.

It's coming slowly, Paul Haydn thought, because we are running ahead of the sun. Then he smiled at his fancy as he looked down at the floor of clouds below him. He watched them change from blanched shapeless ghosts into a foaming sea of sun-streaked waves, their curling crests held motionless, poised but never spent. A traveller, fifty years from now, hurtling through the skies, would find that dawns came even more slowly for planes flying westwards. Or would he be travelling in a plane, fifty years from now? Then suddenly, Paul Haydn noticed that the clouds were no longer a sea beneath him, hiding the real ocean. We're coming down, he thought, at last we are getting near land, we're getting near America. Yes, there was a stretch of the Atlantic, a dark grey sheet of corrugated iron. He sat up abruptly, stretched his back muscles and his legs.

His excitement, controlled as he tried to keep it, woke Brownlee sitting beside him. The other passengers in the plane—the two congressmen and their secretaries and the brigadier-general who had accompanied them from Berlin, the silent worried sergeant who had joined the plane at Frankfurt, the three E.C.A. officials returning from the Rhine-

5

land—were still slumped in sleep, their faces wiped clean of expression, their troubles, their hopes, their failures, their achievements all forgotten.

"Won't be long now," Paul said to Brownlee by way of apology. His smile made him younger, more like the Paul Haydn whom Brownlee had first met in London eight years ago.

Brownlee, still not moving, still gathering all the parts of his mind together that sleep had unlocked and left lying loosely around, answered Paul's smile slowly. He yawned, stretched his arms, eased the muscles on his neck, and rubbed the blood back into his cheek where, as he had slept, it had rested too heavily against the eagle on his shoulder. He said, his smile broadening, "For a man who stayed away so long, you sound pretty eager to return."

"I guess I've been away long enough," Paul Haydn said. Then his grey eyes looked sharply at his friend. "And what's amusing you?"

"The difference that eight years can make in a man."

"Don't know if I think that's altogether funny."

"You wouldn't be altogether pleased if eight years left no differences." Brownlee studied Paul's face. "When we first met in London in 1942, you were a very new lieutenant in a very smart uniform, an enthusiastic young crusader——"

"On the brash side," Paul amended. He shook his head as he remembered himself then. "At least," he added, "I've learned that life is not all that easy." Besides, his watchful eyes seemed to say, I'm not the only one who has changed a lot in eight years. Brownlee was thinner and more worried, his hair was almost white now; and yet, since the war had ended, he had been stationed in Washington, not in Germany as Paul had been. When Paul met him in Berlin only a couple of days ago (Brownlee had been taking the congressmen around the D.P. camps), Paul was as much surprised by the outward changes in Brownlee as he was by their meeting. A lucky meeting, though. If it hadn't been for Brownlee, he wouldn't have had this quick transportation home. And a good meeting, too. He liked Brownlee, even if Brownlee had been his superior officer all through the war.

"Yes, life seemed easier eight years ago," Brownlee was saying. "In spite of everything, it seemed easier. All we had

6

to do was to win that damned war, and then—if we were lucky—slip back into peace. Everything was more black and white, then. You knew where the dangers lay."

Paul Haydn only nodded. He was glad of the stir around them as the others in the plane were wakened and warned of the landing ahead. He wasn't going to get entangled in any more discussions. Brownlee was still very skilful at steering the conversation his way.

Brownlee seemed to be concentrating on fastening his safety belt, too. But he was still remembering Paul Haydn in London, eight years ago, excited about his assignment to the Free French and his work with the underground resistance in Brittany. He had done well in that job, including some extremely active service inside Occupied France. After the Liberation, Brownlee had lost immediate touch with Haydn, but he had kept track of him. Captain in Intelligence, examining German prisoners. Then Frankfurt. Assigned to counter-propaganda. Munich. D.P. camps. Berlin. And the young, smartly uniformed lieutenant with the friendly grey eyes, the disarming smile, the dark close-cropped hair, and the features which had been so regular that they were almost characterless, had become a major with some faded ribbons on his chest. His smile wasn't so ready, now. The dark hair showed some grey at the temples. The regular features had lost their pleasant anonymity and gained a determined, capable look. Now, too, his eyes were watchful; more serious, less amused by life; less expectant of good, and yet—with Paul's essential optimism that even Europe hadn't altogether withered—still hopeful of finding it.

"Why did you stay away so long?" Brownlee asked suddenly.

"Never could get transport."

Brownlee grinned. "You always had a surprising sense of duty, I remember."

"What's so surprising about it?"

"Because you never seemed particularly respectful about anything."

"I agreed I was a brash young man," Paul admitted with a smile.

"With the right impulses," Brownlee said. "And I'm still betting on them." His tone was light, but his alert brown

7

eyes were serious. "Given any thought to the proposition I made at lunch yesterday?"

Paul Haydn hesitated. "Not too much," he said frankly. "You weren't specific enough, I guess."

"I couldn't be. You've got to see this thing for yourself, Paul. I'm not a draft board, you know. I want volunteers."

"Look, I've done enough volunteering. When I'm finished with the army, I'm finished. I've had enough duty to last me the rest of my life." His face was once more determined, guarded. He turned his head away and looked out of the window.

"This isn't an army job," Brownlee said patiently. "Once you've had your leave, run around, settled down and started your career again, come and have a chat with me. By that time, either you'll know what I've been talking about, or you won't care. That's when you can give me a definite answer."

"I'm giving it to you now. Sorry, but I'm—look! There she is! Look—will you look at that?" Paul grabbed Roger Brownlee's arm as if to make sure that he wouldn't miss this, either.

It was New York, its clear-cut buildings squared and neat, its towers and pinnacles gleaming in the early sunlight, its silent streets running like straight dark threads below the myriad shining windows. It was New York, cool, remote, beautiful.

"We're coming in too low," Brownlee said, glancing worriedly at his brigadier-general and the congressmen.

"Suits me," Paul said. He didn't take his eyes away from the window. He said nothing more.

Brownlee took his notebook and pencil out of his pocket and wrote quickly. "Tuck this in your pocket," he said to Haydn. "It's my telephone number." He tore the page from his notebook and held it out.

"At the Pentagon?" That seemed unnecessary, Paul thought.

"No. At my own office. I'm becoming a civilian, too."

Paul Haydn stared.

Brownlee said, nodding in the direction of the congressmen, "This is my last job in uniform."

"But——" began Paul, and then stopped. You didn't ask Brownlee questions.

"Because the job I want to do now is better done as a civilian," Brownlee said quietly.

"But your seniority, your——" Paul stopped again. If Roger Brownlee was giving that all up, then he was really worried. Paul looked at him, and buttoned the slip of paper safely into his tunic pocket. Then, like everyone else in the plane, he concentrated on the landing for the next minute or two.

"Reporters," Brownlee said, looking out of the window as he unstrapped his safety belt. "Time I was joining my congressmen, again. Did I tell you they were very upset about the hordes of new D.P.'s all streaming into our Zone?" He was smiling wryly.

"About time someone was getting upset," Paul answered grimly. Then, as he rose to follow Brownlee who had become very much the capable colonel again, he told himself to forget it, he had had enough of being harrowed and harried, now he was going to cut himself a slice of peace. He was five years behind most of his friends, but he'd still hack himself a good slice. There was plenty to go around.

He stopped beside the sergeant. "Are you going straight to the hospital? I'll give you a lift."

"The colonel said he'd take care of me, sir," the sergeant replied. Normally, he would have a cheerful pugnacious look on that square face with its wide mouth. But now, worried by the news of his wife's illness, he was grim and sullen.

"The colonel may be held back by the reporters. I'll give you a lift."

The sergeant picked up his kit and followed Paul. "Her mother wrote," he began to explain, if only to talk out his troubles, "she said there might be a chance if the wife could see me."

"Then the sooner the better."

"Yes, sir." He looked patiently at the congressmen still asking last questions of the brigadier-general, while the secretaries recounted the bulging suitcases. The E.C.A. men were talking politely if condescendingly to the colonel, who after all had only a military mind. Paul Haydn managed to catch Brownlee's eye, and he nodded towards the sergeant. Brownlee understood quickly enough. He was that kind of man, Paul thought, as he watched Brownlee speak quietly to the general. In a few minutes, the plane's exit was clear. The civilians were somehow persuaded not to be photographed from the gangplank, not to pose there while they made their statements to the Press. They were grouped together on the lower eminence of solid ground, and the sergeant and Paul had a free path before them.

Yes, Brownlee was that kind of man, Paul thought as he stepped out of the plane. He gave his last official salute, colonel sir, and caught an answering smile in Roger Brownlee's eyes.

As he fell into step with the sergeant away from the plane and the little groups of V.I.P.s being photographed, toward the long line of buildings with their stretches of smooth concrete and shining glass, he was still thinking about Brownlee and what he had said yesterday in Berlin. Odd that Brownlee should go off on such a tangent as that. . . . Then Paul remembered these were not the thoughts he had intended to land with. As he left the plane, as he reached good American ground, he was going to have said, "Well, there's the last of Europe. Here's where I begin my own life again. Here is where I find peace." But like most dramatic speeches, it had been left unsaid. Because of Brownlee . . .

A reporter caught up with them. "And how's Berlin?" he asked.

"Ask them," Paul Haydn said with a grin and nodded back towards the plane. "We're just a couple of guys who hitched a ride."

"No story?" The reporter, young, eager, stared at them in disappointment. He had been sure that there was a good story somewhere, when a brigadier-general had got off a plane so hurriedly to let a sergeant and a major get out.

The sergeant shifted the weight of his kit. "No story, Jack," he said decidedly.

"He'll go far," Paul said, looking after the reporter, "as soon as he learns to play his hunches." Then he looked at the sergeant in consternation. "He's only a kid—why, he's a good ten years younger than we are!" A new stage in my life, he thought wryly. He began looking at the men who were polishing the glass and steel doors, at the men inside the hallways and waiting rooms, at the men behind the information desks. In this new discovery, he almost forgot to look at the girls. That would have been indeed a sign that to be thirty-three was practically verging on dotage.

"How about a sandwich and some real American coffee?" he asked the sergeant. And the man, forgetting his nagging worry for a moment as he looked round the enormous building alive even at this early hour with people, his own people, smiled.

"Sounds good to me, sir," he said.

"Yes," Paul said, listening to the voices around him. "Everything sounds good." He smiled, too.

Rona Metford had been sleeping lightly because she had warned herself, last night, that to-day was a day for rising early, a day for a rigid timetable. The plane, flying so low over Manhattan, wakened her completely. She looked at the small clock beside her bed. "Oh, no!" she said. It was five o'clock in the morning.

"There should be a law," she told the plane's roar angrily as it receded to leave peace and sleeplessness. Then she remembered there was a law; so she thought bitterly of the pilot, instead.

But her annoyance didn't last long. Her mind was too full of to-day's plans. She lay in bed, stretching comfortably, enjoying its warmth and softness. Outside the blankets, the little room was cool and fresh, partly because of its green curtains against white walls, partly because the early April air had still a sharp edge to it—last week, there had been snow. She could tell from the bright colour of the gently moving curtains that this morning was sunny and clear-skyed. (On grey threatening mornings, their green was cold and lifeless.) That cheered her. At least, her guests wouldn't arrive for the party to-night with rubbers and heavy coats to jam the tiny hall or with dripping umbrellas to fill the small bathroom.

"Oh, I hope it goes well!" she said to the ceiling. Then she sat up in bed and she looked at Scott's photograph on the dressing-table. Of course it would go well. She blew him a kiss and pulled the green ribbon off her hair. Last night, she remembered with a smile, last night had been a good night. . . . She looked down at her left hand and its engagement

11

ring. Yes, all her recent worries had been pointless. Last night, everything had been normal again, everything had been happy and gay and all the fears of last month had become so many silly shadows. Scott had told her he loved her, in a hundred ways he had told her. She knew just by the way he had looked at her, had talked for her and laughed with her, even by the way he had fallen silent as he watched her. She was the loveliest girl in the whole place, he had said at the theatre. She was the most wonderful girl, he had said as they danced. She was his girl, he had said afterward.

He does love me, after all he does love me, she thought as she hugged her bare shoulders suddenly: I am the luckiest girl in all New York. And she slipped out of bed to run and open the curtains and welcome a new day. Then she turned to the dressing-table to brush her dark hair—it was too long, now, but Scott wouldn't let her cut it. Her large brown eyes, emphasised by well-shaped brows and black eyelashes, laughed at her in the mirror. What did Scott say last night about the curve of the lashes, and the curve of her cheek?— Enough, she told herself, or you'll end by thinking you are Récamier. What sweet nonsense Scott could talk! But as she looked at herself, critically now, she found she was vain enough to be glad that her hips and breasts curved as they did from her slender waist. And she laughed again, and kissed the photograph.

The alarm sounded its warning. Enough, enough, she told herself again, and slipping a dressing-gown around her she ran to the kitchenette to start the coffee. Her quick shower made her still more practical. I'll get to the office early this morning, she thought as she dressed, and I'll clear that desk of mine so completely that Burnett will give me permission to leave early and I can be back here by five o'clock. The guests were arriving at six. Scott would come before then, of course. He was the host, to-night. She gave a last look at the photograph, at the rather solemn face which didn't do Scott justice—he wasn't so cold and intent as the camera pretended he was. His face was much more gentle than that. In fact, the usual adjective that women used for him was "sweet"; that was the gruesome effect that his charm and his smile combined with his height, fair hair, and blue eyes had on them. But what I like most of all, Rona decided as she

12

pulled the blanket and sheets off the narrow bed, is the way he pays no attention to any of them. In the beginning, when she had first met Scott, he hadn't wanted to pay much attention to her either. But he did, all the same. She was smiling as she hurried to the kitchenette to stop the kettle whistling itself hoarse.

After breakfast, there was the usual tidying of the two small rooms which Rona called "my apartment" so proudly. (Mrs. Kasprowicz was coming in later, to clean and polish for three hours. At a dollar an hour, Rona could only afford her twice a week.) It was a simple apartment—the top floor of a brownstone house that had been converted into small flats—but everything it contained was Rona's: Rona's work, Rona's ideas. This is something I've produced, she thought as she stood looking at the living-room. And then she wondered, as she did at least once each day, where Scott and she would live, and when. Perhaps by this summer, he would feel he had saved enough money. Last night, she thought wryly, had been no help to his budget, but what could she have done? Remonstrate gently? And risk making him angry, risk spoiling the evening? He didn't like nagging women or interference. He liked to enjoy his impulses, even if they cost forty dollars.

She had started worrying again. So she picked up a pencil and found a shopping pad and gave herself some practical worries to think about. She must order crackers, cheese. Flowers. Smoked salmon, olives, lemons, nuts. Liver pâté from the delicatessen on Third Avenue. Soda water. Scotch for Scott's father, certainly. Perhaps some of the other men preferred that too. Martinis for the others. Cigarettes, she had nearly forgotten cigarettes. What else?

She must take her party shoes to the cobbler to get the ankle strap fixed. And remind the cleaner to deliver her silk suit by five-thirty. What else, what else? A note for Mrs. Kasprowicz, printed carefully so that there would be no mistakes, about the glasses to be washed and polished. Oh, and ice . . . she must order extra ice.

Then, with a last quick look around her, she went into the small hall. On the telephone table, near the door, she left the instructions for Mrs. Kasprowicz. She glanced in the mirror that hung over the table, readjusted the angle of her neat white sailor hat and tucked away a stray end of the heavy-meshed veil fitting closely over her face. She pulled on her freshly washed white gloves which matched the piqué waistcoat she wore with her grey wool suit, checked the seams of her stockings, and opened the door. The morning paper was lying at the threshold, in time for an eight o'clock breakfast. She lifted it, decided not to take it with her, and glanced at the headlines. The navy plane was still missing in the Baltic: ten young men who would never come back to their families. . . . New York reservoirs were still low. . . . Further investigations in Washington. . . . The case of Dr. Fuchs was still going on, even if it was over. . . . A Communist demonstration in New York against the President of Chile. . . . Nazi trouble rising once more in Hamburg: desecration of graves.

As she laid the paper with a frown on the hall table, the phone rang. I'll be late, she warned herself, but she lifted the telephone. She was hoping it wouldn't be Peggy, her sister, calling to say that she and Jon couldn't come to the party because the baby was sick or they couldn't get a sitter. But it was Scott's voice that answered her. "Hello, darling," he began. And she forgot all her worries, public and private.

Scott Ettley had been wakened at five o'clock, too. His apartment, only a few blocks away from Rona's, lay almost underneath the incoming plane. He listened for engine trouble, and then—reassured that he wasn't going to be killed in his bed with the biggest hangover he had had in weeks—he cursed the pilot as heartily as his splitting head would let him. He made out the time with some difficulty on his watch. Oh, God! . . . He stared angrily at the darkened room, at the litter of living—the scattered clothes, the misplaced books, the tailored cover of the divan which he had ripped off last night, no, it was this morning, and left lying beside his shirt on the floor. He pushed an overflowing ash tray farther away from his nose, and then pulled the sheet over his head as if to blot out all the joys of a bachelor apartment.

Waking is always hell, he thought. Or I'm getting old. Twenty-nine. I can't take night-club air and the great indoor spaces any more. Twenty-nine, and already giving up the simple pleasures of the poor. Forty bucks, that was what simple pleasures cost nowadays. Forty little bucks. But Rona had enjoyed it. Made up to her for the quarrel last week. My fault, of course. She never says it, but she might as well. I know it was all my damned fault. And why am I admitting it now, anyway? Just to add the final touch of joy on a lousy morning at five o'clock and sleep all gone and this head spinning like an empty boat in a whirlpool? He groaned in pity, and lay with his eyes closed. Because he was so sure that sleep had gone, it came drifting back.

When the alarm went off, it was ten minutes to eight. He felt slightly better. But waking, he told himself again, was always hell. Slowly, he sat up. He stayed sitting on the edge of his bed, looking down at his crumpled pyjama legs. Then he groped for his slippers, couldn't find them, and padded into the bathroom on his bare feet. His reflection in the mirror made him feel worse, but a cold shower pulled him half-back into life. He remembered then that he must call Rona.

"Hello, darling," he began, and listening to her voice he began thinking of her as she had been last night. "Hello, beautiful . . . did you enjoy it? . . . Did I? It was the best evening we've had in a long time. Let's have some more. To hell with the cost, Rona. Are we living, or are we living?" He listened to her laugh, and wished he could manage one like that at this hour. "Honey," he said, "by the way—I can't meet you for lunch to-day. Sorry, got to go out of town. . . . No, I'll be back in time for the party. Don't worry. Sorry about lunch, though. . . . I meant to tell you last night, but I was enjoying myself too much, I guess. Forgive me, darling?"

He replaced the receiver. He was smiling now. Rona was pretty wonderful. In spite of Orpen's sneers about man-traps, Rona was wonderful. But the smile left Scott Ettley's face as he thought of Nicholas Orpen, of Rona, of his father, of all the complications in his life. All that was enough to drive him back into gloom, away from the moment of pleasure when he had listened to Rona's laugh over the telephone. Orpen was wrong about Rona. Rona was understanding, Rona was pliable. It was the only way to be

15

happily married—to take the girl you wanted when she was still impressionable and mould her into someone who would be yours forever. Orpen was right about most things, but he was wrong about Rona.

Ettley shaved and dressed with care, choosing a dark grey flannel suit, a fresh white shirt, a navy silk tie. Conservative, he told himself with a grin. He left the apartment before nine, complimenting himself on his speed and efficiency. (He would have time, after all, for a cup of coffee. He might even walk to the office.) He closed the door and double-locked it, leaving behind him the disordered room with yesterday's shirt and stray socks and the bed-covers still lying abjectly on the floor. Marija, who came in to pick up and clean each day, would have everything in order for his return. She was a quiet Esthonian who had never learned enough English to be able to take out her citizenship papers. She was a reliable woman. Orpen had recommended her: he knew her husband.

I must see Orpen to-night, Scott Ettley was thinking as he reached the street. It was a cool, fresh morning. The small trees spaced along the sidewalk were in bud, their black thin branches dusted with green. He skirted an empty ash can, a couple of milk bottles, a dog straining at the end of a leash. I must see Orpen. This waiting and wondering is getting me down. To-night, I'll see him.

Then he remembered Rona's party. After it, no doubt, his father would insist on taking Rona and him to dinner. Her sister and brother-in-law would be drawn in, too. One of those family evenings with Duty raising her ugly head. And every time his father made a tactful allusion to weddings, Rona would try not to look embarrassed, yet her cheeks would colour and her eyes would find something interesting to watch on the other side of the room. But getting married wasn't so easy, not at the moment. Perhaps by Thanksgiving, perhaps by then. Rona would wait another six months: she was his, she trusted him. Some day he could explain to her, and that would make everything clear to her. She would understand. They could be happy together, in spite of what Orpen said.

He stopped for a moment at the corner news-stand and read the morning's headlines. He didn't even bother to buy a

16

paper. Just the same old stuff, ground out day after day. And then he went into Schrafft's, sat at the counter, and drank a cup of strong black coffee. He caught sight of himself in the mirror behind the bubbling coffee pots—a fair-haired man, well-fed, well-dressed, with a look of prosperity about him. He turned sharply away from the mirror, paid the clerk, and left.

CHAPTER TWO

Rona Metford left the office just after half-past four.

"Where's *she* going?" the new typist asked, catching a glimpse of Rona as she passed the open door of the large room where fifteen tables and fifteen typewriters stood in neat rows.

Mrs. Hershey, In Charge, looked up with a frown. She did most of the important typing for the Architecture Department, and so she felt she had to defend Rona. Besides, she liked Rona Metford and she didn't like new girls who thought they were running the magazine after three weeks on its staff. "When you've been working here nine years and become assistant editor of the Architecture Department and learned to finish your job by half-past four, no doubt Mr. Burnett will let you leave early whenever you are giving a cocktail party."

"Nine years. Good grief!" the new typist said in disgust. "And she isn't even married yet."

Miss Guttman looked up from the filing cabinet. "We don't all rush to grab the first man that asks us." She exchanged a small smile with Mrs. Hershey—just a couple of old-timers putting Miss Pert in her place—and came back to her desk. Talking of Rona Metford though . . . "Guess who I saw in the street to-day?" she asked in a lowered voice.

Mrs. Hershey couldn't.

"Paul Haydn! He didn't see me . . . too busy looking at a windowful of ties."

Mrs. Hershey was impressed enough to stop her work, even if it kept her late. "Paul Haydn in New York? Well!"

"I heard rumours that the magazine wants him back here."

"There have been plenty of rumours. But will he come?"

Miss Guttman shrugged her thin shoulders. "He was in uniform, a general or something, perhaps he's staying in the army."

"It might be difficult for him here," Mrs. Hershey said. "I mean, with Rona Metford and all that."

"He's forgotten long ago. He wasn't the kind of man to let a broken engagement worry him. Wasn't that why she broke it, anyway—all those women in Europe?"

"Oh, you can't believe all you hear," Mrs. Hershey said good-naturedly. "He couldn't help it if the girls liked him." She shook her head, pushed a grey curl back into place, and her plump white face looked regretful. She had been sorry when Rona Metford and Paul Haydn had broken off, for she had seen the beginning of their love affair right here in this office; there was nothing like a touch of romance to brighten up life and they had looked so well together, just right, as if they'd never be the ones to disappoint Mrs. Hershey.

"He's like all men," Miss Guttman said gloomily. She looked down at her neat figure in its excellent black suit, and then admired her carefully kept hands. They looked nicer ringless, anyway, she decided. "I think I'll get a waistcoat, white piqué," she announced suddenly. "Wonder where she bought that one she wore to-day? Touches of white, that's what's new this spring."

"Too much laundering," Mrs. Hershey said. Then she suddenly remembered that she was to take care of her grandson to-night, so she couldn't waste any more time at all. Her expert fingers raced over the electric typewriter. "My son and daughter-in-law are going to see *South Pacific*," she explained, her eyes on the clock.

"And I've got seats for *The Cocktail Party* to-night," Miss Guttman said, also suddenly remembering the time. "They say it's good." She began typing too.

Couple of old cows, the new typist thought politely. But she was feeling depressed because three weeks of typing and shorthand had turned out to be more work and less glamour than she had imagined when she had told her friends she was going to become a secretary. She stared defiantly at Mrs. Hershey for inflicting all these letters on her—the dullest, silliest letters of no importance at all—and was startled to see that Mrs. Hershey was watching her table.

But Mrs. Hershey was remembering the morning, nine years ago, when she had pointed out that desk to a dark-haired girl with large brown eyes. "Rona Metford," the girl had said nervously, "I'm Rona Metford." She had been seventeen then, straight from high school. And more willing to learn than some of those college graduates who wanted to work on a magazine, nowadays. Mrs. Hershey looked severely at the new girl. (She'll have to go. Lazy, inefficient, blaming all her troubles on other people. As if we didn't earn most of our own troubles: pity they hadn't taught her *that* in college.) Then she pulled back her attention to the last letter she had to type. She slipped a sheet of paper, carbon and second sheet neatly in place and typed the date expertly to balance the elegantly embossed heading—TREND: A MAGAZINE FOR LIVING. In all her fifteen years with *Trend*, Mrs. Hershey had never quite decided what that really meant. Perhaps that was why so many people bought it, just trying to find out.

"I don't care," Miss Guttman said suddenly, her blonde palomino-rinsed head turned towards Mrs. Hershey. "I'm going to get a white piqué waistcoat."

Mrs. Hershey nodded placatingly, frowned at a word, and typed on.

The white piqué waistcoat which had aroused Miss Guttman's envy was now getting out of the elevator and arousing passions of a slightly different nature in the men hurrying through the lobby.

Joe, the elevator operator, was finishing the story which he had begun on the twenty-third floor about Monday at Jamaica. "Fifty-to-one shot. Breezed in."

"It paid the rent, then?" Rona asked with a smile.

"Sure did. Paid the rent all right." He grinned and added, "This week."

"Good night, Joe." Rona hurried past the row of elevators toward the entrance of the building, before he could add the inevitable phrase that his life was just a series of ups and downs.

"Good night, Miss Metford." Joe's voice sounded cheated of a laugh, but in another half hour or so he would have plenty of customers coming down from the upper floors. He knew them all, had seen them come and go. Not many of them could say they had been working here in this building for twenty-one years. Miss Metford was leaving soon—so they said. Engaged to that nice-looking young fellow with the fair hair and blue eyes. But he wasn't waiting for her, down here in the lobby, to-night. She wasn't expecting him, either, for she was walking past the Coffee Shop where they usually met, out into Fifth Avenue through the big swing doors.

Rona turned east towards Madison, walking quickly, keeping to the right of the sidewalk to prove she was now an old New Yorker. To-night, she didn't even glance at the hats and dresses and ties and shirts and books and glassware which were so invitingly displayed in the small shops all along the street. At Madison Avenue, busy, less formal than Fifth but with its own elegance and high-priced look, she had to wait for a traffic light. And looking up and down the avenue, looking at the buildings with their varied lights and shadows, looking at the spring evening sky so high and blue, looking at the white clouds so admirably placed to balance the skyscrapers, she fell in love with her town all over again. Each evening, waiting at Madison and East Fifty-fourth Street, she'd look at the sky, and then at the buildings, and then at the buses and taxis and people, and—no matter how tired or annoyed or worried she had been that afternoon—her spirits would lift. To-day, she had been happy and excited so that now she felt like singing. The vision of herself gaily skipping across the avenue, hitting a high note, made her smile. The woman beside her, draped in a silver-blue mink stole, her enamelled face expressionless under a riot of roses, looked at Rona curiously for a moment. A man, watching both of them, kept his thoughts to himself. And then the traffic lights changed to green, the buses and taxis lined up, and the three of them crossed Madison quickly, adeptly, now only intent on their own private business.

Rona cut up Madison for a couple of blocks to see how the new building was coming along. Like everyone who had lived in the city for some years, she took a proprietary interest in all the tearing down of old buildings, the piling up of new ones. Only a few months ago, the bulldozers had been biting into the debris of this block. Then the piles had been driven deep for the foundations, the steel girders had started mounting, the concrete had been moulded. Now the building was reaching up into the sky, a fretwork of steel and concrete, and the large open space where the bulldozers had worked was a vast ground floor, black and cavernous behind its protective boarding. There, under bare electric bulbs, mounds of supplies lay in a confusion that the workmen seemed to find orderly. In another month or two, all this would be gone, to the last speck of dust. And the ground floor would have its displays of delicate dresses, or porcelain and crystal, of fragile hats and precious jewels, against a background of soft pale colours and polished mirrors and thick carpets. Modern magic, Rona thought; and standing at the rough gateway cut into the wooden boarding she watched an electrician at work on the long reels of lead piping exposed in an unfinished pillar, with the awe that Cinderella must have felt for the old lady with her wand.

But to see better—although, of course, she mustn't spend more than a minute to-night—and to be out of the way of workmen clearing debris on to a truck, she moved farther along the temporary wooden gangway and put her eye to one of the square holes cut for "sidewalk-superintendents" in the fence. Beside her, a small boy was watching through another square hole cut obligingly at a three-foot height, while he resisted all attempts by his mother to drag him away. She was saying, "But Billy, we've *seen* it! And the men are leaving now. They've nearly all gone." It was true, although the very junior sidewalk-superintendent didn't want to believe it. Or perhaps the huge ground floor, still unbroken into rooms, fascinated him by its size. It seemed all the bigger because only a few men, busy on overtime, were left to emphasise its loneliness. "I'll build a house just like that," the little boy announced, and decided to leave and get home and start right away. His mother ran after him.

Time for me to leave too, Rona thought, and she turned away. A tall man in uniform stepped aside to let her pass over the narrowed sidewalk. Then, even as she had passed, his arm suddenly went out and he gripped her by the elbow and pulled her back. Startled, she looked up at him and saw a dark-haired man with strong eyebrows, a face that was now more handsome than good-looking, a pleasant mouth beginning to smile, serious grey eyes now losing their surprise. "Rona!" he said. "Rona . . ."

She stood staring at him. She half-opened her mouth. When she did speak, her voice was incredulous. "Paul Haydn!"

They stood there, blocking the sidewalk. Then he dropped her arm. "Look," he said, smiling, "we'd better get off this catwalk before we are arrested for obstruction." That took a minute, a minute that gave them time to regain themselves a little, a minute that took away all the naturalness of their voices and made them suddenly self-conscious.

"I wondered who the girl was," he began, and she looked at him. She was thinking, he hasn't changed at all, the same old Paul, he looks different except when he smiles, but he's the same old Paul wondering who the girl was. He noticed the look, and he went on, "the girl who had enough sense to admire a good job of work." He said it simply, and she felt ashamed of herself. She had often imagined this meeting, and she had dreaded it. Now it was here, and there was no reason for those fears at all. At the first moment—well, that had been surprise. But now—we said we'd be friends, she told herself, it's all over and we are only friends.

She gave him a warm smile and said, "I'm glad to see you, Paul. You're looking well. And very impressive."

"Oh, this!" He glanced down at his uniform. "None of my old clothes would fit, and the new suits needed alterations. I'll look less conspicuous in a few days."

"Are you coming out of the army?" She was surprised.

"You didn't expect me to stay in it forever, did you?"

"It seemed that way," she said.

He looked across the street at one of the small smart bars. "Come and have a drink and give me the news. I'm all out of touch with everybody."

"I can't, I'm sorry. I'm late. I've got to rush."

"Still living with—what was her name?"

"Molly Anders? Oh, no, she married." There was a moment of embarrassment for Rona. But Paul Haydn didn't seem to notice it. She was thankful for that. Yes, he thought of her as an old friend. He had probably had so many girls since she had last seen him that she was only a faded piece

22

of the past. Then she smiled at herself, for she didn't quite like that description; but it was, at least, a pleasantly safe position. She held out her hand. "Good-bye, Paul. I must go."

He kept her hand, saying, "Have a heart, Rona! I've been walking around New York all day. I've only talked to my tailor and a couple of clerks, and the waiters and taxi drivers. Couldn't you let yourself be a little late to-night? . . . No?" He let her hand go. "All right," he said, with a grin, "I'll walk along with you. Is that okay?"

"Of course. It isn't far. I live just a few blocks across town." She began walking quickly, and he went with her. "I've some people coming in to see me," she explained, "and I've got to get things ready." For a moment, she had the impulse to ask him to come; he'd know nearly everyone there. Then she decided against that. "Have you seen many of the old crowd?" she asked instead.

"I just got in this morning."

"You mean, this is your *first* day in New York? Since when?"

"Since 1945," he admitted. "I was on leave here then, but I spent most of it in Colorado. I haven't been in New York, properly, since 1942. It's a queer feeling. I went down to Washington Square, to-day, just to have a look at my old apartment. It's gone—nothing but a gaping hole and a lot of bulldozers moving in. And that building you were watching, what used to be there? I was trying to remember when you almost passed me by."

"It was a gallery. Art collections and things. Remember?"

"And where is it now?"

"Moved uptown. The city's moving uptown."

"So I saw. No more trolley cars on Fifty-ninth, business offices on Park Avenue, the U.N. building towering over the East River, and Radio City settling into a respectable middle age."

"It must have been a frightening welcome for you."

"It's what I get," he agreed, "for thinking everything stood still while I was away. But actually it's more exciting than frightening. It's good to see people building. It's good to see them confident."

"That's what I keep thinking," she said eagerly. "But some
23

people go around talking about the country being in the grip of hysteria—the bomb, and spies, and all that. And I just can't quite see how they can believe it, if they'd use their eyes and look around them. We may all be worried underneath, but you don't get this kind of confidence with hysteria, do you?"

He steered her safely across the double width of Park Avenue, circumnavigated a small flotilla of baby carriages and tricycles returning, with balloons flying, from a visit to the Central Park Zoo, and led her along a quieter stretch of side street to the neon signs of Lexington. "You're very serious, nowadays," he said, watching her face with a smile.

"Not altogether, I hope." She smiled back. "After all," she reminded him, "I was only eighteen when you last saw me. That isn't exactly a serious age."

"You still look very much the same, if you want to know. I'd have recognised you at once if it hadn't been for the hat. Don't you wear it on the back of your head any more? And what's all this veiling for? Camouflage?" But there was a compliment in his voice, and she felt unexpectedly pleased. She looked at him, still smiling, but she said nothing. He seemed much older, much older than he ought to be. But she couldn't tell him that. He had a quick glance for everything, everyone on the street, and not just for the prettiest girls either. He seemed—she wasn't quite sure of the word: capable, perhaps. Capable and reliable. She almost laughed. Perhaps it was the uniform, she thought. Paul Haydn had been famous for his charm, in the old days, but reliable? Clever and erratic, they had said about him: life came too easily for him. It probably did, even now.

His grey eyes were watching her. They were amused.

"What's the verdict?" he asked.

She flushed a little. "You're—you're different," she said lamely.

"Is that bad or good?"

Her colour deepened. She laughed openly. "I wouldn't know."

"No," he said, and he was serious again. There was a pause. Then he said, suddenly, "I heard in 1945 that you were married. To a man in the navy."

"Just gossip, Paul. But I am getting married, now." She

24

drew off the glove on her left hand, and said, "There it is."

"Very handsome," he said, glancing at the ring, and then concentrating on leading her through the maze of traffic on overcrowded Lexington. "And is he?"

"Of course!"

"He must be a nice guy."

"Why?"

"To make your face light up like that when you talk about him."

"He's a wonderful guy," she said softly.

Paul Haydn studied a cleaner's shop with interest. Then he said, "I'm glad, Rona."

She said, as simply as she had spoken when she had shown him Scott's ring, "I'm glad you're glad, Paul." And with that, she buried their past completely.

"What about your job at *Trend*?" he asked suddenly. "I heard you were practically running the Architecture Department. Good for you."

"Just more gossip. I'm only an assistant to Mr. Burnett. I imagine what should go inside a room once he has decided its shape. I'm not fully qualified yet, you see."

"You mean as an architect?" He was surprised. "Still following that idea? Then you got a college degree?"

"Yes, I made it. Part-time work and night classes. That sort of thing."

"Not as much fun as Vassar, I'd imagine."

"No." She smiled. "Still, it was either that way or nothing." She halted, looking up at the quiet brownstone house in front of them. She pointed out the green window boxes on the top floor. "My apartment. Now, I'll have to dash in and start spreading canapés like mad."

"Sorry I kept you late. But it was good to see you again." He held out his hand and gripped hers.

"That's the strange thing about this city—the way you meet people so unexpectedly."

"Yes. Now I really know I'm back in New York."

She looked along the familiar street, and she saw it as it must seem to him: a tight wall of houses, busy at this hour, yet lonely, with strangers hurrying to their homes. She said impulsively, "Paul, why don't you come to the party? Jon Tyson will be there."

25

"Jon?" He was delighted to hear the name again. "And how's Jon?"

"He married Peggy—my sister, remember? He teaches history up at Columbia University. Yes, and they've two children. Didn't you know?"

"I'm a bad letter writer," he reminded her. Especially, he thought, when I wanted to cut myself off from everything I remembered.

"You'll know quite a lot of the other guests, too. They'd love to welcome you home. Why not come? It would save you a lot of telephoning in the next few days."

Paul Haydn hesitated. He looked at the lonely street. "Swell," he said. "I'd like to see them all."

"I said six o'clock." She glanced at her watch. "Heavens!" She waved and ran up the steep flight of steps, with the same light graceful movements he now remembered so well. He saluted and turned away. Behind him, an elevated train rattled over Third Avenue. He avoided two children shakily trying out their new roller skates, a dog straining on a long leash across the sidewalk toward a hydrant.

On Lexington Avenue, he went into the first bar he could find, a small place blazing with neon signs outside, stretching its capacity to the last inch inside with booths for eating, welcoming its customers with a blast of music and cold air-conditioning. The early clients were gathered round the bar near the entrance. Uninhibited tweed jackets, Paul noted, and ties strong enough to knock you over. There were some women too. A blonde with pointed breasts and good legs looked at him haughtily. Soldiers are out of favour, he thought, for he hadn't had time yet to catch up on the new poses in the fashionable magazines. He decided that it was a pity though that a pretty girl's hair should be so ragged—as if mice had been gnawing at it overnight—and he chose a seat at the far end of the bar where his uniform wouldn't annoy her.

He looked at the men; they seemed prosperous and well-fed, a peaceful crowd. Even the arguments were good-natured, and the loud voices had no harsh sneering edge. It would be easy for someone coming in here as a foreigner to start generalising: easy to forget that most of the men here must have been just the right age for the war. When we demobilise, we demobilise, he thought. In one way—remembering Berlin as he had seen it only twenty-four hours ago, remembering the new refugees with their small bundles of belongings and the new fears—that idea worried him. In another way, he was cheered: it was good to see people who had been first-rate fighting men throw off regimentation so quickly. The gloomy predictions of some columnists five years ago didn't make much sense now. The adjustment problems were drinking a beer or a rye after a day's work and making vague plans for definite relaxation this evening.

"Just back?" the barman asked, filling Paul's empty glass, glancing at his service ribbons and then at his face. "You'll get used to it," he said reassuringly. "Once had a couple of them things." He nodded to the ribbons on Paul's chest. "Guess the old woman stowed them away in the attic along with her wedding dress." Then his dark, heavy and thickening face concentrated on polishing the glasses until they shone like crystal. His strong broad hands arranged them delicately in their neat pyramid in front of a gleaming mirror. Over his shoulder, he'd throw in a remark to each conversation: the drought, the Dodgers' chances this year, the plane missing over the Baltic, the Rangers in the play-offs at last, this new play called *The Cocktail Party* and what right had any of those psychiatrists to send a good-looking girl to be pegged down for the ants to eat?

The blonde girl had met a friend almost as pretty as she was, with the same hauteur and mice-gnawed hair. (Can this be a fashion? Paul wondered in dismay.) They were both losing something of their grand manner in a heated discussion about ranch-type houses. Paul Haydn, keeping his eye on his glass, hoped that whatever type of house it was, it wasn't as ugly as its name. Or should he have said "new-type name"? He repressed a grimace, for the barman might think aspersions were being cast on his excellent Martini. Yes, Paul thought, one slipped quickly back into the old routine after all: he was half-way to becoming an editor again with an aversion for nouns being used as adjectives. He paid and left the cosy comfort of the bar, avoiding the blonde's carefully ignoring eye. He came out on to the busy sidewalk, hesitated. He was still undecided whether he ought to accept Rona's invitation or not. It was scarcely six o'clock yet.

He argued with himself around the block. Rona had made one thing very clear by the invitation: they were friends, nothing more. She would never have asked him to join the party if she had felt any other emotion when she met him. Not Rona. It was just as well to get that straight, especially if he were going to take his job with *Trend* again. (He wished the magazine would change that damned name, though: what once had seemed on the smart side, now seemed comic. Like a cute inscription on a book's fly-leaf, seen years later when the clever touch made you shudder.) But perhaps he wouldn't become an assistant editor again in *Trend*'s Feature Department. Perhaps he'd find something else for a change. Then he wondered, as he had wondered vaguely for the last month, why he should have been given this late chance to return to his job with *Trend*. What was wrong with the man who had taken his place at the end of the war? In 1945, *Trend* had been a little stilted when he hadn't rushed back to his job with them, especially (they reminded him coldly) especially since they had kept it open for him as they had agreed in 1941. Yet, a few weeks ago, when he had written them hesitantly about a recommendation to help him get started once more in New York, their reply had been effusive. (Come right home, the sooner the better, we love you. Salary advanced to cover war-service years, Feature editorship when Crowell retires next year. Come home, come home, start at the old stand in May.) Flattering, to say the least. Reassuring. Useful, too. But what about the poor devil who had been assistant-editing meanwhile? Ditched? And why? No doubt with a wife and kids: that kind of unfortunate always had hostages to fortune.

I don't like it, Paul thought. Sure, the magazine game was a hard one. Here to-day, failed to-morrow. Yet *Trend* for all its fancy title was a fair-minded place. Its reputation was solid. But I don't like it, Paul thought: I'm not going to be the cause of ditching some guy with a couple of kids to keep in shoe leather.

He looked up at the green shutters on the top floor of the

brownstone house. Perhaps Rona knew what was happening at *Trend*, perhaps she could tell him the score.

Is that the only reason why you are walking up these steps? he asked himself suddenly. But it was too late to answer that question: he was already inside the glass doorway of Rona's house, his finger was already pressing the button beside the little white card with "Metford" in its neat script.

CHAPTER THREE

Paul Haydn pressed the bell again. Behind him, the roller skates were still grating shakily over the sidewalk. Some more dogs were straining towards the interesting hydrant. People, homeward bound, glanced at no one. An elevated train roared up Third Avenue.

Then the front door gave a hoarse warning rattle, as Rona released its catch from upstairs. He grabbed the handle too late, and found the door had locked itself again. He shook his head and grinned. You've a lot to relearn, he told himself. Again he pressed the bell. And this time he was ready, and got in. He was still smiling at himself as he went up the narrow flights of stairs past the doors to the other apartments. He heard Rona's voice calling, "Stop for breath on the second landing!"

She was waiting at the door of her apartment. "Oh!" she said when he came into sight. She was obviously dismayed.

"I'm too early?" He looked at his watch in alarm. It was just one minute after six o'clock. He backed down a step.

"No." She was laughing now, holding the door open. "I needed someone to help with the ice. Come in, Paul. Welcome!"

"Sorry, Rona. Give me a few days to break army habits." He entered the small hall, cursing himself. He had forgotten that six o'clock for cocktails in New York meant six-thirty with luck. He looked round, searching for some place to lay his cap. He put it on the little telephone table, but it looked too conspicuous, too possessive lying there. He picked it up again, and stood holding it, feeling still more uncomfortable.

Rona took it and dropped it on a chair inside the bedroom. "The cloakroom for to-night," she explained. "Now, here's where I'm having a slight battle with the shrimps. I'm beginning to wish I hadn't thought they were a better idea than smoked salmon." She led him into the kitchenette. She tied an apron—a white organdie thing with roses and frills—around the waist of her elegant black suit. Paul looked at her, then at the neat white miniature kitchen, then at the platter of food which she was arranging with some care.

"They're being obstinate, to-day," she went on. She concentrated on removing the few remaining shrimps from their hard transparent cases. "Coy, that's what they are. And yet if you hurry them, you mash them into pieces."

He kept looking around him as she talked. She was more embarrassed than he had been by his promptness, but she was doing her best to tell him to stop feeling worried. "This where you keep the ice?" he asked, his voice as casual as hers. He didn't tell her that, flushed with all the rush and excited by her party, she was the prettiest girl he had seen since he had said good-bye to her.

"Yes. Careful of that refrigerator door, Paul. It swings back on you." She looked up from her work to catch him smiling at her. She raised an eyebrow.

"Your apron," he explained. "Is that what the well-dressed housewife is now wearing?"

She smiled and handed him a bowl for the ice. "The tray is set up in the living-room," she said. "Straight through, you can't miss it."

When he came back to the little kitchen, she was studying the coral-tinted shrimps massed round a bowl of sauce. "Would you try it, Paul? It's supposed to be mustard sauce. All right? I've been tasting so many things that I've lost my judgment."

She watched him anxiously. It was very good, he reassured her. "Now, the lemon peel," she said, remembering the Martinis.

"Anything else I can do?"

"Did the drink tray seem all right?"

"Yes. Everything seems pretty much all right."

"Then why don't you pour yourself a drink and tell me what you've been doing?"

"Oh, I've just been walking around, getting acclimated." He smiled. "I forgot about traffic lights, and I still jump when the elevated roars out of nowhere."

"I mean what have you been doing since—since you left London?"

"Just one job after another," he said lightly.

"Well, where did you collect all that?" She pointed to his ribbons.

"You get one with every fiftieth can of Spam."

She laughed. "You're just the same as Scott," she said. "He won't talk about the war, either. He was in Italy, you know."

"There are pleasanter things to talk about. By the way, Rona, how is our *Trend* nowadays, apart from the interior decoration side?"

"Strictly Virginian this month. March was pure Texan. And it's going to be very Boston and Havad Yad in May." She admired the thin translucent strips of lemon peel which curled delicately from her careful knife. "You'd almost think I liked dry Martinis," she observed.

"Still taste like medicine to you?"

"Still the little country girl at heart," she admitted. "But why were you so serious when you asked about *Trend*? Is it true that you are coming back? Oh, yes, the rumours are flying around." She was suddenly equally serious, almost worried.

"You don't like the idea?" His voice was hard.

"Not that, Paul," she said quickly, looking at him. "We mustn't think back to the old days. You got your freedom again, and that was what you really wanted. I picked up my life. And now I'm terribly happy. So all's well. Isn't it?"

"Yes," he said. "All's well." He turned to look out of the window. He studied the view. Roofs, chimney pots, water towers. And down below, little squares of persevering grass and determined trees, boxed into miniature gardens by brick walls. "Why did you look so worried, there?" he asked suddenly.

"I was thinking of Blackworth—the man who got your job when you stayed in the army."

"Do you like him?"

"Yes. He's popular. That's what makes it so awful. You see, it was my fault—I'm sure it was my fault—that he lost the job. Oh, he's lost it, Paul, even if you don't come back."

He was startled. "Your fault . . . ?"

"Paul . . ." She looked at him uncertainly. "I can't talk about this to everyone. I've told Scott, of course, and Peggy and Jon. You see, Paul, it was like this—oh, it's so difficult to begin, you'll think we are all crazy or something, and yet——"

A bell sounded.

"That's Scott," Rona said quickly. "He was coming early to look after the drinks," she explained as she hurriedly gave Paul the dish of lemon peel, and then went to press the button that released the lock of the front door.

"What about this man Blackworth?" he asked.

"I'll tell you the story once you've seen the Boss. But he will explain most of it, I expect."

"Sounds very hush-hush."

She looked at him as if she were trying to gauge his thoughts. "It is," she said. Then she pushed him gently towards the living-room, and she hurried to open the door of the apartment.

It wasn't Scott who arrived, then. It was Peggy and Jon, slightly breathless after their climb.

"We came early, because the sitter has to get home by half-past seven," Peggy was explaining as she came into the living-room. Then she stopped and stared at Paul Haydn. She was slightly taller than Rona, and where Rona's hair and eyes were very dark, Peggy's were light in colour. But she had the same straight nose, the same broad brow and rounded chin, the same warm smile. She was smiling now as she came forward, her surprise perfectly controlled, her hands outstretched. She had always liked Paul: it was through Paul that she had met Jon, after all.

"Rona found me wandering on the streets on my first day home, and took pity," Paul Haydn explained quickly. But there wasn't much need to explain to either Peggy or Jon. They were never permanently surprised by anything Rona did.

Jon, thinner than ever, his fair hair now losing most of its wave and some of its substance, his attractive angular face twisted into its shy smile, came forward more slowly. Then while Rona approved Peggy's dress and couldn't believe it was that old one, vintage 1946, done over, the two men looked at each other carefully as they shook hands. They had been friends at college, friends (when they saw each other, in typical rushed city fashion) in New York; and then, apart from a few early letters, they had lost touch during the war.

"Congratulations," Paul said, looking towards Peggy. "And I hear you've a family, too."

"Yes," Jon said. He glanced at Rona. As her only male relative, he felt responsibility for her happiness. He wasn't going to let anyone come back and disturb it, not even someone whom he had once liked as much as Paul Haydn.

"It's good to see you all happy," Paul was saying. "And settled." He looked directly at Jon, and Jon accepted the frankness of that look. He relaxed. His smile became easier. He began to ask some questions about Germany. He even answered a few about his days in the Pacific (he had been in the navy) and about his present teaching job at Columbia University.

"You are both being too serious for a party," Peggy reminded them when the doorbell started ringing and Rona hurried away to be the welcoming hostess. "Come and see us, Paul, if you can struggle as far uptown as Riverside and 108th Street. You and Jon can then be as serious as you like, and I'll join in too if you'll let me. Friday nights are good—no classes on Saturday morning for Jon, this year. There are always a few students dropping in to see us then—plenty of arguments and beer and sandwiches. But what on earth is keeping Scott so late?" For she was now looking at the doorway, where two men and three women had appeared, but still no Scott.

Jon, at a sign from Rona, began mixing the drinks, Peggy passed the canapés and a bright smile, and Paul began shaking hands. Still more people were arriving. Some he remembered well, others—although they seemed to know him—were more difficult to place. But gradually, as he sorted them out, he began to recall something about them that made identification easier. The women were the hardest to remember, strangely enough, and the younger ones were cultivating the haughty look that the blonde in the Lexington bar had adopted. He found himself caught up in various friendly groups, passed along from one to the other by a greeting or a phrase. "Hello, there!" . . . "Look who's here!" . . . "Well, well, our military expert. Paul, how *are* you?" And then conversation would begin as if he had only been away a couple of weeks from New York. They were taking his return as normally as they ordered breakfast, but there was a warmth in their voices, a welcome in their handshake that was a tonic. He relaxed, and began to enjoy himself.

Then he found himself in a corner of the room, surrounded by a group of total unknowns. Rona he was partly amused to see—but only partly—had steered two of the prettiest girls in his direction, a blonde and a redhead. Rona, herself, was looking happier now. Had Scott arrived? Paul wondered which man he was . . . that handsome guy in the brown suit, or that one in the blue suit with a quiet smile and a friendly look? That might be Scott. Rona was laughing up into his face. That could be Scott. Paul studied him. He was a reliable sort of man, a good mouth, a fine pair of eyes. Yes, he'd do all right.

Then a thin anxious woman at Paul's elbow pulled him back to the group around him. Why, she wanted to know, was he keeping Germany divided? Another woman, younger and prettier but too intense, stared gloomily at his uniform and announced she was a pacifist. Beside her, a heavy round-faced man told Paul with a bright smile that America was in the hands of reactionaries and warmongers, that was the whole trouble. The dazzling blonde, persisting, said he simply must see the Hapsburg Collection at the Metropolitan, it was out of this world. And the quiet redhead (if there could be such a contradiction in terms) asked him if he had yet seen *The Cocktail Party*? The round-faced man said, with another bright smile, that America had never disarmed, that was the whole trouble. The blonde, edging out the redhead, said he must see the Cloisters, too, the new tapestries were divine and the wild cherry and plum trees would soon be out. Did he remember the view from there, over the garden wall, of the George Washington Bridge spanning the Hudson? The thin, anxious woman began to analyse *The Cocktail Party*. But someone preferred *The Consul*. Nonsense, the round-faced man said with a brighter smile, Menotti was politically naïve, didn't know his brass from his oboe. A youngish man, listening from the background, said, "Absolute rubbish! That's the new Communist line. Don't fall for that, Murray." The too-intense girl laughed along with Murray at such naïveté. "Character assassination," the young man persisted gamely, "but we're getting wise." The round-faced man called Murray said, "You're getting wise? Hysterical, you mean." And he plunged into an emotional argument.

Paul took a deep breath, and tried to move away.

But the redhead, watching Paul through her long dark eyelashes, wanted to know if he enjoyed skiing? She was temporarily routed by the thin-faced, anxious woman, who began to tell Paul all about the situation in Berlin. The redhead, her chin up, said it had been a miserable winter, no snow on the slopes at all. And Murray, finishing his speech, demanded to know why Paul was sending arms to the French.

Paul, his retreat cut off by both blonde and redhead, listening, watching, didn't have to talk at all. There's always a lunatic fringe at every party, he thought, but where on earth did Rona find this little crowd?

Scott Ettley arrived just after the second large group of guests.

"Sorry, darling," he said, kissing Rona, keeping her in the hall to kiss some more. "That damned office . . . I never can get away when I want to." He held her in his arms. "Sounds as if we had a mob in that room. Has Father got here yet?"

"Yes. Peggy's talking to him, and he seems happy. Don't worry."

"He'll read me a lecture about being late." Scott spoke in fun, but Rona didn't feel like enjoying the joke. Why pretend his father behaved in a way he never behaved?

"We've got an extra guest, Scott." We've several, actually, but there's only one I'm beginning to worry about, she thought. She told him quickly about Paul Haydn.

Scott stared at her. "Paul Haydn? Why on earth did you ask him?" He was angry.

"Don't, darling. It's all right. You know that." She kissed him. "Be polite to him. That's the best way to stop any gossip, isn't it? After all, he's going to be around New York now, and we'll keep meeting him."

35

Scott looked relieved. "Was that why you asked him?" It wasn't a bad idea. Treat Haydn naturally, and anyone inclined to a little malicious speculation would be disappointed. Rona had ended gossip before it could start. He pulled her into his arms again, kissed her violently and quickly. "Glad I'm jealous?" he asked.

"Delighted," she said. But she was as surprised as he was by his emotion. She caught his hand and coaxed him toward the room. "I need hardly say he's the one in uniform," she added in a low voice.

"I'll have a drink first," Scott said, catching sight of the uniform beside Mary Fyne's red hair. "And I'll have to say hello to Dad, too." He looked away from the uniform: that was a hell of a way to come dressed to a party, proud of the ribbons no doubt. "Sorry about having to miss lunch, Rona. Just one of those awful days when your life isn't your own." He pushed a soft curl behind her ear and admired the effect.

"Why didn't you tell me last night?" she asked, half-puzzled.

"I meant to. But I forgot. I always forget the unpleasant things." He pressed her hand, gave her a smile that made her happy, and then went toward the tray of drinks, saying hello to their friends, making the usual comments. His father, he noted, was over by the window talking earnestly to Peggy Tyson. Scott waved and smiled, and then poured himself a drink. Rona was talking now to a dark-haired man in a blue suit—something in television, he remembered. Another of her "old friends," but more harmless than Haydn. Rona had been at the impressionable age when she met Haydn; after that, there had been several men hanging around her, but nothing definite, not until Scott had found her. I'll have a second drink, Scott told himself, before I go and shake Haydn by his hand; or perhaps I'll be honest and knock his teeth in.

Over by the window, Peggy Tyson was saying to William Ettley, "I think Paul Haydn needs rescuing. He is getting that slightly glazed look, just like Jon when he is trapped."

But William Ettley, still watching Scott and Rona talking together at the door, said, "They look so happy together. I can't make out why she doesn't fix the date. When Rona

36

invited me to this party, I was hoping they'd choose this day to announce the wedding."

Peggy's attention came back to William Ettley, and she looked at his seemingly placid face. His quiet eyes behind their round glasses were worried. He was a man nearly sixty, short, energetic, heavily built, white-faced, white-haired. He was quick to smile, and his voice was deep, decided, pleasant. Most people, meeting him for the first time, were amazed that this mild-mannered man was William Ettley. Not *the* William Ettley? Not the man who had built up the *Clarion* to be one of the best-informed, most reliable, and completely trustworthy newspapers on the Eastern seaboard? True, the *Clarion* was a small paper, a country news-paper, but it carried both punch and weight. Ettley was the Republican who voted for Roosevelt when his conscience told him to. Ettley was the man who fought ward politics at home, despised pressure groups, believed in bipartisan policy abroad. You could trust his editorials. However you might disagree at the moment, you'd find yourself amazed some months later by the solid good sense that had kept him from jumping to false conclusions.

Peggy said, "Shall I bring Paul Haydn over here? He's been doing counter-propaganda in Germany or something like that."

"I'd like to meet him," William Ettley said. His eyes watched her face. "Peggy, why isn't Rona marrying Scott?"

"But she is!" Peggy stared at him in amazement. "She'd marry him to-morrow if only he could manage it."

"I lunched with Scott last week. I got the impression . . ." William Ettley didn't finish his sentence. He looked around the room a little unhappily. Rona was successful, Scott had said gloomily: how could he ask her to give up her career and only offer her the salary he had? "Why don't they just get married, anyway?" William Ettley asked irritably.

"That's what I'd like to know," Peggy said. Then, recalling his affection for Rona, she restrained her own annoyance. "But Rona can't arrange the date by herself, Mr. Ettley. It's up to the man to decide that, isn't it?" And if I didn't like William Ettley, she thought, I'd tell him that I'm angrier than he is with his precious son.

"Then what's wrong with Scott? The boy's in love with

37

her. That I know." Then he shook his head sadly. "I don't seem to understand him very well in anything."

Peggy was silent. What was the good of criticising Scott Ettley even to herself? She would only end by losing Rona if she didn't fight against this dislike of Scott. She heard herself saying, almost placatingly, "Don't worry, Mr. Ettley. Scott has his own ideas, you know that. But he and Rona will get married soon. And I shouldn't be surprised if he changes his mind about joining your paper. I'm sure he will, some day, when he feels he has declared his independence sufficiently."

Ettley said quickly, with a touch of pride, "I like his sense of independence. I like the way he wants to make his own name. If he chooses to work on a paper in New York instead of getting his experience on the *Clarion*, well—I can understand that. I'm *not* trying to run his life for him. Only, I don't feel he is happy. Not altogether. Happy with Rona, yes. But in his job? You can't blame me for wanting to see my only son enjoying a useful happy life, can you?" He tried to smile over this sudden display of sentiment.

"No," Peggy said gently, "that's what we all want to see." She thought of Bobby, aged five. When Bobby was twenty-five would he resent advice and help? Probably. I did too, she thought guiltily. Ah, well, once Scott was married and had some children to worry about he would begin to understand his father better. She looked at William Ettley, now silent and tight-lipped. "I'll go and rescue Paul Haydn," she said, and made her way adeptly through the tight little crowd.

"Paul!" she said, drawing him away from Mary Fyne and her skiing stories. "Or did you want to stay with the redhead?" she asked him laughingly as they edged their way back towards the window. "Tactless of me. But don't worry, she'll be around. She likes strong men with inscrutable faces."

"What's been happening to women's eyes?" Paul asked.

"You mean the Eastern touch with black pencil? It makes them alluring, the magazines say. I'm afraid they look to me like the wolf dressed as Grandma . . . All the better to see you with."

"Reminds me of the circus. All they need is some flat whitewash over their faces."

"You've become a cynic, Paul. Why, once you——"

38

"Sure. Once is a long time ago."

"Yes," she said. And she looked at him speculatively. "I'm taking you to meet William Ettley," she said. "Remember the *Clarion*?"

"Why, of course." He was suddenly pleased. "Is he still the real old-fashioned American liberal?" He was more than pleased. He was excited. And William Ettley, turning to meet the young man (from Mr. Ettley's point of view, Paul Haydn was very young), felt something of the good will that was offered him. He began talking, quietly, intelligently. And, like Jon Tyson, he knew how to ask questions. Paul answered them straight, admitting frankly when he didn't actually know about this zone in Germany or that problem of military government. William Ettley liked the way he answered, and his questions became more particular. His interest was now more than that of politeness.

Peggy Tyson waited for a few minutes, and then managed to slip away. She had to rescue Jon, this time. He always seemed to get stuck with the most predatory bores, generally women who were dashingly unattractive. Once in their clutches, he stayed caught: he was too polite to ease himself away as the other men did. No wonder that Jon disliked cocktail parties. Now he gave Peggy a look of heartfelt thanks as she arrived beside him. "Paul is looking for you, darling," she said, smiling excusingly to the weirdly dressed woman beside him. If you were to take all the front pictures in the last six copies of *Vogue*, Peggy thought, and jumble them together, you might possibly arrive at this woman's idea of what the best-dressed woman could wear. Long earrings, heavily pencilled eyes; a velvet band round her ageing throat caught with a diamond and emerald pin; a nipped-in waistline that resisted hard; stiff taffeta that crinkled and crackled with each movement.

But the woman didn't let Jon go so easily. The hat with large clusters of grapes drooping over each ear, emphasising the downward lines of her face, shook with regret and emphasis. "I simply must enroll at Columbia and come to your husband's lectures," she said, all of sweet nineteen in her own mind. "He's such fun, Mrs. Tyson, such fun! I never could be bothered with history at school, but I'm *sure* he could teach me anything."

"No doubt," Peggy murmured, and left determinedly.

"In heaven's name!" Jon said feelingly, once they were at a safe distance. "Where did Rona find that?"

"You do pick real beauties, Jon. Think of all the people in this room, and you had to choose her."

"I didn't pick her; she just happened," Jon said, remembering the elderly claw that had laid itself on his arm as he had been talking to a little group of writers. *Oh, Dr. Tyson, I've been waiting to meet you for so long!* . . . He had been turned to stone as if she were the Gorgon itself. No help from any other man, either; they knew when they were well out of it. What made people think that university professors liked being bored?

"Fantastic hat," Peggy said. "Did the vintage grapes fascinate you?"

"All we needed was a wooden tub, and then we could have removed all our shoes and socks," Jon said gloomily. Then he looked at his Peggy, recovered, and smiled. "Come along, old girl, home for us!"

"No one seems to be going home—just yet," Peggy said slowly.

"No one here has a home to go to. Obviously." Then he relented, seeing her disappointment, hiding his own. They didn't get to so many parties nowadays, not with Bobby and Barbara aged five and two respectively.

"What about a really pretty girl for a change?" Peggy asked, looking in the direction of Mary Fyne's red hair.

"I've got her," Jon said quietly.

Peggy actually blushed, and her eyes laughed.

Rona's voice said, "It's supposed to be against the rules for a husband and wife to flirt in public. But don't mind me. I like it." Then her voice became serious. "Poor Jon . . . Did Thelma catch you? I tried to reach you, then I saw Peggy taking charge. No, don't look at me like that. She's totally uninvited. She just——"

"Happened?" Jon asked.

"Yes, that's the word exactly. She arrived with Murray. That's the round-faced man over in the corner. Talking politics, no doubt."

Peggy said, "He's the man who insisted on telling me

about the social significance of the comic strip. Wait until Bobby hears that one! I must say you do pick up some odd friends, Rona."

"Oh, he's just one of Scott's lame ducks." Then her voice became worried. "I don't think Scott has noticed Paul Haydn, yet."

"Hasn't he?" Jon asked with a smile.

"He's going in that direction now," Rona said with relief, as she watched Scott make his way leisurely over toward his father and Paul Haydn. "But what on earth made me ask Paul here?" she added, almost to herself.

"Don't worry," Peggy advised. "A little competition wouldn't do Scott any harm. He's much too inclined to think you're his entire possession." With that little truth she went off to talk to the television man, and Jon found that Mary Fyne wanted to know if he did much skiing nowadays.

Rona, still watching anxiously, saw Mr. Ettley leave Paul just as Scott approached them. Mr. Ettley, his back to Scott, hadn't noticed him. But Scott will never believe that, Rona thought. He felt, and nothing could persuade him otherwise, that his father had never forgiven him for his revolt. And Scott, although he pretended he didn't care, worried about it. He had a sense of guilt which he would never admit, but it made him—well, not exactly difficult, Rona thought loyally, not exactly difficult but—but a little, just a little unaccountable at times.

Now, watching Scott's back stiffen as his father walked over to speak to another group, watching Scott reach Paul Haydn and hesitate, she felt all his unhappiness. Dinner will be awful, she thought in agony; and afterwards, when his father leaves us, I'll have to face it alone. Then she told herself that even if you were really in love, deeply in love, there was always some measure of unhappiness to balance your happiness whole and unattacked; they lived in a world of their own. But how, she wondered sadly, how do you ever find that kind of world?

She said, smiling brightly to one of her guests, "Let me freshen this drink? No, I haven't seen the *Ballet Russe* this season. How did you like it?"

Scott Ettley watched his father leave Paul Haydn, and his

excuse for approaching was gone. Then Haydn, noticing his hesitation, said, "Have a cigarette?"

"No, thanks."

"My name's Haydn."

"I know. Mine is Ettley."

"Oh!" Paul looked away from the young man in the grey suit and dark blue tie towards William Ettley.

"Yes, I'm the son of the *Clarion*," Scott said with a bitter smile. "But I don't work on it."

"No?" Paul was surprised by the sense of attack in the short phrase.

"No." Scott was looking at Paul Haydn carefully. Imitation Cary Grant, he thought derisively.

"The *Clarion* is a paper to be proud of," Paul said. He was studying young Ettley's face, in turn. What's burning into him? he wondered.

Ettley ignored that. "I hear you're going back to *Trend* . . ."

Paul Haydn lit his cigarette carefully.

". . . taking over Blackworth's job."

"Is that how it sounds?" Paul Haydn watched the intense blue eyes. They might be improved by being blackened. Easy, he told himself, easy now: this is Rona's party.

"Yes." Then Scott noticed the grape-laden hat was coming close, and Thelma's quick eyes were interested. He forced himself to relax and smile. "I don't know a thing about Blackworth," he said, "but I don't like what is happening to him. It sounds like persecution to me, frankly. Why don't you ask Murray? He's been at *Trend* for the last four years." He nodded toward the corner of the room, toward the round-faced, heavily built man who was still making speeches.

"You mean that guy who doesn't like America?"

Scott looked puzzled, angry. "You don't have to wear a uniform to be the only one who likes America."

"And you don't have to go around kicking America in the teeth, either."

Scott smiled. "Murray's been up to his little tricks, I see. He likes to shock people." He looked at Haydn and his grin broadened. "He seems to have run up a high score to-night."

Paul Haydn said grimly, "Sure, I've lost my sense of humour. That's it."

Scott, still smiling said, "But what I really came over to tell you was this: when you take over Blackworth's job on *Trend*, just keep away from Rona, will you?" There was a savage bite to the last phrase, all the more bitter because of the quiet voice.

Paul Haydn stared. "Your first name isn't Scott, by any chance?" He broke into a broad grin and relaxed. "You might have said that in the first place. It would have explained everything."

Scott Ettley said nothing. He was standing with a smile on his lips, his eyes cold and hard.

"Don't worry," Paul said, his voice changing once more, "I've never stolen another man's property yet. Good-bye." He put down his glass and turned away abruptly. He said good night to a magazine writer and a reviewer who had made a date to lunch with him this week, nodded to a couple of friends and promised to see them to-morrow, ignored Murray's humorous circle, found his cap, and searched for Rona. She was saying good-bye to Jon and Peggy in the hall.

"You too?" She was polite, a little anxious about something.

"Yes, I must go. It was a grand party," he said. "Thanks, Rona."

"Come home with us, and we'll find some dinner," Peggy said impulsively. "And we'll waken Bobby and let him see a real live major."

"Come along," Jon said. "We didn't get much time to talk at the party." Privately he wondered when he'd get those papers graded to-night. But he smiled at Peggy, thinking she had a heart as big as the Empire State.

"Not to-night," Paul said, "but thanks all the same. I've been travelling. I think it's early bed for me."

"On your first night home?" asked Mary Fyne in her low voice, as she came into the hall. She took his arm, smiling. "Oh, Paul!" She emphasised his first name.

I've been promoted, he thought. Rona was watching him with a strange little smile.

"I'm pretty tired," he said with embarrassment.

"What you need is a good steak and a bottle of wine." Mary's red hair caught the dim light in the hall, her large pencilled eyes glanced at him sideways. "And I cook a very good steak," she said. "You promised you'd come, you know. . . . Good night, Rona. We've had a lovely time."

Paul stared, and then remembered to be polite. Jon was watching him with a sympathetic grin.

Rona said, "Good night, Paul." Her amused smile deepened.

All right, he thought savagely, all right. He took Mary's arm in a firm grip. "Good night," he called back as they started downstairs.

Mary Fyne's pretty face twisted with pain. "Oh!" she said softly, "that hurts."

He slackened his grip.

"You don't know your own strength, Paul." She looked at him with that sideways tilt of her head, and she smiled. She leaned on his arm.

Outside, he dropped her arm and stood irresolute. His anger was leaving him. For a moment, she rested her soft hair against his shoulder. Then she looked up at him, saying in wide-eyed innocence, "I really do have a steak in the icebox. And I've a bottle of wine—at room temperature . . ." A taxi halted at the corner of Third Avenue. She raised her arm and signalled. It nosed around slowly to where they stood.

"Look——" he began.

"Yes, look!" she said laughingly, her hair gleaming bright under the street lamp, her coat falling open to show her neck white against the low-cut black dress. She caught his hand playfully, carried it to her lips, and bit deeply.

"What the——" he began in fury. She laughed again, drawing him into the cab after her. He glanced up for a moment at the lighted windows above the green window boxes. His mouth tightened and he followed her.

"Because," she was saying as she lifted his hand gently and looked at it, "because I like you angry." She gave her sideways glance, her smile deepened into a laugh. "I like men who get very angry."

At the first corner, he leaned over to the driver and said, "Stop here, Joe." He handed the man a dollar as he opened the door and jumped out.

"What——" she began, her voice rising.

"Because I like you angry," he said. "I like you very

angry." He left them, walking quickly. She called him, but he didn't look round.

He went up Lexington and entered the little bar with the neon lights above the door. "Benny's," he noticed now.

The bartender was still polishing glasses. The blonde with the model look was still sitting there with her friend. They glanced at him, but this time they smiled.

"Getting to be an old habıtchewee," the barman said with a gloomy shake of his head. "What will it be?"

CHAPTER FOUR

The party was over. Good-bye's filled the little hall, echoed up the staircase. We had a lovely time. Lovely, lovely time. Rona came slowly back into the living-room, now almost large again in its emptiness. She picked up a battered shrimp from the beige rug, removed an ash tray that had overflowed on to the green and white striped couch, collected half-empty glasses from the top of the little white mantelpiece. The fireplace was filled with stubs and cigarette ash and burnt matches. Only the dark green walls looked clean, she thought, only the walls and the white picture frames and the white and beige curtains now billowing gently as Scott opened both windows wide. She sat down on the red chair right-angled to the hearth. She was holding a couple of dirty glasses in her hand; she hadn't even the energy left to decide where to put them. Scott didn't make any move to come to her, to hold her and kiss her. He was still standing at the opened windows.

From the street, there floated up cheerful good-byes. Murray's voice was calling "Taxi! Taxi!" A woman's voice broke into laughter.

"Why *did* he have to bring Thelma?" Rona said wearily. "That over-aged bacchante . . . " She sighed and then put the wet glasses down on the hearth.

"Thelma asks him to a lot of her parties," Scott said.

"But why repay her at our expense? She gave Jon and several other men a miserable time. Why didn't Murray look after her when he brought her here? Why did we ever invite him anyway? Oh, sorry, Scott—I'm just thinking out loud."

Scott said slowly, still not looking round, "I'm beginning to think Murray's a big mistake."

"His line is so *old*! Two years ago, or three, he could manage to get away with it. But not now."

"What do you mean?" Scott looked across the room.

"Just that he wasn't the least little bit the original talker he likes to imagine he is. He only succeeded in annoying most of our guests."

"Because he thinks differently from them? So we must all talk the same way, think the same things?"

"No, darling!" She rose and came over to him. "I don't believe two of us in the room echoed any point of view, except in a general way of—well, of believing that right is right and wrong is wrong."

"That's all relative," Scott said. "Depends on each man's frame of reference."

"I don't believe that," she said, "except for the small things in life. You can find them as relative as you like. But in the big things, you've got to decide what is right, what is wrong. Or else you've no moral judgment, at all. Like Murray. He's just a parrot, that's all he is." She looked at Scott worriedly, unhappily. He seemed to have forgotten that she was there.

At last he said stiffly, "Sorry if Murray offended you so much. I won't ask him again."

"He made your father flaming mad."

"Dad?" Scott's voice tightened.

That's the trouble, Rona thought. Her worry left her, but standing beside Scott, looking across at the lighted windows opposite and the uneven rows of black chimneys sprouting from the flat roofs, she was still more unhappy. She was waiting for Scott to forget all the things that had irritated him to-night, to take her in his arms and kiss her. She said, appeasingly, "Your father was disappointed he couldn't stay in town. He wants us to have dinner with him next week, instead."

"Yes."

46

"Scott, he *had* to be back in Staunton to-night. Your father would have stayed if he could."

"I suppose so." Scott picked up a withered canapé from a plate on the writing-desk, examined it critically, threw it back. All day, he had been preparing himself for this family dinner to-night, for the hidden tensions, for the seemingly harmless remarks that disguised petty criticisms. Instead, his father had gone back to Staunton. He shoved the desk chair angrily into place.

"Scott!" Rona's voice was near breaking point.

He turned to face her, suddenly noticing her exhaustion. "Darling!" His face softened. "I'm sorry. I had a bad evening, that's all." He took her in his arms.

"Didn't you enjoy the party at all?" She was almost in tears.

He kissed her eyes and mouth. "Yes, it was a good party."

"I'm so sorry, Scott, that I ever asked Paul Haydn."

"He seemed to be enjoying himself."

She smiled, shaking her head. "The same old Paul! He left with the prettiest girl—as usual." Then she glanced round the room. "What a mess all this is!"

Scott kissed her again. His smile had returned, the frown had cleared from his brow. "Forget it. We'll go out and have a quiet dinner together. Then I'll bring you home fairly early to-night."

"Do I look so tired?"

"No, you look wonderful. You were wrong about Haydn. I'm the man who's leaving this party with the prettiest girl. Now what about putting on your hat? The one that's only a couple of roses?"

"All right!" Her eyes were smiling now. "But I'm a bit scared of original hats after seeing Thelma's to-night."

"You aren't Thelma."

Rona said pityingly, "She's so unhappy. What's wrong with people like Thelma?"

He didn't answer that. He looked around the room. "Get Mrs. Kasprowicz to come up here, to-morrow. Just leave everything to-night, Rona. Promise?"

She was tired enough to agree, to try to forget that her budget was already overstrained this week. Parties cost a lot these days. She said, "I don't know how Peggy and Jon manage. Yet they do. And look at them to-night—as smartly dressed as anyone! You know, I always feel so guilty when I remember Jon makes less money than I do. Can you imagine it? He's got brilliant degrees, he's had years of training and study when he earned nothing, and what does he make? Four thousand dollars a year as an assistant professor."

Scott let her go. "Yes," he said, beginning to walk restlessly around the room. "It's bitterly unfair. But what do you expect in a country where a movie star makes more than the President?"

"Scott, I didn't mean it that way. All I was doing was to admire Peggy and Jon. It doesn't make them bitter. Worried, yes. But not bitter. They couldn't be so happy if they let themselves go bitter."

"They don't even know where their interests lie," he said. Why admire fools, even if they were good-natured fools? He halted suddenly, and he turned to look at Rona. "Why did you mention them, anyway?" Marriage . . . was it so important to a woman as all that? Rona and he—they had each other, they were faithfully in love. Wasn't that enough? Provided they could wait together, did waiting matter? Yet, thinking of Jon and Peggy Tyson, remembering the way he envied them even if he pitied them, he could give no true answer to his own questions. Rationally, he could find an argument. But with Rona, he couldn't argue rationally. That was what Orpen said, and what he kept denying to Orpen. I'm going to see Orpen, to-night, he decided. Once I bring Rona back here, I'll see him. Then he remembered Orpen was at a meeting to-night. But he would see Orpen on Friday definitely. He'd tell Orpen then.

Rona was saying, "Why did I mention them?" She gestured helplessly. "I don't really know," she answered slowly. "Or perhaps it was just because Peggy and Jon seem to be living a fuller life than most of us in this room to-night. Fuller and richer. And isn't that better, too? Yet, from the point of view of earning power, most of us could have bought and sold them. That was all."

Scott said, "I've been deciding one thing, to-night. We are getting married. We'll set a definite date for this summer. We've waited long enough." He smiled, and the strain and

48

worry left his face. "Will you take a chance on my earning power?"

"Oh, Scott!" She threw her arms around him. She was no longer tired and unhappy. Her smile was no longer uncertain. He caught her, holding her close to him, kissing her soft dark hair.

"We'll manage," he said. "We'll be all right, Rona. Just trust me." His grip tightened round her, almost desperately.

It was another evening to remember happily—a long, deliberate dinner with gay talk and good humour. Scott's depression had vanished completely. Now, sitting over their coffee cups in the almost deserted restaurant (it was a small French place where the proprietor was glad to see Americans being leisurely over his excellent food), Scott was reminding her of their visit last summer to Mexico. This summer, he was saying, they'd try Canada in August for some fishing. Or they might go in September and make it a honeymoon trip.

"And spend it hunting?" Rona asked, not quite sure about that. A hunting camp wasn't exactly the best place to wear charming negligees. It would be a flannel honeymoon—not lace and chiffon. "Isn't September too early for the hunting season?" Yet, she remembered, Scott had gone on hunting trips to Canada in previous summers, so her ideas about seasons must be all wrong.

"Perhaps we'd better leave that for another time," Scott said. "This year, we may have to economise a little." He smiled. "You won't mind?"

She shook her head. Why would he always assume that she judged everything on its money value? Then she thought that it was wonderful to have a man who was so modest about his own value, and she was ashamed of her irritation. "We'll have a busy summer," she said. "So much to plan for. . . . Oh, Scott, your father and Peggy and Jon are going to be so pleased."

He laughed. "We aren't setting the date for their benefit, are we?"

"No. But they all wish us well." She added happily, "I'm glad your father likes me. It makes everything—easier."

"Now, don't start planning to get me on to the staff of the *Clarion*," he teased her,

49

"I wasn't," she protested. "I know you've made up your mind about that."

"I have." Then, leaning forward on his elbows, watching her large dark eyes, he asked, "What do you really think about my decision to work in New York?"

"I admire it," she said truthfully. "Yet, I'm sorry in some ways."

"For Dad's sake?"

"No, darling." She smiled. "I think of you most of the time."

"What's wrong with the *Morning Star*? Don't you like my working there?"

"I just thought that you didn't particularly like the *Star*."

"I've got to make money, somehow, you know."

She hesitated. Then she put into words, at last, the thought that had troubled her for some months. "If you don't like newspaper work, honey, why don't you give it up?"

He didn't answer for a moment. "When I came out of the army, I thought I'd try it," he said awkwardly. He watched her face. "Besides, you are wrong. I don't dislike newspaper work. There are worse jobs. It's just so damned tedious to begin with. Nothing but police courts and fires. Routine stuff."

"Perhaps they'll give you a break soon and let you handle bigger things." Foreign news, that was what Scott really would enjoy. That was what he wanted, she knew.

"Perhaps," he said moodily. "Oh, well, I'd rather have things as they are. If I had joined the *Clarion*, everyone would have said it was my father who gave me the breaks. He's had an easy life. Plenty of money. Inherited his father's newspaper. It is about time that one man in our family stood on his own feet."

"But your father has! Why, he'd never be standing where he is to-day, if he hadn't climbed there. By himself. And that's what he wanted you to do. He wanted you to begin at the bottom and work up, as he did. And if you were good enough, you'd have been given a chance to show what you could do. It's absurd to say that you shouldn't be given a chance, just because you are his son. You ought to have the same chance as any other reporter on his paper."

"You say he began at the bottom, like any other reporter. I say he was still the editor's son."

"All right, darling," Rona smiled appeasingly. "He was still the editor's son." And a better editor than his father, she thought. He had pulled the *Clarion* out of the strictly local class into a paper whose foreign news was well reported, well edited, and well read. But she couldn't say that—not with Scott's worried frown and tight lips to warn her. And again she wondered why Scott had ever become a reporter at all. He had been a brilliant student in economics. Why hadn't he gone into business? It would have been easier on him if he had broken away completely into another field. Easier on him, easier on his father. That was what Jon Tyson said. Jon had a way of seeing things clearly.

"We'll tell Jon and Peggy on Friday," Rona said.

Scott looked up.

"About the wedding," she explained.

"Friday," he said. "This Friday?"

"They are expecting us then." She looked at him in dismay. "Don't tell me you can't come." But the expression on his face answered her. She said, "Surely if you are working late so much this week, you won't have to give up Friday too?"

"You go and see Peggy and Jon. I'll collect you there, later in the evening, and bring you home."

"All right," she said slowly. She tried to smile. "You really are the most overworked reporter in New York. Five late nights, last week. Four, the week before. They might as well put you on the night desk."

"It isn't work on Friday evening," he said. "I forgot when Peggy asked me that I had already promised Nicholas Orpen to go to a party at his place. Don't worry, I'll slip away early. I'd take you with me, but——"

"It's men only. As usual," she said crisply. She began to prepare to leave. She was intent on finding her gloves, on studying her face in the small mirror from her handbag, on adjusting the two roses caught in a heavy mesh of green veiling to their proper angle on her dark hair.

"Jealous?" He was making a joke of it.

"Perhaps." She tried to smile, too. "But why does Nicholas Orpen always avoid women so much?" And why not let himself be called Nick? she thought.

51

"Perhaps he's afraid of women," Scott said teasingly.

"When I met him, he didn't give me the feeling of being afraid of anything."

Scott was amused. "He's just a very shy, quiet little man. And you only met him once, Rona, for a matter of ten minutes. Perhaps less."

That was quite enough, she thought. "You like him a lot, don't you?"

"He's a kind-hearted sort of guy. With a good taste in music."

Rona said slowly, looking down at the gloves she was drawing on, "He seems to surround himself with young men."

"Who like music, and beer, and a lot of pipe smoke. Just trying to recapture our college days, that's all." Scott was laughing at himself now. Then his voice became more serious. "Orpen actually was a professor at one time, you know."

"I thought he was an instructor," Rona said, trying to remember. "Why did he leave Monroe College?"

"As far as I know—I was only a junior at the time—he didn't get on with the president. And you know the self-appointed dictator *he* was."

"But why didn't Orpen go on teaching elsewhere?"

"He hadn't a chance once the president got his claws into him. Orpen makes a living by his writing. He doesn't ask too much of life, you know."

"He isn't bitter?"

Scott laughed. "Heavens, no. He never talks about it, anyway. He lives quietly, sees his friends occasionally."

All of them men, Rona was thinking. She wished she didn't feel this sense of fear. She looked at Scott's face—at the blue eyes, the excellent features, the finely shaped head with its fair hair waving naturally over the high brow. She closed her pocketbook angrily: she was furious with herself. Jealous, she thought, jealous of a shy quiet little man she had once met when she had been walking with Scott down Third Avenue. Orpen had fallen into step with them for a block, had taken Scott's arm in a friendly way, had dropped Scott's arm when he saw her watching him, had smiled when she spoke and then looked vaguely away as if she weren't there at all. Yet in spite of this, it was odd how she had been left with the feeling that he knew a great deal about her. He had treated her as if she were an old acquaintance whom he disliked. Odd. And ridiculous. She rose from the table.

Scott seemed to have read her thoughts. "Rona, if you want me to stop going to Orpen's occasional parties——"

"You *know* I'd never ask you to do that," she said sharply. She was irritated as we all become irritated when we hear a man loudly offer to pay the cheque he knows someone else will pay. Safe offers always annoyed her. She quickened her pace between the little rows of empty tables.

"Good night, good night," said the proprietor, beaming on his two late guests. "*Au revoir, mademoiselle. Au revoir, monsieur*."

"Good night," echoed the waiter, a little less enthusiastically. After all, it was now half-past eleven. The tips in his pocket were heavy but so were his feet.

"Rona, stop worrying about Orpen," Scott said as he caught up with her at the restaurant door. "Or would you rather have me go to parties where there were only women?"

She shook her head, and slipped her arm through his. I am lucky, she was telling herself as they walked along the darkened side streets towards Lexington Avenue, I am lucky. Scott pays no attention to any other women; of that, I *am* sure. And if I've been worried or unhappy at times, it was only because we've been in love for three years and engaged for almost one, and sometimes that seemed so long. Sometimes, too, there seemed no real reason for being so vague about their wedding as Scott had been, but that was again only her impatience. I'm too impulsive: if I were a man and in love, I'd not even have bothered about an engagement ring; I'd have married the girl and lived in a one-room apartment if necessary. But that probably wasn't wise, however romantic. Scott was wise. He knew very well where he was going. And yet, he could be romantic too. She smiled.

"What was that smile for?" he asked.

"For you," she said. "For the days we had together in Mexico."

He gripped her arm, and they fell into step as they turned into Lexington. The neon signs above the cafés and bars were as bright as the colours on a Christmas tree. The sidewalks were still alive. People were walking home from a movie, from late business, from a visit to friends. A subway

53

train rumbled underground. Taxis were coming back from the theatres, travelling to the little night clubs on the side streets. Far down the avenue, the General Electric Building was crowned with changing lights. The tall graceful spire of the Chrysler tower pointed into the dark reddened sky.

"What about a visit to the Blue Angel?" Scott asked suddenly, as they neared Fifty-fifth Street. "Charles Trenet is singing there." Rona liked Trenet's songs: they might cheer her up, take her mind off Orpen. Why the hell did I mention his name to-night? "Or are you too tired?"

"Perhaps," she admitted. "I'm just beginning to have that old collapsed feeling."

"We'll go to-morrow night," he said. "No—not to-morrow."

Scott was working late to-morrow, she remembered. He was busy all of this week. In a way, it was lucky she was taking night classes at Columbia University—she always had plenty to do to keep her occupied too.

"We'll go sometime next week," he said.

She nodded.

"Now, stop worrying about Orpen's party on Friday night. I'll get away early and come up to join you at Peggy's. I'll get away by eleven, I'm sure."

She nodded again.

"You *are* tired," he said gently.

Yes, she was thinking, I suddenly feel quite tired, quite depressed. I'll go to bed at once. I'll have to leave all that appalling mess in the living-room. I'll get up early and clear it away in the morning. That would be a grim way to start a new day. The joys of being a career girl, she thought dejectedly.

He put his arm around her waist as they reached her house. "You're home, darling. Wake up, Rona. You can't go to sleep until you are in bed. Shall I come up and search for any burglar?"

She found herself smiling, too. That was Scott's oldest joke. "Not to-night, darling," she said. "See you soon." She kissed him, and hurried upstairs.

"I'll call you to-morrow," he was saying.

CHAPTER FIVE

On Friday, just before eleven o'clock in the morning, Paul Haydn walked into the building on Fifth Avenue where *Trend* had its offices.

"Hello, Joe," he said, as he entered the express elevator, "and how's Jamaica this season?"

Joe stared. "Mr. Haydn!" He grinned. "I heard you was back in town. But my eyes ain't what they used to be. Took me a minute to recognise you."

"To tell you the truth, Joe, I barely recognised myself." He looked into the mirror above the elevator door. The grey flannel suit, the white shirt, still looked as odd as they felt. And he had lost his taste in ties: the plue polka dot that he had bought so enthusiastically seemed a bit intense to him now.

"You'll get used to it," Joe said sympathetically. "Just like me. Been married thirty-five years. To-day's our anniversary. I woke up and looked at the wife, and I said 'Guess I'm married all right.' Well, it's good to see you, Mr. Haydn. Hope we'll be seeing more of you around here." He brought the elevator to a smooth halt and opened its door.

"I don't know, yet," Paul said. The elevator door closed behind him. He was left looking at a receptionist sitting very impressively behind a desk. Impressively, because once this landing had been a linoleum-covered place without any pretty girl waiting to receive visitors as they came out of the elevator.

"Yes?" she was proud of the effect she caused.

"I'm Paul Haydn. I have an appointment with Mr. Crowell, the Feature Editor."

"Just a minute please." She slowly lifted a telephone. "Won't you take a seat?"

Paul repressed a smile. He chose an arm-chair in white leather, looked at the light grey rug and then at the prints framed in red against a dark grey wall. "Snazzy," he said, but the girl only gave him a pitying look. Where I come from, she seemed to say, we use this kind of place for an outhouse. He retired into silence, smiling broadly now.

She reported, "Mr. Crowell is not in to-day. But his secretary says Mr. Weidler wants to see you as soon as you arrive."

Paul's eyebrows gave away his surprise.

"Mr. Crowell's secretary will show you——"

"Tell her it's all right, I know the way." He rose and went toward a door. "Straight ahead and then to my left?" She didn't answer, but began telephoning more urgently this time. She stared after him worriedly. She looked much prettier when she was being human, he thought.

He entered a long corridor, with offices leading off on either side. Some of the door were closed: conferences going on. Others stood open, showing businesslike interiors. The waiting-room's luxury was replaced by efficiency. He felt slightly better: *Trend* was a good magazine, a good place to work, except for its name and its waiting-room.

Two or three people walked past him, glancing quickly at him, paying little attention. From the largest office, a grey-haired, pleasant-faced woman hurried out. "Why," she said, stopping in surprise, waving a sheaf of papers at him, "if it isn't——"

"And just imagine, it is!" In spite of his teasing words, he shook hands with her enthusiastically. He had always liked Mrs. Hershey. "It's good to see *someone* I know, around here."

"You're coming back?" she asked eagerly. My, she was thinking, and doesn't he look as nice as ever? More serious, but still as quick to shake your hand as if he meant it.

"I don't know, yet. Some people don't want me back, I hear."

"Why, that's just spite!" So she had heard the rumours, too. "Miss Guttman!" She intercepted a blonde secretary in a neat suit and a dazzling white waistcoat.

"Why, Mr. Haydn! Pleased to meet you again."

"Hello, Annie!"

Miss Guttman's face flushed with pleasure even under the pancake make-up. She laughed and said, "So you didn't forget us." It was a long time since anyone in the office had called her Annie.

"Couldn't," he said. "Couldn't imagine this place running efficiently without you two." That was true enough, in its way. "See you both later. Now I'm——" he nodded in the direction of the Boss's end of the corridor.

Miss Guttman watched him as he walked on. She was only then remembering that she had meant to disapprove of him. "You know, that permanent I got yesterday has just ruined my hair," she said angrily, touching its tight curl. "Ten dollars. I ask you! I could *sue* them."

"Never mind, dear. The waistcoat looks nice," Mrs. Hershey said with a smile.

Mr. Weidler's secretary was waiting for him.

"Mr. Haydn?" She was new, too. And very young. Paul began to feel old, practically tottering on the edge of senility. He would soon be talking in terms of the days when. She took him through a small white room furnished with much white leather and many red-framed prints. (Daumier, he noted with surprise: the realities of life against a cushioned setting.) But the inner office was still the same old place. Even before Weidler rose from his cluttered desk, shook hands warmly, and offered him a battered—but surprisingly comfortable—brown leather chair, Paul Haydn was warned that his hunch had been right. You did not arrive so promptly in this inner office, unless you were considered urgent. Not necessarily important, just urgent. He was glad he had decided to visit *Trend* so soon. This feeling of urgency had bothered him in these last few days.

Weidler, he was pleased to see, was not much changed. In appearance, at least. He was a short stocky man with a red square-shaped face, grey hair bristling from many years of crew cuts, clever eyes, and a ready smile. He was a happy optimist by nature. He had started *Trend* in the thirties when nearly everyone else had been more than depressed about any future. From a small magazine "dedicated to the arts," with departments for literature, painting, and music, it had expanded into "a magazine for living," where the departments had grown to cover many subdivisions. But the emphasis was still on art in general. It avoided politics, personalities, and editorial comment.

Bill Weidler, apart from a good business sense, had been activated by one idea: why keep literature, painting, music separate? They all influenced one another. Why not show that? Show it in terms that the ordinary intelligent man or woman could understand. There were plenty of people in America who wanted to go on educating themselves after they left school or college. ("You get a kick out of recognising a picture, a symphony," Weidler would explain with his broad smile. "It's good to know that when people start talking about Eliot or Faulkner or Le Corbusier, you don't feel dumb. Sure, I'm appealing to snobbery, but who isn't a snob? No closed shop in that. You can call it potted culture, but no reader's going to remain the poorer because he's read us. We don't cheat him.") All you had to do was to make the learning process attractive. None of this silly superior stuff that catered for two thousand minds and repelled the rest—silly, because it defeated itself, it couldn't operate except at a loss: first, a financial loss, then the loss of itself and all its potential influence. And *Trend* had both annoyed and amused all its initial critics by avoiding any loss whatsoever. There were, it seemed, enough ordinary intelligent people to make it pay and expand.

Now Weidler offered Paul a cigarette and turned his chair to look out of the window, too. Just as he had built his magazine's sales on appealing to people's desire to understand more, he had built the magazine itself on his own ideas of human relationships. He hired good men, treated them well, and kept himself approachable. None of this higher-than-God stuff, as he'd put it. It was harder, nowadays, to keep an eye on everything and get to know the men who worked for him. Since the war, and the increasing interest in music and painting and architecture, his staff had doubled. But Paul Haydn was one of the prewar crowd. He looked at Paul shrewdly, lit a cigarette himself, and put his feet up on the window sill.

"Well, Paul, glad you came around to see us so soon."

"Sooner than I meant to, frankly," Paul said. He had only intended to call on Crowell of his old department, and get a general picture of the situation in the office.

"Got tired of having a vacation? Well, the sooner you can start here, the better for us."

Paul Haydn was a little taken back by this reception. He wasn't ready, yet, to discuss definite dates. He owed himself a holiday, a time to choose his future carefully. This was like a second start in life. You didn't hurry it. He said, "I wanted to know how I stood about this job. That's all." He looked around the small room, noting the photographs of a smiling wife and two pugnacious boys, the silver cup for rowing, the Piranesi prints on the wall. "Glad to see this hasn't changed. I got scared when I came into the office, at first. Thought you were branching into the latest from Paris."

Weidler's plain, good-natured face relaxed in a broad grin. "Oh," he said self-consciously, "all that feminine touch? Don't let it worry you. It's there to impress the people who like being impressed. But the real set-up is much the same. We are still looking for the right men to work here." In spite of his smile, a worried look came over his face. He was watching Paul Haydn carefully.

"Frankly," he went on, "we need you back. You know our policies, our market. Crowell isn't at all well—he's been ill, off and on, for the last three years. He wants to resign this September. So, although we are asking you to come back as his assistant editor, you'll be Feature Editor in a few months. That's an important job."

Paul nodded. He was impressed. "I know," he said quietly. "But why am I getting this chance? I thought a man called Blackworth was firmly established as assistant editor."

Weidler's face changed completely. All the good humour was gone, and he looked bitterly unhappy. "Blackworth just wasn't the right man."

"But you've had him four years—nearly five." The wrong men didn't stay on *Trend* four months. Paul said casually, "There's a story going around . . ."

Weidler was very still.

". . . that I've been plotting to get Blackworth removed," Paul went on smoothly. "I don't like that. I don't like that one bit."

"You know it's a lie," Weidler said persuadingly.

"Sure. I've had a lot of exaggerated gossip spread about me in my life, but this particular little item is one thing I'm not going to have tacked on to me. And so I've come to ask you why Blackworth is being kicked out. You must have a good reason. Yet no one can give it to me."

"They just give you the story that you stole Blackworth's

job?" Weidler rose suddenly, swearing, walking around his desk excitedly. "Of course," he burst out, "that's what they want . . . they want to keep you from taking it!" Then he paused, his face redder than ever. He forced his voice to be normal again. He said, "Where did you hear this story?"

"Everywhere I've been, frankly. You know how New York has its little circles that know all about each other as much as if they all lived round a village green. My circle is the writing field—magazine people, agents, newspapermen, critics. My friends say they don't believe there's a word of truth in the rumour about Blackworth; but they've heard the rumour and it's worrying them. Those who aren't my friends just challenge me to my face. I don't like this whole thing, Bill, I don't like it one bit." He rose, glanced at his watch. "I expect you're busy."

"Sit down, Paul, I've plenty of time for this. . . . You are thinking of refusing the job, just when we need you. I know your record, both here and in the army. You had enough experience there with psychological warfare to make you the best man we can find for the job. You were in counter-propaganda, weren't you? You know that two and two make a good clear four. That's why they don't want to see you back here."

"Who the hell are 'they'?"

Weidler came back to his chair. This time, he didn't lean back or stretch his legs comfortably. This time, he sat forward with his hands clasped, his elbows on the arm-rests. His eyes were fixed on Haydn, his hair seemed to bristle with anger.

"I get so damned mad when I start thinking about it," he said. "But I'll try to keep my temper and give you a clear picture. You are looking at a man, Paul, who—only six weeks ago—couldn't add two and two. Sure, that rankles, that bites deep." He paused, and gave a wry smile. "The only reason I haven't let anyone know the full story is that —I didn't want to start a rumour going round that we've been infiltrated by Communists. We haven't!" he added quickly. "Yes, I admit there was an attempt. I found that out six weeks ago. Blackworth has gone. So I've stopped the rot. I've got my eye on one other man—a bit of a loudmouth who may not be guilty of anything except stupidity—he's in the advertising department and I don't see what damage he could do there."

"Name of Murray, by any chance? I met him at a party on my first night home. He doesn't advertise himself very well, I must say."

"But until I know definitely about him, I can take no action. You can't fire a man for what he says."

"If a man went around saying he believed in raping children, you'd fire him quickly enough."

"But politics and morals are two different things, Paul. You can't say a Communist sympathiser is the same as a man who rapes children."

"I'm only saying a man *can* be fired for what he says— if his beliefs are pernicious enough. It all depends on what we feel is pernicious. It's very tough on a typhoid carrier if he has to be segregated from his fellow men, but doctors insist on treating typhoid germs as a pernicious menace to public health. And most of us are very thankful that they do. No one goes around talking about persecution of typhoid carriers."

Weidler didn't answer.

Paul looked at him. What's wrong with him? he wondered. Has he lost his old zest for a challenge? Is he going soft? Or has he suddenly found himself in territory that he never believed existed—like a cautious explorer in a new stretch of jungle? Paul said, "Your story interests me a lot. So Blackworth turned out to be a Communist."

"He says he isn't. I don't know. He swore on his oath he wasn't."

"On his oath of allegiance to the Communist Party?" Paul asked with a smile. "That isn't much help to us who swear on a Bible. Anyway, what did Blackworth actually do? Obviously he did more than talk, or you wouldn't have fired him." His voice was bitter. Then he said, "Sorry, Bill. I'm only a week away from Europe. I can still see people, with stark fear on their faces, starving, filthy, trying to reach our Zone. They've walked miles, they've sneaked past sentries expecting a bullet in their backs, they've hidden in woods and ditches. They are in rags. They've nothing, except their hatred for the nice little guys like Blackworth who betrayed them into the kind of government they've now got. You should

61

see their eyes, look at their bones, at their bleeding feet. All the refugees from tyranny don't arrive in aeroplanes, you know."

He paused, willing to stop there. But Weidler gestured to him to go on.

He went on, "You see, I've been working a good deal among political refugees for the last year. We had to find out if they were genuine. Oh, yes, infiltration is tried there, too. We've caught a number of fakes and phonies. But most of these people are genuine." He paused. When he spoke again, his voice was cold and factual, giving a vehemence to his words that startled Weidler.

He said, "When you've seen the face of a woman, as she tells how her husband disappeared without trace, her elder son imprisoned without trial, no communication allowed, and even the name of the prison only a vague guess; when you look at the thin body of her younger son and see his eyes, and hear how she managed to bring him into the American Zone, walking by night, hiding by day; when you look at the rags on their backs and know that is all they own now, along with each other and the will to freedom which nothing could kill—then you begin to realise just what political persecution *is*. She was the wife of a school-teacher in a small Czechoslovakian village. They had a small house which she kept neatly. They survived the Germans. Her husband came back from the concentration camp where he had spent six years of his life. And why was he kidnapped now? Because, in the last elections, he voted 'No' to the Communist candidate. That was all: he voted 'No.' He had made no speeches, taken part in no organisations against the Communists, had kept silent. One concentration camp is enough for one lifetime, he had said. But when he came to cast his vote, he followed his conscience. There were informers watching the casting of votes. That was all."

Paul Haydn stopped. Then he added, "There are thousands like her and her son. And I come back here and find some people still giving out a lofty line of talk about America's mistakes and its 'political martyrs.' By God, I'd like to take all these little hair-splitters and show them the people who struggle into the American Zone. I'd let them look at the human beings they are betraying by their talk. I'd show them some real martyrs!" Then he dropped his voice. "Bill, don't the people in America *know* what's at stake?"

"I think we do. Most of us do. Most of us sense the over-all strategy against us. We don't always recognise the tactics. But we are learning." Bill Weidler's eyes narrowed. "I think," he said, "that you are the man to hear the full story about Blackworth. You won't go calling me a 'witch-hunter.' It's a strange story," he warned.

In a strange setting, Paul Haydn thought as he waited: he looked across at the busy office buildings on Fifth Avenue, listened to the dim roar of traffic beneath, imagined the busy sidewalks—people working, people hurrying to engagements, people planning a pleasant party with friends, people looking forward to a quiet night in their own homes. What could be more peaceful, more unsuspecting of evil, more comforting?

Weidler began his story, speaking quickly but clearly. "In the last three years Crowell has been pretty sick, off and on. He came more and more to depend on Blackworth as his assistant editor. During the last ten months, Blackworth took over most of his work. I didn't know how far it went, until recently. I've always liked Crowell, and I didn't want to force him to retire. I was waiting for him to admit he couldn't carry on. In any case, Blackworth was next in line for the editorship of our Feature Department." He rubbed his nose, then his head. The story clearly embarrassed him. He cleared his throat and took a deep breath.

"We knew Blackworth as a good writer, a better editor, a young man who was hard-working, clever. His previous jobs had been in a publishing house, and in Washington for two years of the war. I did notice that during the last ten months, the tone of the feature articles was changing. They depressed me. But facts are facts. And here were articles giving facts about America. I began to think that the country was in a hell of a condition, that there were basic wrongs and injustices and corruptions it would be hard to cure. Some letters from our readers would reflect my feelings, but there were others saying 'Good old *Trend*! Tell us more of the real truth!'

"Then one day, just about six weeks ago, a writer I know personally called me up to ask what was wrong with his stuff—we never printed anything he sent us nowadays. He pretended to make a joke of it, but I could feel he was pretty sore. I calmed him down and got him to give me a list of his rejections.

"Perhaps I'd have done nothing more about that (after all, writers *can* be prima donnas) but Burnett, who is now head of our architecture section, came to see me. Blackworth had been running a series of articles on housing. Naturally, Burnett and his department were surprised and interested. Rona Metford—remember her? She's done very well, you know— well, Rona had been making a special study of postwar housing for one of her courses at Columbia this winter, and she insisted that the writer of those articles was lying. She tipped Blackworth off about that, as soon as she read the first article; but no action was taken, for a second, and then a third, article was published. So Burnett was worried. He brought me the three last numbers of *Trend* where Rona had underlined all the oversimplifications and misrepresentations. His own verdict was that the articles were definitely misleading.

"I wanted facts. So I sent for Rona. She made a list of them for me. She agreed that there had been mistakes in postwar housing, but things weren't as bad or vicious as *Trend* made them out to be. The effect of those three articles, as Rona pointed out, was to make our readers think that America was run by cheats and crooks."

Weidler took a deep breath there, shaking his head, a wry smile on his lips.

"I sent her away, told her to keep quiet about it. But I studied her list of figures, and the marked magazines. I called in a couple of other architects, a couple of experts on housing, and a couple of building contractors. By the time they had verified Rona's analysis, I was pretty damned mad.

"Then I checked on the new feature writers who had been printed by us recently. Some of them had written for us before, but it was odd that their articles were usually accepted when Crowell was ill and Blackworth was in charge. In the last six months we had had some articles by writers I didn't know at all—new discoveries, apparently. When I looked at the tone of their work really carefully, I decided to check on their names. I got some expert help on that. And one of them at least was using a phony name. He's an ad-

64

mitted member of the Communist Party. But he wasn't presented to our readers as that. You know those little captions we put on the 'Introduction to Contributors' page? He was listed simply as 'William Slade, writer, lecturer, and collector of rare coins.' Strictly double-headed eagles, I'd imagine. . . . His real name is Nicholas Orpen. Ever heard of him?"

Paul shook his head. "New to me."

"Few people remember him. But I've known about him for some years," Bill Weidler said. "I know a lot about Orpen." He shook his head in distaste, and fell silent for a few moments. Then he roused himself. "Orpen's article was a clever piece. It pretended to discuss the reasons for decadence in American writing. You were left with the feeling that a system such as ours would inevitably result in decadence. It was after this that I decided to take some action. I didn't know how far the thing had gone. But apart from the fact that I had to get rid of Blackworth, I didn't know quite how to do it. It wasn't as easy as it sounds. I wanted no scandal, nothing to ruin *Trend*'s reputation, nothing to stampede our readers away from us. You see?"

Paul nodded.

"In a way," Weidler said, "I felt I was fighting shadows."

"But," Paul reminded him, "if there's no substance, there's no shadow. Anyway, what did you do?"

"The obvious thing. I asked a man at the FBI for advice. He told me the FBI could only deal with people's actions, not with people's political ideas. And there is no law against anyone refusing to buy from certain firms or stores, or from certain writers. People are allowed to have their own prejudices, their own opinions. If I challenged him, Blackworth could always retort that he wasn't forcing our readers to believe anything—he was only publishing what he considered good writing."

"Well, how did you fire him?"

"By asking him about our new contributors. Had he met them? Of course he had—that's part of his expense account. Then I asked about the man who was modestly called a 'writer, lecturer, and collector of rare coins.' Blackworth said he was a nice guy to meet, shy and retiring, that his material was well written, and that he seemed a good man to have as a regular contributor. So then I said, 'If you've met him, you must have recognised his face. For he taught you at Monroe College fifteen years ago. And you know the scandal that broke out there in 1941.'"

Paul said, "Then Blackworth protested it was persecution, not scandal. He probably said that Orpen was no longer a Communist, and he had to live, and you couldn't take his livelihood away from him. Was that his reply?"

Weidler looked up at Paul then. "More or less," he said. "How did you know?"

"They keep repeating their patterns. I had the same defence from hidden Nazis and disguised Communists trying to slip into German newspapers. Same old story. Always appealing to human decency and conscience, although they themselves try to kick all antitotalitarian writers into the gutter. They have no conscience about ruining other people's careers. So, what did you do?"

"I lost my temper. I showed him Rona Metford's analysis. I told him he'd better leave. He wanted to know my exact reasons. But I'd got my temper under control again, and I said he was leaving simply because he didn't suit us. No, he didn't get any libel suit out of me!"

"Then he said that publishers shouldn't be dictators, that all kinds of opinions should be given freedom of expression?" Paul asked.

"But I had an answer for that. I said if he felt free to choose the feature writers, surely I had the same freedom to choose the members of my staff? He had followed his own taste and judgment: that was what I was doing, too."

There was a long silence.

Then Weidler spoke again. "You believe I was right, don't you?" He was still worrying about his decision.

Paul Haydn nodded. He was thinking of his plane trip home, of Roger Brownlee who had sat next to him and tried to enlist his interest in something that had seemed fantastic. Yet Brownlee's guarded generalisations now began to fall into an understandable pattern. But where Weidler believed that he alone had been singled out for this bit of treachery (part of his indignation was based on the feeling he was fighting a propaganda battle all by himself, with little understanding expected from either his readers or his friends), Brownlee saw it all as a widely thrown net where people were often caught because they felt they were alone and helpless.

"I know a man—he was my colonel at one time," Paul said, "who knows a lot about propaganda. He made a particular study of the fall of France in 1940. He came to the belief that France was defeated before the German armies reached her border. I used to think he was a bit hipped on the subject. But—perhaps I was wrong."

"Do I know him?"

"I don't think so." Better not give away Brownlee's name, even to Weidler, until Brownlee said it was all right. "Before the war came," Paul went on, "he used to work for Consumers' Union. He tracked down all the false advertisements, the misleading statements made by dubious manufacturers. He believed that the public ought to know what it was buying. He feels very much the same about propaganda. Take away the tinsel and the gay wrapping paper and let people see what really lies inside. All ingredients to be marked honestly on the outside of the box. Then, if people still insist on buying it, the responsibility is all theirs."

"That makes solid good sense," Weidler said, suddenly interested. "That's an idea worth following through."

"And that is what he means to do. It seems to him that people have been offered a lot of packaged ideas in these last few years without being told what the packages really contain. Just as the people of France were sold ideas such as 'Imperialist war,' 'Patriotism is for the rich,' 'Hitler doesn't mean the destruction of France.' 'Why fight for England?' But by the end of 1940 Frenchmen were beginning to realise that they had been duped. Patriotism was for every man, if he wanted to stay a Frenchman. They weren't fighting for anything except their own freedom. By that time, it was too late to fight ideas with ideas. It was a case, then, of fighting with machine guns too, of underground warfare, of risking torture and death and the destruction of their families."

"I'd like to see you do a series of articles on that," said Weidler. Then regretfully, "Only, of course, we steer clear of politics."

"What has Blackworth been doing? Concentrating on the beauty of abstract art or the joys of travel?"

Weidler looked at Paul Haydn almost angrily. "You've

come back speaking plainly," he said. But he was thinking over what Haydn had told him.

"Yes. And I'm going to add this too," Paul said. "There will be other Blackworths trying to edge their way into *Trend*. Don't think you can relax, now that you've found him out. This is going to be a struggle for power for the next ten or twenty years. Perhaps longer. Some struggles for power used up centuries."

Weidler said, "Will you take this job on *Trend*, Paul?"

Paul hesitated. "I'm closer to taking it than I was," he said frankly. "I need a few days to think it all over. The situation is all clearer to be. But—Bill, why don't you publish the story you told me? Just as you've told it to me? Let your readers know. Let the public see what is happening."

Weidler's frown came back. "You know what *will* happen? There will be a campaign against us. We'll be called fascists, warmongers, American imperialists, witch-hunters."

"You've forgotten to add 'hysteria-inciters,'" Paul said, smiling. "Strange how often they've been using 'hysteria' recently—almost hysterically, in fact." Then, seriously, "We can, of course, let ourselves be blackmailed into silence. That is one of their tactics. We are supposed not to join together and pool our experiences. We have all to keep on worrying in private, and hush everything up publicly. Just like the victims of gangsters' rackets, who are afraid to testify."

Weidler said slowly, "I'd like to talk with that friend of yours. The colonel."

"He isn't a colonel any more. He resigned his commission. He sees he has to act as a civilian in this."

"I'd like to talk with him," Weidler repeated.

"I'll arrange it. I think it would probably cheer you up if you did. You aren't alone in this."

Weidler looked surprised, and then smiled. "God knows I could do with some cheering up."

"Solidarity forever," Paul said with a grin, as he rose to leave. "That's our motto."

He said to himself, as he went down the corridor, "I wanted none of this." He had listened to Roger Brownlee in Berlin with impatience. On the plane journey home, he had been almost angry with Brownlee. And yet, for the last half hour,

68

he had been echoing all Brownlee's worries and thoughts. And now, because of Weidler, he would have to get in touch with Brownlee after all. And soon. I wanted no part of this, he thought. But what other choice was there? Turn your eyes away from the war that was going on, the struggle for domination over your country? And then, later—when it was too late—moan about your blindness, your smugness, your vanity, your cowardice?

"There's no choice," Brownlee had said, "no choice. They've chosen the weapons. Infiltration and control of propaganda sources. We shall have to learn to know them for what they are. Or go down in history as the biggest boobs of all time. For the writing is on the wall, clear to see. It is up to people like you and me, Paul. It's up to people like us, who make our living in an information medium—the publishers, the writers, the producers and directors, the journalists, the columnists, the teachers and the preachers, the editors, the television and radio men. It's up to us. We ought to see the lies and guard against them. We've got to expose them."

In the crowded elevator, lunch-going voices chattered, cutting across each other, forming a rattling pattern of broken sound.

"——I tried it on, and it fit perfectly, so I——"

"——funniest movie in months. Gave me a real yak."

"——and she said, 'I didn't mean that at all.' I said, 'Well, it's a fine thing you always never——' "

"The Yankees are much too big business for me. Now take the——"

"It looks fifty dollars at least. And blue's my——"

"Sure, I read it in the paper. She's getting married on——"

"——the new Prokofieff. Hope Liberty's isn't crowded. I want to hear some other records too."

"Yes, he's serious. Said his drive never brought him anywhere near the green until he changed his——"

"I've been trying for three months to get seats. Isn't worth it."

Paul Haydn broke away from the crowd and hurried out of doors. Joe, staring after him, said to the dispatcher, "Looks as if he didn't get that job after all, Tony. See his face?"

Tony, timing the elevators, didn't listen. "Better take it up again," he told Joe in his rush-hour voice. "Feeding time at the zoo. They'll start roaring like lions if you keep them waiting."

In the busy avenue, Paul Haydn looked at the faces round him. Why didn't I choose to be a buttonhole manufacturer, and then all I'd have to worry about would be the sizes of buttons? And my income tax. Why didn't I stay in the infantry and learn about bazookas instead of psychological warfare? Why did I have to learn all the things I've learned? Why did I have to know either Brownlee or Weidler? Why didn't I shut my ears and stay happy?

He began walking toward the Plaza. If he had to drown his worries, he might as well drown them in comfort.

CHAPTER SIX

Rona arrived early at the Tysons' apartment on Friday evening. Peggy, in a neat blue dress, her hair slightly ruffled, a flush on her cheeks, an apron around her waist, came out of the kitchen for a moment to greet her sister in the dimly lit, long, narrow hall. Jon was helping Rona to take off her new white fleece coat.

"It's darling," Peggy said with an admiring glance, but she flinched at the thought of Rona's cleaning bills. Then she lowered her voice, glancing warningly along the hall. "I've just got Bobby to bed, and he's asleep, I think. Come and help me with the sandwiches. Honey"—this was to Jon— "do get your manuscript all cleared up or we won't have a place for the beer."

"I'll have a look at the children first," Rona said, trying to make the two packages she carried in her arms as inconspicuous as possible.

"Now, Rona, you really shouldn't have——"

"I shan't waken them," Rona said quickly, and went toward the children's bedroom.

"You'd better not," Peggy said with a smile, and went back into the kitchen.

"Watch out for Bobby's train," Jon whispered as he and Rona stopped outside the children's room. "The tracks are all over the place." They listened at the door. Jon nodded

70·

and pushed it open gently. "Asleep, thank heavens," he said.

Rona stepped in alone, and let her eyes become accustomed to the darkened room. Bobby lay quite still in his small bed, one pyjama-covered arm thrown above his head. Barbara, a round rosy dumpling of a child with fine fair hair pressed to her head by the warmth of sleep, lay with her feet on the pillow. The top sheet was twisted into a crumpled heap; the blanket was cast aside. A brown bear, worn with patting, stared glassily at the shadowed ceiling.

Gently, Rona moved Barbara right side up, straightened the pillow, smoothed out the sheet and blanket. Barbara stiffened, screwed up her small fat nose, and tried to rub it away with a vehement fist. Then she slumped still, her eyelids gave a last quiver, and she was deep into sleep once more. Rona placed one of the packages at the foot of the cot. It had no string around it. It could easily be opened in the morning by small fumbling fingers.

Then she moved across the room to Bobby and laid his parcel—tied in innumerable knots, for he enjoyed the mystery of opening them—between the mound of his legs and the wall. She stood looking down at him. By the faint light from the half-open door, she could see the outline of his smooth small face. His fair hair waved like Jon's. (Barbara had straight hair, as if Nature had got mixed up in her gifts.) His eyelashes lay placidly over his pale cheeks. He looked thin and helpless, and somehow very touching.

One eye opened and looked at her gravely.

"I'm asleep," he whispered.

"So I see."

He whipped out a gun with the hand that had been hidden under the blanket. "I'm on guard," he whispered loudly, opening his other eye. He lowered the gun. "But you're all right."

"Who were you expecting?"

"Underslung Dick has been raising a lot of trouble around here."

"What, again?" Underslung Dick had been one of Rona's inventions which everyone was now beginning to regret, everyone except Bobby.

He nodded. "But I guess he's gone to sleep now." He relaxed, stifled a large yawn. "And what did you bring me?"

71

Rona giggled. "You know you aren't supposed to ask that question."

"Only in front of Mummy! What is it? Can I see?"

"Sh-h! Your voice is getting louder." Rona picked up the package. "Shall I open it? It's too dark in here to see the knots."

"What kind are they this time?"

"Mostly granny knots, I'm afraid. You'll have to teach me all over again." She began opening the parcel.

"But I've *shown* you! Aunt Rona, you're *awful* dumb." He looked at her affectionately.

"Yes. And I don't know what we're going to do about it."

He gave her a sudden smile. "Aw, you aren't so dumb," he said comfortingly. He reached out his hand for his present. "Oh!" He sat bolt upright. "A cowboy belt. White. Oh! . . . What's those?"

"Rubies and emeralds. Sheriffs always have rubies and emeralds on their belts."

"Gosh! Thanks . . ." He buckled it round his thin waist, and slipped the gun into the holster. "Just right," he announced and lay down again, drawing the blankets up to his chin. "Sheriff's sleep in their belts," he told her.

"But I think they take their guns out. Might get rusty or something."

"Oh! . . ." He thought over that. "Perspiration?" he asked. He handed over the gun to her.

"I'll put it under the pillow, but don't touch it. Rust is very bad for a gun, you know."

He nodded, his eyes closed over the image of a white belt blazing with rubies and emeralds. "It's tamendous," he said sleepily. "Thanks, Aunt Rona." He smiled and settled his head comfortably on the pillow.

She bent and kissed him, and pushed the hair gently back from his forehead. She left the door only slightly ajar, and went quickly toward the kitchen.

Peggy had buttered the slices of bread. She was now chopping up some hard-boiled eggs. She handed Rona an apron. "I've made the deviled eggs. You mash up the sardines and add some lemon juice. Are they really asleep at last? They were perfect little monsters this evening—one of those inciting-to-riot nights. It always seems to happen on a Friday. Jon's getting the living-room cleared."

Rona smiled. When Peggy was busy, her sentences were always busy too. "How's Jon's book coming along?"

"He'll get it finished this summer, we hope. There isn't much free time to do any writing during term, you know."

"Then Jon has decided not to teach in summer school this year?"

Peggy nodded. No summer school meant they wouldn't make eight hundred extra dollars. Still, the book had to be finished, and soon. Before anyone else published something new on Madison. "Jon's at the War of 1812, now," Peggy said, "but there's still a long way to go."

"And are you going to exchange the apartment for that cottage in New Jersey?"

"I think so. The people who own it seem civilised. He's a schoolteacher and he wants to attend classes at Columbia this summer. So it could work out very well. It isn't a very big cottage, but it would be easy to reach and it has a fine view and a garden. The children will love that. Bobby's getting so wild. He chases around all day."

"He's thinner. I suppose he's growing."

"He's shooting out of all his clothes. I don't know why he is so thin, though. I keep pumping all my best cooking into him." Peggy looked up, worried.

Rona said quickly, "Barbara looks like a butterball. An angelic butterball."

"If you had seen her slinging the suds around the bathroom to-night when I was trying to wash some of her clothes in the hand basin, you wouldn't think she was an angel." That reminded Peggy to look at the socks and vests and sweaters drying on the wooden stand near the open window. She put down the bowl of chopped eggs, and went over to turn the clothes around and keep them from ridging as they dried.

Rona shook her head. "How do you do it all?" she asked.

Peggy gave a short laugh. "Most of us have to do it," she said. "Six million new babies last year. One good thing—Jon says he and all the other teachers are never going to be out of work."

"I wasn't pitying you, Peggy," Rona said. "In fact, I was

envying you." Strange as it might seem to Mr. Burnett or Mr. Weidler, she did envy Peggy. "You're happy, aren't you?"

Peggy stared at her. "Aren't you?" she asked suddenly.

"Of course!" Then Rona's voice lost its defensiveness, and she said shyly, "Scott was awfully sorry he couldn't come here to-night. Because we've decided on the date."

"Oh, Rona!" Peggy put down the salt shaker. "That's wonderful news. When is it to be? Before we go to New Jersey for the summer, I hope."

Rona's cheeks coloured. "September."

"Why wait until September?"

"It will be early in September."

"When?"

"Oh, Scott isn't quite sure yet when he can get his vacation this year—sometime early in September." Rona went on spreading the sardines carefully over the buttered bread, trying to make them stretch as far as possible. "We are starting to look for an apartment next week," she said. "His studio is too small—there's only one room and one closet for clothes, so it would be hopeless."

"What's wrong with your apartment?"

"Scott doesn't like the idea of coming to live there, somehow."

"But he would be paying the rent," Peggy said. "And he could add some of his furniture." Then, as she saw that Rona was still more embarrassed, she said quickly, "Well, I hear it's a little easier to find a place nowadays. Rents are high, of course. But I think you could get two or three rooms in this district for about eighty or ninety dollars a month." Rona's apartment was more than that, she remembered. So that was the reason Scott didn't want to live there. What on earth did he do with his money? His salary wasn't at all bad, and his prospects were good, but he never seemed to be able to save anything.

Rona's cheeks had coloured again. (Scott wouldn't live in this district. "Too far away," he had said, "no one ever comes to see you, and you can't get anywhere quickly.") But the doorbell rang, and Peggy was looking in alarm at the clock—it was exactly eight—and then at the half-finished sandwiches. She took off her apron and left the kitchen, and

74

Rona didn't have to give any evasive answers. From the hall, she heard Jon's voice and then Paul Haydn's. She was staring at the closed kitchen door when Peggy returned.

"Yes, it's Paul!" Peggy said, her voice a mixture of consternation and amusement. "He's just gone into the living-room with Jon. My fault, honey: I told Paul that Friday was always a good night to find us at home. He came early to talk to Jon before the others arrive."

"Well, why shouldn't he come to see Jon? Before the war, they went around a good deal together." Rona was smiling, now that the first surprise was over. "Look, darling, I'm quite inoculated against Paul's famous charm. He's just another nice guy, that's all."

Peggy began to trim the sandwiches. "Why did you break your engagement to him? You never gave me any real reason, you know. And I've tried to keep off the subject ever since. Of course, you were really too young at the time." She looked questioningly at her sister. "Paul felt that, too, didn't he? He thought he was cradle-snatching. And then he was much older than you were—almost seven years."

"Yes. I was too young. And too rigid in my ideas. And I had far too much pride." Rona tried to laugh. "I was an awful little prig, you know. I took everything so seriously. When I think of the high tone I adopted in my last letter to Paul—he was over in London, then—I could really scream with laughter. No wonder he got mad and took me at my word. Probably congratulated himself on escaping the neatest little man-trap he had ever got caught in."

"Now, Rona! You were just so sure that your ideas about life were the only possible ones."

Rona smiled. "That makes me sound worse than ever."

Peggy said quickly, "You were only very inexperienced, that's all."

Rona began to laugh.

Peggy said more quickly, "Besides, he was much *too* experienced if you ask me. Now, don't get me wrong. I like Paul. But——"

"A lot of the stories that went around were just gossip. I know that, now. He's the kind of man who finds himself in —well, situations."

"Such as Mary Fyne at your party?" Peggy asked teasingly.

75

"Such as Mary Fyne," Rona said seriously. "And we pushed him into that."

"We did what?"

"We stood looking at him in horror—just a couple of outraged females. He saw me saying to myself, 'That's Paul, trust Paul to pick the prettiest redhead in sight.' So he left. With Mary Fyne."

"That's what Jon said. Yes, he defended Paul. We argued practically all evening over it."

"You argued?" Rona was amazed.

"Almost a quarrel," Peggy said cheerfully. "But you know what Martinis are! I expect there are more married squabbles after cocktail parties than you'd normally get in a month of Sundays. You see, Jon began telling me the kind of girl Mary Fyne was—and just to prove his point, he repeated what she had been saying to him. He meant to reassure me, I suppose, but I nearly slept on the living-room couch that night. She did concentrate on him for almost half an hour, you know. My fault, too. I rescued Jon from the harridan in the Pinot Noir hat and told him to go and enjoy himself for a change." Peggy began to laugh.

"Well, I'm glad you didn't sleep on the living-room couch because of my party," Rona said slowly.

Peggy was watching her with amusement. Still the little romantic, she thought affectionately. Does she imagine that Jon and I never have some moments of disagreement? "Jon wasn't going to stand for that," Peggy said. "He yanked me into bed with him. He was furious—his old quarter-deck manner. And after all you can't stay mad at someone in a double bed, can you?"

"I suppose not." Rona was smiling now. "Then it ought to be easy to lower the divorce rate. Just enforce double beds and abolish all Martinis."

"One thing I do ask you, Rona. Next time you give a party, don't have Mary Fyne along."

"I don't intend to," Rona said.

"She isn't a friend of yours, is she?" Peggy was now very much the elder sister.

"Not particularly," Rona said, which was a miracle of understatement. "Scott says she's a product of her environment," she added

76

"Strange how we never use that phrase when we are describing pleasant people," Peggy said, with a shrewd eye for Rona's face. So it was Scott who thought *la belle* Fyne ought to be at the party. . . . "Does Scott ask people because he dislikes them?" she asked with a smile. "How original of him." Then her amusement left her, and she listened intently. "That sounds to me like your little angel Barbara. I bet it's a drink of water, this time. Why, that's impossible! She was almost awash before she went to sleep."

"I'll go. You finish the sandwiches."

"If it's another drink she wants, remind her that there's a water shortage, will you?" Peggy called after Rona. Then she wrapped the sandwiches carefully in waxed paper and a dampened towel to keep them moist. Egg and sardine sandwiches would do very nicely; pity she hadn't bought some ham, too. But not at a dollar sixty-five a pound, she reminded herself hastily. She cleared the kitchen table and washed the bowls and knives.

Rona returned. "Another drink," she reported. And she had slipped off the white cowboy belt from Bobby's waist and left it hanging over the head of his bed while he slept.

"Not *too* much?" Peggy asked.

"Only a sip," Rona assured her.

"Good. I do get tired racing to Barbara's cot at five in the morning. Now," Peggy looked round the neat kitchen with the children's clothes drying nicely, "that's all, I think. Jon will look after the drinks." She straightened Barbara's high chair, painted a bright red to disguise the scratches Bobby had made on it in his day. "I'll have to make new curtains," she said, shaking her head at the window. "I've been pricing that plastic stuff. It's quite cheap by the yard."

Now it was Rona who was amused.

"And what's so funny?" Peggy asked.

"You. No one would ever guess that a few years ago all you knew was how to write a Ph. D. thesis on Marcel Proust."

"And how I racked my brain to try and find the answer to him," Peggy said, "while all he really wanted was to climb back into Mama's arms, poor little man. Oh, well—that thesis did teach me how *not* to bring up a son."

They went along the narrow hall to the bedroom to comb

their hair and wash their hands. Peggy was silent, partly because the children were in the room next door, partly because she was seeing something in a new perspective. It's odd, she was thinking—Rona feels guilty because she can afford to buy more than I can. And I have guilt because I got a college education before father died, and Rona couldn't get a degree except by working in an office through the day and taking classes at night. But perhaps that is why we are such good friends, each of us with our little sense of respect for the other. Now, if only Rona finds as wonderful a husband in Scott as I've found in Jon, everything will be all right. Everything, as Bobby says, will be tamendous.

She laughed softly and began to tell Rona of Bobby's new additions to his language.

Paul Haydn and Jon Tyson had got back to normal with each other very quickly. But all the time they were talking, joking or being serious, Paul was watching Jon. And Jon, in his own quiet way, was conscious of it.

"Have I changed such a lot?" he asked suddenly.

Paul said, "I don't think so." He ruffled his hair as he used to do when he was worried. I hope not, he was saying to himself.

"What's bothering you?"

Paul decided to risk it. "Look, I need your advice. Besides, this concerns Rona. Remotely. But still, it concerns her enough so that I think you ought to know."

At the mention of Rona, Jon's face changed.

"This has to do with *Trend*," said Paul hurriedly.

Jon relaxed. "Oh, with *Trend*," he said.

"Rona said she had told you about the Blackworth incident.

"Yes." Jon was surprised, a little puzzled. "I must say I thought it was harsh of Weidler to fire Blackworth because he had slipped up on some contributor's idea of modern housing. That isn't like Weidler."

"That is all Rona knows?"

Jon nodded. "Is there more to the story?"

"Yes. I saw Weidler this morning."

"You did? Getting squared away quickly, aren't you?"

Paul said, "It begins to look as if there isn't much time to waste." He hesitated. Then he said, "I can't tell you the full

78

story, yet. Weidler's all for secrecy, the blasted fool. But I'd like to tip you off—you can smell a dead rat under the floor as quickly as anyone. I'll give you a general direction and let you follow it yourself. Because you and Peggy are the only relatives that Rona has."

"This is a serious business, then?" Jon was alert.

Paul nodded. He stared at the faded roses on the rug at his feet, wondering how to begin. "You're in education, Jon. Do you think propaganda is a powerful force? Could it be dangerous? Supposing an enemy of this country had its sympathisers carefully planted here? Supposing these propagandists were trying to infiltrate such businesses and professions as radio, the Press, films, schools and colleges, the theatre, publishing?"

"That's a damned silly question," Jon said almost angrily. "You ask how dangerous it might be?" He looked at Paul unbelievingly, but Paul kept silent. "This is the twentieth century, with communication easier and more powerful than it's ever been. The trouble with those who see no danger, who think we are perfectly safe if only we invent more hideous bombs, is that they are still living with a nineteenth-century idea of peace. Wars haven't changed much except in bigger and better holocausts. But peace, as we are going to see it in this century, is something quite altered. A lot of new dangers are going to stay with us permanently just because we've invented a lot of peacetime conveniences that make life so interesting. It isn't only armies we have to fear to-day: it's words, words abused and corrupted and twisted."

Still Paul said nothing.

"You see," Jon went on patiently, "a hundred years ago, fewer people could read, fewer people were educated, and fewer people thought they could argue about international conditions. Also, in those days, propaganda spread more slowly and less widely. But now we've got a vast public who read their papers, discuss books and articles, go to the movies and the theatre, listen to their radio, watch television, and send their children to schools and colleges."

"And a public," Paul interposed, "who have enough to do with arranging their own lives without analysing all the things they read or hear. They've got to trust the honesty of those men who deal with the written or spoken word. Just as the journalist, or the movie director, or the teacher, has got to trust the honesty of the businessman and workers whenever he buys a refrigerator or a car or a shirt. Isn't that right?"

Jon looked at him, and then he smiled. "And I thought I had to convince you—you with all your experience in Germany."

"Well, you never can tell who needs convincing, these days," Paul said gloomily.

There was a short silence. Jon, who had been studying his hands spread out on his knees, suddenly looked up. "I think I begin to smell that rat under the floor," he said. "Blackworth is one of the men whom workers and businessmen have got to trust. And he's betrayed that trust?"

Paul said, "I can't tell you the story yet, Jon."

Jon rose and went to a bookshelf heaped with old numbers of magazines. "Rona always sends us a copy of *Trend* each month. Peggy's been reading them—I've been too busy lately. But let me see . . ." He consulted an index of contents with the expertness of the trained scholar. "What has Blackworth been putting out, recently?"

Paul crossed the room and looked over Jon's shoulder. "Try this issue," he suggested, and pointed to the name of William Slade. "Know William Slade?"

"Never heard of him."

"Ever heard of a man called Nicholas Orpen?"

"Why," Jon said slowly, "yes. . . . Didn't he cause an uproar in the university world before the war? He is, or was, a Communist. He admitted that, at the time."

"William Slade is Nicholas Orpen. And if you read that article, you'll see Orpen is still a Communist."

Jon stared blankly at Paul. Then he looked down at *Trend* incredulously.

"Don't blame *Trend*," Paul reminded him.

"So that was why Blackworth got heaved out. . . . And Rona started it all." He looked worried. "I'll keep this to myself until you give me clearance. But—well, thanks for tipping me off."

"I heard the first rumour against Rona to-day," Paul said. "After I left Weidler this morning, I dropped into the Plaza for a drink. I met a man there I used to know well. We lunched together. Then, talking casually, he brought up Rona's name. He had heard at a party, just the night before, a silly story. He thought I ought to suppress it before it got any bigger. Rona, it seems, made a pass at Blackworth. When he turned her down, she cooked up a story to get him fired—just in time for my return."

Jon said, "No! No one could invent such a petty piece of filth."

"Someone has," said Paul. "It's got the smell of a man called Murray who saw me at Rona's party. I'm sure that added the second part to the story—'just in time for my return.'"

"I'll smash his——" Jon recovered himself.

"I felt the same way. But that isn't the way to fight this."

"I know it isn't," Jon said savagely. "But what can we do?"

Paul ruffled his hair again. "And I thought I could let down my guard once I was back in the States. I guess I was in the nineteenth-century state of mind when I was crossing the Atlantic."

"But that story is so damned petty," Jon said, worriedly. "It's the Communists' way of getting back at Rona, is it?"

"Yes. Character assassination, they call it. It's generally petty. If they can't find out anything against a man, they invent it. Some of the things I've heard in my one week home have been unbelievably petty—things you and I would laugh at, if they weren't all part of a big pattern. A tragic pattern for us, if we don't become aware of it."

Jon said, "They may get away with a lot of things, but in the end people will damned well see through them. You can't fool all the people all of the time."

"That was a wise remark—for the nineteenth century," Paul said. "But would Lincoln make it now, seeing totalitarian propaganda as clearly as he would see it? What's the good of realising you've been fooled, if it's too late to do anything except be a yes-man or a refugee or a concentration camp victim?"

"Or fight."

"A pity if being fooled in the twentieth century means the bloodiest civil war on record. State against state—oh, yes, ten or fifteen years of efficient propaganda would boil up imagined grievances—and class against class, groups against

81

groups. No Communist army would need to invade the United States by force. They could walk in after the propagandists had done their work."

"Do the men who are working for Communist propaganda know just what they are getting into?"

"It's obvious some haven't thought everything out: they are following a daydream. But those who are power-grabbers know quite well what they are doing: they don't care what happens as long as they can feel they're the Big Bosses."

"But the dreamers are just as guilty as the power-grabbers, for the results will be the same."

"Is Nicholas Orpen a power-grabber, or is he a dreamer?" Paul asked suddenly.

"Orpen?"

"He interests me. Few people I've met to-day can tell me anything about him. Weidler happened to remember him. And you did. But that's all I've found, so far. The rest of us have forgotten him completely. Is that what he's been aiming for? You know, I couldn't even find a photograph of him in the newspaper files I looked up this afternoon. I spent dinner reading his article in *Trend*. He's clever—the subtlest of the bunch that Blackworth steered into print. What do you know about him, Jon?"

"Well, as far as I remember——"

"As far as that, honey?" asked Peggy, as she and Rona came into the room.

Rona smiled and said, "Hello, Paul, you're looking awfully serious, both of you. What on earth were you discussing?"

Paul said, "Jon was telling me about a man called Orpen."

Rona's smile froze. "Nicholas Orpen?" she asked slowly.

"Do you know him?"

"I met him once, long ago. But I've often wondered about him."

Paul looked at her for a moment. "All right, let's hear about Orpen, Jon."

"I'll pour some beer, first," Jon said. "Or would you rather have rye, Paul?"

"Beer's fine. I like this room, Peggy." He made easy conversation with the two women while Jon went into the kitchen. Peggy was pleased with his compliment. She liked the room too. It had been simply awful, she told him proudly,

82

when they had first come to the apartment. But Rona had helped her paint the woodwork, and all the hideous standpipes running up the walls had been covered with asbestos and then disguised by the curtains, and Jon had fixed the bookcases. As for the furniture . . . well, it was frankly bits and pieces; but even if it couldn't claim a Period, sandpapering and waxing had revived a lot of unexpected charm.

"Once the children are older," Peggy said, "we can get a room the way we want it. But now, I come in here and find a tricycle beside the waste-basket, or a rag doll put to bed on a couch, or a brick castle under the coffee table. I've asked Rona what style of interior decoration you could call that, but she's no help." She smiled to Rona, trying to draw her into the conversation without any success. "Are you still living in a hotel, Paul?" What's gone wrong with Rona? she worried.

Yes, meanwhile, Paul explained. He was hoping, however, to sub-let a furnished apartment from a friend of his. It all depended, of course, on where he'd find a job.

"You aren't thinking of leaving New York?" Peggy asked in amazement, glancing involuntarily at Rona. But Rona, fortunately, wasn't listening, and the doorbell rang at that moment to save Peggy's own embarrassment. She hurried into the hall to welcome the new arrivals.

Rona was thinking of Orpen. What was it that had made Jon and Paul so serious? She felt cold, suddenly. She rose to close one of the windows. Paul went to help her, and for a moment or two they stood beside each other. "Paul——" she began and then stopped. Then she shook her head, pretending to smile and forget what she had been going to say. I've been exaggerating all my worries recently, she thought. Better stop it, Rona. And you can't turn to Paul for advice either. She moved quickly away from the window and faced the door. The other guests were arriving. Introductions, light remarks, smiles, laughter.

Perhaps it wasn't anything too serious about Orpen, Rona thought, as she watched Jon being an excellent host and Paul a helpful guest. At this moment, it looked as if Jon and Paul hadn't a care in the world.

CHAPTER SEVEN

It seemed now as if there were an enormous crowd in the Tysons' living-room, for it was quite full. But there were only ten people altogether. Robert Cash, Milton Leitner and Joseph Locastro were all third-year students. Cash was a small fair-haired man with a thin white face, a serious mouth, and glasses. Milton Leitner was dark-haired, with heavy eyebrows, a prominent nose, exceptionally fine eyes, shoulders too broad for his height, and a watchful expression. Joseph Locastro was also dark-haired with a thin aquiline nose, a broad smile, and long legs which were a bit of a nuisance to him as he sat on the floor. But he put up with the discomfort of a coffee table pressing against his shinbone, for his girl, Edith, was sitting on the floor beside him. She had come down to New York from Vassar for the week-end, and he had brought her specially to meet Peggy Tyson.

Peggy was delighted with the compliment, and as she listened to Edith (Peggy hadn't been able to catch the second name, as usual) she admired her fair hair and excellent skin. Peggy was always happy when one of her husband's pupils fell in love with a girl who was both pretty and good-natured as well as intelligent. She had been worried in case Joe's girl would turn out to be one of those dreary hairy-legged creatures, breathing an atmosphere of boiled milk and women's wrongs. So Edith (proud of Joe) and Joe (proud of Edith) and Peggy (proud of both of them) were having a hilarious session beside the coffee table as they discussed the ballet, the price of restaurants, Edith's term paper on Petronius, apartments, Cape Cod, Joe's term paper on the Federalists, Maurois' new book on Marcel Proust, and painted furniture.

The other two guests were the Burleighs, a young instructor from the English Department and his wife. Frank Burleigh, heavily built to match his name, was sitting in one of the arm-chairs. Opposite him, leaning forward anxiously, was Robert Cash who was asking him about Kafka in his serious, determined way. Burleigh's eyes were closed, as if he were thinking of his answer to the long question. (Actually,

84

he was wondering how he could get his hero talking again: Moira had dragged him away from the novel he was writing in order to come to the Tysons' party, and although it was always pleasant to come to the Tysons', he was left with his hero's mouth opened at the top of a blank page.)

"Well, in Kafka," Burleigh said, rousing himself, "you've got to remember his environment. His form of personal uncertainty is something that belonged to his particular *milieu*. No, I don't think anyone else should attempt to model himself on Kafka. Unless he lived as Kafka in Kafka's way. And then, it would only be an echo." Robert Cash, who intended to write a novel some day, didn't believe it. He began to show Burleigh where he was wrong.

Paul Haydn and Milton Leitner were discussing Germany with Jon. That left Rona sitting on the couch beside Moira Burleigh. She was a cheerful young woman with a hearty complexion, forgotten hair, a slap-dash manner, and a way of expressing herself which she always called "frank." Rona was doing her best to listen to Mrs. Burleigh, but the room was small enough to let parts of the other conversations drift in, too, and somehow they all seemed more interesting. She had to pull herself away from summer theatre at Cape Cod, from Kafka's insecurities, from concentration camp psychology, back to Mrs. Burleigh's stream of consciousness. Rona had already been informed that the Burleighs lived upstairs, that they had twins almost two years old—just Barbara's age, that a sitter had been engaged until half-past ten, that Mrs. B. hated the city, that she had been a college president's daughter, that her husband taught English at Columbia, that her husband was writing a novel. "And don't be worried if he calls you Jane," Mrs. Burleigh rattled on, "he's got a heroine called Jane who looks just like you. He's always doing that, calling people by names in his book almost as if his imagined world were more real than this one. I tell him he isn't really being very flattering to people, but he goes on doing it. Tell me, how's Scott Ettley?"

"Scott Ettley?" Rona lost all interest in the other conversations.

"I'm so sorry he couldn't be here to-night. I was looking forward to seeing him after all those years. I hear he's changed. I'm so glad. He really was an awful brat."

Rona said, "Scott? Did you know Scott?"

"Why, of course! We grew up together. My father was president of Monroe College and that's just on the outskirts of Staunton. Do you know it at all?"

"Yes, I've been to Staunton to visit Mr. Ettley. And then, Scott went to Monroe."

"Did you know about Monroe?—It isn't named after Doctrine Monroe at all. It was Obadiah Monroe who founded it. He made his money out of the East Indies and then built a college, just to keep up with old Elihu Yale."

Rona said that was interesting. And there was a slight pause. Then Mrs. Burleigh darted back to Scott again. "So you're engaged to young Ettley? Well, I'm glad he has got someone reliable."

Rona smiled politely and hoped it was a compliment.

"He really had such a miserable time when he was young," Mrs. Burleigh went on.

"Scott?" Rona asked in amazement. She was remembering the Ettleys' comfortable house and large garden with the woods and hills rolling westward. In front of Scott's home, there was a winding river edged with trees and farmland. And to the east, only five miles away, were Staunton's church spires and busy streets and small factories, for it was one of those typical New England towns where light industries are set squarely down in rural countryside.

"Yes indeed!" Mrs. Burleigh took a deep breath and plunged on, delighted to tell everything. "You see, he really *was* such a brat. When we were to be taken to visit his house, we used to pretend we were ill so we needn't go. Imagine! I think it was his mother's fault: he had to have the best of everything, nothing too good for her little boy. His toys! But he'd never let us touch them unless we let him boss us around. So we'd fight. After all, when he was brought to visit us, he used to commandeer all the best toys we had. And at school—he used to get a black eye at least once a week. Sometimes, I'd be almost sorry for him. And then he'd do something to me that made me wish he had gotten two black eyes." She laughed merrily, and looked at Rona as if she were expected to be amused also. Rona was too busy being thankful that Scott wasn't here to-night, after all.

Rona said to Jon, who was passing some sandwiches around the groups, "Let me help!"

But Jon said, "That's all right, Rona. Milton is giving me a hand."

So there was nothing else to be done except to sit on the couch. And although you might try not to listen, it was difficult to shut out Moira Burleigh's insistent voice.

It was saying: "Then I was sent away to boarding school, so I didn't see much of Scott after that except for Christmas parties. He was awfully handsome in a pretty-pretty way. And proud. He couldn't dance very well. But instead of letting us teach him, he'd stand at the doorway and watch us disdainfully. I'm sure he wished he had a limp and could pretend he was Lord Byron."

"We all have our little attitudes," Rona said, smothering her anger and trying to laugh. Poor Scott, surrounded by girls like Mrs. Burleigh. "Scott did awfully well at college," she added defensively.

"Brilliantly. And he seemed to be very happy, too. I told you he changed completely, didn't I?" Mrs. Burleigh said delightedly.

This time, Rona returned the smile.

"Yes, I do blame Scott's mother," Mrs. Burleigh went on, not knowing when to leave well enough alone. "After all, his father isn't the kind of man who would think that his boy was superior to all other children. When Mrs. Ettley died, his father took him in hand. But——" She shrugged her strong shoulders and sighed. The damage was done, she seemed to say.

"But what?" Peggy Tyson asked from across the room. "You sound dismal, Moira."

"I was just telling your sister——"

"How mothers can be disasters," Rona said quickly.

"Out of kindness," Moira Burleigh added. She looked indignantly at Rona: did you think I was going to be tactless?

"Marcel Proust, for instance?" Joe Locastro asked with his broad smile. "We've just been dissecting him. Professor Tyson, I didn't know your wife was an authority on Proust."

"I'm not," protested Peggy happily.

Robert Cash looked up with interest, and left Dr. Burleigh.

There was a shifting around of people, a loosening and reforming of groups. Only Joe Locastro and Edith stayed together, and he was holding her hand determinedly.

Rona escaped thankfully in the direction of Milton Leitner, who asked her formally about Scott Ettley, whom he had met at other parties here. And then, once that politeness was over, he began talking about his plans for the summer—he wanted to go West, this year. There was a job in Cheyenne he'd like to have. It would be good to get away from the family and see how another part of the country lived.

"There's no doubt that the hand that rocks the cradle rules the world," Mrs. Burleigh was informing a startled Paul Haydn. "Whatever ideas Mrs. Schicklgruber let Adolf get away with certainly changed a lot of lives. Whenever you see a man behaving antisocially, you may be sure his mother didn't teach him how to conduct himself. Those delinquent children we worry about—shockingly bad mothers, that's what they have."

"See, Peggy," Jon said, "you've a big responsibility ahead of you. Moira doesn't think that fathers count, so I'm out of this."

Frank Burleigh said, "St. Augustine wrote rather forcibly that all children were born sinful. Perhaps some just stay that way."

"Oh, no!" cried Edith and Rona together, and then there was a free-for-all argument, with everyone joining in. At its stormiest height, with politics and the Russian question edging in sideways, Milton Leitner looked toward the door. "Hey Bobby!" he said. The room was silenced and everyone turned to look.

Bobby was standing there, blinking in the light, his pyjama trousers slipping over his small hips. He was clutching his white cowboy belt in one hand.

"Why Bobby——" Peggy said, coming forward. "Why——"

"I had to go to the bathroom," Bobby announced in his clear, light voice. Then he looked at his mother and then at Rona. "And someone took off my belt," he said accusingly. He held it out.

"Hi-yo, Silver," Joe said. "That's a fine belt, Bobby."

"Have a sandwich, Ranger," Bob Cash said.

"I'm not a ranger. I'm a sheriff. And *someone* took *off* my belt." He looked at Rona, and then at his mother.

Peggy started to step over Joe's legs to reach Bobby. She glanced at the new cowboy belt and then at Rona, quietly saying, "It seems that aunts can cause just as much trouble as mamas."

Rona reached Bobby first. She said, kneeling beside him, "I did, Bobby. You see, I suddenly remembered . . ." She caught Paul Haydn's eyes watching her, and she halted.

"What did you remember?" Bobby asked, standing very straight, still accusing, still unconvinced.

"That a sheriff doesn't *hide* his belt under the blankets. He hangs it up above his bed, and then everyone who sees it knows that it's a sheriff who is sleeping there!"

Bobby considered that.

"I couldn't tell you about it because you were asleep," Rona added. His face suddenly lost its determined frown. He smiled.

"That's all right," he said, in such an imitation of his father that Joe Locastro choked and had to fake a fit of coughing to cover his laughter. "But I *was* simply furious."

"A sandwich for the Sheriff?" Milton asked, giving as broad a smile as Locastro.

"I'll have a doubled egg," the Sheriff said, having reconnoitred the possibilities in the refrigerator before he had gone to bed.

Jon said. "We've finished the deviled eggs, Bobby."

"Oh!" He looked as if he might have expected this.

"I'll make you one for lunch to-morrow," Peggy said.

"Promise?" Bobby asked quickly.

"Sure," Jon said. "We'll have a tremendous lunch to-morrow. Come on, Sheriff, say good night and we'll get going."

"I haven't said hello, yet," Bobby reminded him.

"Well, say it all together. Saves time." He swung Bobby up in his arms.

"Hello and good-bye," Bobby said, beginning to laugh. He waved the belt triumphantly. "Hello and good-bye. Hello and good-bye," he chanted as he was carried down the hall.

Peggy watched them go, and Joe and Edith watched Peggy. Joe gripped Edith's hand more tightly. We'll get married in June, he thought. I'll find a way, somehow.

"Bobby's growing. I suppose that's why he's got thin," Moira Burleigh said, thinking proudly of her two sturdy girls.

Peggy looked anxious. I'll take him to see the doctor, she decided. Next week, I'll take him.

Burleigh rose. "Our sitter departs at half-past ten," he reminded his wife.

Paul Haydn said quietly to Rona, "We're going down town in the same direction. Let me know when you want to leave."

"Thanks, Paul. But Scott said he would call for me. And I'm staying a little longer, anyway." She faced him frankly. "I want to find out about Nicholas Orpen, to tell the truth."

"Nicholas Orpen?" repeated Mrs. Burleigh at Rona's elbow, her hand outstretched for a hearty grip. "That Red? Why he ought to be put up against a stone wall and shot!"

Paul and Rona and Milton Leitner exchanged glances. Bob Cash's lips tightened.

"He killed my father," Mrs. Burleigh said. "It only took a few months and Father was worried into his grave."

"Now, Moira," her husband said gently.

"*I* know what happened!" she said angrily. "Orpen was discharged because he had too many parents complaining about him. He said he wasn't a Communist, then! But just a month later, when he wanted to be called a martyr, he admitted he was a Communist all right."

Everyone looked bewildered except the Burleighs, to whom it all made good sense seemingly.

"Parents complaining about him?" Rona asked faintly. All her fears were surging back. Paul looked at her worriedly.

"Yes. Orpen never seemed to realise that teachers only held jobs because people paid fees for their sons' education. Once they found their sons were arriving home all raving little Commies from Orpen's classes, they had something to say about it. After all, they were *paying* Orpen to teach!"

"Now, Moira," Burleigh said again, "you know this always upsets you."

"I'd like to meet Orpen some night. With an axe!" Moira Burleigh said as she left.

"Golly!" Edith said. "Wasn't she *mad*?"

"Lizzie Borden up to date," Milton Leitner said.

There was a short difficult silence. Everyone was embarrassed by Mrs. Burleigh's fierce emotion.

"That's the wrong way to talk," Milton said gloomily.

"Yes," Paul said.

Milton looked at him and frowned. "What I meant," he said in his deliberate way, "is that she helps the Communists."

"That was what I was thinking," Paul agreed.

"She's a very exaggerating kind of person, I think," Rona said stiffly. "She has some very weird ideas."

"Sorry about all this," Peggy said, coming back into the room with Jon. "I've never seen Moira so upset. Whatever happened?"

"I mentioned Nicholas Orpen's name," Rona said. "That was all."

"Oh!" Jon said, his bewilderment vanishing. "Nicholas Orpen."

"I'm sure Moira didn't really mean what she said," Peggy said appeasingly.

"She did." Robert Cash's voice was unsympathetic. "That's just the kind of reactionary who is running America."

"Well," Peggy said, trying to please everyone, "we've got to remember that reaction is inspired by action, isn't it? If you hit me over the head, Bob, I'm not going to forget it, am I?" She emptied some ash trays. "Who's betting on the Yankees this year? Jon, you've got to take me to one of their games this spring. I simply must see Yogi Berra, just once."

"Is he an East Indian?" Edith asked, and raised a storm of laughter. "Well, I know very little about baseball!" she protested.

"He's only called Yogi because he stands on his head before a game," Joe said, admiring the blush on her cheek.

"Bobby is sure he does that so as to be light-footed," Peggy said with a smile. Everything was all right again, no one was going to start any wild arguments. The silly thing about political discussions was that most of the statements were only people's opinions or people's guesses. It was ludicrous to watch tempers being lost. If people had to upset their digestions and ruin their sleep, at least let them argue on facts and dates and figures. That was Jon's way. She glanced with respect and love at her husband.

Jon had been silent in those last few minutes. Milton Leitner noticed it, too. And because he was interested, and felt that Jon could have said much more about Orpen, he wouldn't let the topic die away. With all a young man's tenacity, he said, "Professor Tyson, do you know anything about Nicholas Orpen?"

"Why?" asked Jon in surprise.

"I've met him. I just wondered."

Robert Cash looked at his watch. "I'll have to leave," he said. "I've got a theme to finish to-night."

Joe Locastro climbed to his feet and pulled Edith up after him. "Time to go, too," he said. "Edith's staying with friends away down town, so it's a long journey. No, don't worry, Mrs. Tyson! I know the way out. See you soon. And thanks."

Milton Leitner was smiling as he watched them say goodbye and leave. "Joe's a good guy," he said, "but all he's interested in at the moment is getting married."

"They've more things to talk about than Nicholas Orpen," Peggy suggested, and the men smiled. "But why did Bob leave so early? He usually stays until one o'clock, and even then he's arguing all the way down the hall toward the elevator."

Milton, who had been a good friend of Bob's for two years now, said nothing. He stared at the rug in front of his feet, conscious that Tyson was watching him. Then he looked up suddenly and said, "I'd like to hear about Nicholas Orpen."

Paul and Rona were waiting, too. "Well," Jon said, "I don't know all the details, actually. And I didn't hear what Moira Burleigh said to-night to throw you all into such embarrassment. But here are some facts. Back in 1940, there was quite an argument going on, as you may remember. The colleges and universities were full of pickets with placards saying it was all an imperialist war. The students and faculties were deluged with leaflets denouncing warmongers and reactionaries. Speakers were appearing on the campus, haranguing us all not to fight.

"The president of Monroe College—that was Moira Burleigh's father—had a difficult time of it. He was a New Dealer, and sympathetic to a lot of his young men's ideas on how to make a better United States. But he saw the war

92

as a war of survival. Most of the faculty agreed with him in principle, although there was the usual division of opinion among them about what should be done. But one small group insisted it was an imperialist war, and attacked the president bitterly. Nicholas Orpen was the leader of that group.

"By the beginning of 1941, there was practically a state of war at Monroe College itself. The president tried to keep it all hushed up, of course—I think he made a big mistake there. For the more he concealed his motives, the more they could be misinterpreted. And then, he lost his temper.

"About Easter, I remember, there were headlines in the papers. 'College Professor forced to resign. Freedom of speech endangered.' That kind of thing. I was working on my doctorate at Columbia then, and I was doing some teaching on the side. We were all worried. We didn't like any attack on freedom of speech. We saw it as a danger that could spread to every university. So we joined in the general criticism against Monroe's president. Orpen did a bang-up publicity job. He suddenly stated that he was a Communist, and forced the issue. He was hailed as a martyr, and even non-Communists felt a bit guilty about that. Every university and college in the country was arguing about it.

"And then, just two months later, Russia was attacked by her ally Germany. Overnight the pickets and the slogans disappeared from the campus. And Nicholas Orpen, a sacred martyr for two months, suddenly found himself ignored and forgotten. And anyone who did remember him by December of that year, when the Japs attacked Pearl Harbour, only cursed him as another false prophet."

"What about his Communist friends?" Peggy asked. "Did they abandon him?"

Paul Haydn said, "Why should they? They were caught off-base, too. It's my bet he was only following orders when he admitted openly that he was a Communist. After the imperialist war became a holy crusade, all he could do was to slide into the background and stay there—until non-Communists had forgotten his speeches. He hasn't gone around reminding people of his imperialist-war effort, has he?"

"But people don't forget so easily," Rona said worriedly. Scott, she was thinking, Scott ought to be warned. Orpen isn't a friend at all. That kind of man has no real loyalties except

93

to his own purpose. But how could you warn Scott? He obviously believed that if Orpen had made mistakes in the past, then that was a long time ago. Scott was tolerant, Scott was loyal . . .

Paul was asking her a question. "Don't they forget?" he said gently.

"We forget too much," Milton Leitner said bitterly. "Look at the ex-Nazis in Germany and all that 'pity us' line they're handing out. They murdered my grandfather in a gas chamber. They murdered my uncles and all their families. *I* won't forget."

"I wish Bob had stayed to hear all this," Peggy said. "It might have made me seem less stupid when I talked about actions and reactions. You know, if Communists ran a party like any other political party, like Democrats or Republicans or Socialists, all they'd get would be the usual election name-calling. But every time something hidden and secret about them comes to light, they are distrusted more and more. Don't they see that they get what they earn?"

Jon smiled as he listened. She sounded despairing that educated men should be so blind. Peggy was so sincere, so transparently honest; it was difficult for her to imagine that there were other standards of behaviour in the world among educated men. It wasn't a matter of blindness; it was a matter of obedience, of letting other men do your thinking for you.

The telephone rang, and Peggy went to answer it. From the hall, she called back softly for Rona. And Rona, rising quickly, said half-worriedly, "That's probably Scott." Probably, too, he was going to be late. She glanced at her watch as she left the room.

Milton Leitner said quickly, as only the men were left together, "By the way, you wondered how I met Nicholas Orpen?"

Jon tried to be noncommittal, but Paul Haydn stopped examining *The Witch Cult in Western Europe*, which he had picked up from Jon's desk.

Leitner said with a smile and a glance over his shoulder at the hall where Rona was now safely telephoning, "It all began right here, in this room."

"What?" Jon said, sitting up erect and spilling an ash tray.

"Bob Cash and I met Scott Ettley here, you know."

"What's this?" asked Jon, worried and annoyed, trying to brush the ash into the rug, picking up the stubs and matches with distaste. "Scott Ettley?"

"Oh, he doesn't know the score. He's a decent enough fellow. Some friends are using him, that's all."

"How?" Paul Haydn asked crisply. He laid the witchcraft book back on the desk, made a mental note to borrow it as soon as possible, and came forward to take a chair facing Leitner.

"Well, we met Ettley here on a Friday evening, and liked him. He asked us to go and see him—just some fellows and a lot of discussion. That suited Bob and me very well. We went to Ettley's studio. We had a good time. I met a man called Murray, and he seemed to take an interest in me. All very flattering. A week later, this guy Murray phoned to ask Bob and me to go with him to a party on Park Avenue. Sure, we went! A duplex apartment, plenty of food and drink, a lot of people—some famous names here and there, a lot of music and talk and argument."

"Who was giving the party?" Paul asked.

"A funny old girl with butterflies in her hair. No kidding!"

"Was her first name Thelma?"

"Yes. I never did get her second name quite straight. No one was using it, you see. Everyone just called her Thelma."

Peggy returned to the room. "Free for all?" Peggy suggested, wishing she had caught the beginning of the story.

"So it was a good party?" Paul asked, but it sounded more of a statement than a question.

"Yes. Bob thought it was first-rate."

"And you?"

"I guess my new buddy Murray didn't know that some people don't like being patronised. He kept handing me a line about his admiration for Jews—as if they were a separate race, just as Hitler said. Then I noticed there was a group, three men and a couple of pretty girls, who were trying to make me feel I was the wittiest guy they'd ever met. I'm not all that good."

"And Bob Cash meanwhile?" Paul asked. Jon kept silent, his mouth tightening. He made a small gesture to Peggy, who changed her mind about speaking.

"He was getting the same treatment from another little

group. They were agreeing with him about the difficulties of being an artist in an economic set-up such as ours. He lapped it up."

"And then?"

"We were invited next week to another party by some of our new friends. I didn't know if I wanted to go. There's just so much butter that I can swallow. But Bob was keen, so I went along with him. I guess if Bob had learned to be more sensitive about his religion, he might have been warned too. But he's a Christian, and he's never had to listen for double meanings."

Peggy looked upset. "Milton, you know it doesn't matter what religion a man has as long as he is a decent human being."

"You know it, I know it—but some people don't," he said bitterly. "And that applies to my own family, too," he added harshly. "I've a battle on my hands right now. They want us to keep different, and I'm telling them the hell with that, we're Americans. That's what we are. Stop building a wall around us, stop emphasising differences, that's what I keep trying to tell them. And they look at me as if I were some kind of traitor." He looked at Jon Tyson. "But I'm building no wall, and no one is going to persuade me to do it."

Rona came into the room, then. She looked pale and unhappy. She sat down very quietly, and lit a cigarette.

"That was the trouble at Orpen's, you see," Milton Leitner went on. Rona looked up at him, quickly. She had to strike a second match.

"That was where the party was held this time?" Paul asked.

"Yes. A stag affair. Music, talk. But there was too much damned sympathy for me. Look, to-night, have you been making me feel I was a Jew, and I ought to be sorry for myself, and what kind of system are we living under where discrimination is a settled policy? That was the line I was handed. I left early. And I never went back to any more of those parties."

"You were asked?"

"Sure. Murray and one or two of the others kept calling me. That crowd give a lot of parties. Discussion groups, they call them. Bob has been going regularly, though. He loves

96

them. He meets writers and people who can give him advice about his novel, and he talks his head off and they listen respectfully. He's one of the intellectuals now. That's his idea."

Rona said, stubbing out her unsmoked cigarette, "What is Orpen like when you talk to him?" Her voice was too controlled, too lifeless. Paul looked at her sharply.

"Oh, he's just a vague little man," Milton replied. "He doesn't say much, keeps in the background almost. At least, that's the way he behaved when I met him. He lives on a dreary street, and the house looks shabby. But he has fixed himself up quite nicely. His room looks civilised."

So it all began here, Jon was thinking bitterly, here in my apartment. This is where the path to Orpen's door started. What fools both Scott and I have been. . . . I'll drop him the hint. Murray and Thelma . butterflies and grape clusters my God! And then Jon began to wonder morosely if any of his other pupils had been steered in the same direction. But no, he thought sharply, that's insulting Scott's intelligence. Scott liked Milton Leitner, and Robert Cash just tagged along with Milton as he usually did. Scott's mistake was to have a man like Murray at any of his parties, that was all. I'll drop him a hint.

"Civilised!" said Peggy bitterly. She was thinking of what might happen to Robert Cash. Perhaps it was already happening—he had left early, trying to hide his anger, just because someone had mentioned Nicholas Orpen in a disrespectful tone of voice. She looked anxiously at Jon, who was saying nothing at all, just sitting there brooding. That was a bad sign.

"I'm going to get some more beer," she announced. "Or would anyone join me in some tea?"

"I must leave," Rona said, and rose abruptly.

"But Scott?"

"He couldn't make it after all. He was detained. He got deep into a talk with a French journalist who used to fight in the underground. Perhaps he'll get a story out of it. So . . ." Rona smiled for everyone's benefit, ". . . I told him to stay with it. It's a long way up here, you know."

"What a shame, Rona!"

"I'll see Rona safely home," Paul said.

"You don't have to bother," Rona said. "Really, Paul."

"Well, I'd like to think of you getting safely home," said Peggy. "It's midnight, now."

Rona laughed. "Still worrying about mugging in the Park?"

"Just avoid the Park at night!" Peggy said, less amused.

"All right, darling," said Rona with mock obedience as she went to find her coat. But she made no more polite protests when she found Paul waiting for her in the hall.

Peggy started to prepare quietly for bed. In five hours, Barbara would be brightly awake. So she left Jon and Milton talking together in the living-room. And she was fast asleep by the time Jon came to her. She didn't waken when he moved her gently over to her own half of the bed. But as he kissed her, and smoothed the sheet over her bare shoulders and kissed them too before he covered them, she stirred sleepily and smiled and drew her body closer to his. He relaxed then, his arm lying over her waist. But he couldn't fall into sleep. He was staring at the shaded windows, going over in his mind all he had heard, going over it and over . . .

Paul shook hands at the main entrance to Rona's house. It had been an easier journey back here than he had imagined. In some ways, he added. Rona treated him naturally as a friend. In some ways, that was easier; in others, it reminded him very sharply of what he had lost. Each time he saw her, he felt that more bitterly. I may have to avoid seeing her, he thought. It made him feel all the more wretched to realise that she seemingly didn't feel this way at all. Her whole life was bound up with Scott's now. That was her one interest.

"I'll wait here until you open your door," he suggested.

"You're as bad as Peggy. I don't think I'll find any thieves around." But she smiled, and shook his hand, and went quietly upstairs. She turned, when she reached the landing, to give him a wave. "Good night, Paul," she said softly. Then she was out of sight.

He waited, listening to her footsteps. Then he heard a low voice calling, "Okay. All clear," and a door was closed.

He left the hallway, and went out into the street, closing the front door behind him, rattling the handle to make sure the door had locked. He crossed over the street and stood for a few minutes watching the light in her living-room. Then it was switched off.

A policeman came out of the shadows, looking at him closely. "That's okay, Bud," he said. "She's gone to bed, can't you see?"

Paul grinned and moved away.

"I'll keep an eye on her. Particularly," the cop called after him, with an answering grin.

Paul walked toward Park Avenue. His footsteps made him feel still more solitary. This was the bad hour of a night, the hour when you realised you were alone.

CHAPTER EIGHT

Paul Haydn slept as little as Jon Tyson that night. At six o'clock he gave up the struggle, rose, and pulled back the heavy curtains from the window. It was grey and bleak outside, as bleak as in this room. Spring was coming late this year. April looked like early March. It was tweed-suit weather.

He shaved, had a shower, and dressed. He took one more look at his room, decided that the people who lived alone in hotels must be the ones who filled the cafés and bars of New York every night, and left. At this hour, the corridors were silent and the elevators quiet. But downstairs, the hotel was already functioning. Early arrivals and departures were grouped at the desk in the lobby, while their families waited for them, half-hidden behind the large potted palms. Down a shallow flight of marble stairs, soft-carpeted, there was the giant dining-room. He found it closed, with chairs up-ended on tables and vacuum cleaners humming. But farther downstairs, near the entrance, the coffee shop was open with a fine welcoming fragrance of bacon and eggs. He entered it, after buying a newspaper at the cigarette stand, along with a couple of magazines from the hundred on display. After breakfast, he would get a haircut at the barber shop across the lobby, and have his shoes shined; and he'd telephone Brownlee from one of the booths at the coffee shop door. Then he thought, I'm slipping back into New York ways all right: I'm accepting all those little timesavers and conveniences without an eyebrow raised in astonishment.

He chose a table rather than the counter so that he could read in peace. He would order ham and eggs, a double orange juice, and plenty of coffee. Luxury, he thought again. He wondered what the travelling salesman sitting at the table next to his would say if he were to lean over and exclaim "Luxury!" Paul knew what he would get. A startled look, a hasty conciliatory smile, and a quieting "Sure, sure!" Then the man would pretend to read his paper again, but after a minute or two he would look up and say, "You a stranger here?" And by a stranger he meant foreigner. For he himself might come from a small town or farmlands, but he wasn't a stranger to New York. He knew what to expect. If he hadn't found it, he would have been the one to do the exclaiming, a very forthright and frank exclaiming. (American tourists complain so much, they said abroad.)

The waitress repeated her question, pencil waiting. She smoothed an imaginary wrinkle on her crisp organdie apron, and studied her white buckskin shoe. I'll get a slightly darker shade next time, she decided, looking at her nylon stockings.

"Sorry?" he half-said, half-asked.

"Hot buttered toast or hot rolls or bran muffins? Marmalade or strawberry jam? Cream with the coffee? Prunes, figs, or would you prefer cereal?" She lifted the double-paged menu and snapped it shut. "It's all on the dollar ten breakfast," she explained. She straightened the clean ash tray, placed a napkin in front of him, added an extra knife.

"You choose," he said with a smile, "I'm bewildered."

She gave him a startled look.

"All right," he said, "just bring on everything you can think of. And make that a double portion of ham and eggs." He began reading the newspaper, turning through its fifty-four large pages carefully. Luxury, he thought again. Then he wondered how long it would take him to forget that this *was* luxury—three weeks? Three months? And he would be accepting all this as something completely natural, nothing to be amazed over, just as the travelling salesman accepted it over at his table as he dropped a tip and lighted a cigar with the band left defiantly on.

"Sump'n funny in the papers this morning?" the waitress asked him as she brought him the orange juice and found him smiling broadly. Then she moved briskly over to the next table, slipped the tip into the pocket of her neatly cut green uniform, and began wiping the table carefully with a damp cloth before she began to set it afresh with its white mat and clean silver for the next customer.

Paul waited until nine o'clock had arrived before he telephoned Roger Brownlee, colonel retired sir. By that time, he had had a lot of conversations—with the waitress, the barber, the shoeshine boy, the doorman, a hotel clerk, and a couple of visitors in the lobby. (One was a farmer all the way from Ohio, the other was a locomotive engineer in town for a convention.) They were quite free with their opinions. That was another thing about the United States—no scarcity of opinions. But at nine, he called a halt to his one-man Gallup poll. And as he waited for Brownlee to answer his ring, he found he was more anxious than he had admitted. What if Brownlee wasn't in town, what if he wasn't in his office on a Saturday morning? Then what? A week-end of waiting and worry.

But Brownlee answered. He didn't sound too surprised to hear Paul Haydn's voice. He was pleased, but not surprised.

"I thought it was about time to see you," Paul said.

"Fine. What about twelve-thirty? At the Central Park Zoo? I'll meet you on the terrace there for lunch. All right? Fine. See you then."

That was all. Paul Haydn found himself smiling. Same old Roger, whether he wore a colonel's eagles or an understated suit from Brooks.

He left the hotel then. He had plenty to occupy him for the next three hours. Yesterday he had visited the Bowery, the day before that—the upper east side. Harlem, Riverside, the Battery, Washington Heights, Greenwich Village, Broadway, Yorkville—he had covered nearly all the island on foot during this last week. Just our roving reporter, he thought, as he stepped into the busy street.

Men and women were hurrying to work. The trucks were backing up against the sidewalks. The buses were filled to

101

standing room. Cars were parked in continuous rows. Taxis sounded their horns impatiently. Another day, another dollar.

The terrace, which ran the full length of the Zoo's cafeteria, was already crowded when Paul Haydn arrived at twenty minutes past twelve. Although the day was still cool, and the morning had been overcast, the children were out in full force. They were not going to let a little thing like weather keep them away from their Saturday visit to the Zoo. On the broad terrace, the small green tables were optimistically shaded with large sun-umbrellas. Mothers and fathers were concentrating on carrying out the trays which they had piled high with food chosen from the self-service counter indoors, while some small boys proud of being alone were trying to reach their tables with their plates unspilled. All was confusion and happiness. Voices in every degree of possible tones, high and clear, low and muted, deep bass, pleasant, harsh—and in every degree of excitement, from the two-year-old eating chopped chicken to the independent little boys ploughing into hot dogs—formed a busy orchestra tuning up before a major performance.

Paul saw a free table, a small one for two, and made his way quickly toward it. It was at the edge of the terrace, next to the low wall topped by flower boxes. Sitting there, he could look over the flowers to the large quadrangle of pavement and grass plots and fruit trees which surrounded the central part of the Zoo—the pool and rocks on which the seals were now posing to an admiring audience. The new grass was brightly green, the fruit trees had a sprinkling of pink dust over their thin black twisting branches. The sun was coming out after all, the skies were going to be blue again, the bright balloons were being sold from white carts, the children in their gaily coloured clothes were scattered like confetti over the sombre grey paths. And on the terrace, the excited talk went on around Paul, the babel of happy sound, the clatter of plates, the arguments, the advice, the admonitions. (Yes, we'll see the lions being fed. . . . Tie that balloon to your chair or you'll lose it. . . . Eat it all up, now! . . . I *know* the sun is shining, but keep your coat on! . . . If you don't drink that milk . . . Have you lost the spoon *again*?) But four children at the table beside

102

Paul's were silent. Some time earlier that morning their clothes, thin and cheap, had been clean. Now they were dirty and torn. The youngest of the children was a girl scarcely three, the others were boys reaching up to perhaps nine years old. They had walked here from the far east side, probably, for a day in the Park. They were waiting silently, their faces and hands streaked with dust from the nearby playground, their eyes fixed on the oldest brother who had just arrived at the table with five frankfurters and five bottles of milk. Now, he was smearing each frankfurter with mustard and presenting it—in right order, the youngest got hers first—with a solemn air. If he had been carving a Thanksgiving turkey, he couldn't have been more serious, more patriarchal.

"Hello!" Roger Brownlee said, pulling out the iron chair opposite Paul with one hand while he placed a tray with the other on the table. He looked thin and spare in a dark flannel suit; his brown felt hat was pushed back on his white hair. "Hope you like frankfurters," he said in his quiet voice, indicating the tray. "Thought I'd save time. Damn, I've slopped the coffee." He placed a paper napkin under each cup. "Well, how's everything?" He glanced with a smile at the children, then at Paul, who still seemed a bit startled by his sudden appearance. "You look well," Brownlee went on, borrowing the mustard from the children.

"I've been having a lot of exercise," Paul said, keeping his voice in the same low conversational tone as Brownlee's.

"Oh?"

"Just having a look at everything."

"Plenty of parties, too? Some nights on the town?"

Paul laughed. "Not exactly. Things didn't turn out the way I planned, somehow."

"What have you been doing besides walking around?"

"Reading. Catching up on all the opinions. Listening to voices, looking at faces. Just catching up . . ."

"Formed any opinions of your own?"

"Yes."

Brownlee's thin face relaxed. "I was glad to hear from you."

"I'd like your opinion on something."

"Oh?" Brownlee hid his disappointment. Was that all? Then, looking at Haydn's face, he decided there was more to come. "Don't look so worried," he advised. "We're enjoying ourselves at the Zoo, aren't we? Always liked this place." He looked round the masses of children, the preoccupied parents. "Cheers me up. Makes me feel human beings can be normal. Well, what's your question?"

"When you spoke to me before——"

"Yes, I remember," Brownlee said quickly. No need for any mention of Berlin.

"——you were pretty vague about a lot of things."

"I thought I was clear enough."

"Yes, in a general kind of way. But you didn't give me any specific examples of what you were talking about. I see now why you didn't. You wanted me to see them for myself. How were you so sure that I would see them?"

"New York's a strange place. It's like a collection of small towns. You have all kinds of circles and groups, you have all kinds of opinions."

"And as someone whose friends were mostly in the writing or publishing field, I'd——?"

"Exactly. You were bound to see something of their problems. Besides, you had all the training for seeing them quickly. Your last few years made sure of that."

"I've been to visit Weidler, the editor of *Trend*. He has offered me my old job with plenty of future attached."

"I was wondering how long Blackworth would last as assistant editor."

Paul glanced quickly at Brownlee. "I think Weidler should meet you. He has handled the situation well, but I don't think he knows what is the next step. He's keeping everything quiet. As if that's the way to ward off future trouble. . . ."

"Are you taking the job? Is that your problem?"

"Half of it."

"The other half?" Brownlee asked.

"It's all connected. There's a girl I used to know pretty well. Her name's Rona Metford. She's in trouble, I think. She doesn't know it, but there seems to be a storm cloud moving up over her. She's engaged to Scott Ettley. Do you know him?"

"Only through his father's name. I've heard he's a pleasant young man. But I doubt if he will ever be the man his father is."

Paul Haydn said, "Better not let him hear you say that." He was silent for a few moments. "The truth is that I just don't like young Ettley. But then, he's engaged to Rona, and that makes me critical."

This time, there was a long pause, while Brownlee seemed only to concentrate on sugaring his coffee. "I don't quite see your problem," Brownlee said at last. "It's nothing I can solve, is it?" He smiled, shaking his head.

"Well, what do you know about a man called Nicholas Orpen?"

That ended Brownlee's amusement. "Does he come into the picture?" he asked very quietly. Then, in a normal voice, "Let's finish our coffee and take a short walk to settle our lunch."

Paul Haydn relaxed. Brownlee knows something about Orpen, he was thinking. If only I get the whole picture filled in, I'll know where Rona stands.

"When I was a kid," Brownlee said, looking at the next table, "I used to come to Central Park every Saturday, hauling my brother along by the hand. We used to walk fifteen blocks to get here."

"And then fifteen back?"

"Sure. Fifteen blocks back with our feet trailing." Brownlee was watching the children at the next table with a smile. They were leaving now. The oldest boy clamped his young brother's cowboy hat more firmly on the back of his head, wiped his sister's hand clean of mustard before he took a firm grip, and told the other two to stop horsing around.

"Good officer material," Roger Brownlee said, watching them drift off the terrace. "He's the kind of kid who'll always get the jobs to do. He's too damned efficient to be passed over. If anyone wants a nice quiet life, all he has to do is close his eyes and ears and let someone else wipe the dishes."

They rose. Paul led the way toward the steps, scattering the pigeons and the sparrows who were lunching on the terrace too. "Where shall we walk? Past the bears, up towards the Mall?" Paul asked.

"We are doing all right as we are," Brownlee said, as they reached the cages on the north side of the Zoo. Men and women as well as children were standing in a group to watch the lions and leopards. Others were watching the tiglon as he paced in his bad-tempered way; his stump of tail drew the usual comments.

"Here are some interesting object lessons for to-day," Brownlee said, stopping for a moment at the tiglon's cage. "Half lion, half tiger, so unhappy that they say he chewed off his own tail. Clearly a schizophrenic. Warning to all to keep ourselves as undivided as possible. A Dr. Klaus Fuchs personality, if ever there was one."

They walked. "And here," said Brownlee, watching the three gorillas, "is a practical case to disprove the theory that equal environment produces the same results. The nasty-looking one has had to be separated from the other two, who manage to tolerate each other in the same cage."

"Better be careful what you say about him. He's got his eyes on you."

"He gives me the creeps," a woman's voice said at their elbow. "Look at his five fingers! And what do you call *them* —the yellows of his eyes?"

"He gets more like your brother Joe every week," her husband said. "Boy, he knows when he is being insulted, doesn't he?" For the gorilla's large mud-black eyes swung round to fix themselves on the speaker.

Brownlee and Paul left the crowd. "I'm always sorry for the animals behind the bars," Brownlee said. "They are kept clean and well fed, which is more than you can say for the victims in concentration camp countries, but . . ." He shrugged his shoulders.

They left the Zoo, following the path through the underpass which led them northward in the Park toward the children's playground at Sixty-seventh Street. There, Brownlee bought a couple of bags of peanuts from the man with the candy stall, and tossed one to Paul. "Let's go feed the squirrels," he suggested with a smile.

They left the path and its crowded benches, its baby carriages and chess games and roller skates and tricycles, and climbed up through the grass and trees toward a ridge of rocks and scattered bushes. Paul Haydn was warning himself, *Don't be the first to start talking about Orpen.* But his impatience grew. He tore the cellophane bag open, and some peanuts scattered on the grass.

106

"Take it easy," Brownlee said, "that bag has got to last you for another hour."

Paul, trying to smile said, "What about this rock? It looks like a good place to sit."

Brownlee looked round. At some distance boys were playing a game of baseball. A young couple sat under a lime tree in bright green flower. A nurse helped a baby to walk on the grass, watched glumly by a leashed Scotty. The paths behind the fringes of trees seemed far away and they were becoming still more crowded with walkers. The benches were now full. It was Saturday afternoon with the sun making its bow after all, coats were coming off, faces were being turned to the first warm rays. "This will do," Brownlee said, sitting down. "Find yourself a soft corner. It's dry, at least." He looked over again at the boy and girl under the tree. The boy was now stretched on his back, his head in the girl's lap. "Well, I suppose when you are twenty you can't get rheumatics," Brownlee added, opening his bag carefully and holding out a nut to an inquisitive but hesitant squirrel. It advanced and retreated and then advanced some more.

"You asked about Orpen," Brownlee went on quietly. "I've quite a file on that little lad. What do you want to know?"

"Anything you can tell me."

Brownlee's story of Nicholas Orpen followed the same pattern as Jon's account, last night. Only, Brownlee could carry it farther along. When Orpen's role of martyr flopped so badly, he had kept a tactful silence until Pearl Harbour. But after that, he went into free-lance writing. He got published frequently, for he wrote well and Communists were enjoying much reflected glory from the Red Army. His theme was always the same—an impassioned plea for a "second front" at a time when there weren't enough landing craft to get adequate supplies or reinforcements across the English Channel. He didn't sound too repetitive, though, for he took the precaution of using a variety of pen names. Responsible men who knew the capabilities of the Western allies at that time began to wonder if Orpen didn't want a second front then so that it could fail, and the Red Army would seem all the more glorious by contrast.

"In fact," Brownlee said with a smile, "some of us used

to call him the Voice of Moscow. That's now important Orpen was. He was confident, too. He even tried for a job in O.S.S. But he didn't get it. The next we heard of him was in a good-will project subsidised by a philanthropist who wanted close international co-operation. By the end of the war, Orpen was over in Europe as one of the chief men of that outfit. He was helping quote anti-Fascist refugees unquote. He travelled around, and when he came back here he had a lot of articles all ready to be printed. He wrote well, as I said. He was a most persuasive character. His angle? 'I was there, I saw it all, I speak for humanity.' He was published widely. He proved the Communists in Greece were not Communists at all, just Greek agrarian reformers or something. He proved the Poles were all just waiting to welcome the government that had come from Moscow *via* Lublin; the other Poles, the ones who had fought on all through the Battle of France and the Battle of Britain, were mere fascists. He showed that elections in Rumania and Bulgaria were all free and honest; that business prospects would be far better for the United States once real democracies were set up in Eastern Europe; that the Czechs had never been happier than when the Communists seized power. It was all good spadework. And plenty of people over here believed him, and repeated what he said. Helpful bunch of little sweethearts, they were."

Brownlee paused and watched the squirrels now surrounding the rock, their small grey bodies erect, their front paws folded across their smooth bellies as if begging for more food and still more.

"After Masaryk's mysterious death, Orpen's popularity dropped. In fact, for a few months he was very quiet. Now, he has begun writing again, always under assumed names, but he is leaving foreign politics strangely alone. I don't like it, Paul, I don't like it one bit. He is still doing good spadework, but it is against the United States now. And you can see by his past record that he's an expert tunneller."

"What's his line, nowadays?"

"Still the Voice of Moscow. In particular, he has been attacking the corruption of the American Press, the menace of the FBI to our freedom, the hysteria of spy-hunting, the war-mongering of our draft laws. In general, if there is anything bad he can magnify, he certainly does. If there is anything good about the United States, he never mentions it. If there are two interpretations to be put on any American problem, only the worse interpretation is made. He says he's fighting for the oppressed and the exploited; but he never mentions slave labour in Russia. He talks of witch-hunting; but he never mentions purges in Eastern Europe. He talks bitterly of intolerance; but he never mentions the Believe-and-Obey rules of Communism. He speaks of peace most glowingly; but he never mentions that Russia has more soldiers and more equipment than any of the Western countries. Yes, he talks of peace, while he is fighting a war in secret. He and a few hundred men like him."

Roger Brownlee looked gloomily over the broad stretch of grass falling away to the crowded paths. "He is fighting a war against *them*," he said, pointing to the people sitting on the crowded benches or strolling slowly in the sunshine. "Comrade Orpen doesn't trust the way they vote. He has no respect for their opinions. He and some seventy thousand comrades are quite sure that almost a hundred and fifty million people are fools—only the Orpens are right."

"Yes," Paul said slowly, "he is pretty contemptuous of the rest of us, isn't he? If I were to join your counter-attack against Orpen and his friends, that would be a good enough reason."

Brownlee fed some more squirrels, favouring the smaller or more timid ones that had been forced into the background by the self-assertive. "If?" he asked, at last. Then, "What's holding you back, Paul?"

"I want to know what I'm getting into, frankly."

Brownlee looked up at him suddenly, shrewdly. "We aren't amateur spies, if that's what you mean. We are only tackling a job that needs doing, a job that no agency in this country can deal with. We are simply a group of volunteers—men and women who make our living by newspapers, magazines, books, radio, movies. All we are doing is to fight ideas with ideas. Counter-propaganda in other words."

"I don't want to get into any organisation," Paul said, "that could lead to thought control. In the end, there wouldn't be any difference between Orpen and ourselves."

"I'd agree. But there are a lot of us working together as

volunteers. We're from different parts of the country. Politically, we're a mixture—Democrats, Republicans, Liberals and Norman Thomas Socialists. As far as religion goes, you'll find Catholics and Jews and Mormons, Christian Scientists and Protestants like you and me. We've some agnostics, too. It would be pretty hard to produce thought control with that variety. The only thing we have in common is a real loyalty to our own country. We happen to like it a good deal." Roger Brownlee stared at the grey rock beneath his feet. "It seems that quite a number of us have been worrying about Orpen and his friends for the last few years. All we needed was a little organisation—it wasn't easy for a man worried by suspicions to do very much entirely alone."

Paul nodded. He said gloomily, "Weidler would agree with you. He told me yesterday, when I went to see him, that he felt he was fighting shadows. It was he, by the way, who first mentioned Orpen's name to me. Blackworth was seemingly one of Orpen's prize pupils. He was gradually ousting anti-Communist writers and planting articles by people like Orpen in their place. Did you know about this?"

"We guessed."

"Weidler is hushing it all up like a fool."

Brownlee said slowly, "Not so much of a fool."

"But his silence plays right into their hands."

"A frank statement of the case would also play right into their hands. Blackworth would sue to the hilt. And he would get away with it—unless his Communist Party card was discovered, which it won't be. And unless the FBI caught Blackworth breaking the law in some way, there's nothing they could do."

Paul was silent.

"You see," Brownlee went on, "the fellows like Blackworth are cowards. They run no real risks, they can't be arrested and tried. They sit in a nice cosy job, take capitalist money, and talk very bravely against capitalism when there are no capitalists around to hear. The most we can do to them is to expose their hidden propaganda. We pull their teeth, in other words. Whenever they write or publish an article—or a speech, or a review—pretending to be just ordinary American Liberals, we write an article on the same subject and give the full facts. That's the job we have to do;

just show the misrepresentations and lies for what they are."

"There's another job we have to do, too," Paul said.

"We?" A smile of real pleasure came over Brownlee's thin worried face.

"Yes. I'm in on this," Paul admitted.

"Well, what's the other job?"

"We have to find out any men who are in a position, as Blackworth was, to destroy other people's earning power. He had obviously a list of anti-Communist writers who were to be suppressed and sabotaged. They have no comeback at all against men like Blackworth."

"Yes, that's a problem. There we need the help of men like Weidler who saw what was happening to his magazine. Weidler will be on guard, from now on."

"But Blackworth gets off pretty easily—he'll find another job because of all this secrecy, while the writers he black-listed probably had a hard time paying the rent. And what about a writer's confidence if he keeps getting rejections? Take away his confidence, and his career is over. I suppose that is what the Blackworths hope for." Paul Haydn frowned. "What do you want me to do?"

"I'll send you your first batch of homework on Monday."

"What's that?"

"You'll be allocated certain magazines and periodicals. Just read them thoroughly. When something needs to be answered, just let me know at once. We have to get a reply published immediately, if possible in the same magazine or periodical."

"And if that isn't made possible for you?"

Brownlee smiled. "That happens rarely. Most Americans are like Weidler: they don't like being tricked by disguised Communists. But when we find any who seem to enjoy it, then we find them—interesting." He rose, and stretched himself stiffly. He emptied the last crumbs of peanuts on the ground and watched the squirrels pounce boldly. "We get no pay, of course," he reminded Haydn. "We are doing this work for"—he looked down at a daring squirrel now cling-ing to his trouser leg—"less than peanuts. That's why we all have other jobs. So take Weidler's offer. And you can start helping the non-Communist writers to pay their rents again. By the way, it is possible that Orpen may find you interesting as the future Feature Editor. Has he any other contacts at *Trend* that you've heard of?"

"There's a man called Murray." There was distaste in Paul's quiet voice and open dislike in his eyes. "I met him at a party on my first night home."

"Oh, you argued?" Brownlee shook the squirrel gently to the ground.

"No. I was still too dazed about being back in New York."

"Lucky. Don't argue with Murray."

"Look," Paul said defensively, "is this part of my homework? Because I shan't enjoy it."

"No. It's a sideline." Suddenly Brownlee's voice was bitter. "I am curious about Mr. Nicholas Orpen. I think he's much more than a glib propagandist. He lives comfortably, he travels a good deal. Who pays? He doesn't write so much for high-priced magazines, he has no private income. So where does he get the money? And why?"

They began walking toward the nearest path, Paul was thinking about Milton Leitner's story last night. "Yes," he said, "I suppose Murray could lead me to Orpen eventually. The only trouble is that I don't like Murray and he doesn't like me."

"If he is told to make friends with you, he will," said Brownlee. "It may only be to persuade you that certain writers are worth publishing. To Murray, you'll be just another fool to have your head turned by parties where people are obviously impressed by your brain power. Don't flinch when they claim you as a true intellectual with real Liberal sympathies. They mean it to be flattering. And in some cases, flattery works."

Brownlee sidestepped two boys roller-skating along the path. He watched them go, their arms flailing rhythmically, their feet flashing in the sunshine. A gaggle of small girls played "run sheep run." A father showed his young son how to feed pigeons. Three young mothers pushed baby carriages and gossiped leisurely. Two old men sat on a bench with a chessboard spread between them and debated their next moves slowly, while the little group standing around them watched in silence. Brownlee looked at all this and his face tightened. "Don't get me wrong," he added unexpectedly, "if any other group in America starts using those Communist tactics for

112

their own purposes—if any ex-Bundists or hidden Fascists begin propaganda or infiltration, we'll be after them too. If anyone wants to spread his ideas let him do it openly, not hide under false pretences."

Paul Haydn, marking the intensity of Brownlee's face as he spoke, said, "You've declared war, I see."

"No. War has been declared on us. I'm just taking up the challenge. And so are you. And so are most of us." He smiled, then.

They said good-bye at the Sixty-seventh Street entrance to the Park. Brownlee continued up Fifth Avenue toward the Metropolitan Museum to have a look at the visiting Hapsburg Collection before it left New York. Paul Haydn turned south, following the continuous row of trees that stretched along the Park side of the avenue. He walked smartly, as if a lot of his worries had dropped from his shoulders. His decisions were made, and he felt they were well made. The lazy holiday in the Southwest, which he had planned in Berlin, would have to wait. He would start work at *Trend* as soon as possible. And instead of admiring the mesas, he could wonder at New York's changing skyline.

He looked at the new buildings on the east side of Fifth Avenue, at some with pleasure, at others with criticism. From architecture it seemed that his thoughts slid naturally back to Rona. But it didn't take much to make him think of her, these days. I'm just the man, he thought bitterly, who didn't know what he was throwing away until it was too late. When he was back at *Trend*, he would have to avoid her. It could be done; the staff was larger now, the offices were more spread out. He would avoid her. She would never notice, and he would, at least, not be reminded so constantly of what might have been. And with that decision, he buried his last hesitation about joining *Trend* again.

He was now approaching the southernmost limits of Central Park. Before him lay the canyon of Fifth Avenue. The afternoon sun caught the different colours of its buildings, the sky—now high and blue, with the early morning clouds all drifting out to sea—emphasised their varying shapes. The rows of windows gleamed; the flags drifted lazily over the heads of the masses of people who jammed the sidewalks; the river of buses and taxis flowed slowly, steadily. He hesitated when he reached the Square, where General Sherman sat on his bronze horse with Glory, womanlike, leading him firmly toward Bergdorf Goodman's jewellery counter. Then, following General Sherman's direction, Paul crossed over to the Plaza. The fountain wasn't playing, and the smoothly shaped nude on its pinnacle was now a Nymph Surprised by a Drought, but the bright tulips and promenading pigeons and the gaily dressed children told everyone this was a holiday: this was Saturday afternoon, almost three o'clock.

Saturday afternoon, and what the hell do I do? Paul Haydn wondered. It was too late to go out to a ball game. It was too late to call up his friends—most of them would be trying to find spring in the country, anyway, planting rose trees, painting porches, going fishing and catching their first sunburns, or trying to lower their golf handicaps.

Across Fifty-eighth Street, he saw a new movie theatre. It was showing a Jean Gabin film. He walked toward it, past the placid rank of elderly horses and ancient carriages waiting for young men to take their girls for a ride in Central Park, past the couples strolling slowly arm-in-arm. Well, Paul Haydn thought, as he looked back at the Plaza, he could always spend a Saturday afternoon in finding out how much French he had forgotten.

II. Antithesis

CHAPTER NINE

It was the end of April, a cold wet Sunday that covered the churchgoers' spring clothes with heavy coats and umbrellas. Scott Ettley arrived at Rona's apartment at eleven o'clock. "A filthy day to go apartment hunting," he said gloomily, as he hung up his raincoat in the hall closet.

"Perhaps it will clear." Rona was looking cheerful in spite of the weather. She pointed toward the living-room, neat and welcoming. A small table covered by a gaily-checked cloth was set for breakfast beside one window. The azaleas Scott had sent Rona for Easter were now planted in the window box, and still in bloom. "See, I've everything ready. I've just made the toast and coffee. You'll feel much better once you've had something to eat."

"How did you guess that I hadn't had breakfast?" he asked, beginning to smile as he followed her into the little kitchen.

"Because you never look after yourself properly."

He caught her in his arms and kissed her. "Darling, it's good to see you. Even a wet Sunday morning seems different, then."

"It's funny . . ." Rona began, and then concentrated on heating a pan for the eggs. "Scrambled?" she asked.

"Perfect. But what's funny?"

"The way everything smooths out when we are together. I

wish people and things would leave us alone. We do very nicely by ourselves, don't we?"

He nodded. Then, half-smiling, "What people and things, Rona?"

"Oh—just life." She beat the eggs, added a drop or two of water, salt and pepper. She watched the nut of butter foam in the pan, and poured the eggs into it. "Just work, and duties, and work, and people. Perhaps we ought to go and live in Alaska or some place." She reached up suddenly and kissed his cheek. "Cheer up, darling."

"I'm sorry I couldn't see you last night," he said. "Last week was damned busy." If only we could be left alone, he thought. Rona is right. There's too much duty, too many people in this life.

"Oh, Scott, I wasn't grumbling. Please, don't think . . ." She said no more, but the smile had left her eyes. She stirred the eggs, and pretended to be very busy.

"You don't grumble," he said quickly. "Only, you can't like the way we have to disappoint each other. I don't enjoy it, any more than you do."

"I know you don't."

"What did you do last night?"

"Oh, very prosaic! I did some laundry. And I read up on that architecture test." She kept her voice cheerful, although it hadn't been exactly her idea of how to spend a Saturday evening.

"Still serious about becoming fully qualified?" he asked.

She dished the eggs neatly. She said, "Why not be qualified, anyway? I'm more than half-way through the course, you know. Or don't you want an architect in the family?"

"Might be useful," he said with a laugh, and carried the plates into the living-room. Rona took off her apron, and brought the coffee and toast.

"Some day," she said, "I can design our own house, and then we needn't go apartment hunting any more. I'll do a study for you that will really knock your eye out."

They sat down to eat.

"Meanwhile," said Scott, "what lousy apartment at what extortionate price have you found?"

"Let's wait until we reach a cigarette and our last cup of coffee, shall we?" Rona kept her voice gay, and started talking about yesterday's parade down Fifth Avenue. But she was thinking that the few apartments on her list didn't sound too hopeful. Perhaps they ought to live in the suburbs or in one of the new outlying housing developments. But Scott had already pointed out that if they lived any distance from Manhattan, then he'd be away from home a good deal. What with his work and all that, he might even have to spend several nights in the city each week. Not a pleasant prospect, he had said. And she had agreed.

"How is *Trend*?" he asked suddenly.

"Still holding up. The great excitement is that Miss Guttman has got engaged. She's going to live in St. Louis."

"I hear Haydn's back." His voice was too casual.

"Yes, he came about two weeks ago or more," Rona said, just as casually.

"Is he bothering you?"

Rona looked up at him, startled. "Oh, darling," she said, beginning to laugh, "I haven't seen him at all, except once in the elevator. His office is in a different corridor from mine, you know."

Scott still looked worried.

Rona said, "I think he's avoiding me, to tell you the truth. Doesn't that amuse you?"

"Not very much, frankly. Why the hell did he come back at all?"

"Scott, he's done more than his share in Germany. You couldn't expect him to go on volunteering to stay in the army forever, could you?"

"The army's just his level," Scott said angrily. "But why did he have to go back to *Trend*?"

"Why should he turn down his old job because I'm going to be there for another five months? That wouldn't make any sense."

"I just hate his guts, that's all," Scott said gloomily. "I don't trust him one bit."

"I *am* flattered," said Rona, laughing again. "But you don't have to worry, honey. He is not the wolf he used to be. He's just a very efficient assistant editor."

"Better than Blackworth?"

"Certainly as good." Rona thought it wiser not to mention the fact that Paul Haydn was probably better, judging by the

117

number of writers who seemed to be interested in his return. "He's a sympathetic editor, apparently," she added. "But that's only office gossip."

"He's working his way in pretty fast," Scott said bitterly.

"Well, he knows the job. And he always did have a lot of friends in the publishing business. You see, he actually enjoys the work he's doing. That's why he's so good at it, I suppose."

Scott said nothing at all. His lips tightened.

Rona, suddenly realising she had been tactless—although heaven only knew, she hadn't been thinking of Scott's lack of enthusiasm for his newspaper job—said quickly, "Here's the last cup of coffee, darling. Now, what did you find out this week about apartments? Anything possible?" She tried to quell the annoyance that attacked her, nowadays, when she found herself apologising for having worried Scott. It is all very well to be sensitive, she thought, and I'm sensitive enough too, but it's going to be a depressing life if we've got to guard ourselves continuously from saying wrong things. Scott knows by this time that I wouldn't ever try to hurt him. Why can't he let it go at that? She looked down at the table-cloth and hoped he hadn't noticed the gleam of sudden tears in her eyes.

Scott began talking about apartments. He was as depressed as she had become.

"Well," she said at last, rising and beginning to clear the dishes on to a tray, "let's not get worried about it. After all, apartment hunting is something of an adventure. We can laugh at the grim and grisly places. And when we do see something we like, but it's far too expensive for us, we can plan on getting something like that some day. Can't we?"

"Why can't we find a decent place at a decent rent *now*?"

She looked around the room. "I think we could make any apartment look fairly decent. It only takes some thought and work."

"And money," he reminded her as he carried the full tray into the kitchen.

"Less money than you think, Scott. Don't you remember this apartment of mine when I first took it? The fact is, the more ideas you have the less you need to spend."

"All right," he said, beginning to smile, "I'll take your word for it. You certainly did a good job here." He caught her round the waist and kissed the nape of her neck. "Hey!" he said, holding her back to look at her head. "You've had your hair cut."

"Only a little. You like it?"

"Yes," he admitted. "It looks all right. Why didn't you tell me you were going to have it done?"

"It wasn't a very important secret, was it?" She kissed him. Then suddenly she pointed to the kitchen window. "Look, it isn't raining any more. We're in luck. I'll get ready and we'll set out. What is our first stop?"

He pulled out a list with three addresses. "I brought the car," he said, "so that will save time."

"I've got a list, too," she called back as she went to the bedroom. I'll wear my saucy sailor hat, she thought, and the rainmaker can go jump in Croton Reservoir. Scott came to lean against the bedroom door and admire the way she fixed the tight veil over her face. She smiled happily, picked up her freshly laundered gloves and a crisp white handkerchief to tuck into her pocket.

"You know what you are?" he asked. "You're a cute little trick."

Her smile deepened. She took one last look in the mirror and gave him her hand. "Come on, honey," she said. Her excitement was infectious. He followed her into the hall, smiling broadly. She stopped at the mirror above the telephone table, drawing him to stand beside her. "See?" she asked.

"Yes." He kissed her cheek. "We look pretty good together."

"Just right, if you ask me." She hugged him quickly. "Now, let's be the almost-married couple trying to look very serious, very sedate, very budget-minded. That should impress any old superintendent or grouchy landlord, shouldn't it? Oh, Scott, let's make to-day a lot of fun."

He nodded. He was thinking, the only time I'm really happy is when I'm with Rona and I let myself forget everything else. But life wasn't all just Rona. Life was something he had to deal with, not dream through. He led the way downstairs, his brows drawn into a frown, his lips tight, his jaw more marked in outline.

As they reached the street door, Rona glanced at him and wondered what was wrong now. And all the lightness left her heart.

By five o'clock, they parked the car on a street near lower Lexington Avenue and Gramercy Park.

"That's the lot, then," Scott said, checking the lists of addresses, giving a final look at the classified advertisements in the Sunday *Times*. "West side, east side, all around the blasted town." And we had to choose a week-end when the elevator operators and doormen were on strike, he thought gloomily. All the pickets had been out.

"That place on West Eightieth Street wasn't too bad," Rona said. "We could make it look very pleasant, actually."

"It looks like hell now." He threw the *Times* on to the back seat of the car. "The only possible apartment we've seen to-day was that last one. And it cost a hundred and twenty-five dollars a month."

She kept silent.

"We can't afford more than eighty a month. So solve that problem."

"We'll have to look for an apartment outside of Manhattan, that's all."

He started the car. And Rona was too tired to argue further, either with Scott or herself. If only, she thought, Scott wasn't so determined on what he wanted. . . .

They drove in silence through the centre of the city. Then Scott turned the car into Park Avenue. They swept smoothly along its broad clean surface. On the sidewalks, in front of most of the apartment doorways, pickets were parading slowly, quietly. A few people walked determinedly for the sake of their health, even on this grey Sunday afternoon.

"If we could pay a rent equal to my entire salary," Scott said bitterly, "we could find something here."

Well, she thought, we can't; so why worry about it? Besides, few of the people who lived here had begun house-keeping on Park Avenue when they were first married.

"Even if I worked for twenty years," Scott went on, "we'd still be unable to afford this sort of place."

"Who cares, darling? I don't. Do you?" If anyone did care, she thought, he ought to remember that others had done it;

120

or did Scott only see a future in the same job at the same salary for the rest of his life? She couldn't quite believe that. What on earth was Scott trying to do—depress her still more? Then she was angry with herself, angry with Scott, angry with Park Avenue.

"Of course I don't care," he answered. Something was amusing him, now. He gave a short laugh and nodded towards the people who were out for their Sunday walk. "Look at them! A bunch of overdressed, overstuffed Park Avenue——"

"Scott!" She tried to laugh, too, to take away the sharpness from her voice. Would it make Scott happier to see people poorly dressed and badly fed? "These people probably don't live here any more than we do. See!" She pointed to a New Jersey car that was parking near a corner to let a family descend in all its Sunday finery. "That's one of the things that I like about New York. When you meet people on the street, you can't tell from the way they are dressed where most of them live or how much money they make. That New Jersey family, for instance . . . we'd have thought they were New Yorkers if we hadn't seen their car's licence plate. And I couldn't tell whether the man owns a grocery store, or works in a delicatessen, or runs a bank, or sells bicycles, or is the best carpenter in Trenton. I couldn't guess whether his family had lived in America for twenty or two hundred years."

Scott was too busy watching the traffic to reply.

"I shouldn't be surprised if the New Jersey family probably looked at us in this smart little car and made their guesses, too. If they disliked us for being the gilded rich, I'd be a little amused, wouldn't you?"

Scott said nothing, but waited patiently for the traffic light to turn green.

Rona felt his silence. "Cheer up," she said, her voice suddenly cold. "We do have a very handsome car even if we can't afford an apartment to go with it."

The edge in her voice cut through his silence. "Rona!" he said sharply. Just like a woman, he thought, bringing up the subject of the new car sideways. He needed this car; it wasn't an extravagance. They'd both enjoy it, didn't she see that?

"Scott," she said sadly, "won't you ever compromise? If you are so worried about money, why don't you let me keep my job when we get married—just for a little time, anyway?"

"I'm not the one who worries about money."

"You do. You hide the worry, and it twists inside you and makes you bitter and spoils everything. This is one time in our lives that shouldn't be spoiled by anything." She was almost in tears.

"Nothing is being spoiled." He was emphatic about it as if he were persuading himself that it was true.

She stared at him. Didn't he even guess the effect his constant criticism was having on her? At first, she had listened to him, thinking how clearly and honestly he saw everything; he wasn't afraid to speak the truth as he saw it. But it seemed more and more, as if his idea of the truth was one-sided. "I wish," she said slowly, "I wish you'd stop generalising so harshly about everything. Why, sometimes I begin to think you're a foreigner jumping to conclusions about America. Give it a chance, will you?"

He looked at her. His voice softened. "You're tired. Let's have a drink, and then dinner, and then a Broadway movie. How's that? Or perhaps there's a show we could take in." His voice was gentle, understanding. It was his way of apologising.

She said nothing for a few moments. Then, "Yes, I suppose I'm tired," she said. It was all or nothing with Scott, she thought. Either he cancelled Saturday night abruptly, leaving her to mope around the apartment, or he was filling up Sunday as packed as it would go. Then, at that thought, she was angry with herself again. She must be more tired than she actually felt. Suddenly, she noticed that they were almost at Fifty-ninth Street. "Why, we've passed my street!"

"I'm taking you to a party," he said. "That's what we need to cheer ourselves up."

"But I'm not dressed for a party."

"You look wonderful just as you are. Thelma is having a big affair to-day. She's been pestering me on the phone all week to bring you along."

"Thelma . . . the female with the grapes in her hair?"

Scott laughed. "You women!" he said affectionately. "Is Thelma never going to live that down?"

"But I don't know her. I only met her once, when Murray brought her to our party." And I don't like Murray, either, she thought.

"She's a quaint old type. But I hear she always manages to

122

gather quite a crowd of celebrities at her parties. It might be fun to go."

Rona watched him anxiously. "Will Murray be there?"

"Everyone and anyone will be there. So I've heard, at least."

"Is Murray a friend of yours?"

"Oh, I just know him, that's all."

"Isn't he a friend of Nicholas Orpen's?"

"Is he? Could be. I wouldn't know. Well, here we are. . . . A place to park, and all." He drew the car neatly in to the curb.

Rona, looking in amazement at the building before which they had stopped, was too startled to reply. So Thelma lived on Park Avenue. Why on earth had Scott attacked all its inhabitants so bitterly if he liked Thelma well enough to come to her party? She sat still. "I'm not really very keen on a party at this moment," she said. "To tell you the truth, I——"

"Darling, you look swell. You'll be the smartest girl there."

"It wasn't that."

A disapproving doorman appeared beside the car. "You can't park here," he said. "We need a space for taxis."

Scott obeyed, but he was angry. He had to drive for almost a block before he found a place to leave the car. "There was plenty of room," he said, looking over his shoulder at the doorman. "What the hell does he think he is?"

A man doing his job, Rona thought wearily. And whether you approve of him, or not, depends on whether you're parking a car or trying to find a taxi.

"Come on, Rona." Scott was waiting for her with a smile. He caught her hand, pressing it gently as he drew her out of the car. "Let's have some fun."

She got out of the car. Scott, she suddenly realised, had been as tired and disappointed by their search as she herself. She left her hand in his, and they walked slowly toward the expansive blue and gold awning that sheltered the doorway to Thelma's apartment house.

"Where did you hear this talk about Murray and Orpen?" he asked. "Just more office gossip?"

"Actually, it was at Peggy's. Remember the night you got entangled with a French journalist and couldn't come up to
123

collect me, after all? There was quite a discussion going on, that night. I only heard the end of it—I was out of the room when it began. In fact, I was speaking to you on the telephone. I got back to the living-room in time to hear Orpen's name linked with Murray's." She hesitated. Then she added, "You know that Orpen is a Communist, don't you?"

"He was one. But he's had nothing to do with politics for years. I'm pretty sure of that."

"Scott, I've been worrying how to tell you, but——" She hesitated. Then she kept silent as they passed the doorman, now standing impassively in his blue uniform beside the large glass doors.

"What, no pickets?" Scott asked him quietly. "There's a strike on, isn't there?"

"This house settled," the man said. He turned away, angry. I'm no scab, his stiff back told them.

Scott gave Rona a reassuring smile. "Well, we don't have to walk up, at least." He led her into the entrance hall—a long stretch of marble floor and grey carpet. Windows facing an inner courtyard were draped with white satin splashed with large red roses. Red chairs, green couches stood like a guard of honour against the dark charcoal-grey walls. White and gilt sconces held diffused lights. An enormous bowl of waxed flowers stood on an ebony-black table.

"You've been worrying how to tell me about what?" Scott asked, as they began walking down the long hall.

"About Orpen. I heard a lot against him."

"Why didn't you tell me before this?"

"Frankly, I didn't know *how* to tell you. You like him, don't you?"

"He's all right." Scott caught her elbow and guided her toward one of the elevators at the left side of the hall. "Who was talking about him, anyway?"

"Mrs. Burleigh. She's the daughter of the president of Monroe College—the one who died just after Orpen left."

"Moira Burleigh? Thank heaven I wasn't there to meet her that night." He said to the elevator operator, "Fourteenth floor."

"I didn't particularly like her," Rona admitted.

"She made my life miserable for years. All the kids used to run a mile when they saw her coming. Is she still the same

124

old Moira? I bet she is. Honey, I'll give you one piece of good advice: only believe half what she says and don't believe that too much. She's a comic character, straight out of Sheridan or Molière. Last time I saw her, years ago, it was at some Christmas party or other. She had braces on her teeth, and pink satin slippers."

Rona laughed. "How on earth did you remember that?"

"Have you seen the size of her feet?"

"Didn't you dance with her?"

"Not her weight," Scott said decidedly. "I kept near the door, ready to escape whenever she came toward me. We had quarrelled steadily ever since we were kids. Mother used to make me be polite to her and the rest of her family. But at that dance I didn't have to be polite to anyone unless I wanted to. Did she talk about it? I bet she did." He grinned, watching the embarrassment on Rona's face.

"She lives beside Peggy," Rona explained as they left the elevator. They had come out on to a broad landing with a single door—a private hall furnished with high dark chests and dim tapestries in fourteenth-century château style.

"Poor Peggy," Scott was saying commiseratingly as he pressed the doorbell, "you'd better warn her. By the way, how are Jon and Peggy? I hear Jon's been phoning me once or twice, but I always seem to be out. I'll give him a ring soon."

The massive door opened. A manservant with the air of a respectful undertaker stood aside to let them enter. Again there was a hall, long and broad, dimly lit, leading eventually into a room through an arched entrance. The room was filled with people, standing closely bunched together or moving around like a restless tide. Some guests had overflowed into the hall. From adjoining rooms came the rise and fall of voices and laughter.

"Quite a crowd," Scott said approvingly. Rona, feeling her heels sink deeply into the Chinese rugs, watching the room of haughty Sargent portraits that overlooked the Spanish chests and high-backed Italian chairs, repressed a smile. She gripped Scott's hand suddenly.

"I told you it would be fun," he said, his eyes on the people milling around the room ahead. "We'll find Thelma in the library or music-room. Come along, darling."

But although Scott was smiling encouragingly, although he had an expectant look on his face, it seemed to Rona that the sudden glance he gave her was anxious. "I'm not too afraid," she said, smiling back. She lowered her voice. "I got a glimpse of Thelma. That was all."

Thelma left a group of guests and came forward at that moment, a wide smile on her thin face, her arms outstretched in welcome. Her coarse dark hair was braided with gold ribbon; a short pleated tunic, elaborately draped, belted with a narrow gold cord, flounced over black satin trousers tightly fitted at the ankles. The thongs of gold sandals were laced round her bare feet. The nail on one of her big toes was broken.

"*Darlings*!" she cried. "I'm *so* glad. This is *too* wonderful, but wonderful!"

CHAPTER TEN

When Scott had said that everyone and anyone would be at Thelma's party, he had described it accurately. There was a sprinkling of faces whose names needed no repeating— two actresses, a poet, a composer, a producer, a couple of novelists, a playwright, three film stars, and a well-known journalist. (But most of them didn't stay long, Rona noted. They had come to make an appearance and once that was done, their ranks thinned out.) There was a second group consisting of faces whose names, when they were made known, were easily recognised. (They stayed longer than the first group, but some of them were beginning to leave too.) And the third group, which was waiting determinedly for supper, was one whose faces and names were not recognisable at all. But everyone had one thing in common—they were all as well-fed and well-dressed as the people Scott had disliked on the avenue outside.

The party wasn't helping Rona's temper one bit. She was feeling critical of everyone—including Scott and herself. She could blame her mood on the fact that she never accepted invitations from people she disliked; this afternoon, she had let herself be persuaded into breaking this rule, and now she was suffering because of it. Or was that fair to Scott? She hadn't been persuaded. She had been curious. If Murray were at this party, perhaps Nicholas Orpen would be found here too. She looked for Orpen continually, but she couldn't see him.

So here she was, standing in this monstrous music-room with its Louis XV chairs, Lalique vases, velvet curtains, Oriental rugs, all pushing a spinet and a piano into the background. Like everything else in this strange apartment, there was a clutter of wealth, a total disregard for suitability. And now she was listening to a bald-headed man in a baggy tweed suit, who had proudly announced he was the only businessman in the room. (He seemed to think it a distinction that he might be taken for a writer or an actor.) He was, of course, exceedingly polite; they were all extremely polite. They had drifted, those unknown faces, those unheard names, in a constant stream toward Rona. They all seemed to know who she was, and there had been plenty of conversation.

Perhaps that was what worried her. It was a kind of purposeful conversation as if they were sounding out her opinions. In a way, she felt as if she were being interviewed for a new job. If she gave an answer which was approved, she could see a little glow of interest in the polite faces. If she answered in a way that wasn't approved, she noticed that the faces went quite dead—a cold expressionless mask slipped over them and she might have been speaking to a blank wall. The strange thing about this approval or disapproval was its uniform quality. All those who had been talking to her, seeking her out (for she had made no move to join any group once Thelma had snatched Scott away leaving Rona to fend for herself), seemed to agree in all their points of view. She had noticed this after the third encounter with one of Thelma's guests. She had begun to test it on those who spoke to her afterward. The result was unmistakable: their reactions were always the same. If she said the Marshall Plan was a good thing, a dead face looked at her. If she said the Marshall Plan was a grave mistake, an interested eye told her to go on. It was the same with every topic that came up—whether it was the U.N. or ballet, the Atlantic Pact or the latest novel, the Communist trials or a new play, everything was measured

127

from one political line of judgment. These People (for that's how she was beginning to think of them) not only thought exactly the same way, but saw everything in a political light. I might as well be reading *Pravda*, Rona thought.

Fun, Scott had said. . . . But to her it was completely comic in another sense. True, a newspaperman had an inquiring mind, and here was certainly a story ready for the writing. The apartment furnished by the power of money, with no taste, no discrimination. The silly woman playing hostess to a group of people. . . . Just what *are* they? Rona wondered.

She was listening at this moment to the bald-headed businessman who was explaining, more in sorrow than in anger, that the universities were in danger of losing their liberties through this ill-advised inquiry into teachers' politics. And as she listened, she was studying the clothes and faces around her. Communists? Fellow-travellers? Yet if anyone ever owed anything to capitalism, they certainly did. They were apparently educated, obviously well-clothed and well-nourished. Then she looked for Scott. He was in an amiable group near the door. Seemingly, to judge by the interested faces around him, Scott wasn't running into any difficulties. Yet she knew, from hearing him talk at her own parties, or with Peggy and Jon Tyson, or with other friends, that Scott's political ideas coincided a good deal with her own. Something is wrong with me to-day, she decided. I'm seeing far too many implications; I'm going slightly crazy.

"Now don't you agree?" the bald-headed man asked.

"Agree?" she echoed in embarrassment.

"If we all support the men with real courage in the universities, the men who refuse to be blackmailed into telling what politics they have, then we have a real chance of keeping our liberties, don't you think?"

"But why should a teacher hide his politics? I'm a Democrat, and I don't care who knows it."

"Surely you see the dangers? It is all a gross invasion of our privacy."

"When the census man arrived to interview me last week, I told him much more about myself than the fact that I was a Democrat," Rona said with a smile. "And when I came home from Mexico last summer, I listed everything I had bought for the customs officer. In a sense, that's an invasion of privacy too; but it has got to be done, hasn't it? To protect us from crooks?"

The dead look spread over the man's face. He smiled, not convincingly, and after a brief safe remark about the water scarcity this winter and the rainmakers now at work, he saw a friend in another corner of the room.

Perhaps I *am* going crazy, Rona thought. She looked around the crowded music-room, suddenly feeling alone. Very much alone. Scott was no longer standing near the door. She would have to search for him, plead a headache, and get out into some fresh clean air.

A woman, quiet, middle-aged, stubbed out a cigarette on the ash tray beside Rona. "Did someone bring you here?"

Rona, surprised, said yes, a friend had brought her.

"That's what happened to me," the woman said. "But I'm leaving. Like to come along?"

Rona said she couldn't, not yet.

"Fine friends you and I have," the woman said bitterly, and turned away.

Rona's face flushed. She watched the woman walk determinedly out of the music-room.

"We haven't all got her courage," a thin high voice said quietly beside Rona. "Have a cigarette?" the voice deepened unexpectedly. Rona turned to see a man, less tall than she was, with a smooth pale face, thin red hair, horn-rimmed glasses, and a tendency to be overweight. He was holding a glass in his hand, and he obviously had held several in the course of the afternoon. She remembered that he had been hovering vaguely near her for the last half hour, talking to no one, listening, ignored, a solitary kind of figure to be at a party.

"No, thanks," she said. "I was just about to——"

"——find Scott and ask him to take you away?" The voice began low and ended high. But it was still very quiet, almost hushed. "Don't look so surprised. You are Rona Metford, aren't you? Yes, we all know about you. And how are you enjoying your education?"

Rona stared at him blankly. The constant little smile still played over his face, but his eyes were unhappy.

He went on, "What do you think of the party?"

Rona didn't answer him.

"You aren't enjoying it? In spite of all our efforts?" His voice was mocking. Then it became serious. "I've been listening to your conversations. Do you mind? My manners were always bad, I've been told."

Rona looked for Scott. He still hadn't come back.

"Sit down, shall we? Please. I'd like to talk to you." There was a note of earnestness in the comic voice that caught Rona's attention. She sat down on a yellow satin chair and watched him light another cigarette.

"You don't have to get mixed up with this crowd," he said. His thin high voice broke in the middle of the sentence and slid into baritone. "This isn't the place for you." He looked round the room and shook his head.

"What about you?"

"I'm supposed to belong here." He shrugged his shoulders. "But I go away. Last time, I went as far as Texas. I try to make up my mind. I argue myself into thinking I've got enough courage. I come back. I hope to see everything has changed, so that I won't have to act. But things aren't any different, either with Thelma or with me. And I can't speak out. So I go away again." He took a long drink. Rona watched him, wondering what he was talking about. It obviously made sense to him. He added, "I keep looking for people like you, or like that woman who left. But she left, didn't she? And you'll leave, too. That's it, they all leave."

Rona said, "Why do you keep looking?" She was baffled. Perhaps he was drunk after all, and her first guess had been correct.

"To give me a little more courage," he said with an uncertain smile. He looked at the people in the room. "They don't look very terrifying, do they?"

"Are they?" She tried to keep her face serious.

"Only when you know what's behind them." He was watching her now. "You don't believe me," he said almost sadly.

"I—I don't know quite what we are talking about."

"Don't you? Or are you afraid, too, of looking a fool by putting your thoughts into words?"

He was far from drunk, she thought. "All right," she said. "What are these people? Communists?"

"I know of only three in this room who admit they are.
130

The others? They say they aren't. They are the non-Communist Communists."

"Everyone here?" She looked at the doorway in alarm, but Scott still wasn't there.

"No, not all. That woman who left; you; that silent man over there in the grey suit; that worried young man by the spinet . . . and a few others. But either they'll walk out as the woman did, or they'll be flattered into coming again."

"Flattered? I've been far from flattered to-day."

"What? You don't want to be considered a great brain?" he asked with a return to sarcasm.

"I've no pretensions about that."

"Ah—then you'll be quite safe. If you have courage, too, that is."

Rona looked at him. He was a man in love with the word courage.

"Moral courage," he said bitterly, and finished his drink. "Come on, let's find the bar."

"But——"

"The circus hasn't begun yet. You ought to stay and complete your first steps in political education."

"Charles, you'll get drunk again," Thelma said, appearing beside his chair. She looked down at him dispassionately. He was the first man, Rona thought, who seemed to rouse no emotion in Thelma. The effect on Charles was odd. He rose to his feet, making the most of his five feet four inches. He looked at Thelma, not with hatred but with almost a touch of shame in his disgust.

"I like getting drunk," he said, his low voice rising to its highest pitch. He kept staring at Thelma. She laughed and turned away, leaving them. "Silly boy!" she said. But her mouth closed in an angry line.

Rona said hurriedly, "I have to leave." She watched Thelma's gold-braided head as it made its way toward the spinet. When Charles didn't answer, she looked at him. He was still standing as Thelma had left him. His smooth face was now emotionless, but the knuckles that gripped his empty glass were white. Suddenly, the glass cracked and splintered. He threw it into the fireplace behind him, bringing Rona to her feet. No one else seemed startled. Someone laughed.

131

"Your hand!" Rona said, searching for a handkerchief.

He looked at her gloomily, sadly. Then he left her, as abruptly as he had first spoken to her. Blood dripped on the blue and gold rugs, leaving a thin small trail to the door.

Rona watched him leave. If this party is a circus, she thought, I'm afraid Charles is one of the clowns. Then she quickly forgot Charles. At the door Paul Haydn was standing. He looked around the room, hesitated, and then came straight toward Rona.

"Hello," Paul said, "you look frightened."

"I've lost Scott," Rona said, trying to keep her voice gay. "What on earth brought you here?"

"I thought you needed some reinforcements." He, too, was speaking lightly. He had meant to avoid Rona, but when he had come into the room and had suddenly seen that look of real fright on her face, he had broken all his resolutions.

"I guess I do," Rona admitted. "I've had a very odd time. But what I meant was—why are you in this place?" She was remembering their last evening together at the Tysons' some weeks ago. Paul Haydn's conversation then did not match an appearance here.

"You don't like it?"

"To be quite candid, it's the phoniest dump."

He grinned. "You flatter me. Actually, it was Murray who brought me along."

"Murray?" She was startled now. Then she looked at Paul disbelievingly.

"He's been very polite, recently." Paul was still smiling.

"I always avoid him at *Trend*," Rona said pointedly.

"I don't seem able to," said Paul.

They looked at each other for a moment.

And then, the sound of someone playing the spinet caught their attention. The talk around them died down.

"Have a chair," Paul said, pulling a spindle-legged bench near them. "We are evidently going to have a few cultured pearls thrown before us. We might as well catch them in comfort."

More people were crowding from the hall into the room, chairs were being pulled together, there was a minute of noise and bustle and then silence again. A blonde girl with a good

132

figure, well displayed in a black sweater, was leaning over the spinet. She wore heavy gold earrings and rows of gold bracelets that jangled as she moved her arms. "Sing, Anna!" someone called. "Sing!" And Anna, in a clear sweet voice, began to sing while the white-haired man at the spinet accompanied her with simple chords. At the end of each ballad, the applause was wholehearted. During the singing, the silence was unbroken. From the other rooms, beyond the hall, the talk and laughter had died away.

At first, Rona listened quite naturally. She liked ballads. She liked the girl's voice. She liked the way people joined in the choruses. And then she noticed that she wasn't enjoying it as she ought to have. There was an intensity on many of the faces that was unnecessary, and when they sang they would look at each other with a smile as if they shared some secret. Rona stopped looking at Anna, and began studying the faces around her. Here and there, someone felt the same way she did; and he would look uncertainly around him, a little worried or perhaps amused. But the others were caught up in a private world, intense, exciting.

"Sing 'Guadalajara' again, Anna," a man called.

So it was sung for the third time, and sung with attack and feeling.

"It's a good song," Paul said, watching Rona.

"Yes, I've always liked it." Her voice was hesitant, and low like his. In Mexico, she had heard it constantly, played gaily and charmingly. Down there, it was a ballad. Here, it was given another meaning.

"But . . . ?"

"There's no need for them to be so intense about it," she said angrily, still speaking in almost a whisper.

Paul Haydn said nothing. In front of them, a man sitting cross-legged on the floor looked round with a disapproving frown.

"Paul, am I dreaming things? See how these people draw together. Emotionally. They're sharing some secret understanding. Aren't they?"

"We'll be thrown out," he said, and then frowned back at the man who was still disapproving. "You must learn to disguise your feelings," he added with a grin.

133

"But don't you feel this odd atmosphere?" she whispered. "Oh—I know it's silly, it's perfectly silly. I'm going crazy. People can't be so childish."

"You're insulting children," he said gently. "But you aren't going crazy."

She stared at him for a moment. "Paul," she began anxiously, but the man in front of them turned around with a commanding hush. So she kept silent, but she exchanged a smile with Paul as the man began drumming with his hands on the floor accompanying the rhythm of "The Song of the Plains." It was a song Rona had always liked for its drama, but now as she listened to the drumming hands and heels, beating out the gallop of a troop of Red cavalry through a Park Avenue apartment, she wanted to laugh. Only, inside her, there was a deep irritation, an unexplained anger, that turned the laugh bitter.

At the doorway, she saw Scott at last. With Thelma. Thelma's gold-braided hair had slipped a little. She was wildly excited, madly applauding. Scott was looking grave, almost worried, perhaps bored. Rona waved and attracted his attention. He nodded. He was smiling now. Then he caught sight of Paul Haydn beside her. Scott was no longer smiling as he left Thelma and started to plough his way across the crowded room. But it was a slow job, and he had to stop while the singer made a little announcement. "My voice is giving out," she said with her charming smile. "So just once more—the last one. What shall it be?" Cries of disappointment, calls of "More later," suggestions for songs, all crossed and meshed into each other. There was a sudden sharp lull, as the girl held her hand up for silence. Her bracelets jangled prettily. "What shall it be?" she asked again.

"'From the Halls of Montezuma'," Rona called in her clear voice.

There was a shocked moment followed by a babel of voices.

"Well," Rona said with a smile to the man in front who had turned to stare, "it has a good marching rhythm, too."

Paul Haydn bent his head to hide his wide grin. "Naughty," he said, "that was very naughty of you, Rona." The grin deepened and he began to struggle with a laugh. There were

134

some others, too, who were trying to smother their amusement.

But someone did laugh, a loud high laugh that brought complete silence once more to the room and swung every head toward the piano. Charles, his red hair disarranged, his white face excited, his hand bandaged roughly with an incongruous guest towel, had climbed on to the piano stool. He stood there, balancing himself precariously, holding up his glass. "Time for a toast," he shouted in his high thin voice, beaming around the room.

"Stop him, someone!" It was Thelma leaving the doorway, struggling to reach him.

Charles turned to look at her, slipped and regained his footing. "Time for a toast," he repeated. "I give you, ladies and gentlemen, I give you the theories of Karl Marx—the opium of the intellectuals!" He raised his glass still higher, and he lost his balance, falling with a smashing clang into the open piano. Waves of wild chords jangled through the room as Charles's bandage got caught in the piano wires. He was climbing out now, slowly, choosing his exit by way of the piano keys. The discordant crashes overpowered the chorus of voices.

"He's drunk again," the man on the floor said angrily, as Charles was at last pulled free.

"Poor Thelma," said his companion, "she'll really have to put him away some place."

Rona turned to Paul. "Who *is* Charles?"

Paul watched the red-haired, white-faced man telling everyone to give him another drink and he'd oblige with plenty more toasts, he'd been thinking them up for months. He answered grimly, "Didn't you know? He's Thelma's son."

"Oh, no!" Rona said nothing more. Charles was trying to shake himself free from a restraining hand. He was now inviting everyone to come and start on the smoked turkey and salmon and baked ham in the dining-room. "Arise!" he called. "Arise, ye prisoners of starvation!"

It was at that moment that Scott reached them.

"Time to leave," he said angrily. He looked at Paul Haydn, his eyes narrowing.

Rona, still watching Charles being persuaded out of the
135

room, only nodded. The spinet sounded a chord, the singer leaned on one elbow and brushed back a lock of gold hair. She smiled and began to sing. It wasn't about the Halls of Montezuma or the Shores of Tripoli, though. It was "Guadalajara," for the fourth time that evening.

Rona got up, smiled to Paul and began to leave. Scott hesitated for a moment, and then followed her. The music lovers looked at them angrily, motioned to them to wait until the song had ended. But Rona, and then Scott, reached the hall. The other rooms were empty now. The dining-room waited with its large table decorated with food— Charles had been right about the smoked turkey and baked ham. But Charles, himself, was nowhere to be seen.

"I'm sorry," Scott said, as he waited for the stiff-faced butler to find his hat. "That was a shocking performance." He took her arm, trying to smile. But he looked tired and worried. She noticed the drawn look at the side of his mouth, the lines at his eyes. "Let's go and have dinner," he said, but he couldn't disguise his anger. "Let's find a quiet place." He held a tight grip of her arm all the way down to the street. They didn't speak at all.

He helped her with excessive politeness into the car. It was then she knew just how angry he was. As he edged the nose of the car out toward the stream of traffic, his anger suddenly exploded. "Why the hell is Paul Haydn following you around, everywhere, all the time?" Then as they waited for a line of cars to pass them, he reached a hand over and gripped hers. "Why do you do this to me, Rona?" he asked.

So that was it. She relaxed. But still, she was thinking, we are going to talk frankly at dinner. We must. I've had a lot of questions boiling up for months, and I've always taken them off the fire and laid them aside. To-night, they are going to be served up, and Scott will give me the answers. And then, with everything cleared off, we'll be able to begin again. We'll reach right back to the happiness we had last summer, and we'll start from there.

She felt the tears sting her eyes. She leaned over quickly and kissed his cheek. "I'm sorry, darling," she said. "But why did we go to that frightful place? We ought to have known that anyone as awful as Thelma would have no taste in anything."

136

He swung the car out into the avenue. "Don't worry, I shan't take you there again."

"Let's write off Thelma and Murray completely," she said eagerly.

Scott was watching traffic. Usually, he liked to take chances. To-night, he was being more cautious than usual. "What did you think of Charles?" he asked.

"I became very sorry for him," she said slowly.

"For that little drunk? He's a manic depressive, you know."

"But who made him that way?" she asked quietly, thinking of Thelma.

"Made him?"

"Yes. What could you do, if you had a mother who filled her house with people like that? He's still loyal to her, which is odd. She forfeited that, long ago, I'd think."

"Loyal? Do you call him loyal to Thelma?"

"Loyal enough not to go to the FBI and tell everything he knows."

"What on earth would the FBI have to do with him or Thelma?"

Rona said, "I don't know about such things, Scott. But I just supposed that Charles, knowing what he knows, must feel he's got to tell someone. Unless he believed in Thelma's politics. And he obviously doesn't."

"You've been reading too many accounts of those Washington witch-hunts, Rona." He was smiling, shaking his head over her simplicity.

"I haven't been studying them enough," Rona said sharply. "I've been too quick to disbelieve a lot of things. But from now on—oh, Scott!" The car swerved and avoided hitting a woman who had stepped off the sidewalk before the lights changed. A taxi, behind them, screamed to a sudden halt, and the driver's red face leaned out to yell what he thought of Scott's brain power.

Scott ignored the vehement descriptions, but his mouth tightened and his jaw clenched. Rona, remembering now how he hated scenes, began to wonder what he had felt this evening when the fireworks started. And she had been to blame. She knew that. Charles had laughed at her request for the Marines' hymn, and that had given him the courage to climb on the piano stool. Poor Charles, even his little protest had been so ineffectual. Drunk, everyone had said. Drunk? His voice had been clear enough, on either of its octaves.

"We'll have dinner at Carlo's," Scott said suddenly. "His place is open on Sunday, I think. Hungry?"

"Yes." It had been a long time since breakfast together, a very long time since they had set out this morning with nothing to worry them except a list of apartments.

At dinner, they talked a great deal; and Scott explained and argued patiently. Yes, he agreed, Thelma was an idiot. And Murray was a fool. The others? Surely Rona wasn't going to let a crackpot like Charles influence her? Or perhaps she had so disliked the apartment that everyone became equally dislikable.

"No," Rona protested, "I felt I could have liked many of them, if they had stayed normal people. But they aren't. They are laughable. Laughable and frightening, too. I didn't imagine anything. I just happened to be feeling observant to-day, that's all."

Scott said with a smile, "Rona, don't go round talking that way. People will think *you* are laughable. And you aren't."

"But I wasn't the only one who felt it. There was a woman who left very angrily. She wore a red hat with a white bow on it."

"Oh yes, I heard her go. Her boy-friend deserted her for the little girl who sang." Scott was amused.

"Well, Paul Haydn felt it."

"Haydn?"

Rona bit her lip. "I'm sure he did. Just as I was so sure you did, too."

Scott said, "Well, perhaps you're right about this thing. Perhaps they are a crowd of Communists. I guess I'm not quick enough to know."

"Frankly——"

"Yes?"

"I don't think you are."

He was startled. Then he began to laugh.

"I mean it, Scott. You're much too honest to realise when people are deceiving you."

"Who is deceiving me?"

138

She hesitated. "Nicholas Orpen," she said slowly.

"Rona," Scott's voice was firm, "Nicholas Orpen is my friend. I've known him for years, ever since he taught me at college. He isn't a crook or a cheat. He's a man of sincere convictions. He believes in the good of mankind. He's honest. He's had a lot of rough treatment in his life, but because other people turn on him is no reason for his old friends to turn on him. I don't agree with his politics, just as I don't agree with many of my friends' ideas on religion. But that doesn't make me avoid them. So why avoid Orpen? He isn't a criminal. Besides, even if he once stood up and said he was a Communist, that doesn't mean he is a Party member now. I don't discuss these things with him, but I did hear he's been out of Party affairs for several years now. So why worry? Is it some scandal you're afraid of?"

"No. Much more than scandal," Rona said impulsively. "I've been thinking about Blackworth."

"Who?"

"Blackworth—the assistant editor at *Trend* who got fired just before Paul Haydn came home. I've been thinking about him. I've been reading all the issues of *Trend* in which he was acting as Feature Editor. And I don't like what I read, Scott. Oh, it isn't just a matter of agreeing or disagreeing with the writers that Blackworth published. It's much more than that: they are a kind of—a kind of corruption. Thoughts *can* be corrupted, Scott. And then standards of behaviour get corrupted, too. That's what frightens me—not scandal."

"Oh, Rona, come! We are mostly intelligent people with fairly reliable judgments. We don't corrupt so easily."

"Blackworth was corrupted," she said quietly. "Because what he did to Weidler was complete treachery. Look, Scott, an editor has got to trust all his assistants and associates. He's got to delegate a lot of power. He's got to be able to trust the men who take his money. And Blackworth betrayed that trust. Isn't that corruption? If Blackworth had been honest, he would have resigned from *Trend* and gone to work for a Communist magazine."

Scott rose from the table. "Time we were getting you home," he said, calling the waiter for the bill. "We're beginning to talk in circles."

"I'm not," Rona said. "I'm just getting things straight."

"Fine," he said. "We'll go on from this point, another night. But there's just so much politics that I can take at one sitting." He was frowning now, counting the tip.

"Yes, Scott," Rona said wearily. She rose and left the restaurant. On the sidewalk she waited for him, looking up at the lighted apartments above the shops. The windows were unshaded. She could see the rooms on the second floor quite clearly—bookcases, a vase of flowers, pictures on the walls, the colours of the ceilings. In one room, people were moving around, quite heedless of any eyes that might be curious. Let them all look, what is there to be ashamed of? No, she thought, we aren't a secretive people. We don't go around hiding our lives. Or our thoughts. Or our intentions. We are what we are, take us or leave us. Foreigners think we are fools. Simple, they call us; naïve; big-mouthed. But, at least, we aren't hypocrites. Is that why, at first, we can be so easily deceived? Is that why we get so angry when we start finding out that something is being hidden from us?

Scott came out, at last. "Still so serious?" he asked.

"I was wondering which made Mr. Hull angrier—the bombs on Pearl Harbour, or the fact that the Japanese were waiting in his office outside to continue talking about 'peace'?"

"How did you ever reach Hull's office?" He took her arm, and they started walking toward the car.

She looked up at the unshaded windows again. "By way of the second floor." She pointed. "And by Thelma's party this evening."

He looked puzzled. "I don't follow. But if you are still worrying about the people you seem to have met at Thelma's, then forget them. They aren't important." He smiled and shook his head.

"They think they are. If they didn't take themselves so seriously, I'd stop worrying about them."

"They were more of a joke than anything." He glanced at his watch. "It's later than I thought," he said in surprise.

"Too late for our movie?"

He looked up. She saw that he had forgotten his earlier invitation. He said, awkwardly, "It's getting pretty late."

She put aside her disappointment. "Well, come up and have a drink at my place. That won't take so long."

He hesitated.

"Or have you any other plans for the rest of this evening?" she asked. "I seem to get in the way, these last months, don't I?"

"You're talking nonsense to-night," Scott said with a laugh. "It's been a hard day, you know. I was only thinking of that." He pulled her more closely to him as they walked, slipping his arm around her waist. Then his voice changed, and he said, "Rona, I blame all this on Paul Haydn. You've been worried and upset ever since he got back."

"Scott, that's——" She stopped, drawing herself away from his arm, turning to face him.

"Yes, you have. That's our whole trouble recently. What's wrong, Rona? Don't I measure up to his standards?"

"Scott, you're——"

"You've changed. You don't love me the way you once did."

"*I've* changed? No, I haven't."

"Do you mean *I* have?" He gripped her wrist.

"You aren't the same," she admitted slowly, painfully.

"I love you, don't I?" he asked, almost bitterly.

She said, again slowly, quietly, "Yes. Yes and no. Oh, Scott, what's happening to us? Something is standing between us, something, something."

"Paul Haydn."

"He *isn't*!" Her anger broke out of her control. At this moment, she hated Scott as much as she loved him. She struck his arm away from her wrist. She turned and ran.

Scott Ettley looked after her in amazement. "Rona!" he called, "Rona!" Then he began to run after her. But before he could reach her, a Madison bus had halted at the corner; its doors opened and Rona jumped in. The bus was already moving away from the corner as he reached it. He rapped on its side, but it didn't stop. He stood, looking after it, cursing.

"Too bad," a man said at his elbow. "But give a bus driver a green light and there's no holding him. Write the company, why don't you?"

"Who asked you?" Scott said and turned away. He walked quickly back toward his car, his face flushed, his mouth tight. He cursed the driver again. He cursed the interfering idiot at the street corner. He cursed himself.

When he got into the car, he sat still for some minutes.

And now, he was only thinking of Rona. I've lost her, he thought wearily. I've lost her. . . . Then he roused himself. "I haven't," he said aloud, "I haven't lost her. And I won't. I'll give up a lot, but I won't give up Rona."

He started the car, and drove slowly towards Rona's street. Her windows were in darkness. But even if they had been lighted, he couldn't have stopped. It was half-past ten. At eleven o'clock, he had to be at Nicholas Orpen's. (Thelma had been quite explicit about that. "Eleven o'clock, without fail," she had said.) He would call Rona to-morrow. Early. Perhaps even later to-night, after the visit to Orpen was over. He glanced up at the dark windows once more. No, he would call her to-morrow, perhaps even at midday. She would have to learn a little discipline too.

As he drove away from her street, back to his apartment where he could leave the car safely and then walk to Orpen's, he had lost the fear that had gripped him outside of the restaurant. He was still thinking of Rona. But now he was half-amused, half-angry.

CHAPTER ELEVEN

By eleven o'clock on Sunday night, Third Avenue was already half-asleep. Only the bars and cafés were still lit. A few taxis, their tyres jolting over the trolley lines, sped under the shadows of the El. The small shops lay in darkness; the genuine Second Empire tables, the Biedermeier chests, the positively real antiques, the crystal candelabra and painted porcelain vases, the sun-spray clocks and gilt spindle-leg chairs, all huddled together in the black windows. Keeping them company, the garbage cans stood waiting at the closed entrances to the walk-up apartments overhead.

A man in shirt-sleeves was having a quick cigarette at a darkened doorway. A woman waited patiently while her dog nosed round a curb. A group of people straggled home from a neighbourhood movie. Two policeman walked slowly, steadily, covering their beat. A man and a woman passed, arguing. Four people in evening dress waited at a corner for a taxi. A drunk went his lonely way. A cat prowled, alert and suspicious. An elevated train roared, half empty, up the avenue.

Scott Ettley left Third Avenue, entered the street where Nicholas Orpen lived, and approached a drab row of houses standing grimly across the road from a blank soot-grimed wall of garages and warehouses. Farther east, new apartment houses had their uniformed doormen and smart chauffeurs; westward, beyond Third Avenue, the brownstone houses had been converted into expensive small apartments. But here, the row of brownstone houses hadn't been painted for years; there were no window boxes, no bright-coloured doors. The steps were peeling, the railing sagged, the basement area was heaped with overflowing garbage.

It was a forlorn stretch of street, dark and forsaken at night except for the parked automobiles that hugged the curb. Orpen's front room was on the top floor. Its windows, heavily shaded, showed only a crack of light. The other windows of the house were in darkness. Here, most people went to bed early. If, to begin with, Orpen's neighbours had been surprised by his late visitors, they had learned to accept that as normal. "He's a writer," they would say with a shrug. That explained a lot of things. And in New York few questions were ever asked, anyway.

Scott Ettley gave his accustomed ring and waited. The door opened automatically, letting him into a cramped hall, poorly lit by one bulb, cluttered with a shabby baby carriage and a battered tricycle. There was a box telephone on the wall at the foot of the steep staircase, but Orpen had installed his own upstairs: he didn't like exercise.

Scott climbed the narrow stairs, treading as quietly as possible on the cracked linoleum. There was always the smell of cooked food hanging around each narrow landing. From behind the closed doors of the apartments which he passed, there was either deep silence or heavy snoring. The other tenants in the house had work that took them out early in the morning. Often, they would be rising, getting breakfast, even as Orpen was going to bed. ("He's a writer," they'd say with a shrug. He wore tweed jackets and old flannel trousers, even on Sundays. He kept no holidays, either. Or perhaps every day was a holiday to a writer. A lazy kind of life, sitting around.)

143

Orpen's door stood closed. But as Scott knocked, again using his own signal, it opened at once. He entered a comfortable room, well furnished with a massive desk, a table, arm-chairs, bookcases, and an excellent phonograph with a huge horn. Heavy curtains were drawn across the windows. Reading lamps gave a quiet look to the whole room. The pile of records near the phonograph, the books on the mantelpiece and chairs, the heap of folded newspapers and magazines on the table, all increased this feeling of peaceful living.

Orpen was taking off his glasses, polishing them quickly before he put them on again. Behind him, on the desk near the windows, were pages of manuscript covered carefully by a huge sheet of blotting paper. He was a man of less than medium height, slender, with a thin quiet face. Just a very ordinary-looking man, with a slow, gentle way of talking. His sparse hair was mid-brown, his eyes a mid-grey. His skin was sallow. (There were days on end when he never left his two small rooms.) Yet his movements were quick, decided. His gestures were emphatic. His accent, carefully trained, was indefinable.

Now, as he took Scott's outstretched hand and gave it a quick, brief shake, he could have been—with his friendly smile, his watchful eyes, his tweed jacket, his background of books—a middle-aged professor at a New England college. He might have discarded his instructorship at Monroe, but he had never discarded its ways.

"Come in, come in," he said, closing the door and locking it. He waved Scott to the most comfortable chair, and opened two cans of beer that stood waiting on the table.

"Well?" he asked, when he too was settled in an arm-chair facing Scott. With an impatient movement, he switched off the lamp beside him. "My eyes," he said wearily. "I'll have to get stronger glasses." Then he sat, quite motionless, watchful. Scott waited, but it was he who had to speak first.

"Thelma gave me your message," Scott said uneasily. He glanced at the clock on the mantelpiece. It was six minutes past eleven.

Orpen followed his glance. "You must learn to be punctual," he said with his quiet humourless smile. He pulled his

144

pipe out of his jacket pocket. "Well, what is wrong? You don't look particularly happy."

"I had a little trouble to-night," said Scott. "Rona." He had meant to mention Rona only at the end of this meeting, but Orpen had a way of making him blurt everything out in the first few minutes.

"Ah? Didn't she enjoy the party at Thelma's?"

"It was you who told me to take her there." He couldn't keep a note of reproach out of his voice.

"And now you see for yourself," said Orpen with considerable bite to his words.

Scott looked up at him sharply. The light beside him got in his eyes; he couldn't see Orpen's face clearly.

Orpen was pulling out his tobacco pouch, filling his pipe methodically.

Scott rose, and began walking around the room. "I told you it was too soon to take Rona to one of Thelma's parties. She isn't ready for that, yet."

"Nor will she ever be." Orpen's voice was angry. He lit his pipe, his eyes narrowing. "Come back and sit down, Scott. I didn't bring you here to argue about Rona Metford. I've told you before, as your friend, that she isn't the girl for you. When I think of all the women you could have fallen in love with——" he broke off, and flung his hands up in mock despair. He was being amused, now.

"I'm in love with Rona," Scott said quietly. "We're getting married. In September." He came back to his arm-chair then.

"Are you?"

There was a note in Orpen's voice that kept Scott from answering.

Orpen went on. "You aren't staging a small revolt by any chance? That would be foolish. At this stage of your work. I'm speaking as a friend, Scott."

Scott shook his head slowly. "It's just that I'm—well, I'm tired of all this . . ." He hesitated.

"All this what?"

"All this play-acting. I'd like something definite, something that achieves real results."

Orpen said sharply, "Smoke screens have their uses in any battle. Believe me, Scott, there's nothing irrelevant in this fight. Everything is at stake. And every means must be used. *Every* means," he insisted, "no matter how irrelevant, how trivial it may seem. You do as you are instructed, you ask no questions, and we'll get results."

"I've always followed your instructions," Scott said. He thought of all the nights in those last six months, when he had had to curtail an evening with Rona, even cancel it, for the sake of Orpen's meetings, Orpen's arrangements.

"But until you got tied up thoroughly with this Metford girl, you didn't evade my orders."

"I don't evade them," Scott insisted.

"You've been getting restless."

"But——" Scott began.

"But what?"

"I've begun to feel you don't trust me," Scott said with some hesitation.

"What makes you feel that?" Orpen looked amused.

"Four years ago, when I was discharged from the army, I came to you. I told you how I felt. I knew, from the old days, that you'd agree with me."

"And I did," Orpen said.

"You did more than that. You made me believe I could be of some real use; you said there was real work waiting for me, an essential job to be done."

"Only after I had talked with you for over a year," Orpen reminded him sharply. Then he smiled. "You make me sound a very slap-dash recruiter," he added. "Not that I ever doubted your sincerity. But we need more than sincerity, you know. We need discipline, determination."

"I've tried to give proof of that, too," Scott said quietly.

"Yes, you've done very well. You've been accepted. You've followed instructions and kept yourself clear of suspicion. You've learned most of the disciplines. Except patience, I'm afraid."

"But I don't seem to have done anything of importance," Scott argued.

"You've been working with me. You don't think that's of any importance?" For a moment, Orpen was angry. Then his mouth relaxed once more, and he said with amusement, "Because I've been your friend for so many years, you are quite sure I'm of no importance?"

"I didn't mean it that way."

"No? Well, perhaps my job is of no importance." And yet, the expression in his voice showed that he didn't believe what he had suggested. Suddenly, he rose from his chair. He went over to the desk. He spoke over his shoulder, as he searched among some papers. "Have you decided about Rona Metford?" he asked quietly.

Scott looked up. Orpen's voice had warned him. "What has Rona got to do with all this?" he asked quietly.

"Everything."

"I don't see——"

"You'll have to see, Scott. You have only one choice. If you want the assignment that is waiting for you." Orpen returned from the desk to his chair. He was carrying a sheet of paper.

"An assignment?"

"Yes. Difficult. But important. We consider it of prime importance." There was no doubting Orpen's sincerity as he emphasised these last words.

Scott's face changed. He sat forward on his chair, alert, expectant. But he waited for Orpen to explain, as if to prove that he had learned the discipline of patience. It wasn't easy, though. He could tell from Orpen's smile that this assignment was as important as he had hoped for.

Then Orpen looked down at the piece of paper in his hand. He pursed his lips. Scott waited.

Orpen said, "About Rona Metford. . . . Until now, I've always spoken to you as a friend. I've listened to your explanations, I've watched your compromises, and I've waited for you to realise that you can't put your own wishes before your duty to the Party. You've been persuading yourself that you can handle Rona, that your personal life was your own affair. Now, I'm going to speak to you officially. Your personal life is our affair. We can risk no breach of security. And Metford is dangerous."

Scott said, "She isn't politically mature, I agree. I haven't tried to educate her. You told me to avoid political discussions. But, if you let me handle this, she can learn to follow Party doctrine without ever having to become an accepted member. That would be safe enough."

Orpen threw back his head and laughed. "Safe? My dear

Scott, safe? After this evening at Thelma's? I got full reports on that, you know."

"But she has had no instruction. If you will let me——"

"Nonsense. She's completely unreliable. She has already done a lot of damage. She lost Blackworth his job at *Trend*. She put the finger on him."

"By accident. She didn't even know what she was doing. She's told me the story."

"Yes, *her* story. Did anyone else notice the way Blackworth was selecting articles for publication? Did that fool Weidler see that Blackworth was 'slanting' his use of material? No. He had to wait until Metford put that word into his mouth. And what is Blackworth's report on her?" Orpen held up the sheet of paper, angrily, almost threateningly. "She said he had been printing one-sided arguments amounting to distortion. Distortion! Blackworth gave *Trend* the only true facts it has ever published."

Scott looked down at his hands. He interlocked his fingers. He said, "Blackworth made a mistake in publishing those articles on housing. Rona's been making a study of that for almost a year. It was the one thing on which she could trip him up—she had the facts and figures. If he hadn't published that series, he would still be working at *Trend*."

Orpen stared at him. Scott's face flushed as he realised what he had said.

Orpen said, "*Our* facts are the real facts. They show the United States as we see it. That is the only realism, the only truth." Then his voice quieted, and he said softly, "She is beginning to corrupt you. You have proved my point about her. She is unacceptable." He let the report on Rona fall beside his chair.

Scott said nothing. He rose. He stood with his arm leaning on the mantelpiece, his head bent, his eyes staring down at the narrow black hearth with its scattered pipe ashes and cigarette stubs and burnt matches.

Nicholas Orpen rose too. He never remained seated when another man stood over him. He went over to the table and picked up a newspaper. "We're in danger, Scott," he said. "We are at a moment of crisis. This wave of hysteria, this witch-hunting . . ." He dropped the paper in disgust.

148

"We need men like you, loyal, dependable, intelligent. Men who have attracted no attention. Men who can remain unnoticed. Yes, Blackworth was a fool. I agree. But not for your reasons. He misjudged his margin of security. . . . He took five years to build up; he came hurtling down in one morning. And every time that happens, we not only lose a good position, we have to work against increasing curiosity, increasing suspicion. But you aren't a fool, Scott. You've calculated every step of the way. Your only mistake has been Rona Metford. And even with her you've been efficient."

Orpen paused. His voice changed again, became cold and hard. "But you are reaching a point where she's an extravagance you can't afford. We don't trust her. You keep telling me she is ignorant. We don't trust her to stay ignorant. She will find out. And your work will be undone. Your usefulness will be over. You will be discredited. Do you know what happens to those who are discredited?"

Scott left the mantelpiece. He paced across the room. He stopped by the phonograph, looking down at the pile of record albums on the floor at his feet. On the evening he had spent here listening to them, had he been calculating each step of the way? Or had he willingly shut his eyes and let each step be calculated for him?

Orpen was repeating, "What happens to those who are discredited? They are discarded. Once they are discovered, we must write them off as a loss. They may have to wait years before they can be of any real use. Or they may have to change their names, their identities, start all over again where they can't be recognised. It's a slow, wasteful business. It sets us back. Do you think we can feel any particular confidence in those who've let themselves be discredited?"

"No," Scott said at last. He sat down on the nearest chair. He covered his eyes with his hand.

"What's your decision?" Orpen asked sharply. "Are you with us?"

"You can trust me," Scott said slowly, with difficulty.

"I want a direct answer. Don't be a fool, Scott!"

Scott raised his head. "I'm not the only one who's a fool. What about Murray?"

"What about him?" I told him, thought Orpen angrily, to keep a better guard on his tongue after Scott reported his indiscretion at Metford's party. "What about Murray?"

"He brought Paul Haydn to Thelma's. What was Haydn doing there?"

Orpen relaxed. "Murray's been testing him. Haydn's a simple-minded soul. He's got no ideas of his own."

"Hasn't he? Rona told me that he agreed with her about Thelma, about Murray, about everything that happened this evening."

It was Orpen who was silent this time.

"Do you know Haydn's war service?" Scott asked.

"Of course we know," Orpen said irritably.

"Do you know that a lot of his activities were only cover for Military Intelligence?"

Orpen said, "And did Metford tell you this, too?"

"Not in these words. But she gave me the lead without knowing it. When we were having dinner, to-night, I asked her about Haydn. I've been wondering about him."

Orpen half-smiled. "I see how you can persuade yourself that she could be useful to you instead of dangerous. Rona Metford might be good cover for your activities—isn't that what you're trying to prove to me? But only if you hadn't this assignment, only if you were to be an ordinary Party member." He paused and let the significance of his last words sink deep into Scott Ettley's mind. "You see, she would have doubts about the job we are giving you. She wouldn't accept it without questions."

"What is it?"

"Once you know that, you've accepted it. There is no turning back. If you are accepting it, meet me to-morrow night. At the northwest corner of Fifty-ninth Street and Madison Avenue. At half-past nine."

"To-morrow? Orpen, give me time!"

"There's no time to give. If you don't meet me, I will have to report that you have broken with us. And you must take the consequences."

"My God, don't you see——"

"Yes, I see." Orpen came over to Scott Ettley and laid a hand on the young man's shoulder. "Scott, haven't I given up my own personal ambitions, my own private inclinations?

150

I am not asking you to do anything that I haven't done myself."

Scott Ettley nodded. He didn't speak. He rose as if to leave. "I'll see you to-morrow. Half-past nine," Orpen said crisply. "You'll be told about your assignment then." He smiled. "You are going to meet some of those really important people you've been wondering about. You're moving into the big league, Scott. You're leaving the Murrays and the Blackworths and the Thelmas far behind you." He held out his hand; his voice was friendly and conversational once more. "I'll be glad to get all this settled before I leave New York. I'm going on Thursday, so we haven't much time. You see? Good night, Scott." His grip was strong and brief.

The door closed silently behind Scott Ettley. He made his way cautiously, quietly, downstairs. In the street, a rising wind caught a torn sheet of newspaper and circled it over the roofs of the parked cars. The wind had an edge to it. The lights in the distant high buildings were cold and bleak.

He started walking. He didn't know where. Nor did it matter. It was four o'clock, and a new day dawning, before he reached his own street at last.

CHAPTER TWELVE

Next morning Rona waited in her apartment until after nine o'clock. But there was no telephone call from Scott. Twice, she almost phoned him. And then, each time, she decided against it. She was always the first to apologise, she told herself bitterly. After all, who began this quarrel?

She walked restlessly around the small living-room, leaving the morning mail unopened, the *Times* unread, the bedroom untidied, the breakfast dishes unwashed. She went over yesterday's events again, recalling what she had said and done, as if she hadn't lain awake most of the night remembering. What had started all this, anyway? Admitting that she had been wrong to act so impulsively, so childishly, when she had run away from Scott, why had she done it? Because she had lost her temper when he had challenged her about Paul Haydn? Yes, that had angered her. It was so untrue.

Scott knew she loved him, knew she thought only of him. Why did he keep torturing her—and himself—with this talk talk talk of Paul Haydn? She had given up many of her friends for Scott, she had stopped meeting them because he didn't particularly like them. Even at the last party she had given, at least half of the guests had been Scott's choice. And those who had been her friends had come only because of old loyalties, just as she had invited them with the feeling that it had been far too long since she had seen them. When she had welcomed them, it had been with a sense of guilt. When she had said good-bye, they had made gestures (half-sadly, as if they knew quite well she was moving slowly away from them) toward seeing her soon again. And she had made the same gestures, equally cordial, equally well-intentioned. Yet, later, she had refused their invitations because Scott was meeting her for lunch that day, or Scott had asked her to keep that evening free, or Scott had said, "Let's go dancing on Saturday."

Oh, she told herself angrily, don't blame it on Scott! You are as much to blame as he is. You're in love, and you're a fool like all women in love. Then she stared at her white face and reddened eyes in the mirror over the mantelpiece.

No, Rona, she thought, there's more to this quarrel than Paul Haydn or anyone else. That's what is really worrying you. And you can't find any answer. Do you love Scott Ettley? Or have you been spending three years of your life imagining yourself as a woman in love? Did you want a love affair as badly as all that? Her unhappy eyes, filling with tears, and her trembling lips answered her. She loved Scott. That was all and everything.

She turned away from the mirror, and went to search for her hat and her bag. She was going to be late this morning. She was going to be very late.

She had to take a taxi. She would cut down on lunch to-day. And she began persuading herself that the quarrel would straighten itself out. It was all too silly, too childish, to be taken seriously.

In the *Trend* building, the early morning rush was now flagging. Rona had the express elevator to herself. She was

152

glad that Joe, with his sharp eyes and quick tongue, was off duty (Monday was his day for the horses at Jamaica). The relief operator was a stranger with troubles of his own.

She walked quickly, past the receptionist, down the long corridor, until she reached her small office. It was more of a cubicle than a room, but at least it was her own and its window gave plenty of light. She squeezed round the desk that filled most of its space, jammed her hat and gloves into a small closet, dropped her handbag on her chair, caught up a notebook and pencil, and went into Mr. Burnett's office next door.

He had already begun to detail work for the October issue of *Trend* to the small group that formed his department. Harry Jimson was taking notes as usual. Phil Arnim was lounging on the window sill, a sure sign that he was memorising hard. Burnett looked up as Rona entered. "Had a good week-end? Found an apartment?" he asked, and then —after a quick glance at Rona's face—he looked down at the mass of material scattered in front of him. He went on explaining, suggesting, and drew the attention of the others back to the desk and his pointing pencil. The idea now under consideration was a comparison between present-day architecture, with its emphasis on bringing the outdoors inside, and the treatment of gardens in ancient Rome and modern Japan.

"Rona," Burnett said finally, "you'll be responsible for the classical methods. Find the details of the way the Romans placed their gardens in the centre of their houses, open to the sky, a kind of courtyard around which the rooms were built. It will take some research, but it will make a nice spread. We'll use colour plates where possible. Keep checking with Harry, here. He's doing the modern American use of terrace and window gardens. You'll be surprised how your two subjects will dovetail." He waved his pencil to tell them that was all, meanwhile. "Oh, by the way, I've some examples here of Roman mosaics, Rona. You might find them interesting." He began to search for the book.

"There's a guy in California," Harry Jimson said as he picked up his notes and began to leave, "who brought his terrace and pool right into his living-room. All he needs is some lampreys and a few slave girls to toss to them."

"And a hole in his roof," Phil Arnim added, following him slowly. "He ought to buy my place. I've been patching the darned roof all week-end. Now, if I had known, I'd have knocked out a few more shingles, planted the zinnias in the hall, and started wearing a toga around the house." He gave Rona a smile and closed the door of Burnett's office behind him. His face became serious as he turned to Jimson. "Say, Rona isn't looking too good this morning."

"Monday," Harry Jimson suggested.

"Wonder if she's heard that damn' rumour?"

"It can hardly miss her."

"How does a thing like that get started, anyway?" It was a rhetorical question, and they both knew it. They parted gloomily. They had known Rona ever since they had come to work at *Trend* after the war. "It doesn't make sense," Phil said angrily over his shoulder.

Rona came out of Burnett's room. "Then you'll knock some sense into it, Phil," she said. "Did you draw the Japanese approach to nature?"

"Yes. On account of I was over Tokyo twice in a bomber."

"I've always liked the idea of a room with three walls. Provided you've a piece of scenery to fill up the non-existent fourth."

"Provided you've the climate to keep you from getting head colds." They went into the art reference shelves together, and began choosing the books they might need. Phil Arnim talked on. He even got her to laugh before he left her.

Rona carried the volumes she had selected into her office, and spread them over her desk. She had a good deal of work ahead of her. That, she decided, was what she needed—a stiff job of work. First, she would get some broad ideas gathered together. Then, she'd narrow down the field and dig more deeply. Later, she would have to visit the Frick Library and the Metropolitan Museum. But that stage would only come when she knew exactly what she needed.

She sat down at the desk, pulled the most interesting of the books in front of her.

"Busy?" a bright voice asked. It was Miss Guttman, looking coyly round the door. Her sharp face had softened, her whole manner was positively girlish, since she had become engaged. Her left hand was very much in view as it held the edge of the door. She glanced down at the square-cut diamond and said, "I won't take a moment. The mail got mixed up this morning, and Mr. Haydn got this by mistake. He asked me to bring it to you." She relinquished the hold on the door slowly, and came into the room, handing out an envelope. "Looks like a billey doo," she said. "Plenty of it, too."

"Probably some incensed Southerner disagreeing with our ideas on porticos. Thanks, Miss Guttman."

"Did you hear about Mr. Crowell? He's in the hospital. Serious."

"That's bad news."

"Isn't it?" Miss Guttman still didn't leave. "I've a problem, it's awful," she said. "I've been worrying about it all weekend. You know, Hubert's having an extra bathroom built beside the guest-room. He's just got back from St. Louis; he says the house is going to look gorgeous. Well, this new bathroom, it's tiled of course. In a kind of mauve, a very delicate shade. And I'm worrying whether the towels and curtains should be just a little darker, with more blue in them. Or would you have them more pink? Not too deep—just a hint. It's a problem, isn't it?"

Yes, Rona said, that was quite a problem.

"Of course, orchid would look stunning."

Yes, indeed it would.

"Only I've got orchid in the powder-room—you know the big closet at the hall entrance, well, we're making it a powder-room. What do you think? Or burgundy would look good. I like dark towels. Burgundy with a pink monogram?"

"Perhaps you ought to see what the stores have to offer. It's easier to decide that way," Rona said, trying to be polite. Miss Guttman's pleasure was something you couldn't destroy.

"Perhaps," Miss Guttman said reluctantly. "Well, I'll have to run along. Did you get an apartment yesterday?"

"No."

"Looks as if you got a cold instead."

"I'm all right. Didn't sleep very well. That's all." Rona turned over a few pages of the book in front of her.

Suddenly, Miss Guttman looked worried. "Oh!" she exclaimed, backing away. At the door she turned to say,

"Don't let that gossip trouble you. None of us here believe a word of it." And she left, very suddenly for Miss Guttman.

Rona stared after her. And then she picked up the letter which had brought Miss Guttman here. Paul Haydn, she thought with a smile, was determined to avoid her. Yesterday, at Thelma's, he had only come over to talk to her because she had looked so much alone. If only Scott could see how Paul kept out of her way here, in the office, perhaps he wouldn't . . . She frowned, cut off that direction of thought, and opened the large envelope, addressed in neat, thin handwriting. The postmark was New York. And the word URGENT was printed carefully up in the envelope's left-hand corner. Inside, there was a sheet of paper, well filled with the same thin careful handwriting. And there was also a second envelope, sealed, bulky, unaddressed. Across its front was written: "To be opened only as directed."

She picked up the letter, looked with amazement at its Park Avenue heading, turned the sheet quickly to see the signature. It was, simply, *Charles*.

The letter was as simple and direct as its signature. It was dated precisely: Sunday evening, April 30th, eight o'clock.

The party is still going on. I am left in peace, meanwhile, in my room. Later, along with some departing guests, I shall slip out. And mail this to you. Why? Because I feel that I can trust you. I also feel that no one will expect me to get in touch with you. So I am not endangering you.

I know now what I must do. The problem, still unsolved, is *how* to do it. I am unwilling to hurt Thelma. That is the whole trouble. It always has been the trouble. But if anything happens—and I think, now, that it is likely to happen —then the problem is solved for me. It will be at that moment, when I shall be morally free but perhaps not physically free to speak, that I shall need your help.

Keep the sealed envelope *safely* until Saturday. Keep this letter with it, for the two explain each other.

If you have not heard from me by that time, take the letter to someone in a responsible position, someone whom you can trust, and let him open it. Tell him what you know about me, and he will understand what to do. Perhaps Weidler, the editor of *Trend*? He has had a little experience, recently, that will make him listen. There are many people whom you can trust, but few of them will listen. That has been part of my trouble, too.

Meanwhile, as you wait for me to get in touch with you, keep the envelope and letter safe. Safe. Say nothing to anyone, nothing at all. Please.

I beg you to be careful, to do only as I ask you. Why should I ask *you*? You were the only face in that room, to-night, that looked as if you were troubled by what I did. The others were angry or amused. You were troubled. Speak about me to no one. Forget you read this. Do only as I beg of you. Please. Until Saturday, one way or the other.

Charles

P.S. I am writing this in longhand. (1) The typewriter would be heard by Martin.
(2) *Am* I drunk?

Rona read the letter twice over. First, she was incredulous, almost annoyed. Then, its desperation reached out and touched her. It was the postscript that finally decided her. No one who wrote such a neat hand as Charles was anywhere near being drunk. Had he only made a pretence of drinking too much? And why? Then she thought of the small quiet man, with his smooth white face and his thin red hair, his pathetically comic voice, his watchful eyes masked by his round glasses into a vacuous stare. He had sat in his room, the door locked, listening to the distant sounds of music and laughter; and he had written this letter not even daring to use a typewriter as if he had been a conspirator. And who, she wondered, was Martin?

Charles made such a pathetic little conspirator. Even his seriousness seemed, as you remembered Charles, mostly comic. Then, as she half-smiled, she read again, "There are many people whom you can trust, but few of them will listen. That has been part of my trouble, too." And she stopped smiling.

She placed the envelope and letter together again, and slipped it all into her handbag. *Say nothing to anyone, nothing at all.* Not even to Scott? Not to Peggy or Jon? And where was she going to keep the letter and the enclosed envelope safely? When Charles got in touch with her, she had better tell him quite clearly that he wasn't to try anything like this again with her. As if, she thought bitterly, I haven't plenty of troubles all of my own. But where to keep the envelope? She had only a filing cabinet and a closet in her office—nothing was locked. Burnett's safe was always open—he was careless about shutting things away. Mr. Weidler's safe? But how could she ask him, what excuse could be given? You just didn't approach the Boss and ask him to keep this please. One of those deposit boxes in Grand Central Station? That would mean a special journey for her . . . a nuisance, whatever way you looked at it. A hat box or the medicine cabinet in her apartment? Yet Charles had sent his letter to her at the office, as if he hadn't wanted it to lie around her apartment. He could easily have got her home address from a telephone book.

Why, she thought in sudden amazement, I'm taking the little man seriously. She opened the reference books, angrily and began reading determinedly about Roman courtyards.

Miss Guttman waited until Mrs. Hershey had come back with a collection of notes from the Monday morning conference in Mr. Weidler's office. Then, her voice low so that the other girls in the main office couldn't listen, Miss Guttman said, "I think Rona Metford has heard."

"Heard what?" Mrs. Hershey's round placid face looked blank.

"The rumour . . . *You* know."

Mrs. Hershey frowned. "It hasn't reached the office, has it?" It had been wandering around the restaurants at lunchtime last week. On Friday, Mrs. Hershey had had a few sharp words to say to Miss Blenton, who worked over at *Modern*, when they had been having their weekly lunch date and gossip together. As if anyone who knew Rona Metford would ever believe that she chased a married man and then did him out of his job just in time for an old beau to get it. Mrs. Hershey's face coloured with anger at the thought. Any attack on Rona Metford was an attack on *Trend*. That's how she saw it. Besides, it was all ridiculous. She and Miss Guttman had decided that on Friday afternoon.

Miss Guttman looked down at her left hand, moved her third finger just enough to let her ring catch the light. "The girls were all talking about it in the washroom this morning." She paused. "Would she do a thing like that?" she asked slowly.

"Now, not you too!" Mrs. Hershey said angrily.

"I'm *not* saying she did." Miss Guttman was hurt. She started typing. "One thing is sure," she paused again to add, "Scott Ettley isn't going to like it." Then she went back to the problem of burgundy towels with pink or blue monograms.

Mrs. Hershey said nothing. She pursed her lips and began to read her notes. But the frown didn't leave her brow. When she finished dealing with the most urgent of her letters, she rose and left the room. Mrs. Hershey bustled around a good deal; none of the typists, not even Miss Guttman— who was now thinking of midnight blue towels but would Hubert like anything so daring?—paid any attention to her sudden departure.

Mrs. Hershey went straight to Paul Haydn. "It's none of my business, I suppose," she added at the end of her story. "But someone has got to deal with this."

Paul Haydn nodded. When she left, he arose and went to see Weidler. "Something's got to be done," Paul ended grimly, after Weidler had heard him through without one interruption.

"But what?" Weidler's face, weathered red from a week-end of gardening and golf, was furrowed with worry. He turned his chair to stare out of the window. He said slowly, "This explains a side remark I was given at the Club yesterday. In the locker-room, a publisher I know said he had heard we were having trouble at *Trend*: that was what happened when we took women into business—cartoonists would have to think up a new angle to the joke about big executive chasing pretty secretary."

He swung his chair back to face Paul. "You believe this story about Rona Metford and Blackworth has been purposely invented? That's hard to swallow, Paul."

"There never has been any malicious gossip about Rona before. Why now?"

Yes, Weidler thought, it could be a story to cover up the

reasons for Blackworth's dismissal. And certainly the Communists would blame Rona for that. "But who'd invent such a rumour? Who'd spend good time on a thing like that? Pretty cheap occupation for a grown man."

Paul said nothing. The rumour was not only invented but spreading, that was what worried him.

"That publisher I was telling you about—he said he'd been running into the darnedest trouble with one of the books on his recent list. It was a factual report on Soviet espionage, with a chapter on that scientist Fuchs. An important book. Well, in several bookstores—good, reliable stores where he knows the men in charge and they are as honest as you or I—he was puzzled because the book had low sales. So he sent someone to investigate, quietly. His man wandered into the stores in question and found that either the book was badly displayed or not even displayed at all; piles of copies were tucked away behind a counter, for instance. And you know who was responsible for smothering the book? Just one clerk. Out of ten or twenty reliable clerks there was one weasel who made a point of attending to that book. He had put it where book buyers wouldn't even notice it. Now, who's going to believe that? Yet the publisher checked with some of his business friends, and one or two admitted that they had been finding some difficulties for the last five years whenever they handled a book the Commies didn't like. Small difficulties, things you can't bring out in the open without looking a fool. It's hard to believe that pettiness can be organised into a weapon. That's what makes me so damned mad—the pettiness."

"Yes, it's petty. But it injures a lot of people, all the same," Paul said. He was still waiting. "What about Rona Metford?" he asked point-blank.

"Well, you know we can't tell the truth about Blackworth."

"You could tell the truth to Rona. That would explain this attack on her. She's bound to hear the rumour. Some kind friend is going to tell her she doesn't believe a word of it, and then give the full details."

"This is a hell of a way to spend a Monday morning," Weidler said, looking at the pile of correspondence on his desk. "All right, let's have her in. No, you stay here. I'll need your help, Paul." He picked up the inter-office phone and asked Miss Metford to come and see him. Then he sat back in his chair again. "Don't worry," he told Paul, "I'll give Rona the full details. We can trust her to keep them to herself?"

"Yes."

"By the way, I'm meeting Roger Brownlee for lunch to-day. He called me first thing this morning." Weidler looked at his watch. "Don't let me be late."

"He didn't waste much time in reaching you," said Paul. "I told him about you only on Saturday."

"Oh?" Weidler was interested.

"We wandered around Central Park and fed the squirrels."

"Did he think I was wrong to hush up the Blackworth affair?"

"No," Paul admitted, still obviously disagreeing with that decision.

"Well," Weidler said with a smile of relief, "that's one small ray of comfort on a bad morning."

Paul was watching the door. "I think I heard Rona's voice," he said. He looked at Weidler, who was no longer smiling. They exchanged a glance. Just a couple of men, Paul thought, who wish they were twenty miles from here at this moment.

Rona entered. She looked pale and depressed. She was carrying, Paul Haydn noticed with surprise, her handbag. She had also brought a pencil and a notebook for any emergencies.

Weidler, pacing around his room nervously, didn't waste much time though. First of all, he gave her the full story about Blackworth. Then he told her the rumours about herself that had been spread around. And, at the end, he gave Paul's explanation.

Rona looked incredulous, and then horrified. Then she almost laughed. "It's so—so silly," she said. "That story about me, I mean." She looked at Paul then. "I've dragged you into . . ." She couldn't go on. She bit her lip. She sat quite still, looking down at her handbag.

Weidler said awkwardly, "It is I who feel responsible." He paused. Then suddenly, he was angry. "No, we're not responsible. It's Blackworth's friends who are responsible for all this." He quieted his voice with an effort. "I am sorry that we had to tell you, Rona, but it seemed the best thing to do. You won't say a word of this to anyone?"

She shook her head. "I'm glad you did tell me," she said. "It is always best to know, even if you don't want to believe." Then her face brightened as if a new idea, a comforting idea, had suddenly been discovered. Scott . . . Scott, she was thinking, had heard this rumour. He couldn't believe it, but it made him miserable, and all he could do was to pick a quarrel with her over Paul Haydn. I'll phone him, Rona thought, I'll phone him and tell him that I'm sorry, I understand, but he knows that the rumour is a lie.

Paul Haydn, watching her, wondered what she was thinking. Out of bad news had come something good, seemingly.

"That's the way to take it," Weidler said approvingly. "At first, you feel everyone is against you, that you can trust no one. Then you begin to realise that there are about seven million people outside these windows who are all on your side—if they knew, if they realised what was happening."

That's fine comfort for Rona when Ettley hears the rumour, Paul thought bitterly.

"Yes," Weidler went on, "in all this city there's probably only a few thousand against you. That's what I thought out, one day, and it helped. A lot. Don't forget that, Rona. There's a clear seven million on your side in this city alone. Now, I've a luncheon engagement——"

Rona rose to leave. Then she hesitated as she looked down at her handbag again. "Mr. Weidler," she began, "I wonder——"

"Is it urgent, Rona?" Weidler asked, looking anxiously at his watch.

"No, that's all right," Rona said. She walked to the door, and Paul Haydn followed her.

In the outside office, he said, "What's the extra worry, Rona?"

She pretended to laugh. "Do I show it as much as that?" She glanced at the secretary's back now disappearing into Weidler's office. They had this room to themselves for a few moments.

"Paul, have you a safe in your office—one you keep locked?"

162

"There's one in Crowell's office. I'm using it now."

"Would you keep something in it for me?" Her voice was low, hurried. She kept watching Weidler's door. "Just for a few days. Please."

"Of course." But he looked at her curiously.

"I can't explain. Yet." She opened her handbag and took out an envelope. She slipped it quickly into his pocket. "You'll keep it safe?"

"Sure."

Behind them, Weidler's secretary returned to her desk. Rona smiled to Paul and left. He waited for a moment or two before he followed her, making polite talk to the secretary.

In the corridor, he met Murray looking appropriately gloomy for a Monday morning. Murray's round face showed no sign of recognition.

"Hello," Paul said, "that was quite a party at Thelma's last night. Sorry I had to leave early."

Murray looked at him, much in the same aggrieved way as he had tackled Paul on their first meeting. Then, he had stood in a corner of Rona's living-room and expounded America's mistakes in Germany while he stared disapprovingly at Paul's uniform. Now, he was edging along the corridor trying to escape, but he still had the same disapproving stare for Paul's shoulders. "Yes," said Murray, not too convincingly, and moved farther away, his eyes shifting to Paul's tie.

Paul went toward his room.

"Haydn!" Murray called. "I'll have to break that lunch date with you to-morrow."

"Too bad." Paul went into Crowell's office which he was using temporarily. He closed the door firmly, and went over to the safe. He placed Rona's envelope carefully inside it and locked it. But he was thinking about Murray.

Whatever it was that had happened, Paul was sure of one thing: Murray's friendly interest in him had died as quickly as it had begun. He began to wonder what he had done at Thelma's party to get this brush-off from Murray. For that was what it was. And another thing he could be sure about, he would never be invited to attend one of Mr. Nicholas Orpen's discussion groups. It was probably Orpen who had

163

passed on the word to Murray to stop bothering about him. Murray didn't do things on his own initiative. He probably asked Orpen's permission to brush his teeth.

Hell, Paul thought, what mistake did I make yesterday at Thelma's?

CHAPTER THIRTEEN

That evening, when Jon Tyson returned from the University around five o'clock, bringing with him a stack of blue-covered examination papers, he found two of his pupils being entertained in the living-room by his family.

Milton Leitner was listening to Barbara, busy with her favourite story book. Her short legs stuck straight out in front of her as she sat on the rug like a miniature Degas ballet dancer. Her fine smooth hair was held back from her forehead by a narrow blue bow, and beneath this touch of gaiety her round, pink-cheeked face frowned as she studied a printed page. "Now, *I'll* read," she was saying in her high light voice. She cleared her throat and began to recite "Jack and Jill," her small forefinger tracing the printed lines, her eyes fixed with concentration on the book which she held upside down. Now and again, she'd glance up at Milton with a smile just to make sure that he was understanding everything.

Bobby, fully armed with his six-shooters, was explaining to Robert Cash the mechanism of a rather battered train which still ran fairly well if you pushed it.

Jon said "Hello everybody" as if this happened every evening. He gave Peggy a hug and a kiss, and dropped the pile of blue books on his desk. Peggy glanced at Robert Cash and then back to Jon, a question now in her eyes. But Jon only smiled and hoped he didn't look as surprised and puzzled as he felt. He hadn't seen Bob Cash, outside of his classroom, since that evening when the Burleighs and Rona and Paul had been there. Usually Bob Cash was one of the students who came to him with questions after a lecture. But in these last few weeks, Cash seemed to be avoiding him. At this moment he was looking worried, almost nervous, glancing over at Leitner as if to say, "You got me here. You'd better do the explaining."

Bobby abandoned Robert Cash and came running to Jon to get his share of his father's welcome. But Barbara only looked up and said, "I'm busy." And she gave Milton one of her glancing smiles.

"Come on, Cleopatra," her mother said, "let's get our bath before supper."

Barbara quickly turned the page for the last verse, and came upon an illustration too. She righted the book without a sign of embarrassment, and stared down at the coloured drawing. "And broke his crown," she said slowly, and stared again. "Where is it?"

Milton said, "And broke his crown and Jill came——"

"Where is it? Where *is* it?" She stabbed at the illustration with annoyance, her eyes as solemn and accusing as if she had discovered a misprint in the Oxford English Dictionary. Milton looked puzzled.

Peggy said, "It's all *there*, darling. See, there's Jack falling down and Jill tumbling after him, and there's the pail of water and the hill and the——"

"Where is the crown?" Barbara asked angrily. "Where is it?"

"Oh!" Milton said, and looked at Peggy. "It isn't that kind of crown, Barbara. Not a crown with gold spikes. It's this crown, the crown of his head." He showed her.

"Come on, Barbara," Peggy said, glancing at Jon and Robert Cash. Barbara rose, putting aside the book slowly, pulled out a crushed pleat in her skirt, felt her crown again, and then suddenly darted at her father. She hugged his legs and he swung her high in the air. She waved to Milton, while Bobby collected a wheel of his engine and Peggy picked up the Teddy bear and one-armed doll which had been playing house under Jon's desk. Peggy glanced at the stack of test papers, waiting to be marked. Well, she thought, I'll get some sewing done to-night. Then she hurried after the children. Baths first, while she washed their clothes; then their supper, and Barbara put to bed. By that time, Milton and Bob would have gone—or would they? She began worrying how far she could stretch the beef stew now simmering on the kitchen stove.

The doorbell rang as Peggy pulled a nightdress over Barbara's half-dried hair. Bobby, still in the tub, was navigating his ferry-boat with the handle of the bath brush.

"Stay there!" Peggy said to Barbara, and to Bobby, "Stop kicking up such big waves!" She hurried to answer the door. It was Rona.

Rona didn't explain her unexpected visit. And Peggy noticing the serious, set expression on her younger sister's face, asked no questions. Besides, a shriek from the bathroom drew her back there at a run. A major wave had soaked Barbara.

"Oh, Bobby!" Peggy administered a well-placed slap and evoked a sharp yelp of protest. She looked at Barbara's freshly ironed nightdress now clinging to her fat stomach in wet folds, and she shook her head helplessly. "You'll need sea boots in here," she warned Rona.

Rona was smiling now. She had slipped off her shoes and stockings, and was fastening a towel round her waist. "I'll straighten them out if you get the food ready for the little brutes," she said. "Come on, brute!" She pulled Bobby out of the bath, handed him a towel, saying, "Don't grumble, now. You made it damp."

Peggy nodded gratefully, hurried to get a fresh nightgown for Barbara, and then retreated to the kitchen in time to rescue the stew from burning. She counted the pieces of meat worriedly. The children, Rona, Milton, Bob, Jon . . . There wouldn't be enough. Not enough vegetables, either. Perhaps some spaghetti? Rona and I can take spaghetti and say we are on a diet or something, she decided. Damn, she thought angrily as she smelled the stew, this is the first time we've had meat in three days. And then she reprimanded herself sharply for being so inhospitable.

Rona carried Barbara, all very pink and white and dry, into the kitchen. "First batch," she said, fastening Barbara into her high chair. "Where's the mop, Peggy? I'll swab the deck for you."

When she returned with Bobby, her face was serious. "Jon's having an unpleasant interview," she said. "I couldn't help hearing."

"No one would say this apartment was well silenced." Peggy too had heard enough from the living-room to feel

166

worried. Then she exchanged glances with Rona behind Bobby's interested eyes, and they said nothing more.

By half-past six, the children were fed and Peggy was tucking Barbara into bed with a story. Bobby, who usually spent the last half hour before his bedtime with his father, was giving his wandering attention to Rona as she read to him in the kitchen. "Won't they go *away*?" he asked with annoyance. And then his ears heard the sounds he had been listening for, and he slipped off his chair and flapped in his bedroom slippers into the narrow hall to stand beside his father as the visitors left.

Listening, in spite of herself, Rona thought Jon's voice sounded cheery. Certainly, there had been no bitter argument. And Robert Cash was saying good night evenly. She was suddenly happier. I'll tell Jon about my troubles at dinner, she thought. And then I'll leave early so that he can get on with his own work. But if I only tell Jon and Peggy about everything—well, not everything; Charles' letter couldn't be mentioned, but it was the least of her worries now—at least, if I tell Jon and Peggy, they can give me some advice. Jon's the kind of man whose judgment you can trust, sane and kindly and never dogmatic. Even if you don't take his advice, you respect it, and you feel a bit better too, somehow.

But Peggy, coming back into the kitchen to see that the stew was thoroughly heated again, said, "Rona, let's keep conversation fairly light at dinner. I know from your face that you've got something to tell us. But leave it until we have coffee, will you?"

And Rona nodded. She could always give a description of Thelma's party at dinner. That was light enough. And it would be an introduction, too, for what she would tell them afterward.

Over coffee in the living-room ("To-night, we'll leave dishes and everything," Peggy had said), Rona was finding her story hard to tell. Darkness was falling. The house was at peace now, the children were asleep, and yet the room's shadows and the silent audience made the story seem twice as serious, twice as difficult to relate.

"Well," Rona said at its end, "there it is. . . . I don't know

167

why I ran away like that. But it is a definite quarrel. Because I phoned Scott just before lunchtime. He was out. I left a message. He didn't answer it."

"Perhaps he didn't get the message," Peggy said, but she looked worriedly at Jon. She switched on the light beside the couch as if to cheer up the room.

"I've had the feeling all day, and I can't shake myself free from it," Rona said, "that—that——"

"What, Rona?" Jon prompted gently.

"That we'll never be married." Rona turned her face away from the light. She began to cry. Her tears were as unexpected as her words. Jon and Peggy stared at each other.

Jon was saying, "Rona, people quarrel, people make up. Don't take it so hard." Why the hell hadn't Scott telephoned her?

Peggy said, "Scott can't possibly believe that rumour. If he does, then he isn't worth marrying." As she spoke, the doorbell rang. "I'll get it," she said with annoyance and hurried from the room.

Rona searched for her handkerchief and gave an attempt at a smile as Jon handed over his. Jon was thinking moodily of this evening. First there had been Bob Cash. Milton Leitner had brought him along to Jon for some frank advice: Bob had decided to join the Communist Party, and he was trying to persuade Milton to go along with him. Milton had been arguing all week-end with Bob, and then this evening he had managed to get him to come here for a discussion with Jon. Bob's people lived two thousand miles away. It was up to Jon, Milton had argued, to try and put forward their point of view. And Jon, although he probably wouldn't have agreed with Bob Cash's father on many things, had done his best. All he had managed to do was to persuade Bob to think over his decision, to wait until summer, to hear other sides to this question. But even that half-defeat was a half-success. Jon had put forward his points of view, some of which Bob couldn't answer. Bob had left, obviously going away to search for the answers. There would be more talks, more arguments, more answers to be found—a long, troublesome, and wearying job, yet someone had to do it.

So first, there had been Bob; and now there was Rona. No, first there had been Joseph Locastro. This afternoon

Locastro had come to Jon and said he was leaving the University at the end of his junior year, he was taking a job, he was going to get married. Just like that. It had been more difficult to argue against Joe's decision than it had been to marshal facts to persuade Bob. It wasn't easy to show a young man that what he chose to do to-day was going to shape the whole pattern of his life. Life didn't seem a matter of cause and effect when you were young. That took bitter learning. Joe—Bob—Rona. Love, politics, love. A pretty indigestible sandwich for one day, Jon thought wryly.

"What is keeping Peggy?" he asked, suddenly conscious that Peggy and the new visitor were talking in low voices in the hall. Rona, looking out of the window, watching the soot-rimmed bricks of the darkening houses opposite, hadn't even realised that Peggy was delayed.

Then Peggy came in, her face flushed, her mouth trying to look cheerful, and she announced casually, as if all this were perfectly understandable, "Here's Mr. Ettley to see us, Jon!" She turned on another lamp and began to draw the curtains, if only to avoid watching Rona meet Scott's father.

William Ettley came forward to shake Rona's hand, moving in his quick energetic way. His quiet eyes, watchful behind his glasses, looked at her both worriedly and affectionately. He shook hands with Jon, too. Then he selected the nearest chair and sat down. He crossed and then uncrossed his legs. He took out his cigarette case, opening it, shutting it, opening it.

"In a way," he said, his deep pleasant voice re-establishing its usual decision, "I'm glad I found you here, Rona. For I came to talk about you and Scott. I'm worried about you both, frankly. Why are you breaking your engagement to Scott?"

Peggy, who had until this moment been thinking that Rona was taking everything much too seriously and just wait until she had a family to worry about and the monthly bills to be met, sat down on the couch and watched Mr. Ettley anxiously.

Jon, noticing Rona's horrified silence, said quietly, "You are a jump ahead of anyone here, Mr. Ettley. Who says the engagement is broken?"

"Judging from what Scott told me this evening, I assumed

169

it was. I met him at five, and we had dinner together. I've just left him. He had to be back at the office at eight o'clock. A pity. I wanted to get him and Rona together." Mr. Ettley chose a cigarette at last. "I've got to return to Staunton to-morrow morning," he explained.

He looked in turn at the three faces watching him, his eyes resting finally on Rona's. Then he said to her, "You didn't break the engagement?"

Rona shook her head. "No." She glanced down at the ring on her left hand. She said bitterly, "But I shall, if Scott wants me to."

"He doesn't!" Mr. Ettley said quickly. "He's in a terrible state about this whole thing."

"What did Scott tell you?" Jon asked.

"Well—merely that Rona and he had gone apartment hunting, yesterday, and then there had been a quarrel, and then Rona left him." Mr. Ettley took a long time to light his cigarette.

"I think he must have told you more than that, Mr. Ettley."

"Yes. Sideways. He's very unhappy, he can't talk much about it. But . . ." Mr. Ettley looked at Rona. "There seems to be a very bad misunderstanding. I'm glad, now, that I *did* come up here to-night."

"Why didn't Scott get in touch with Rona to-day, and clear this all up by himself?" Jon wanted to know.

"He did try to get in touch. She wouldn't talk to him on the phone."

"I wouldn't what?" Rona asked.

Peggy said quickly, "Scott is mistaken about that. If Rona's phone was busy, why did he assume she wouldn't talk to him? Really, Mr. Ettley, I do think Scott is acting like a spoiled——"

"Well, we can clear up these misunderstandings quite easily," Jon interrupted, giving Peggy a warning smile as he silenced her. "Why don't you call Scott at the office, Mr. Ettley? Tell him you've seen Rona, and that she's as miserable as he is. He had better get in touch with her as soon as possible."

"No," Rona burst out, "no, I don't want it that way.

170

Scott can call me by himself, without being prompted by anyone. I telephoned him to-day and left a message. Now it's his turn." Then her voice quieted and she said, "I think Scott doesn't want to marry me, that's all. And he sent you here, Mr. Ettley, because he thought that this would be the easiest way to break it to me."

"He didn't send me, Rona," Ettley said unhappily. "This is my own idea. He doesn't know about it."

"But he knew you just wouldn't go back to your hotel and forget about it all. He knew you wouldn't leave New York without trying to do something about it."

No one said anything at all to that.

"Rona," Ettley said at last, "Scott's very upset about all this. He's in such a state that I know—I'm sure he wants to marry you."

Peggy said irritably, "Then what's been preventing him?"

"He thinks Rona is still in love with Paul Haydn. He told me about that," Mr. Ettley said unhappily.

"But Paul Haydn wasn't here at Christmas time, and we all expected Rona and Scott would be married then," Peggy said. She looked at her husband and then at Ettley, almost attackingly. "Didn't we?" she asked angrily.

"Oh . . ." Rona began. Then she rose and left the room. Peggy followed.

"What are you thinking?" Ettley asked Jon Tyson.

"I'm thinking what I would do if I were in Scott's place," Jon said slowly. "And, to tell you the truth, Mr. Ettley, I don't see myself behaving the way he is."

"There's more to all this than we are told," Ettley said. "Scott won't speak frankly about it, trying to protect Rona, no doubt. But, you know, if she's in love with him, you'd think money wouldn't hold her back. After all, most young men begin with little. And most girls accept that. It's a kind of—challenge to them. The way your wife manages this home of yours, for instance."

"Has Scott been telling you that Rona thought money was important?"

Ettley didn't like Jon's tone of voice. "I know he worries about that a good deal," he said stiffly. "He's now worried, too, because Haydn's job is a good one, paying twice as much

171

as Scott's, perhaps more. You know of course that yesterday Scott and Rona had a pretty miserable day apartment hunting. Scott insists that they can't afford more than——"

"Look, Mr. Ettley," Jon said, "I'm sure of one thing. Scott's been giving you the wrong angle—altogether."

"He's always been honest with me," Ettley said, rising, stubbing out his half-finished cigarette. "He's a determined boy, and at times a pigheaded one. I grant you that. But he's always been completely honest. I'm proud to say he's never told me a lie in his life."

"Knowing Rona as you do, why do you let yourself be persuaded that she's the only one to blame?"

"I don't think she's the only one to blame, Professor Tyson. I think this whole mess could be straightened out by a little frank talk on both sides. But there is one thing that is certain: I may not know Rona so well, after all. And I do know my own son. I don't enjoy seeing him being made as unhappy as he is."

"I wouldn't say Rona has been very happy, recently," Jon said bitterly. "You only have to look at her to see she isn't the same girl she was six months ago."

There was silence for a few moments. Then William Ettley nodded. "I see that to-night," he admitted. "You know, I think I'd like to have a talk with her. Is she staying here for the evening, or may I take her home?" He smiled apologetically. "I'm afraid my temper is short, these days."

"My fault," Jon said. "I began it."

William Ettley said, "Family loyalties are strange things. They sneak up on you when you don't even suspect they are anywhere near you."

"Yes," Jon said. "I'll go and see if Rona's ready to leave."

William Ettley paced around the little room. Family loyalties, he was thinking, family affairs. . . . Once you start worrying about them, you even forget newspaper headlines. Strange there, how my temper flared up when Jon Tyson questioned Scott's honesty. I've often criticised Scott myself, he thought. I've criticised the way he always arranged things to suit himself. That, I admit, has always been his weakness; that was why, to be frank, he didn't like the army. I thought he might have learned something there, but he came out rebelling against everything he had seen and felt.

172

If he had been promoted, perhaps it would have been different. But what am I saying? Scott *can* submit to discipline—to his own discipline. Even as a boy, he amazed me sometimes by his determination in following his own decisions, however unpleasant they turned out to be. He can wear a hair shirt if he feels he has made it himself. He can wear it, even enjoy wearing it. But let anyone else try to . . .

At that moment, Rona came back into the room and Ettley's train of thought was cut short. She was wearing her hat and jacket, she was pulling on her gloves. She said, "I'd like it very much if we could ride downtown together."

And William Ettley, watching her face, seeing no sign there of recrimination, no petulance round her mouth, no sullen temper in her eyes, wondered if Scott knew just what he was in danger of losing. Then he smiled, and took Rona's arm. He realised, at that moment, that he believed more in Rona than he had let Jon Tyson think. Or himself, either. When he said good night to Jon and Peggy, there was an added warmth in his voice and his handshake.

Peggy stood in the hall, looking at the closed door for a few moments. "It all depends on Scott and on Rona," she said sadly. "All the good will in the world won't have any results unless they really mean what they say."

Jon was at the telephone. "I'm going to phone that son of a bitch," he said savagely, glancing at his watch. "He'll be in the office by this time, damn him to——"

"Jon!" Peggy said, pointing to the children's room.

"Okay, okay," Jon said, lowering his voice.

"Remember you're a professor, now, honey," Peggy said with a smile. But she hoped Jon would speak bluntly to Scott. Someone had to, someone who didn't care if he hurt Scott. That was the trouble. Rona and William Ettley were always trying to soften any blows for Scott. That was the trouble. But that was what she did to Jon, and what Jon did for her. If you loved someone, that was what you did instinctively. So, where did that leave Scott Ettley? Was he in love, or only half in love? Was that all he ever could be, half in love with a girl and the other half kept for himself?

Peggy cleared away the dinner dishes. By the time she had washed them, Jon came back from the phone. "No," she
173

said, "I'll dry. You'd better start working on those exam papers, Jon." She glanced worriedly at the kitchen clock. It was five minutes past nine. "Well, what did Scott say?"

"He wasn't there. He isn't in the office to-night. I hung on to that phone until I made quite sure of that. He wasn't expected, either."

"Jon!"

"Yes. Exactly." Jon's voice was grim. Never told a lie in his life, William Ettley had said.

"Perhaps he's at his apartment?"

"I tried that, too. No answer."

Peggy found a dry dish towel. "Stop worrying, darling. Get those old tests graded. I'll be with you in a few minutes." And let's say nothing more about this, her voice suggested.

Jon went through to the living-room and turned on the lamp at the desk. When Peggy came to join him, she brought a length of green material, her sewing-box, and an envelope of paper patterns. She didn't speak, but concentrated on spreading the cloth over the rug and pinning the pieces of pattern in place. Jon watched her as she sat back on her heels, studying her jigsaw puzzle. "If I juggled it a bit," she was saying to herself, "I might have enough for a dress for Barbara too."

Jon rose, walked over to where she knelt, bent down and kissed her.

"Thanks, darling," Peggy said, smiling up at him. "But what for?"

"I just felt like it. I'm a lucky guy."

She rose and hugged him. "And that's for you. Oh, Jon, I'm a lucky girl."

Then they both went back to their work.

CHAPTER FOURTEEN

Just before nine o'clock, even as his father and Rona were saying good night to the Tysons, Scott Ettley left his apartment. He was inconspicuously dressed, and he didn't take a taxi. Instead, he walked toward Fifty-ninth Street and Madison at an unhurried pace, and the route he followed was haphazard, as if he were out for an evening stroll and found much to interest him in the shop windows which he passed.

He reached the busy intersection, its sidewalks still crowded, its garish lights warming the faces that passed under them. It was five minutes before the half hour. He went into a large drugstore for a pack of cigarettes, and then glanced through its rack of fiction near the door. He found nothing to buy there seemingly, for at half-past nine he returned a cheap-edition novel to its proper place, and then went out into Madison Avenue. Nicholas Orpen was buying a newspaper from the corner stand at Fifty-ninth Street. He looked at Scott for a moment, didn't recognise him, pocketed his change, and started walking toward Fifth Avenue. Scott lighted a cigarette and followed him.

He might pretend to smile at Orpen's precautions but he enjoyed them. They emphasised his sense of excitement, his feeling of immense responsibility. And he knew he had been right in his decision. This, he told himself, is something bigger than anything else I know; this is bigger than Rona or I. We aren't important, not compared with this. And it is all the more important with each sacrifice made for it. I have come so far, I must go on. Or everything I have done is meaningless, and everything I have believed is blankness. His face still had the same look of unhappiness that it had worn all of this day, but now there was a certain look of grim satisfaction round his lips. Nothing that was good was ever achieved easily. Power, as Orpen had so often told him, was for those who had earned it. Those who would not make the sacrifice would gain nothing in the end.

By the time he had followed Orpen by bus to Columbus Circle, by subway to upper Broadway and Seventy-second Street, by foot to Eighty-sixth Street and Amsterdam Avenue, Scott Ettley was beginning to lose some of his enthusiasm for Orpen's precautions. No one was following them; no one was interested. Orpen liked playing conspirator. Or was he hoping to impress Scott with the importance of to-night's meeting? Ettley couldn't guess. But he was relieved when Orpen at last spoke to him as they waited together in the darkness for a cross-town bus.

"Well?" Orpen said. "Made your mind up?"

"I'm here."

"You use your head . . ." Orpen said with a smile.

Scott Ettley looked at him.

". . . in following a man," Orpen added. "You learn quickly."

Yes, Ettley thought, Orpen had always been a good teacher: discipline first, complete obedience, and then praise. Scott Ettley's feeling of animosity disappeared. He admitted, grudgingly, that Orpen had given him a little lesson in caution and security that he was always going to remember. Then he wondered what had aroused this sense of criticism toward Orpen. And he was uneasy. Orpen's sardonic smile made him all the uneasier. Orpen had felt that animosity, that grudging submission. And Orpen seemed to know the reason why it was there. Then even that proof of Orpen's infallibility aroused Scott's annoyance again. Determinedly, almost bitterly, he forced himself to stop brooding about Orpen, to think only of the meeting, to try and recapture that sense of excitement and responsibility that had silenced his unhappiness as he had followed Orpen from Madison Avenue and Fifty-ninth Street.

"What next?" Scott Ettley asked, smiling, outwardly at ease again. A bus was approaching, now.

"We'll keep separate on the bus. We'll walk together after that. I've some things to ask about, before we appear at the meeting."

Scott nodded, and drew apart slightly. He searched for his fare. Another passenger joined them, and they boarded the bus as strangers. But as the bus followed the short run through Central Park, taking them eastwards once more, Scott had a good idea of what Orpen would ask. Orpen would want to know what had Scott decided to do about Rona. What *can* I do? Scott thought as he stared out at the Park's black shadows, at the high towers rising into the dark sky with a blaze of lighted rooms, what can I do except let us drift apart? Didn't Orpen see that this couldn't be hurried, that you can't love a girl one day and then pretend to forget her on the next? And if Orpen challenged him with being a coward, he would admit it. He couldn't face Rona. He wasn't able to do that. All right, so what? Orpen had won. Wasn't that enough? Careful, Scott told himself, stop this

176

bitterness against Orpen. It isn't he who has won; it is something bigger than Orpen or Rona or myself, something bigger than all this city and its lighted sky and the millions who stare up at it.

When the bus stopped at Fifth Avenue, Scott Ettley got off first, and it was Orpen who had to follow him, catching up with him as he walked slowly down Fifth Avenue on the tree-shadowed side by the Park's east boundary. "Am I going the wrong way?" he asked Orpen.

"No, this will do," Orpen said with a narrow smile. He began his questions and they were mostly what Scott Ettley had expected.

Scott answered briefly, without hesitation. It was a good feeling to know that he could recognise Orpen's next move. A new stage in my life, he thought. Until now, Orpen had done all the leading. Then he noticed that Orpen's worry (he was always most sardonic when he was worried) wasn't altogether directed at him. Orpen *was* worried. Orpen was disguising it. Orpen had troubles of his own. Scott Ettley became so sure of this that he didn't even allow his amusement to be shown when they approached Thelma's apartment house on Park Avenue. In the last three blocks he had guessed it would be their destination.

"You may have to wait a little," Orpen said, glancing at his watch. "It's an important meeting to-night. We have a visitor. A tourist. From Prague."

Scott was impressed. A tourist? That was very high level indeed. And there was an odd quality in Orpen's voice that strengthened Scott's interest in the visitor from Prague.

Orpen noticed his glance. "You probably won't see him," he said brusquely, putting Scott into his proper place once more. Then, in marked silence, they entered the apartment house.

Orpen was annoyed with himself. I was too abrupt, he thought. Then he smiled, this time with real amusement. He was thinking of the way he had helped Scott Ettley all along this road. From the beginning, he had advised and taught and cautioned and protected and persuaded. It was on his strong recommendation that Scott had reached this stage of his career so quickly. Or did Scott really believe that everyone in the Party got the same chance? Was he congratulating

177

himself on his special virtues that had marked him out from the others? Orpen's smile turned into a laugh quickly covered by a fit of coughing.

"Don't worry about the night elevator man," Orpen said, as they waited in the private lobby to Thelma's apartment. "Or about the night doorman. Souls of discretion." His amused eyes seemed to be saying, Yes, Scott, I can still tell you a thing or two.

The door took some time to open, this evening. When it did, the butler stood there. But his coat was off, and his face was smiling. They entered quickly, and he double-locked the door behind them. He held out his hand to Orpen. From the music-room, its doors closed firmly, came the sound of someone practising Chopin, not well, but determinedly.

"Bill!" Orpen said in way of greeting, as he gripped the man's hand.

Scott Ettley hoped he hid his surprise. He shook Bill's hand, in turn. Bill? Scott had always know him as Martin, the very correct and stupid butler who was the only servant who stayed in the apartment. The rest of Thelma's servants left after dinner. It was difficult nowadays, Thelma had often explained to her friends, to find any servants who would live on the premises. Most seemed to have homes of their own and wanted to get back to them each night. It was a common enough explanation in New York housekeeping, and no one had ever disbelieved it. Everyone had thought, privately, that Martin might be a stiff-necked old idiot, but Thelma was lucky to have him around especially when Charles started getting drunk.

But now Bill was walking ahead with Orpen, and Scott Ettley was left to follow. Bill took them to a narrow door in the hall, opened it, and gestured for them to enter. He listened to the sounds of the piano from the music-room, and smiled. "Thelma may not play good, but she plays loud," he remarked. "That's all we need, anyway." He closed the narrow door and led them into a short dark passage. It was Scott's guess that these must be the servants' quarters, now so little used. But the sound of the piano could still be faintly heard, ebbing and flowing as Thelma interpreted the emotion of the music.

"Where's that son of hers to-night?" Orpen asked suddenly.

"Charles started drinking at ten o'clock this morning. He's in his room, dead to the world." Bill's voice held no interest.

"I always feel happier when he is out of the house," Orpen said.

"Better this way. Then we don't have to worry about him returning unexpectedly. He's so drunk he wouldn't recognise Thelma," Bill said cheerfully. "If you lived in this place, you wouldn't be afraid of Charles." He opened the second door in the corridor. "You wait here," he told Scott Ettley. "Oh, by the way," he added, dropping his voice almost to a whisper, "when we meet Peter remember he's all for the formalities. A great stickler is Peter. Comrade this, Comrade that. Just his European way. But remember!" There wasn't any humour now in Bill's voice. He and Orpen exchanged a look. There was a tightening to Orpen's lips. Bill was impassive.

"Peter is next door, now?" Orpen asked in a low voice.

Bill nodded. "He seems anxious to see you to-night."

There was something almost ominous in the phrase. Scott Ettley thought he saw a shadow cross Orpen's face. But Orpen was saying "Good!" as if he meant it. Then Bill gestured impatiently, and Scott entered a small empty room, poorly lit, sparsely furnished. Bill closed the door behind him.

Scott sat down on a hard wooden chair and waited obediently. As the minutes dragged on, he became almost paralysed with nervousness. Suddenly, he remembered Nicholas Orpen's words to him last night: "You're entering the big league, now." He fumbled with a pack of cigarettes. It had been more comfortable in the minor leagues, he thought. He loosened his tie, relit his cigarette, and then studied the furniture. What, he was wondering, what is this job I've to do? The question had lain at the back of his mind all day, all evening, ever since Orpen had told him about it yesterday. But he hadn't allowed him to speculate about it, not until this moment. Why even speculate now? He had accepted it. Orpen had made sure of that. All that was left to know was the assignment itself.

Then it seemed to Scott Ettley, suddenly, as if the walk here with Orpen had meant something after all. Orpen had been preparing him. But for what? Scott began organising the trend of Orpen's questions. Rona . . . his father . . . when had Scott seen his father? This evening? How was his father? Still friendly? . . . A silly question, a question Scott had only shrugged off with bitter annoyance. How could he explain his father's emotions to-night? Orpen wouldn't have believed them. But now, lighting his third cigarette, he began to wonder. And as he began to wonder, he felt the coldness of fear beginning to chill his excitement.

The door opened. Bill's heavy white face, expressionless, looked into the room. Bill's short broad forefinger beckoned him. He was on his feet at once, grinding out his cigarette under his heel, following obediently. All speculation, all fears and hesitations left him. He entered the next room. He was quite calm. He even enjoyed this feeling of cold fatalism. This was it.

The room was almost as small as the one Scott had left. It was as barely furnished, as poorly lit. The window, too, was tightly shaded. And it must have been closed, for the air was warm and heavy with tobacco smoke. Four men were grouped round a card table, three of them talking quietly. There was Orpen who didn't even glance up at Scott, as if he were disowning him, and two men in early middle age, as sedately dressed as Orpen, unplaceable. The fourth man, small, solidly built, sat a little apart. He held his cigarette in a strange way, thumb uppermost. His face was quite expressionless; his eyes missed nothing. He was saying nothing at all, but he dominated the room.

Scott Ettley, at a quick gesture from Bill, took an empty chair. It creaked as he sat on it, creaked with each deep breath. He was embarrassed and he sat motionless, trying to control his breathing so that the uneasy noise would stop. How ridiculous, he had time to think, to be facing one of the most important steps in my life, and to be worried only by a loose-jointed chair.

And then Bill began to talk. It was a thorough examination. They knew everything about him, but they still asked questions. Orpen was silent, as if his job were already over. And the man from Czechoslovakia said nothing at all. It seemed as if he were examining the examiners.

Scott answered promptly, without hesitation. He could thank Orpen for that. The others seemed satisfied. There was a short pause, almost an unspoken agreement.

180

Then the man called Bill said quietly, "Here is your assignment. You will leave the *Morning Star*, where you have gained four years of useful experience. You will go to your father. You will tell him that you've reconsidered your decision, that he was right and you were wrong, that you now want to work on the *Clarion*."

Scott Ettley stiffened involuntarily. The chair creaked ominously. He controlled himself. I have already accepted the assignment, he told himself. I have already accepted it.

"You will tell your father that you'd like to have a chance to work in the field of foreign news. He will be pleased by that choice. By the end of next year, his present editor of foreign news will be ready to retire. You understand?"

Ettley nodded. There is no turning back, he thought, no turning back. I'm too deep in, too deep in. He looked at the watchful faces. He said slowly, "I understand. Completely."

Bill's factual voice went on. "You will leave New York, live in Staunton, work hard and efficiently, justify every promotion that comes your way. That is all you have to do. Meanwhile."

Ettley nodded again. He could say nothing. He could not even regulate his own thoughts.

"You will dissociate yourself from all your present political contacts," Bill said. "You will express no political opinions of any kind. Is that clearly understood?"

There was a pause. "Yes," Ettley said, "yes."

The visitor from Czechoslovakia leaned forward. He spoke in English, correctly, not too distinctly, but forcibly. "Comrade Ettley does not want this assignment?"

Ettley faced him frankly. "I have said I will do it. I will do it." He looked at Orpen. How long had Orpen known that this would be his job? How long? Four years ago, when Orpen had persuaded him to work on the *Morning Star*?

"These are your instructions," Bill said. "Simple, but difficult. We rely on you. We consider this assignment of prime importance. Start on it at once. There's no time to waste. You will report to us on your father's reactions to your proposal by the end of this week, at the latest."

Again there was a pause. Again the visitor leaned forward to speak. "Does Comrade Ettley find some difficulty we have not thought of?"

Scott Ettley looked at Orpen again. The other eyes followed his. Orpen was studying the stains on the card table.

"Well?" asked the man who had come from Czechoslovakia. There was a harshness, a coldness, in his voice that startled Ettley.

He blurted out, "A difficulty has arisen. I met my father to-night. We almost quarrelled. He refused all explanations I tried to give him about—about the end of my engagement to Rona Metford."

Orpen looked up then, his lips compressed. He stared at Ettley.

"Your father is an ally of this girl?" Bill asked quickly.

"Sentimental nonsense, comrades. We waste our time," the foreign voice said. "We have no place for weakness, Comrade Ettley."

"Comrade Ettley's good faith need not be questioned," Orpen said unexpectedly. "He thought this girl would be an asset in his work for the Party. We decided she would be a liability. I advised him of this, last night. He accepted the decision. As he has accepted all our decisions. I do not pick men who are weak, Comrade Peter."

Bill was watching the foreigner's face. "But you weren't such a good judge of the girl's usefulness," he said worriedly, angrily. "Wait in the next room," he told Scott Ettley abruptly.

Ettley rose and walked stiffly to the door. He closed it quietly as the argument began. He was remembering the way Orpen had stared at him, unbelieving, almost accusing, challenging disloyalty. And then Orpen had defended him when the Czech had criticised. Or had Orpen been defending Orpen? There's some hidden battle going on, Scott Ettley thought suddenly, there's a stuggle for power, a . . .

He looked over his shoulder swiftly. It had seemed to him, there, as if a door farther along the passage had closed quietly. For a moment he halted, wondering if he ought to go and investigate. Then he thought that it might be another candidate for another assignment, another man waiting for examination in another small room. Or it might have been a draught of air from an open window. In any case, he must not hang about this corridor, he must not appear to be eaves-

182

dropping on the argument he had left behind. He imagined the comments of the Czech comrade if he were found loitering here. Ettley's face still burned with the sting of those last remarks. He opened the door of the room where he was to wait, and he entered quickly, leaving the corridor without another glance behind him.

A struggle for power, he was thinking again. . . . And then he discarded that notion as ridiculous, nonsensical. Men such as Orpen or Bill were not interested in personal power. They were caught up in something bigger than that. Personal politics did not enter into the picture at all: they couldn't. Just as personal wishes, personal desires couldn't. Then he began thinking about himself, about this job on the *Clarion*.

When the door opened at last, it was Orpen who came into the room. "All right," he said briskly, "you can leave, Scott. The next meeting which you will have to attend will be on Friday. Here, same time. We'll come separately. Take care, won't you? You will then report the results of your talks with your father. We expect to hear good news. And then, you'll get final instructions." He turned as if to leave. At the door, though, he looked back at Ettley. "Why didn't you tell me about this attitude of your father's toward Rona Metford? I gave you the opportunity."

"I didn't realise——" Scott halted awkwardly. He couldn't find an explanation. "I don't know," he said frankly, unhappily. And then, to change the subject, "Friday? But will you be in New York on Friday?" Last night, Orpen had said he was leaving on Thursday. For abroad, Scott had guessed. Whenever Orpen travelled abroad, he gave few details; you could measure the importance of his trips by the casual way he'd mention them.

"That's been cancelled, meanwhile." Orpen's voice was expressionless. "And, by the way, so are my instructions to you about giving up Metford."

"Cancelled?"

Orpen studied the younger man's face for a moment. "You look like a man reprieved," he said, almost sadly. If only he had accepted my decision, Orpen thought, he would have spared himself a lot of pain in the future. Better to break with the girl now, instead of in a few months or a year—as soon as her usefulness was over, anyway. "Slip out quietly," he advised abruptly. "Don't speak to Thelma." And he left the room at once, as if he didn't want to stay away from the meeting next door any longer than he had to.

Scott Ettley reached the main hall to the apartment. It was empty. He walked quietly toward the front door. The music, which had stopped for the last few minutes, was beginning again. This time, Brahms was under Thelma's attack and defending himself vigorously. Scott glanced behind him. He thought, but again he couldn't be sure, that he saw a brief movement far down the hall near the library door.

He hesitated. His first impulse was to investigate. But his instructions had been to keep away from the front of the apartment: *Don't speak to Thelma.* He opened the massive front door, and then he closed it without leaving. He stood motionless beside it, his eyes on the other end of the hall. He saw Charles slip out of the library, moving quickly and silently on slippered feet. And Charles saw Ettley. He checked himself for a moment, stared down the broad hall with that stupid expression on his blank white face. Then he moved on. But this time Charles was walking unsteadily. This time, Charles was drunk.

Scott waited until Charles disappeared towards his bedroom. Then he went back into the narrow corridor, his decided footsteps sounding their warning. Bill was out to face him in one moment. "What is it?" Bill asked. He had his butler's coat half-drawn over his shoulders.

"Charles. He's wandering around. He isn't drunk." He had spoken softly, but, from the silence in the room behind Bill, Ettley knew that his words had been heard by all of them. He might be accused of sentimental nonsense but no one could say he wasn't alert.

Bill regained himself. He closed the room door quickly, and moved quickly toward the hall. "Did he see you?" he asked, his eyes narrowing.

"Naturally," Ettley said. "He's probably seen all of us."

Bill swore under his breath. He looked back at the room worriedly, as if he were trying to imagine the reactions of the visiting comrade to all this. "Better get out," he told

Ettley, his voice sharpened by sudden fear. Then pulling his coat into place, he strode angrily up the hall.

As Ettley slowly closed the front door behind him, Bill was entering the music-room. Thelma's startled voice was saying, "Martin, what's wrong?" And the notes she had been playing changed to a harsh discord.

CHAPTER FIFTEEN

"But I must see you," Scott was saying anxiously. "Rona, I've got to see you. I've news for you. I phoned you three times this morning before you left for the office. Rona—Rona . . . Are you there? Do you hear me?"

"Yes." She looked down at the telephone on her desk. It had been impossible, in the office, to leave it unanswered. At home, she had let it ring. Odd that yesterday she had waited desperately for a call from Scott. To-day, she wanted to avoid it.

"Rona, we'll have lunch together. When shall I meet you?"

"I—I don't think it's of much use." Not now, not remembering last night and Mr. Ettley's worried arguments. Did Scott really think of her in that way? "Scott, it's no good. I saw your father last night."

"Look, Rona, don't let any of his ideas worry you. Dad jumped to a lot of wrong conclusions. I saw him this morning before he left for Staunton. He's feeling different about a lot of things, now."

"Are you feeling differently, too?" she asked bitterly. "And if so, which way?"

"Rona! For God's sake—listen, we're getting married next month. How's that for news?"

"Next month?"

"And we're going to live in Staunton."

"What?"

Scott laughed. "Yes. No more damned apartment hunting. We're going to live in Staunton and I'm joining the staff of the *Clarion*. How's that for news?"

She couldn't answer at all, this time.

Scott said, "I'll wait downstairs for you at twelve-thirty. Good-bye, darling." There was a click as he hung up at the other end of the line.

"Scott!" she said, and then she replaced the receiver slowly. At first, she could only stare at the books in front of her, at the coloured plates and photographs piled on her desk, at the few notes she had jotted down this morning.

If only Scott had given me that news on Sunday, even yesterday, she was thinking. How differently I'd have felt about it then. I would have been as excited, as happy as he is. But now—all I feel is nothing, nothing at all. I've gone numb. I've been shuttled around too quickly, I've lost all sense of direction, I don't know where I am or where I'm going. I don't want to see Scott to-day. Or to-morrow. I need time to get my balance again. I need time to forget what I felt last night as I listened to his father, I need time. For I still love Scott. That's my trouble.

And then, as she pulled her notes before her again and lifted her pencil, she stopped thinking about herself. She was thinking about Scott and his news. What had made him change so completely? If there was one thing she could have sworn was true, it was simply that Scott would never have gone to his father and admitted that he had been wrong for four years. Did she understand him as little as he seemed to understand her?

"Busy?" Miss Guttman's voice asked. "I won't disturb you, but I do need some advice. You're the interior decorator around here, aren't you?" She laughed gaily. "It's the dining-room. I like chartreuse, but Hubert, he doesn't see it at all in chartreuse. What would——" Her eyes fell on Rona's left hand. "Why, your ring! Did you leave it in the washroom?"

"No, it's safe," Rona said. She had boxed and wrapped it this morning, ready for mailing. Now it lay in her handbag, waiting to be registered at lunch-time.

"Anything wrong?" Miss Guttman asked half-anxiously, half-eagerly.

Rona couldn't resist saying, "He wants us to get married next month."

"June?" Miss Guttman looked at her blankly. "Why, that will be two of us leaving to get married in June." Her voice became primly polite. "How nice," she said, and she turned to

186

leave the office, the chartreuse dining-room now of little interest. "How early in June?" she asked from the doorway.

"I don't know," Rona said.

"And you've nothing ready! Isn't that just like a man?"

"That's the least of it," Rona said, and went on writing.

Miss Guttman shrugged her disagreement. "It's too big a rush," she said warningly. But her advice went unheard, seemingly.

Miss Guttman returned moodily to her own office. In the corridor, she met Paul Haydn with some manuscript under his arm. He gave her his usual smile and greeting.

"Did you hear the latest?" she asked him. "Miss Metford's getting married early in June."

"Is she?" he said, and went on his way to Weidler's office.

Now why did I have to go and blurt that out? Miss Guttman wondered miserably. It came so quickly to my tongue that I couldn't stop it. Well, he's probably glad to hear it, an end to those nasty rumours anyway. Miss Guttman comforted herself with that thought, and went to tell Mrs. Hershey what a wonderful man Scott Ettley was. "He saw it was the only way," she insisted. "But poor Rona Metford! I wouldn't like to think I was forcing a man to rush my wedding."

"We don't have to be so sorry for Rona Metford," Mrs. Hershey said with a smile. "I don't think it would take much forcing to get a man to marry her."

Miss Guttman looked down at her pretty hands. "Yes," she said slowly, "she's got everything, hasn't she?" She sighed, then. "I suppose she'll get her photographs in all the papers. She'll make a beautiful bride."

"Oh, there's more to marriage than good looks," Mrs. Hershey said encouragingly, thinking of her own daughter-in-law.

Miss Guttman looked at her sharply. Then she clicked two sheets of paper and carbon into her typewriter, and began to type furiously.

"I've got mixed news for you," Weidler said to Paul Haydn when he arrived. "It's good for you, bad for poor Crowell. His wife just phoned me."

"He's got to stay in hospital?"

"He'll never leave it." Weidler stared at his desk moodily.

Crowell was just his age. Crowell had been with *Trend* ever since it began with a skeleton staff and two rooms. . . . Then Weidler rose quickly and stood by the window. "Well, that's the way it is," he said. "You're the editor, now. Who's the man for your assistant? Anyone in the office? Or do we bring in someone new?" He had his own ideas already formed, but it was his way to ask for advice. And there were occasions too, when he even took it. Now, thinking of Crowell, he felt that it wasn't wise to centralise authority. Better delegate it around; then, if anything happened to himself, *Trend* would go on without big changes. Once he had prided himself that he was the magazine. But now—well, the magazine itself was the important thing. It could live, long after he was dead. "Tough on Crowell," he said suddenly. "He was always so damned energetic that none of us ever took this illness of his very seriously. He was the best editor in the business."

"And a generous one," Paul Haydn said slowly. "He taught me all I know about the job."

"Yes," Weidler said, "yes." He turned away from the window. "How is it coming along?" The remark was made to take Haydn's mind off Crowell. Weidler knew well enough how the job was going. Haydn would be as good an editor as Crowell in another few years. It took time to build your staff, your magazine.

"All right." Paul laid a thin pile of manuscript on the desk. "I thought you'd be interested in this."

Weidler began examining it, but his thoughts were still on the new changes in staff, now made urgent. "We don't want to hire any more Blackworths," he said. "I suppose they'll keep trying. At least that's what your colonel told me."

Paul suddenly remembered Weidler's luncheon engagement yesterday with Roger Brownlee. "How did you get on?" he asked.

"He seems a pretty sound guy." Weidler was impressed.

"He would have to be."

"Yes, it's quite a job he's tackled." Weidler looked up from the manuscript. "Do you want me to read this? It seems well written. Controversial, but interesting subject."

"Yes. Interesting altogether. It's just as Brownlee said: they keep trying."

"Oh?" Weidler was suddenly alert. He looked at the author's name again. "Never heard of him. You know him?"

"It's another pen name for Nicholas Orpen."

Weidler stared down at the title page. "Of all the damned impudence! Are you sure?"

"Positive. I got Brownlee's office to check on it. Orpen used that pen name several times in 1945. He did rather well with it; so well, in fact, that he admitted it. Pride of authorship breaking out, I suppose. And perhaps he was confident in 1945 that everything was going his way. But he hasn't used it during the last five years."

"Why use it now?"

"Who would remember? If Brownlee's file on Orpen didn't exist, who would know? Only someone here or there with a long memory, someone who probably wasn't in any position to do anything about Orpen."

"But the fool—why didn't he invent another name?"

"John Smith?" Haydn grinned. "He's got enough pride to want some credit from his dear comrades. Or perhaps he enjoys the feeling that we're stupid and he's bright. Anyway, he used the name."

"Of all the damned impudence," Weidler repeated.

"They've plenty of that," Paul agreed. "Actually they got their wires crossed. Murray was softening me up, you know; until yesterday that is, when he obviously got the word to score me off his useful-list. And this manuscript arrived last Friday. Too bad, wasn't it?"

"How did you recognise the pen name?"

"I didn't. I just felt uneasy when I read the article. It's very persuasive. All about the Philippines. It seems that the Huks have nothing to do with Communism. They are just honest, patriotic agrarian reformers."

Weidler flung the manuscript across the desk. "What are you going to do about it?"

"I'd like to publish it."

"What?"

"Yes, just as it stands. And this is what I'd like to have printed at its head." Paul handed over a typed sheet of paper.

Weidler began reading. " 'Wallace York, the author of the following article, is one of the pen names used by Nicholas

189

Orpen. We thought our readers would find this presentation of Mr. Orpen's Communist point of view an interesting one. We have invited other articles on this subject from two other writers, one a Republican and one a Democrat. They are men who have recently spent some months in the Philippines, and their points of view will be published in our next two issues. We thank Mr. Orpen for giving us this chance to show our readers so clearly the present Communist line on the Philippine question.' "

Weidler looked up with a smile. "Can we get away with it?"

"Why not? It's the truth."

"But have you proof? Proof to back it up before twelve men on a jury?"

"Proof, too."

"Okay!" Weidler began to laugh. "And once I thought I could keep politics out of *Trend*. A magazine devoted to the arts!"

"It still is. Politics is an art we are just discovering again."

"I'll read Orpen's article," Weidler said. "Of all the damned——"

Haydn nodded and left.

His telephone was ringing as he got back to Crowell's office. His office now? He'd go up and see Crowell in the hospital to-morrow. To-night, he had to see Roger Brownlee. He picked up the phone. "Haydn speaking." I know what's wrong with me, he was thinking, too much damned duty and work. I've been running to catch up ever since I got home. It's about time I relaxed for a night or two. "Who is it?" he asked sharply. He turned his eyes away irritably from the calendar in front of him. May—June, the page read. June . . . to hell with June. "Who is speaking? Sorry. I can't hear you."

"You *do* sound angry," the woman's voice said delightedly, coming through more clearly now. "It's Mary. Now, Paul, don't tell me you've forgotten." She laughed as if that were a charming little joke just waiting to be shared.

"No," he said slowly, trying to remember who Mary was. Mary . . . Mary Bartlett was SHAEF, Paris, winter of 1944? . . . "Of course not. How are you? It's been a long time."

"I'm glad to know it has been a long time." You could hear the smile in her voice.

"What on earth are you doing in New York?"

"Not very much at the moment. I'm free for lunch if you find that interesting."

"Look," he said, suddenly doubting, "is this Mary Bartlett?"

"As in pear? No. Wrong." She wasn't laughing now. "This is Mary Fyne. Still mad with me?"

"No," he said, puzzling it out. Then he remembered the red-haired girl at Rona's party, the one who liked them angry. He glanced down at his hand and the smile left his face.

"And I've stopped being mad with you, too," she said softly.

"That's a relief. I'm sorry about lunch to-day. Just can't make it."

"Oh. Too bad."

"Yes. Well, thanks for——"

"I'm giving a party to-morrow. My address is——"

"Yes, I remember it," he cut in.

"Do you?" Her voice was ice-cold, now. "But you can't make the party either?"

"I don't think so. I've already——"

"You know what, Paul Haydn? I begin to believe you can't make anything." She hung up.

Sweet little character, he thought savagely. He pushed away the phone. Then he tried to laugh the whole thing off. But to-day, it couldn't be laughed away so easily. "If you find that interesting," her voice had said. Interesting? Nothing was interesting if you weren't interested. That was the trouble, that was what was wrong with him. You're getting damned critical in your old age, he told himself angrily. You're too damned hard to please.

He concentrated on work until lunch-time, clearing off a batch of final proofs. Routine work, he thought as he lifted his hat and walked down the corridor, routine work; nothing like it for deadening the nerves. He'd go over to Carlo's to eat. He'd meet some of the crowd there. Tom Averil, Harry Meyer, Chuck Johansen. The old crowd. . . . But Tom was now a book reviewer with a comfortable house in Scarsdale and a pretty wife to match. Harry Meyer had settled down in New Jersey, commuted without a murmur, kept bringing the conversation round to tulips and the twins. Chuck Johansen ran his fastest mile, these days, as the Sports Editor of the *Morning Star*. He was married, too, and putting on weight. There would be the usual jokes—now, take Paul, he's a smart guy, how's your bachelor apartment, Paul? Yes, they'd make the same old jokes, but it was only a form of politeness. You knew when you were lucky, they'd say. But not one of them would give up the privilege of grumbling about the ills, or the wife's new haircut, or the kids' reports from school since television came into the house.

"Hello, Mr. Haydn." It was the receptionist, now quite unfrozen. "They say it's a nice day out." She flashed her warmest smile.

"That's fine."

"About time that rain stopped, even if we do need it."

He nodded and got into the elevator. Joe complained about the weather too. He didn't hold with that rainmaking: interfering with nature, the track at Jamaica yesterday was a mud puddle.

"A bad day?" Paul asked.

"Cleaned me out. The landlord will have to wait for the rent this week," Joe said with a grin. "Guess we all have our bad days."

"Guess we do." Paul stepped out of the elevator. Scott Ettley was standing in front of the Coffee Shop door, facing him. The two men looked at each other without a sign of recognition. Haydn pulled on his hat and made his way through the crowd towards the revolving door. He needed cigarettes, but he wouldn't stop to buy them at the newspaper stand. He wasn't going to join this line, here, and see Rona step out of the elevator into Scott Ettley's arms.

As Rona reached the ground floor, Joe was saying, "Guess the landlord will have to wait for the rent this week." He didn't expect an answer, she was too busy looking for her young man. She's got him jumping through hoops, Joe thought as he looked at Scott Ettley: he's been here for ten minutes and more. Spring is in the air, even if it isn't in the weather. Nice looking couple they'll make, too.

192

"Rona!" Scott took her arm, drawing it tightly through his, leading her toward Fifth Avenue. "We've got to celebrate. What about the Sherry-Netherland?"

"I——" She tried to break free.

"Now look, Rona," he said, his eyes serious, "I've been through several kinds of hell since I saw you. But I've got it all straightened out, now." He smiled encouragingly. "We're going to the Sherry-Netherland."

"I'm not hungry," she said. She was trying to keep her determination. But it was difficult. She should never have seen him. Never? Never again? She bit her lip, and turned her face away. He tightened his grip on her arm and led her up Fifth Avenue.

"Or would you rather have the Plaza?" he asked.

"I—I don't care. I'm not hungry."

He looked at her worriedly. "What's wrong, Rona? I'm sorry. If I've hurt you, I'm sorry. But I've got everything clear now. Everything's all right."

"Let's go into the Park," she said. "We can talk there."

"Right," he said. "We'll talk." About the future. At least, that was settled. No more worrying about what lay ahead, no more doubts, no more waiting. It was settled. It might not be his choice, but there was a great relief in putting aside all hesitations, all inaction. Last night, there had been moments of bitterness, of pride in revolt. But he had conquered that. It was a good feeling to know you could master yourself. Now that he had accepted what he had to do, he felt happier. And he had Rona.

"We'll talk, and then we'll have something to eat," he said. "That's a good idea."

The sun had come out, drawing the lunch-time crowds into the avenue. The women's gay new clothes looked appropriate for the first time this spring. The men were in light-coloured suits. The shop fronts invited admirers, and the pace on the broad thronged sidewalks was leisurely. Taxis and private cars edged along the crowded road, jostling for position with the large green and white buses.

They crossed the Plaza, scattering the pigeons. The miles of park ahead of them lay covered in bright green. The rocky crags and fields and lakes and winding paths were hidden by the trees, now in full leaf. The new grass had spread over the earth. Fruit blossom and flowering shrubs added their round clusters of white and pink.

"Too many people around," Scott said suddenly, halting. "We'd have to walk a couple of miles to leave them behind." It was true. The paths leading to the Zoo and to the lake were both crowded. All the benches were filled with people relaxing for a brief hour in the sun. "We'll go for a ride," he said, and led her back towards the rank of horses and carriages standing along Fifty-ninth Street.

"No," she said.

"Yes," he said angrily, and he took a firm grip of her arm. "What's wrong? Afraid I'll make love to you?"

Rona didn't answer him.

The cabby had seen them coming. The blanket was already drawn off the horse, the door of the carriage was held open. The horse looked round, watchfully, as if calculating their weights.

"Take you as far as you like. Nice drive round the Park. See the magnolias and the cherry trees. Take you ten miles if you want that." The cabby's smile was broad, partly toothless. He was a round-faced elderly man, with a red-veined nose. At the moment, he was trying to look romantic, helped by his top hat and tightly buttoned topcoat. The carriage, if not elegant, was clean, and the wheels had been recently given a coat of white paint.

"Only a short ride," Rona said.

The round face looked disappointed. "On a nice day like this?" Then he shrugged his shoulders and climbed up to his seat with scarcely a creak from his stiff legs. Still, a short haul was better than none at all. He clucked his tongue, and the horse began its leisurely walk, its polished harness jingling, its fat haunches gleaming in the sunlight.

Scott was watching Rona's face. "This isn't exactly the way I thought you'd welcome my news," he said with a touch of bitterness. But even that didn't rouse the girl sitting beside him. He caught her waist and kissed her.

"Oh," she said. "Oh, Scott!"

"What's the trouble? Tell me." He kept hold of her hands. She said, "Oh, why wasn't it you who came to Peggy's last night, why wasn't it you who took me home?"

194

He watched her face, suddenly realising that whatever troubled her was more serious than he had guessed. "I tried to see you, yesterday," he said gently. "I went round to your apartment before I met my father for dinner. You weren't at home."

She didn't answer. Her face tightened. She was thinking, why does he lie? To be kind to me? For the note she had left for Scott, the note she had tucked securely into the hinge of her letter box downstairs, had still been there when she returned home with William Ettley last night.

Scott said, "What on earth has my father been telling you?" He was angry now.

"Don't blame him. He talked to me very kindly, very worriedly. But, from his questions, I suddenly saw myself as you must see me. Why did you talk to your father as if I had already broken off our engagement?"

"I didn't! Good God!—When I met my father yesterday, I was sick with worry. He noticed it. He jumped to the wrong conclusions. I probably wasn't very coherent. You see, I've been worried for some time, worried about—well, worried about what I'm doing with my life. I've been trying to work out a solution for about six months. Perhaps even longer than that. Then, yesterday, everything came to a head. I made the decision to— to join the *Clarion*, after I left my father last night." He slipped an arm round her shoulders and held her firmly. "And that is all, honey. When a man gets worried about himself, he isn't good company. I'm sorry if I gave my father the wrong impression about us."

She was watching his face now. "What does your father think about your decision to work on his paper?"

"He's pleased, of course."

"But wasn't he surprised?"

"Yes—at first. But he understands."

And I don't, Rona thought unhappily. She looked at the shabby seat facing her, at a patch of leather peeling off a widening crack.

"We'll live in Staunton," Scott was saying.

She listened to the natural voice; so calm, so assured. She remembered how he had hated Staunton; he had talked contemptuously of its smugness, its small-town snobberies, its bourgeois pretensions, its double standards. She glanced up at him sharply. But he was smiling, looking so confident and happy that she could say nothing.

He said, "Yes, we'll leave New York. That will solve a lot of problems." The meetings. . . . The visits to Orpen. . . . Paul Haydn. . . . Yes, Staunton would solve a lot of problems.

"Not all of them," she said.

"What do you mean?"

"Because there's something wrong somewhere." She bent her head. She lowered her voice still more. "I just can't—I just *can't* understand. The more you explain, the less I understand. You say you've been worried for months. Well, so have I been worried. There's something—oh, I don't know how to explain it, I don't even know what it is that gives me this feeling of belonging to you less and less. Perhaps it's because you really don't belong to me at all. Do you?"

He stared at her, his face pale, the lines at the side of his mouth deepening. "What do I belong to?" he asked at last.

She shook her head. "We've said enough." She opened her purse.

"No we haven't." The intensity in his low voice startled her. She looked up and met his eyes. "What do I belong to?" he asked again, gripping her hand.

"To yourself," she said.

Suddenly, he laughed outright. He released her hand. "Do I never do anything that I don't want to do?" he asked mockingly.

Only if it suits you, she thought. But she found she couldn't say it. She bent her head and searched in her purse and grasped the ring in its box. She put it into his hand, and looked away. On the track beside the road, a fat woman in a heavy sweater cycled determinedly. On the grass beyond, a young couple sat with their arms around each other under the trees. A gaunt man lay stretched on his back, his shirt opened at the neck, his shoes off, staring at the white clouds above him.

Scott looked down at the box, neatly wrapped and decisively addressed. Then he caught her left hand and stripped off its glove. "No," he said, "no, Rona! Not after what I've been through to get you. No, you don't!" He ripped the paper and string from the box, crushing them into a tight

196

ball. He lowered his voice. "I need you, Rona. I want you. You know that."

"I don't even know that, now." Then she raised her voice and called to the driver, "We've gone far enough. Please turn back."

The red face looked round at them in surprise, but only for a moment. He noted the tears on the girl's cheeks, the angry white face of the young man. They weren't an advertisement at all for a romantic drive under the chestnut trees. He turned the horse and let it have its head. It broke into a fast homeward trot.

Scott Ettley said slowly, "Is this all because of Paul Haydn? You can't find the courage to tell me the truth?"

She shook her head. "I love you, Scott."

"Then why——"

"Because it takes more than love to make a marriage, that's why. Love, yes. But there are other things, too. Trust, for instance, that isn't abused. And loyalty that's fully returned."

"You never criticised me until Haydn came back," he said bitterly.

"No," she protested. "Weeks before he came back, I began to—Oh, stop this talk about Paul Haydn! You've hurt me enough."

"He won't get you."

"Stop this!" She was angry, now. And in her anger, with the tears still on her cheeks, her large dark eyes widening in indignation, her lips parted, her skin alive with colour, it seemed to him that she had never been more beautiful.

He said tensely, "I'm not going to lose you. You're mine. If I lose you, no one else is going to get you. You're part of my life." He gripped her left wrist, and thrust the ring back on her finger. She gave a little cry of pain. He held her hand so that she couldn't free it.

Under the trees, on the paved path, a man walked with his jacket folded over his arm, hat in hand, his eyes on the leaves above him. A woman held a tight leash on a terrier straining for a squirrel. Two girls and two sailors had paired off. A boy raced on skates. A mother pushed a large baby up the steady hill. Two old men sat on a bench with a chessboard between them, dappled in the shaded sunlight.

Scott said, "You say I've hurt you. Now you've hurt me. All right—we're quits on that. We'll start from there. We'll forget to-day, we'll forget this last week-end. We'll remember only the ones we used to have."

The buildings were coming near, the tall shapes pointing into the sky, the masses of grey and yellow and white and silvered stone. A flight of pigeons turned, wings gleaming in the sunshine. Up there, on the pinnacle of a high roof, a hawk lived.

"We'll remember last summer," Scott said. "We'll start from there, again."

The carriage rolled briskly out of the Park, round General Sherman's little square. The tulips were massed in deep rows of pink and white. Men and women, sitting on the statue's steps, their faces turned toward the sun, were motionless as the flowers. Others, walking quickly back to the offices and stores, clustered at the corners to wait for a break in the constant stream of cars and buses.

"I'll come to see you this evening," Scott said. "As soon after six as I can make it. We start from there." He smiled and his face softened. He released her hand. The carriage had stopped, the driver was descending to open the door.

"That's five dollars," the cabby said, his eyes now business-like.

Scott pulled his wallet out, and counted the notes. No good complaining. These old sharks knew all the tricks.

"There you are," Scott said, handing over the exact amount. The man was watching him with amusement. Scott turned quickly. Rona had gone.

"Your hat, sir," the cabby said, with mock politeness, and picked it up from the cracked leather seat. He stood, hands on hips, watching the well-dressed back of the young man who was pushing his way through the crowd. Good-looking young fellow, too. Well fixed. Plenty of everything except tact. "Making a girl cry in the Park," he said to his horse as he fastened on the feed bag. "That's no way to behave in our carriage, is it, Snowflake?"

Then he climbed up on to the dashboard and sat there, tilting his hat forward to shade his eyes, his legs crossed to show grey wool socks wrinkling over tight-laced boots, while he measured the passing prospects with a careful eye.

CHAPTER SIXTEEN

"Congratulations, Miss Metford."

Rona halted as she walked through *Trend*'s reception-room and looked inquiringly at the smiling girl behind the desk.

"I hear you are getting married in June." And wouldn't Guttman's nose be out of joint, the girl thought. Pink bathtubs and puce doormats and monogrammed artichokes.

Then the phone rang, and the pretty receptionist was saying, "Yes, Mr. Pillsbury. No, Mr. Pillsbury," and Rona could escape into the corridor.

Most of her department were still out to lunch. Phil Arnim was wandering around though. He came in to sit on the edge of her desk and chat about their new assignment. He had got an angle at last, something to group his ideas around. What about Rona?

"I've done very little," she admitted. "I'll work late." Then she remembered Scott. "I'll have to work late to-night," she repeated. It was one solution, not a very brave solution.

"Had a good lunch?" Arnim asked curiously. On his way back to the office, he had seen Rona and Ettley on Fifth Avenue.

She shook her head.

"I thought so. You look just the way my wife does when she begins dieting for summer. The minute she stops wearing a fur coat, she starts saying she doesn't want any lunch."

Rona half-smiled.

"It's a fact," Phil went on. "I've timed her each year. Regular as a Capistrano swallow."

"Oh, Phil!"

"She is too. I got up some courage this spring and asked her why. And you know what she tells me? She can look at herself in a store window when she's wearing a fur coat, and where she begins and the coat ends doesn't matter much. But when she wears a suit and looks at herself when she's passing a window—that's the warning bell. Know those lonely little buoys that swing with the waves way out in the Narrows? That's what she hears, seemingly." Phil swung himself off the desk. "Well, this way I don't pay the grocer's bill. I'll go back to bringing the cherry trees into the living-room, and I'll leave you to splash round your little Roman fountains. Have fun."

But at least, he thought, I left her smiling, which is better than I found her. "Rona's got some kind of a battle on her hands," he confided to Harry Jimson who had just returned from lunch.

"Who hasn't?" Harry asked sourly. But then, he had just been through a disagreeable hour. His mistress—a nice shy little blonde she had been, last year—was now wanting an apartment, no less. And why should she have to go on working in the nightclub while his wife just sat around a house all day?

The sun filtered in through the south windows, the offices filled up once more. Down the corridor came the clatter of typewriters, the hesitating voice raised in dictation, the click of urgent heels on polished floors, a sudden laugh, the ring of telephones, a sharp discussion, the banging of the washroom door. . . . The afternoon's work had begun.

At five, when the last frenzied rush to clear up the day's business was starting, Rona phoned down to the Coffee Shop for a sandwich, coffee, cigarettes and an evening paper if they'd got hold of one for her. She was relaxing at her desk, opening the brown paper bag which the delivery boy had just brought up, when Phil Arnim looked in to say good night.

"It's going pretty well," she told him, pointing to the litter of notes and diagrams on her desk. "To-morrow, I'll be ready for some field work at the Metropolitan and the Frick. Then you and Harry and I can get together and really start the job moving." She unfolded the sandwich from its neat waxed-paper wrapping, spread the paper napkins on the radiator cover, and laid out the cardboard container of coffee, the wooden spoon and the cubes of sugar. "Have a pickle?" She offered him the last item in the paper bag.

"Give it to the pigeons," Arnim suggested. "Well, glad everything's under control. Don't work too late." He gave her a cheery grin and left.

Silence began to fall over the floor of offices. A few solitary noises—a single typewriter, a fit of sneezing, someone whistling off-key, occasional hurried footsteps—told Rona that others were working late too. She finished the sandwich quickly for she was hungry, wished she had ordered two, and then lighted a cigarette while she sipped the coffee. She picked up the newspaper. Something called the *Amerasia* case was going to be reopened. Strange, she thought, I was here in New York when it all happened and I don't remember a thing about it. What does that make me—too preoccupied with my own life or just plain stupid? Or perhaps that's the same thing. . . . I bet I'm not the only one who's a little bewildered by the newspaper to-night, and most of us will say, "I can't believe this, surely it's all exaggerated!" and we'll throw the paper aside and try to forget it.

She folded the newspaper and put it away, persuading herself that she had indeed her own problems and she couldn't even worry about them or she'd never get this job done. She rose and began clearing the napkins and container and pickle into the brown bag, keeping herself from thinking about Scott by making her movements brisk and decided, by feeling businesslike and ready to face another couple of hours of work. It was six o'clock now. She sharpened her batch of pencils afresh, found some more paper, and settled at the desk once again. She began reading and making notes.

Footsteps came down the corridor and entered the main office. Then they stopped. The silence seemed to deepen. Rona, looking up from her work, listening in spite of herself, called, "Hello, there!"

Paul Haydn answered, "Hello, yourself!" He dropped the magazine that had caught his attention back on Phil Arnim's desk, and came toward Rona's room. He was as surprised and as embarrassed as she was. "Hello," he repeated. He held out a manuscript. "I came along to leave this with Burnett. It's a good article, I think, but it's more in your line than mine. Would you have a look at it?" Then he saw the books on her desk. "No, I guess this is the wrong time to ask you," he added with a smile.

"I'll have a look at it to-morrow," Rona said. She took the typescript and saw the neat memo clipped on its title page: *Would Miss Metford please check on the facts in this? Many thanks. P.H.* She smiled, too.

He turned to leave. "Congratulations, by the way."

201

"About what?"

"About June. I hear you are getting married then."

"Oh," Rona said, and the smile left her face. "That's just another false rumour. Now."

He noticed then that the ring on her left hand was missing. He didn't know what to say.

The telephone rang. Rona glanced at her watch. Six-thirty. Scott. It was probably Scott, calling to see why she hadn't reached home yet.

Paul Haydn stretched out his hand to answer it.

"No!" she said. "No, Paul. Please don't."

He looked at her, making his own guesses. She turned her head away from him, pretending to look out the window at the roofs and penthouses and water towers. The phone kept on ringing, as demanding and insistent as Scott's own voice. It is true, she was thinking, Scott only belongs to himself. His way is the only way, his decisions are the right decisions. There is something almost ruthless, terrifying and ruthless, in his single-mindedness. Even when he hesitates, even when he seems to be arguing with himself, there's never any real doubt in his mind about what he will choose to do. It's odd, she was thinking, that I must have felt this all along, that I must have smothered all these fears because they seemed so disloyal; it's odd that, suddenly, during this last week-end, they couldn't be smothered any more. What happened in these last few days to let my fears all take shape in my mind at last? Or has this hideous climax been a personal crisis for Scott, and I've felt it? Oh, ridiculous, stupid. . . . Perhaps I'm a fool.

She looked at the phone. She almost reached out to take it. But she drew back.

Paul Haydn said, "Whoever is calling you wants to reach you. Are you sure you ought to let—let whoever it is keep ringing?" His voice was expressionless, his eyes pitying. She is still in love with Ettley, he thought.

"Yes," she said unhappily, "yes. I'm sure." How can you marry a man you're afraid of? The telephone stopped ringing. She took a deep breath.

"Well," Haydn said, glancing at his watch, "I'll get going, now. I'm meeting someone at half-past seven." He looked at her again. "You know, it might do you good to come along, too. You need dinner, I think." This wasn't an evening to work alone in an office.

"No. But thanks, Paul."

He hesitated.

"You see," she explained frankly, "I am not going to add to the gossip that has been spread about you."

"You mean about Blackworth and you and me?"

She nodded.

"Hell," he said angrily, "are you going to avoid me just because of a rumour?"

"Haven't you been avoiding me?"

"Well . . ." he said slowly, "I had a reason. I don't have it now." He glanced at the telephone.

Rona's face coloured.

He sensed her embarrassment and wished his tongue hadn't been so quick. "All right," he said. "Sure you won't come along with us to-night?"

At the door, he turned to say, "By the way, you saw the evening paper? Nasty business, isn't it?"

"I didn't read very much. It gave me an attack of guilt, somehow. We are just so busy with our own lives—that's our only excuse, isn't it?"

"Yes. Although there wasn't much that anyone could do. He didn't have many friends, did he?"

She looked at Paul in surprise. "He?"

"Charles."

"Charles?"

"Yes. Don't you remember Thelma's son? The funny little guy with the red hair and the seesaw voice? It's in the evening paper. Didn't you——? Look, here it is!" He came back into the office, picked up the paper, and found the paragraph.

"What?" she said in sudden panic, hardly able to believe what she read. "Charles killed himself?"

"Jumped out of a window. And he injured a harmless old man on the sidewalk. Sort of pathetic that. Everything Charles did, he bungled, right down to the last moment."

She put down the paper. "No," she kept saying. "Oh, no!"

He had never seen her so upset. She hid her eyes.

"Did you know him?" Haydn asked. "Sorry, I didn't realise . . ."

"I only met him that one time," she said quickly. "On

Sunday. And I really didn't believe him. Not altogether. Perhaps I could have helped. Perhaps I could have——" She broke off. She sat very still.

"No one could have saved him. Look, here's the newspaper report. It lets Charles down as lightly as possible, but it's easy to see he was going to be sent to an alcoholics' home. And he resisted. He jumped out of a window right in front of the two men who had come to take him away."

"*What* men?" she asked sharply, her voice rising. "And *where* were they going to take him?"

"Rona," he said in alarm. "Take it easy, there!"

She rose quickly. "That envelope I gave you—it was from Charles." She was already at the door, hurrying through the main office into the corridor toward his room.

He followed her quickly. He unlocked the safe and handed her the envelope. She was calm now, calm and determined.

She said, "I got this letter on Monday morning. Read it. It will explain."

He read the letter. "Yes," he said at its end. He was frowning. He repeated aloud Charles' sentences: " 'But if anything happens—and I think, now, that it is likely to happen —then the problem is solved for me. It will be at that moment, when I shall be morally free but perhaps not physically free to speak, that I shall need your help.' "

Too late, Rona thought miserably. Poor Charles . . . I was of no help.

Paul Haydn said, "He saw this coming—not suicide, but being shut away in some 'rest home.' If his mother agreed to that, then he felt free to speak out."

"But when they came to take him away, he jumped from the window of his room," Rona said. Then, watching Paul's face, she asked, "Or did he jump?"

Paul said slowly, "They didn't need to kill him: they had him, all right."

"In a sense they did kill him."

Haydn nodded. "This letter alters things a good deal. What other witnesses were there? What about the servants? Frankly, I think we'd better hand this letter over to the police."

"What about the enclosed envelope? Charles suggested

204

someone like Weidler to open it. Why didn't he suggest the police?" Rona looked at the envelope in her hand, and then she dropped it on the desk, quickly—as if it were a flame that seared her fingers. She drew back half a pace, looking at the envelope. "Weidler will be home in Westchester," she said almost to herself.

"He isn't even there. He left for Chicago this afternoon. He will be back on Saturday."

"But the envelope should be opened at once. Paul, what shall I do?"

He looked at the envelope, but he didn't touch it.

"You take all this seriously?" she asked him.

"After a death—yes," he admitted.

"It must be opened," she said, still looking at the envelope. Or Charles' death might mean nothing at all.

"I know a man," Paul said slowly. "He would know what ought to be done." Then he faced her frankly. "There may be nothing of importance in that envelope. But it must get into the right hands, whatever it contains. You agree?"

"Yes." Who else could help? she wondered. There was Jon Tyson, there might have been Scott. But the most she could get from them would be advice, just as Paul was advising her. She didn't need any more advice; she wanted action. "Is your friend in New York?" she asked.

"Yes. Actually, he's waiting for me to pick him up now. We planned to have dinner and then go on to St. Nick's for some wrestling."

"You trust him?"

"Yes. And he knows a lot of people. That may be important for quick action."

"All right," she said.

Paul Haydn picked up the telephone and began dialling. "You know," he said as he waited for an answer, "you are trusting *me* a lot."

"Well, you ought to know about this kind of thing. After all you were in Military Intelligence, weren't you?"

He looked at her in surprise. "Now what gave you that idea."

"Why, you were always so silent about your assignment in London, I thought it was hush-hush."

"Plenty of hush-hush jobs that weren't Intelligence," he said. Then he spoke into the telephone. "Roger? This is Paul. Look, something urgent has turned up. Could you come over here, right away? . . . Yes. . . . Good. . . . See you."

Now it's all out of my hands, Rona thought. But did I act wisely? What else could I do? Strange that I should have admitted so frankly that I trust Paul Haydn. Eight years ago . . .

Paul was saying, "Do you mean to say that you actually believed I was in Military Intelligence? Well, I suppose that's one flattering rumour to have spread around. Except, it makes me feel I'm getting more credit than I deserve." He was embarrassed.

"Oh, I didn't talk about it," she said quickly. "Only once, in fact—and that was after you were out of the army, too."

He seemed to have thought of something. "Quite recently?"

She looked at him in amazement, half-smiling. "On Sunday. I was arguing with Scott about something, and I brought up Military Intelligence to prove a point. You know, Paul, you *are* a bit of a detective."

And on Monday, Orpen's stooge Murray dropped me, he was thinking. Any tie-up? He said with a grin, "Am I?"

It was her turn to look embarrassed. Had he guessed that she had been defending him on Sunday? (Scott had called Haydn an idiot. "Not so much of an idiot or he wouldn't have been in Military Intelligence." That's how it had been.) "How long will it take your friend to reach here?" she asked.

"About ten or fifteen minutes. Here's the most comfortable chair. Cigarette?" His voice was suddenly impersonal, matter-of-fact. He began talking about St. Nick's Arena, a nice safe unembarrassing topic unless you were really interested in wrestling.

"Do you go there often?" she asked, grateful that she could stop thinking about either Charles or Scott.

"I'm hoping to write an article on the fine old American myth of the good one and the bad one."

"How's that?" She was beginning to smile.

"Well, in wrestling as it is done over at St. Nick's, the hero begins by losing. That's the way you know he's the good one. Also, he's got a fine innocent face. He fights clean—no fouls.

And he falls for all the bad one's tricks, unless the public yells its warnings. He's taken in, sometimes, even when they do warn him. He can't believe, a fine upstanding guy, that there could be any malice aforethought in a friendly handshake. So he takes a lot of punishment. But he doesn't give up. Meanwhile, the bad one is being booed all around the ring. The public yells its hate at him. The more he wins, the more he's hated. And then, just in the last couple of minutes, the good one suddenly loses his temper and starts winning. The crowd cheers itself hoarse, and everyone goes home feeling fine: that's the way life should be—the good one winning, the bad one losing, and the public being wise to it all, right along."

"A comforting myth," Rona said.

"Harmless, too, unless you confuse it with reality."

She had been studying his face. He's changed so much, she was thinking. "Paul," she said suddenly, "what kind of work *did* you do in the army? Or can't you talk about it?"

"Sure. But no one has wanted to listen." He laughed. "That's what they call the veteran's readjustment problem." Then he began to talk about Brittany and the resistance movement there. "When D-Day came," he ended, "and the Bretons found that Normandy had been chosen, they couldn't believe it. They were all prepared for a landing in Brittany, you see. Every bridge, right down to the smallest foot bridge, had been mapped, and a unit was waiting to attack it and hand it over to the Allies. Every crossroad, every junction was marked. The demolition squads were alerted, the men were well trained, they had collected stocks of weapons. And then the news came through—not Brittany but Normandy. Normandy, where the comfortable farmers had no complete scheme ready to put into operation. The Bretons—well, I saw men break down and weep. That's the kind of people they——"

He heard footsteps in the corridor. He rose and went to the door. "This way," he called.

Rona turned to see a small, thin, white-haired man enter the room. He looked at her with alert brown eyes. He didn't seem surprised by anything. As Paul introduced him, he gave a reassuring smile and a firm handshake. Some of her nervousness and hesitation subsided.

Paul was saying, "Why not tell us how you first met Charles? And what he said to you? We'll begin from there." He smiled reassuringly.

Rona nodded. She began the brief story.

Roger Brownlee listened, as quietly as he had entered the room. Then he read Charles' letter to Rona. And then this evening's newspaper report which Paul laid before him. Finally, he looked at the envelope lying on the desk.

"I'd like you to open it," Rona said. And somehow she hadn't any more doubts. She rose, smiling to Paul. "I think I'll go back to my office and clear up my desk," she said to him. "This matter is all out of my hands, now, isn't it? And to tell you the truth, I'm glad." She glanced over at Brownlee's serious face. He had slit open the envelope and he was glancing through its contents quickly. He was frowning, his lips pursed.

He looked up suddenly. "This matter is out of all our hands, I think. It's clearly something for the Federal Government to consider."

"As serious as that?" Rona stared at Paul.

Brownlee held up three sheets of paper, closely written. "This is a detailed report. It's extremely serious, Miss Metford."

And no questions to be asked about it, Rona realised from his face. And although she was still curious, she was relieved too: this left her completely in the clear. She could forget about the sealed envelope.

"Will you tell what you know about this man Charles?" Roger Brownlee asked.

"Would that be important?"

"Yes. It would explain his letter, just as his letter is made clear by the report he enclosed. You will be a witness on his behalf, you see. His handwriting will be another witness, and so will the postmark on the envelope addressed to you. This man couldn't have been drunk on Sunday as everyone supposed. He wasn't in any state of alcoholism that would justify his being sent to any institution. Actually, he begins his report by saying that he found drunkenness was a very useful act to put on—it let him be taken for a harmless idiot. All the evidence we have here supports that."

"Poor Charles," Rona said slowly, pityingly.

"He may have the last word, after all," Paul reminded her.

"Is this phone switched on to a direct outside line at night?" Brownlee wanted to know. When Paul nodded, he began dialling. "We'll have to cancel this evening's plans. And I think Miss Metford had better go along with us."

He didn't say where, but Rona made her guess. If her statement could be of real help, she'd give it. It was, she thought, like seeing a street accident. If it was only a matter of insurance or a smashed fender, most passers-by melted away to avoid any trouble. Who wanted to get into a police-court case? But if someone was hurt, people would stop to help pull him free of the car. They didn't think of avoiding the nuisance of being a witness in court, then. "I'll wait for you in my office," she said.

She walked slowly down the corridor, her head bent, her face troubled. She was still thinking of Charles.

She met Mrs. Hershey bustling toward the washroom. "It's always the nights I've promised to baby-sit that I find I've got to stay late," Mrs. Hershey said breathlessly, smiling quickly, rushing on, her grey curls bobbing with excitement.

"How's your grandson?" Rona remembered to ask.

"Fine, just fine," Mrs. Hershey called back. "Three years old next month." My, she doesn't look like a girl that's getting married in June, Mrs. Hershey thought. "Oh, congratulations! I nearly forgot!" She smiled and hurried into the washroom.

Congratulations . . . One solitary typewriter, pecking away half-heartedly in a remote room, echoed the word mockingly. Congratulations . . .

Roger Brownlee finished telephoning, and swung round in the chair to face Paul. "All sewed up," he said, with considerable satisfaction. "I got the man I wanted. Nothing like going as near the top as possible. He was getting ready for a dinner-party. But we needn't keep him long. All we have to do is to tell what we know about Charles and turn over his letter and statement."

"Where do we see your man?"

"At his house, to save time. Eight o'clock. He will have rounded up a stenographer and a couple of his agents, by then."

"Charles' report had better be good," Haydn said, thinking of the men whose evening plans were now being altered. It was hard to believe that Charles could furnish anything important. He couldn't even stand on a piano stool without falling into the piano. He couldn't even jump out of a window without crippling an old man. He bungled everything he did.

"Have a look for yourself," Brownlee suggested, pointing to the sheets of paper on the desk. "You'll be interested. Friend Orpen's name leads all the rest." And then as Haydn still hesitated, he added, "You'll have to look at this material, Paul. You've got to be able to confirm it when we hand it over this evening."

Paul nodded. He sat down at the desk and began reading.

Charles had arranged his statement in numbered paragraphs, neatly and tightly written. There were signs of speed in the way he had used short phrases, punctuated with dashes, instead of sentences. But his words were vivid and exact, and when he talked about himself—as if to explain his motives and establish his honesty—much could be read between the lines. The information enclosed was certainly startling, probably valuable. But Haydn found, as he finished reading the three closely written pages, that it wasn't only the facts that interested him. Strangely enough, it was Charles himself who held his attention.

Paul handed the statement over to Brownlee. Then he leaned back in his chair, seemingly looking out of the window. But the yellow light of the setting sun on the brick and concrete walls formed only a vague image in his mind, a background to the vivid picture of Charles' terror, his indecision and weakness and amazing courage.

It was obvious from what Charles had written that he was still trying to protect Thelma as far as he could. She always had been a woman who took up one fad after another. Since the death of his father fifteen years ago, Charles had become accustomed to being exposed to Thelma's whims. He had become accustomed to seeing their apartment filled with peculiar acquaintances, to having no real friends of his own.

Six years ago, Thelma suddenly discovered politics and social significance. Charles, then nineteen years old, waited for that fad to pass, too. Instead, Thelma's interest deepened. The people who came now to her apartment were most admiring and respectful. She felt, for the first time in her life, that she was not only accepted but even sought after. Charles tried to convince her that the new friends—all Communists and fellow-travellers—were only finding her useful for her money and for her large apartment in a respectable building. Thelma didn't listen. Instead, she became a Party member and an intimate friend of Nicholas Orpen. It was then that Charles began to drink heavily, to leave New York on unexpected trips, to spend weeks and months with strangers in parts of the country where he was unknown.

And then, about three years ago, Charles returned unexpectedly from one of those trips to find a new butler—Martin—in complete charge of the apartment. He became aware that something of grave importance was going on in his home, something organised by Nicholas Orpen. Now, Charles didn't start drinking again. He stayed sober, pretended he was too drunk to notice much of anything, and kept both eyes and ears wide open. He didn't consider he was spying; the numerous visitors to his home were invaders. His motive was simply to gather enough evidence to prove to Thelma that she was underwriting graver trouble than she realised.

Charles had to go slowly, carefully. It took him almost two years to gather the information he wanted. And then, its implications suddenly terrified him. Although Thelma had no important part in the main business carried on in her apartment, she couldn't be so easily extricated as he had once hoped. For the last six months, Charles was plunged in doubt and hesitation. He had even started going away on his lonely trips again. He knew what to do, but he couldn't bring himself to do it. Recently, Thelma began to turn against him. She was listening to Orpen more and more. There had been open hints and threats: he was a useless alcoholic; he would have to be sent away to be cured. On Sunday, after a week of brooding, Charles made his first revolt.

He had made it, Paul Haydn thought, perhaps to goad Thelma into taking action. If she sacrificed him to Orpen, then all his feeling of loyalty to her would be cancelled out. He would be free, then.

"Well," said Brownlee, looking up from the curious document that Charles had left as his last will and testament, "it all makes a nasty picture. But there's enough here to give some very good leads. A few months of careful investigation, and Comrade Orpen will have his cell all nicely swept out. But why did this fellow take so damned long to pass on his information?"

"Thelma."

"But the longer he waited, the more deeply his mother was entangled. Didn't he see that?" Brownlee looked down at the sheets of paper in front of him. He said, "Some people seem to think that patriotism is only something to be taken out and dusted off when a war is on. Don't they realise they've got certain clear obligations even in peacetime?"

"Charles did produce some patriotic impulses in the end."

"If he had produced them earlier, he would be alive to-night. And his mother is in one hellish fix now. For his death will have to be investigated, too. She's caught in a double current."

They were both silent.

Roger Brownlee began putting the sheets back into their envelope. At last he said, "Well, I'm grateful to Charles for having enough guts to write this out. Orpen's the leader of this cell, that's clear. Martin was planted by him as a butler in the apartment three years ago. Both of them were always present at the small secret meetings in the servants' quarters. You will notice an odd thing—the meetings were always on certain nights. Does that mean Orpen could depend on a certain elevator operator being on duty at that time? Yes, there's quite a lot of investigation to be done on this branch."

Then Brownlee fell silent, too, thinking of the foreign visitors whose occasional visits to the secret meetings had been carefully recorded by Charles. There had even been strange visitors from abroad who had actually stayed for a few days in the apartment on the pretence of being old friends of Martin's. They remained concealed all day, and only went out at night. Martin took them their food, and the other servants were given a holiday (paid, so that they asked no questions). Charles had shown remarkable intelligence in noting down the dates of their visits, in listening for their party names. and in trying to establish their nationalities. He was right in attaching so much importance to the foreign visitors.

"Yes," Brownlee said, "Charles was no fool in some ways."

"He had plenty of courage, too," said Haydn. "He must have taken some terrifying chances. Did he really listen from that box-room next door to the room where the meetings were held?"

"That can be proved. If a hole is found bored in the wall of the box-room, and hidden behind an old wardrobe trunk, then Charles is telling the truth. But why didn't he get in touch with the FBI? My God, think of all the material they could have gathered by this time."

"He did as well as he could," Haydn said. "His upbringing wasn't exactly the kind to make him a decisive character. Thelma had a big hold over him. He admits it. It must have cost him something to admit it so frankly."

Brownlee nodded. "If I seem harsh, it's because I hate to see a wasted education, a wasted life. Heavens knows there are plenty of men who have had far less than Charles ever had, in money or in opportunity, and they make a better showing than he did. He was just another hair-splitter. I suppose you could say that hell is paved with vacillations." Brownlee thought over that, and then smiled. "If Hamlet had been a ploughman's son, do you think he would have spent so much time hesitating?"

"Well, a ploughman's son starts with one advantage—he doesn't call a spade an agricultural implement."

Brownlee's smile widened. He rose, looking at his watch, and said, "Another five minutes. We are better waiting here than in the street. We haven't far to go. Only over to East Fifty-seventh Street." He lit a cigarette and walked across to the window.

"You know," Paul Haydn said, still thinking of Charles, "it is strange that anyone so emotionally disorganised could be so careful in his planning."

"You're thinking of the way Charles hired a detective to follow Martin? Yes, that was astute. The detective agency can confirm that Martin made regular visits, with a brief-

213

case, to the consulate. Charles' statement that the brief-case was filled with dollar bills on Martin's return, and then—after a secret meeting—was empty again, is damning."

"It took some courage to go into Martin's room," Haydn said slowly, "even if he knew that Martin was spending the night with Thelma."

Brownlee curled his lip in distaste. "Martin and his comrades get paid off in foreign money. Thelma gets paid off by Martin. I wonder what all the little party idealists would think of that?"

"It might make some of them less enthusiastic for Thelma's musical Sunday evenings."

Brownlee paced around the room. "Charles said that those Sunday parties were negligible. Was he only trying to protect his mother?"

"Well, to anyone who didn't know the value of propaganda, they'd seem negligible. Just a collection of well-fed and well-dressed men and woman thinking how advanced they were, how daring. But you and I see them as the first little steps down a long gradual slope into the kind of corruption that Martin is caught in. If Martin wanted to break free now, knowing what he knows, would he be allowed to do it?"

"Hardly," Brownlee said with a smile. "Once you are deep into a conspiracy, you don't get out so easily. Both Orpen and Martin are up to their chins in this bog. All they can do is to hang on to their ideology and make no false move."

"Do they never have doubts?" Haydn asked, almost of himself.

"They gave up freedom of thinking long ago. Or else they wouldn't be in their present position of power. The Communist who thinks for himself never gets very far in his career as a Communist." Roger Brownlee placed the envelopes inside his jacket, and buttoned the pocket carefully. "Don't let me get run over by a taxicab this evening," he said with a grin.

"I'll tell Rona we're leaving," Haydn said, reaching for his hat.

Brownlee said, "Fine. By the way"—he was folding the newspaper, tucking it casually under his arm—"I think I'll ask for a nice quiet watchdog to look after Miss Metford

214

for a week or two. Just in case Charles got excited and defiant at the last moment, and yelled something about a letter."

"They'd never trace it to Rona," Paul said. "That's why Charles chose her." He hoped he sounded more confident than he suddenly felt.

"Warn her to mention this letter to no one. Not even in the future, when all this mess has been swept up."

Paul nodded, his lips compressed, his eyes thoughtful. Together, they entered the corridor.

"I hope she isn't one of those young women who take half an hour to put on their hats," Brownlee said. But Rona was waiting for them, ready to leave.

"I didn't feel like any more work," she explained, trying to keep her voice light and make a joke of it. But she was worried and depressed. Scott; Charles' death; Burnett's annoyance when he found she was making so little headway in her work. I'll have to stay late every night this week, she thought gloomily, or else I'll never manage this assignment. That means cutting evening classes, and the term is nearly over, and I've cut too many classes already this spring. That thought led her back to Scott Ettley. . . .

"Don't worry, Miss Metford," Brownlee said as they waited for the elevator. "We shan't keep you long. Then Paul can take you to his favourite restaurant and buy you a steak."

"Do I look so hungry?" Rona asked, beginning to smile. But she glanced nervously at Paul. We're being pushed together, she thought. Everything that has happened in these last days has pushed us together. Even Scott has done his share.

They entered the elevator, and it was Brownlee who made the conversation. It seemed as if Paul Haydn had nothing to say at all. "Yes," Brownlee went on, for the benefit of the interested operator, "there's nothing like steak to keep you optimistic. Pessimists are always hungry people. That's why Caesar balked at having Cassius around the place—a perpetual skeleton at the feast."

As he talked, Rona hoped it was all as simple as that. I'm reaching a stage, she thought, when everything is piling up right on top of me, and I don't seem to be able to struggle free. Yet, I must. I must.

215

She glanced into a shop window as they reached the avenue, to catch her reflection. She was surprised to see how normal she looked. Then she glanced at the scattering of people, walking slowly up the avenue for an after-dinner stroll. How many private worries, how much disappointment and unhappiness did they hide in their own hearts? They looked normal. But so did she. Just a girl, in a grey suit and a white straw hat, walking between two men toward the edge of the broad sidewalk, while one of them signalled with a newspaper for a cab.

Then Paul Haydn spoke. He said quietly, "Scott Ettley is just behind us." He said it as though he had been expecting this.

"You can't speak to him," Brownlee said to Rona. "Sorry. But we haven't time, you know."

"I don't want to speak to him," she said in a low voice. She didn't look around. She slipped her arm through Brownlee's. He felt her hand tremble on his wrist. He was suddenly aware of a tension between Rona and Paul, a tension that had nothing to do with Charles' death. "There's a taxi," she almost cried out, "there!"

"I'll take Miss Metford. Make sure he doesn't follow us," Brownlee said opening the door of the taxi and helping Rona in. He gave Paul the address quickly before he followed her. Only then, as the cab drew smartly away, did he look back at Scott Ettley. He saw a tall fair-haired man in a well-cut suit starting forward to hail the next taxi. But Paul had stepped forward, too.

"I'm sorry," Brownlee said vaguely, only knowing there was some good reason to feel sorry for this girl. He found he was patting her hand to comfort her like an ageing great-uncle. Not a role he particularly enjoyed. Still . . .

"Just a minute," said Paul Haydn.

Scott Ettley ignored him completely. He was signalling a cab. His mouth was bitter, his eyes narrowed.

"Tell Nicholas Orpen——" Paul said quietly, and left his sentence unfinished.

Ettley swung round to face him. For a moment, he was caught off guard. His face was startled and tense, almost waiting. He paid no attention to the taxi that had drawn up at the curb behind him.

"Tell Nicholas Orpen not to bother thinking up any more fancy pen names for the stuff he sends us."

Scott Ettley's face was under control again. He was half-angry, half-contemptuous. "In the first place, I'm not likely to meet Orpen. In the second place, deliver your own messages. And in the third—you keep away from my girl."

"Hey!" called the taxi driver. "Who's taking this cab?"

"If I were you," Haydn said slowly, "I'd let Rona make her own decisions."

"You would, would you?"

"I would. And another piece of advice——"

The driver leaned over toward the window. "Are you taking this cab or ain't you? Make up your mind, Jack!"

"——stop pushing Rona around, will you?" Haydn said.

They eyed each other.

Ettley raised his right fist and swung.

"All right," Haydn said, ducked, and hit hard with his left.

"Hey!" the driver shouted. "Keep offa my windows." He reached over to close the door which he had opened expectantly.

"You've got your fare," Haydn told him, picking Ettley off the side of the cab and shoving him inside. "Take him to the East River and dump him in with the garbage." He slammed the door.

The driver started his meter, swung his cab out into the main-stream of traffic. "Sit back and relax, can't you read?" he said warningly over his shoulder as his passenger grabbed suddenly at the door handle. The way I see it, he thought, is I'm doing a public service getting this fellow off the street. Any guy who leads with his right is just naturally asking for trouble. "Better get some ice on that jaw," he advised. That's me, he thought, helpful Harry, the kids' counsellor.

There was no answer.

Okay, okay, so I've got one of those talkative fares. "Where to?" he asked briskly.

CHAPTER SEVENTEEN

"No, thanks all the same," Rona said, "really, Paul, I think I'll go home now." She flinched as an elevated train hurtled up Third Avenue a block away, suddenly flashing into view with its warning roar. Then it had passed, and the street was quiet once more, a few lights in the windows already switched on against the gathering dusk, a few children playing on the sidewalk, a few people walking in their city-solitary way.

Rona smiled apologetically, excusing her nervous jump as well as her refusal. But Paul wasn't accepting any excuses to-night.

"You are going to have the steak that Brownlee recommended," he told her. "You aren't going to let me eat it alone, are you?" He took her arm and persuaded her toward Lexington Avenue and a bright neon sign over a narrow window. "Benny's" it read. "Neat but not gaudy," Paul said, "not compared to other neon signs, that is. I'm one of Benny's 'habitchewees,' and it hasn't killed me yet." He smiled down at her and added, "Besides, no one who knows you is going to be there."

"That isn't what worries me, Paul." She still hesitated.

"No? Then it must be the boiled egg or that can of spaghetti which is welcoming you home so urgently."

It may have been that unappetising truth, or his smile, or his decision, or the explanation she owed him about what did worry her in accepting his invitation—but, at any rate, she found herself inside Benny's.

It was a long narrow room with the bar itself, backed by pyramids of gleaming glasses, jammed near the door. Benny, presiding behind the dark polished counter in a crisp white shirt and apron, gave a welcoming nod. His customers, perched on the top of red leather stools, glanced round to look who's here. Some of them gave Paul a nod of recognition and then turned back to their own discussions. A pretty blonde in a black sweater smiled and said, "Hiya!"

"Just fine," Paul said.

"So I see," said the blonde, looking with critical appreciation at Rona.

"Two old-fashioneds, Benny," Paul said, and led Rona toward one of the half-dozen booths that filled the back half of the room. A wide opening in the rear wall showed a small kitchen, clean and bright, with a white-capped cook watching a charcoal broiler and a row of copper pans hanging overhead. The tables in the dark wooden booths were covered with red-checked tablecloths. "Benny picked up several ideas when he was in France," Paul told her. "The steaks are good. But don't try the apple pie. If Mom ever baked it like that, the boys would still be in Europe."

"This is cosy," Rona said with approval, settling into the privacy of their booth, taking off her hat and smoothing her hair as she looked around the crowded little room. Cheap brown wood furniture; crude seascape murals with stiffly bending Cape Cod clam-diggers scattered around flat bays, lighting that blazed from painfully functional fixtures. But in spite of this odd mixture, there was a feeling of friendly warmth, of easy relaxation and good humour. Even the man who took their order for tenderloin rare and baked Idahos seemed glad to see them.

"Yes," Paul said, watching her gradually relax. "It's a home away from home to a lot of lonely people."

"How's your new apartment? You managed to find a sub-let, didn't you?"

"Until September. Oh, it's all right. Quiet." He grinned. "And I get tired of my own cooking."

"Didn't you find someone to come in and cook for you?"

"Only if I were really to eat at six o'clock each night. They want to get home for their favourite television shows, you know."

"And you cook?" She was a little amazed at that new idea.

"Fine hand with a can-opener," he admitted.

Benny brought over their old-fashioneds and was formally introduced. "Pleased tomeecha," he told Rona with a broad grin. And he seemed to be telling the truth. He talked with Paul for a minute or two, just enough to establish the right feeling of welcome. His wife was having trouble with the new garden—not a thing up yet, except the radishes and

219

the grass. Too much grass. Nothing but mowing at the weekends. All this rainmaking. Still the trees were bigger and greener than they'd ever been.

"A solid type," Paul said, watching Benny walk with his slightly rolling step (Benny had always admired the navy) back toward the bar. "There's as happy a man as you can hope to find. Nothing to grumble about except the weather or his income tax. He did his stint footslogging over Europe and settled his conscience. Then he invested his savings in this little place, married a girl from Brooklyn, left the lower east side and moved out to Queens, got himself a couple of kids and a ranch-type house—by the way, how did that word sneak into the language?—and some green grass to mow on Sundays."

"How do you know he has nothing to grumble about except the weather and taxes?"

"True," he admitted. "I ought to have said he didn't let himself grumble. Benny's got one good rule. He says he found it in a ditch in Normandy. To be happy, you've got to know what you want; but you've also got to know when to stop wanting."

"When I was young," Rona began, and then hesitated.

"And what are you now?" he asked with amusement.

"Well, when I was very young, I used to think that if one were grown up, with enough money to buy a chocolate éclair each day, then one would be happy." She smiled at herself. "And I don't even like chocolate éclairs any more," she added. Then, watching him smile, she was shocked to find she had stopped worrying. Here I am, she thought, at the end of one of the most miserable days in my life—certainly the most terrifying and horrible—and I'm chatting about chocolate éclairs.

"What's that thought?" he asked quickly.

How does Paul always seem to know? she wondered. She said, embarrassed and retreating, "That was a nice man. I didn't feel so frightened after all."

He stared for a moment, looked at Benny and then discarded him, and then at last guessed her meaning. "Nice— if you are on the right side of the law," he said.

"Yes," she admitted, recalling the quiet watchful man who had asked occasional questions, well-placed, well-pointed, as

220

she told the story of Charles, and the letter. "Is he really important?" He had been polite, kindly. Not at all terrifying.

"I guess so."

"I suppose Mr. Brownlee stayed to go over the details with him?" Then she glanced at Paul's face. "You don't want to talk about it?"

"That's something we'll have to forget, Rona."

"Altogether? I mean—even afterwards, once everything is cleared up?"

"Altogether."

"Oh." She studied the cubes of ice in the squat glass in front of her. She pressed one against the slice of orange. "All right, Paul. Don't worry. I shan't talk about it. I can't forget, but I promise I shan't talk."

"Good," he said, noting she had been careful not to mention Charles by name. *I can't forget.* . . . Nor shall I, he thought grimly. "Another?" He looked at her glass.

She shook her head. "This is my first real meal to-day," she said as she watched the steaks being carried toward them. "Oh, how wonderful! Mr. Brownlee was right. This is what I needed." She picked up her fork and knife. And that was the end of conversation for the next ten minutes or so.

"Why didn't you want to come here?" he asked at last, still puzzling over her resistance. Was she worrying about the gossip that was being spread around? Was that the only reason? He hoped it was.

"It isn't fair to you."

"Let me be the judge of that, Rona."

"But you see," she said, cutting into the heart of the matter as determinedly as she had cut into the steak before her, "but you see, Paul *you're* the reason Scott blames for our broken engagement. He's been throwing you at me in every argument we've had recently."

"Well," he said slowly, "considering we didn't give him any real excuse——"

"I know. But he believes it." As if, she thought suddenly, Scott was determined to believe it; as if he wanted that excuse. Wanted it subconsciously perhaps, not quite realising he wanted it, but still wanting it. Yes, that had been true of Sunday. But to-day? The excuse that he had created had come so alive in his mind that he could see nothing else.

221

"You look afraid," Paul said. I don't like what's going on, he thought. I've never seen Rona look like this before. What has Ettley been saying? What has he been doing? I ought to have broken his jaw to-night. Not the intelligent way to settle an argument, but a very satisfactory way to imprint a lesson.

"I am," she admitted unexpectedly. "I am afraid."

"Of what?"

She looked up at him, then. "I don't know," she said. "That's the silly part. I just don't know."

"Did Ettley threaten you?"

She sat very still. Scott hadn't meant any of those threats to-day. He had only lost his temper. "You'd better be careful," she said, trying to change the direction of the conversation, "or Scott's going to pick a fight with you. He'll smash your jaw or something."

Paul had a sudden fit of laughing.

"It isn't a joke," she tried to remonstrate. "Scott has quite a temper, you know. And he is terribly angry, he really is."

Paul stopped laughing as he heard the concern in her voice. She's concerned for him, he reminded himself; if I got a broken jaw, she'd be politely sorry. "You're in love with your Scott?" he asked bluntly.

She nodded.

"Then why the hell don't you stay engaged to him?"

She pushed aside the empty plate. She hesitated. But the food and drink had given her courage. "Once I was in love with you. Yet I didn't stay engaged to you. Why? Because we wouldn't have been happy married. And when I marry, I'm going to stay married. Happily. That's one dream of my extreme youth I'm not going to compromise on. That's one idea that isn't a chocolate éclair." She avoided his eyes. She picked up her hat, began gathering her handbag and gloves, and half-rose. "Now I've been thoroughly rude. I'm sorry, Paul. I'd better go."

He reached over the table, pushing her gently back on to the bench, saying, "No, Rona. Did you never think I needed some frankness, face to face? Your letters were too polite, too stilted. I even got the idea that a broken engagement didn't mean very much to you. You were very young, very

222

beautiful; and you needed someone to take you out, give you a good time. That's what I thought when I got your letters in London."

"You thought that of me?" She was horrified. But she let go of her gloves and bag and hat.

"It's hard to find the right explanation in letters. Words are cold things without a face to watch as you listen to them."

She sat very still, looking at him. She said, "But those days are all over now."

And looking at her, he said, "Yes." If he had said anything else, she would have risen and walked away. "Yes," he repeated. "We are talking now as old friends. That's all, Rona." And all's fair in love he told himself, doubly fair when you lose twice. "But I still need a footnote or two to your letters. Why couldn't we—eight years ago, that is—why couldn't we have been happily married?"

"We could have been. But we wouldn't have stayed that way."

"Why not?"

"I don't like jealous wives."

His mouth tightened, but his grey eyes looked at her frankly. "You think I'd have turned you into that? You believe all the gossip was gospel truth?"

She smiled in spite of herself, knowing now what she did about gossip. She looked over her shoulder at the blonde who was sitting at the bar. "I don't believe gossip, now," she said. "But I still think you don't say 'no' harshly enough to women. Can't you snub them when they need snubbing?"

"Perhaps it takes a woman to do that properly," he said bitterly. I've been learning, he thought grimly, looking down at the small scar still left on his right hand. Five teeth marks, once. Then his voice changed. "I was a fool," he admitted. "Blame my vanity, Rona. I had more than my share of that."

"Oh, Paul!" She reached across the table and touched his arm. Her dark eyes were gentle, there was an appeal in the curve of her pretty lips. "You wanted a footnote to my letters? Yes, I think you ought to have had that at least. But I had too much pride to tell you then. You see, I knew you didn't really want to marry me. Or else you would have married me before you sailed overseas."

"Was that why I didn't marry you?" he asked. He shook his head slowly, a smile of bitter amusement on his lips.

"Then why?"

"How old were you in 1942 when I sailed?"

"Eighteen." She looked at him in a puzzled way.

"And I was almost seven years older. Strike one," he said. "And what relatives had you to depend on, if you needed them?"

She was startled. "Well—Peggy," she said slowly.

"Who had her own life to live. And what relatives had I?"

"An aunt in Fresno, and a cousin in Oregon."

"Neither of whom has ever seen me. And how much money had I, beyond my soldier's pay?"

"Nothing. But that didn't matter, Paul."

"And what chances did any G.I. think he had when he left this country in 1942?"

She traced the pattern of the checks on the tablecloth with her coffee spoon.

"Your witness," he said, almost angrily. Sure you were a fool, he told himself. But a girl of eighteen, left alone with a child to bring up, wouldn't have had much of a break. Before she could fight free, she would be a middle-aged woman. That's the way he had seen it eight years ago. It might seem stupid now, but now was 1950 and a war over and a safe return. It was easy to be wise, now.

"I must have hurt you, Paul," she said. "I'm sorry. But I thought—I began to think . . ." She looked at him, her large dark eyes troubled.

"Forget it," he said brusquely. "I made a mess of everything from beginning to end. I got what was coming to me." He mustered an amused smile. "It knocked some of the false pride out of me, I hope."

She said, "It's strange—how you can think you know another human being so well, so well that you can guess his feelings and his thoughts. . . . And yet, you can't. Why don't people explain more? Why don't we ask more questions when we are puzzled?"

"But would we always get honest answers? How many of us know ourselves well enough to be able to give an honest answer? Sure, we hope it's honest. We try to make it honest. But there's a difference between effort and achievement."

"It's a lonely world, Paul. Can we never know anyone, then? Never know anyone in the way it really matters?"

"Perhaps we expect to win that too easily. Perhaps it has got to be earned."

"You mean—through pain? Not physical pain, but what you suffer here, and here?" She touched her heart, then her forehead. The gesture was simple, yet pathetic in its questioning.

He said nothing for a few moments. He sat watching the sudden eagerness in her eyes, the sudden hope that brought her face into life once more. "Yes," he said, "that may be the only way."

Benny suddenly appeared beside them. "Everything suitcha?" he asked anxiously. "Just came over to see that you folks were being treated all right. What about some fresh coffee? Hey, Joe, make with the mocha over here!"

"The steak was wonderful," Rona said, still watching Paul's face. For a moment there, before Benny had spoken, she had seen it unguarded. But now Paul was in control of himself again.

Benny grinned. "How's about a piece of pie? Apple pie?"

"Not to-night. Just coffee," Rona said.

"No Camongbert? Best Winconsin Camongbert."

"I'll try that," Paul said. "Got to support home industries."

"You from Wisconsin, too?" Benny said, looking at Rona inquiringly.

"I'm from Pennsylvania," she admitted.

"That's like most of the people who come in here. They're from every part of the country except Nyork. Guess I'm the only original Nyorker in this room," he said with pride. Then he laughed. "And if I had been born two days sooner I'd have been an Italian immigrant travelling steerage with his mom and dad. That was real smart of the old lady." Then he signalled to the waiter and gave the order, and with a nod and an approving smile he walked with his nautical roll toward his quarter-deck.

"Here's another original New Yorker," Paul said, looking at the door. It was Roger Brownlee, who had just entered. He paused for a moment, glanced quickly around the room, saw them and made his way toward their booth.

"I didn't know he was coming to join us," Rona said in

surprise. But she was pleased, too. And reassured. For Brownlee looked unworried and even cheerful.

"He probably wanted to make sure you got that steak," Paul said, rising to welcome Brownlee to the table.

Brownlee said, "That's right, Paul. Just checking up." He sat down beside Rona, saying that he would have some coffee with them. The conversation became easy and light.

But Paul was still watching the door. And, as he had expected, a young man entered and went up to the bar. The stranger was dressed in a quiet blue suit and a grey felt hat. His face was thin, unobtrusive, watchful. He had dark eyebrows, dark hair. Then, leaning on his elbow casually and looking around him as he waited for his glass of beer, the dark-haired man in the blue suit let his eyes rest on the booth where Brownlee sat. When he finished his beer he left the bar, walked slowly past the booths toward the men's washroom. Paul looked at Brownlee and saw a smile in his keen eyes. Paul relaxed; his guess had been right. And when the man came out of the washroom, he walked in his casual way past their table. For a full moment he looked at Rona, seeing her clearly now in the corner of the booth.

He looks like a good watchdog, Paul thought, and he has a capable pair of shoulders on him. That was reassuring. It was possible that this FBI agent was an unnecessary precaution, just the very solid proof of Roger Brownlee's careful thought. But it was a good feeling to know that he would keep an efficient eye on Rona for the next week or two.

"Do you live with a friend, Miss Metford?" Brownlee was asking.

"No. I've got a little apartment of my own."

"Why don't you stay with Peggy and Jon to-night?" Paul suggested.

"No, Paul. I'm all right now. I don't have to bother them."

"It might be an idea to see Peggy to-night," he said doggedly. For if Charles had given Rona's name away, if he had mentioned any letter sent to her, then to-night would be the time for a search of her apartment.

But Rona shook her head. I can't tell Peggy and Jon about breaking my engagement, she thought miserably. Not to-night. I can't talk to them, yet. To-morrow or the next day. When I've got accustomed to the idea that I'm alone.

To-night, I would only feel twice as alone if I were to see Peggy and Jon together. "I'd only worry Peggy," she said, her voice strained, a forced smile on her lips. "And then Jon would start worrying too. He's got plenty of troubles right now, without adding me to them."

Paul looked at Brownlee who nodded, as much to say, "She'll be well guarded to-night and the next night. Stop worrying." Suddenly, too, he realised why Rona didn't want to see Peggy and Jon to-night. Yes, he thought, there's a couple who aren't just two separate individuals. There's a couple who have learned to know each other, to form a third personality which they share equally. They will never think of the world as a lonely place. Was this what Rona meant when she had talked of loneliness? Was this what Rona wanted?

Paul said, "Only, they may have been expecting you to call them to-day. And they may be wondering why you haven't." He waited. "Would you like me to phone them and tell them you are all right?"

Rona nodded. Then she said, "Would you let them know I've—I've broken the engagement?" The easy way out, she thought. I guess I've still too much pride and too little courage. She looked down at the checked tablecloth.

When Paul came back from the telephone booth, he found Roger Brownlee ready to leave. He was giving Rona his address and telephone number, just in case she ever wanted to reach him quickly. "Oh, by the way," Brownlee said very quietly, "I almost forgot to tell you that you can stop worrying about everything we discussed earlier this evening. It's all under control. You and I, and Paul here, have only one thing left to do—and that is to keep quiet. No comments at all, not even on any newspaper headlines we may see in the future. You will do that, Miss Metford?"

"Yes."

"Good enough." He smiled, in a way that surprised Paul Haydn, as he gripped her hand. "You'll see Miss Metford safely home?" he asked Paul.

"I'll see that it's all safe," Paul said. Then he watched Brownlee walking toward the door. "You've made a friend, my girl," he said to Rona.

"I think he would be a good friend," Rona said. "And
227

I'd rather be on his side than against him. Yes, I'm sort of glad he is on our side."

"Our side . . . how do you mean?"

She dropped her voice to a murmur. "Well—I'd say that our side is Charles' side. I'm for the ordinary man, doing no harm to anyone, who gets pushed around until he can't stand it any longer. Yes, that's it. I'm against the men who push other people around—or plan to push them around." Our side, she thought, remembering the way she had said it so naturally. "What about Peggy and Jon? Did you tell them my news?" she asked quickly, looking away from the watchful grey eyes.

"Briefly."

"Were they—were they disappointed?"

"No . . . Jon seems pretty mad with Ettley."

"Why?"

"Oh, something that happened, I guess." I'll let Jon tell her, if he ever will, that Ettley lied last night about working late. "Anyway," Haydn went on, "Jon sent you his love. And congratulations."

Rona looked up quickly. "Now, Paul!" she said angrily. She was hurt. "Jon wouldn't say a thing like that!"

Paul cursed his stupidity. "I'm sorry." Actually Jon's language about Ettley had been highly colourful, completely un-academic, and totally unrepeatable. Women, Paul thought, are the damnedest creatures. Then he wondered what she would have said if he had told her he had slugged Scott Ettley on the jaw, only a couple of hours ago. Perhaps that might have chased her back into Ettley's arms, with her woman's ministering-angel complex fully aroused.

"What did Jon actually say?" she asked.

"Well, seemingly Ettley has been telephoning this evening. Last heard from at half-past seven. Peggy answered, to begin with. She was trying to keep Jon away from the phone. But at half-past seven, Jon took the call."

"Yes?"

"That's all."

"You told Peggy and Jon I was all right?" she asked anxiously.

"Yes," he said.

"I *am* all right."

228

"Sure," he said. You're just about as happy as I am, he thought.

Rona began to put on her hat. He remembered to look for her gloves under the table. They were there, all right. She took them from him, a smile in her eyes. "You've a long memory," she said.

"Occasionally," he said.

"Paul—I can't thank you for—for the way you've helped me to-night."

"I did nothing. Just persuaded you to keep me company over a steak."

"You would have had company without me, I think." She smiled openly now. "She's very pretty," she added, looking at the blonde girl who was eating supper with some friends.

"That's one of your lonely people," Paul said. "Her husband was killed in the Pacific. She had a baby. And then it died two years later. She saved up and came to New York to try some modelling. She isn't quite good enough. So she works in a hat shop. She lives near, and she likes the way Benny kids her. She's his most favoured customer, although she can only buy one beer a night. She makes his wife's hats, and she gets her dinners free. When I saw her at first, I thought what a ninny, what a complete little daffy-down-dilly who thinks life is just a parted smile on the cover of a fashion magazine."

"That," Rona said, "is what is known as a bolt and a jolt, isn't it? I really asked for it." She walked out beside him, looking at the blonde girl in the black sweater with a new eye for the deceptively calm and carefree face.

They said good night to Benny, who called, "Hurry back!" His best friend in the army had been a Westerner, and whatever Benny liked about a place or about people he adopted as his own. That parting call, echoing Colorado, followed them out into Lexington Avenue.

Rona was smiling. "Yes, Paul," she said, "you've done an awful lot for me to-night. Thank you."

Behind them, some thirty paces away, a youngish man in an unobtrusive blue suit and a grey felt hat seemed to be taking the same direction as they were.

III. Synthesis

CHAPTER EIGHTEEN

Wednesday, Thursday, Friday—days of lowered skies, of clouds wrapped round the peaks of the tallest buildings, days of a spring that seemed turned back to winter. Depressing, everyone said.

Depressing, Rona agreed. Wednesday, Thursday, Friday—all alike this week, all of the same pattern with no word from Scott. Days of sleeping and rising and eating and working, of being polite, neat, orderly, of smiling and listening and hiding all worry.

For the word had somehow got round *Trend*'s office that Rona Metford had broken her engagement. Like all mysterious pieces of news, no one knew who had started it. But it seemed credible: Rona wasn't wearing Ettley's ring; she was working with frenzied concentration; and Paul Haydn had stopped avoiding her.

Mrs. Hershey, genial and kind-hearted, didn't know what to make of it. Rona's getting on now, she thought worriedly: twenty-six, going on twenty-seven now. And women of twenty-seven, although they looked as young nowadays as girls of twenty, were still women of twenty-seven who couldn't afford to go around breaking a second engagement.

"And such a long engagement, too," Miss Guttman said. To cheer Rona up, she resumed her visits with the problems that troubled her. Her present predicament was a breakfast nook. "How would you have it?" she asked Rona. And Rona, whose first impulse had been to say, "I wouldn't," resisted giving the truth and said instead that at the moment all she could think of was mosaic floors and Roman fountains.

"She's taking it badly, poor dear," Miss Guttman reported to Mrs. Hershey. "Imagine giving up three years of your life to a man and then having him turn you down!" Which led, in the typists' office and the washroom, to a long discussion on the demerits of men. But everyone who agreed was congratulating herself privately that her man wasn't like that, of course.

Harry Jimson, over in the Architecture Department, said, "Well, Phil; it looks as if Rona isn't leaving us. So there goes your chance of promotion." Phil Arnim, who had thought that out for himself—who wouldn't, with a family to bring up?—only answered "Tough on her," and went on with his work.

Jimson was thinking of his wife and his blonde and his debts. "Guess there isn't much future around here," he said. These damned women—either taking jobs from men or taking all the money they earned. Takers, one and all. "Guess I'll clear out some day and try San Francisco," he added gloomily. A new start, that was all he needed. He liked that idea the more he thought of it; he liked it so well that he concentrated on it and went no further in his argument. He never even reached the next stage in reasoning: a new man was as necessary as a new start if defeat wasn't to be repeated. "San Francisco," he said again, "that's the place. Civilised. We're nothing but machines in New York." He looked angrily in the direction of Rona's room where she was hard at work. Her worries didn't seem to bother her. Just another machine. Women had no real emotions.

Arnim said, "Better get on with your job, Harry, or old Burnett will be down on top of you."

Harry Jimson nodded, lit another cigarette, and frowned out at the cold wet world. Even the weather in New York had gone to hell. How could anyone work at all if he was as worried as this? Women were all on the surface, all natural pretenders. He glanced at Rona's room again. They put on a good act of working. Or loving. He discarded his cigarette, lit another, picked up his pencil, and thought of his mistress. Did she really mean to go to his wife? Did she? Or was that part of the act, too?

But Rona's work was not pretence. It was a necessity, a necessity to keep her from thinking about herself.

Scott had taken that last glimpse of her on Tuesday night, when she got into a taxi with Roger Brownlee, as her definite answer. That is what I wanted, she told herself as Wednesday passed and Thursday passed and Friday was almost over. But it was difficult to end the habit of thinking about Scott, of waiting for Scott, of listening to each telephone ring with the rising hope that it would be his voice that would answer hers. So she tried to lose herself in work.

It wasn't easy. Her mind had at least two subcurrents flowing through it, fighting each other to rise to the surface. Her anger had passed. So had her wounded pride. But she was left with pity, regret, longing, aversion, momentary dislike that would twist back to love again. She was left with memories strangely mixed, a sense that this was all stupid and needless and negligible, a feeling that this was all inevitable.

I'm to blame, she would tell herself. . . . No, I'm not, she would think. But who was? Was Scott to blame, either? Then who was?

And she would set to work again, to force herself into thinking of something that had nothing to do with Scott and herself, something practical and urgent enough to deaden the pain in her mind. But it wasn't easy.

If Scott had come to see her, if Scott had called her—what then? Yes, she might have forgotten everything else except that she was still in love with him. For she couldn't forget that. And like most women, after having told herself that her decision was made and well made, she now had moments of wondering if she had been right. But this wasn't a matter of going back to a shop and telling a resigned salesgirl that the colour wasn't suitable after all. This was a pattern of life. Once made, it couldn't be unmade so easily.

I was too quick, too angry, I was too cruel, she'd think. Or was I too slow? Ought I to have seen the shape of our lives a year ago? It would have been easier, last summer, if I had never gone to Mexico with Scott; easier if I hadn't accepted his ring and started planning our marriage. I was worried at Christmas when the wedding was postponed; I was afraid at Easter when we avoided even talking about it; I was too happy when it was so suddenly settled, only a few weeks ago. I persuaded myself, too much, that everything was bound to come out all right. But—but why couldn't everything have come out all right?

And there she was, the circle completed, back at the question she could not answer. She could find no real explanation, she couldn't rationalise her actions because they had sprung from something deeper than reason.

That's a frightening excuse, she thought. And then she'd leave her bewilderment, leave it and concentrate on work. Here, at least, was an understandable world. Here, at least, you could see cause and effect.

Scott Ettley had his own emotional battle, but it was less complex because he could focus his bitterness on Rona and Paul Haydn. Some of the anger he felt was kept for Nicholas Orpen, only he had to repress it, silence it, and turn it aside. Orpen's decisions were right. They had to be right; is was no use questioning them. Yet, it was Orpen's fault that he had lost Rona. For months now, Orpen had interfered, and for what purpose? None, as far as the wishes of the Committee had turned out. They had reversed Orpen's judgment. But, by that time, Rona's suspicions had been roused. She had sensed that their marriage was threatened. Or had she? Wasn't Rona using all their difficulties in those last months as an excuse to suit herself? And Haydn?

And so Ettley turned most of the blame on to Haydn. And Rona. Rona had betrayed him. When he needed her, she had left him. And in that scene on Fifth Avenue on Tuesday evening, when he waited outside her office only to see her leave with a stranger while Haydn stopped him from following her—well, she had made a fool of him.

That would be the last time that Rona would ever make a fool of him. That would be the last time that any woman would make a fool of him. He had his work. From now o~

that was all he would think about. Orpen would be pleased, he thought bitterly.

Orpen . . . how had everything come about, just as Orpen would have planned it? He hadn't planned it—that was impossible, a stupid idea. Yet it had come about. Orpen had always been jealous of Rona. That was the whole truth. That was the reason for Orpen's opposition and interference. All his other explanations were only excuses. But if Rona was loyal, if Rona had planned no betrayal, then no outside interference would have had any effect. No, the weakness lay with Rona. So why blame Orpen?

Who would have thought, he wondered in pain and anger, that Rona could have done this to me?

I'll cut her out of my life, he thought, I've strength enough for that. This moment, now, is where the past is forgotten. All that is over—all the mistakes, the bitterness, the self-torture, the delusions. This moment is where the future begins.

And the future will be what I help to make it. That's what I think about, now.

CHAPTER NINETEEN

On Friday morning Orpen telephoned Scott Ettley. "I couldn't get seats for the theatre to-night," he said.

Ettley said, "Too bad." So the meeting, which had been arranged for Thelma's apartment that evening, would not take place. It was hardly surprising. Charles' suicide was being given a lot of adverse publicity in the newspapers in the last two days. "Well, I'll drop by for a chat," he suggested. The meeting was bound to be somewhere, Ettley thought. It must. His news about his father was too important to let drift.

"Do that," Orpen said. But his voice had none of the enthusiasm that Ettley had expected. He sounded tired, uninterested. And then Orpen, without waiting for any further talk, hung up. Ettley was left with the receiver at his ear, his next sentence spoken into blankness.

What's wrong? he wondered. Orpen might be depressed, but 'en when he was depressed you could always depend on to rally for a few bright, seemingly meaningless phrases.

234

Orpen enjoyed playing conspirator even to the point of deluding any curious telephone operator.

Ettley replaced the receiver thoughtfully. Orpen was not only depressed. He was worried. "What's wrong?" Ettley asked aloud, frowning.

And that was the first question he put to Orpen when he arrived at his apartment just after five o'clock that evening.

The grey mists had lifted suddenly. The skies were showing blue, the high New York blue skies that promised a clear sunset and no rain to-morrow. Orpen's street was busy at this hour. The warehouses were loading the last delivery trucks, the garages were open for business, the parked cars along the curb had children playing beside them with roller skates and skipping ropes. Some boys were throwing a ball around, missing the cars expertly and confidently. A woman in a bright cotton dress rested her elbows on a window sill, folded arms folding in fat, faded hair bristling in curlers, and talked to a man returning from work.

Outside Orpen's house, there stood a battered baby carriage. Two young girls with lipstick and long wide skirts, hemlines drooping above snow-white ankle socks, rocked its bundle of pink wool and chattered about their boy-friends. They fell silent for a moment, giving Scott Ettley a side glance, a hidden smile, and then they ignored him, but their voices were louder and their laughter was more intense. Until he rang the bell, waited briefly, and was admitted by the complaining door, he was the gallery to which they played. When he had entered the house, they went back to their own conversation. They felt pleased and excited. He hadn't looked at them, but that didn't matter. He had inspired a good performance, and Betty Grable and Lana Turner could now become Mae O'Neally and Francis Roth again and wait for their evening dates to show up.

Inside the house, there was a workman kneeling in the dark hall, shining an electric torch on an opened outlet. The house superintendent or handyman or perhaps a combination of the two, Scott Ettley thought, noticing the open tool box beside the man; an electrician would have stopped work by four-thirty. Then Ettley, turning his face quickly aside as if the telephone box on the wall were more interesting, mounted the stairs rapidly. He had never seen any superintendent in this house before. But then, he usually came late in the evening, when the man would be in bed or down in his basement room.

As he reached Orpen's floor, Ettley looked over the rickety handrail and waited. All he could see was the faint glow from the torch far below in the hall. No footsteps following him. He felt better for having been careful. He gave his accustomed knock on Orpen's door, and tried to enter. But, to-day, the door hadn't been unlocked in preparation for him. He heard Orpen's voice, low, asking, "Who is it?"

"Scott," he said, keeping his voice just as low. The door was unlocked, then. He entered, puzzled and wondering.

He might have been more puzzled if he could have seen the superintendent, motionless, sitting back on his heels, the torch playing over the loose wires in the wall, his head cocked to the side as he listened to the mounting footsteps, a smile on his lips as he counted the flights of stairs and each landing passed. The door upstairs closed. It was Orpen's, all right. Orpen was the only tenant on the top floor.

The man rose, leaving the torch still trained on the opened wall socket. He opened the front door quietly and stood there, propping it ajar with his foot, while he lighted a cigarette in full view of the garage opposite. Then, with a nod for the two girls at the baby carriage—one of whom said, "Hi, Joe!" and then started explaining to her friend that Joe was the new super the landlord had sent round to fix up this dump and about time too—he turned back into the hall and let the door close quietly. He began screwing the protecting plate back into place over the wires. To-morrow, he thought, I'll have to work on that cracked plaster. Or perhaps the tenant who lived below Orpen could be persuaded that the plumbing overhead was faulty.

Scott Ettley closed the door behind him. Orpen's room was in disorder, as if it hadn't been cleaned out for days. It needed airing, too. In the searching light from its high window, without shaded reading lamps to soften its sagging ceiling and cracked plaster and stains on the rug, it looked both frowsy and decrepit.

"What's wrong?" Ettley asked, watching Orpen standing gloomily by the littered fireplace.

236

Orpen didn't answer that. "You're early," he said. "You're taking chances." There was a fleeting smile round his colourless lips.

"What chances?" Ettley smiled. Orpen loved to play the conspirator, he told himself once more.

Orpen roused himself and walked slowly over to the window. The briskness in his movements had gone. They were tired, like his voice. He stood behind the curtains, looking down into the street.

"I thought I might as well find out," Scott explained smoothly, "where and when the meeting is to be held tonight."

"You sound eager not to miss it," Orpen said. "Admirable, most admirable." He gave a short laugh.

Scott Ettley stared at his back. "What's wrong?"

Again Orpen didn't answer. But he turned and came back to the centre of the room, to the table with its pile of newspapers. He stood there, hesitating, looking down. Then Ettley saw that Orpen's face was paler than he had ever seen it, and that the lines under the eyes had deepened.

"Where's the meeting?" Ettley insisted.

"The meeting?" Orpen repeated, as if he had only half-understood. "It's at eight o'clock. Eight o'clock."

"I asked *where* is the meeting." Ettley looked at Orpen still more closely. "When did you last have any sleep?" he asked. "Or are you ill?"

"Ill?" Orpen's small bitter smile appeared and vanished. "Ill . . . yes, that might be it." He sat down on a chair, leaning his elbows on the table, resting his head on his hands.

"For God's sake, Orpen!" Ettley began in alarm.

Orpen said slowly, "Don't worry. I'm not ill." He took off his glasses. He drew a hand over his brows, over his eyes, and let it rest at his lips.

"Look," Scott Ettley said, his relief giving away to irritation, "you aren't the only one with troubles. Don't you want to hear my news? Don't you want to hear what's been happening?"

Orpen raised his head, letting his hand fall on the table, and looked at the younger man. Again, the brief fleeting smile appeared, a smile with no humour but—so it seemed to Scott Ettley—much pity.

"Rona has left me," Scott said. He turned away, unable to face Orpen. "Doesn't that give you something to crow about?"

There was a silence. "I'm sorry," Orpen said at last.

"Sorry?" Ettley's anger was released. "You sorry? You made everything as difficult as possible from the first. It was you who started the trouble."

"I?" Nicholas Orpen's voice was almost inaudible. "Is that the way you see it, Scott? Didn't you start the trouble for yourself?" He pressed his hand wearily to his eyes again, and then replaced his glasses.

Scott turned to stare at the older man.

"You can't divide your loyalty," Orpen went on. "If you've come for advice, here's what I say. There are two things you can do. And only two. The first is that you devote yourself to your work, give all your obedience to the Party, and be glad that Rona had the impulse to break with you. The second is that you can return to Rona, tell her everything, ask her to stay with you, and renounce your loyalty to the Party. That's your choice."

"Orpen—are you——"

"No, I'm not crazy. That's the only choice you have."

"Renounce my . . ." Scott couldn't finish the question.

There was silence in the room for a long moment. From outside came the shouts of boys playing in the street, the heavy roar of a truck pulling out of a warehouse, the warning horn of a car turning into a garage.

Scott said, "Do you realise what you've just suggested?"

Orpen nodded. "Yes, I know."

Scott took a deep breath. Orpen is proving me, he thought, this is the final test. "I won't betray the Party," he said flatly. "It is more important than I am, or you, or Rona."

Orpen rose, lifting his hands helplessly. He walked back to the window, and stood there, hidden by the curtains, while he looked down at the boys playing in the street. He said, his voice expressionless and clear, "It would be easier for you to break with the Party, now. Later, if you have doubts—later, if you find your conscience refuses to let you go on—later, it will be hell. An endless and torturing hell. The more deeply you are involved and the more you know—the more dangerous it is to leave. You see that, don't you?"

238

Ettley smiled. "But I don't see myself ever getting into the position of quitting." He watched Orpen's back. And he suddenly noticed, by the droop of the shoulders, by the bent head, an admission of hopelessness. Of defeat, almost. "Orpen," he asked sharply, "what the hell's wrong?" There was real concern in his voice. Have we run into trouble? he wondered anxiously. But how? Everything had been working so smoothly, so well.

Orpen came back to the table. He looked searchingly at Scott Ettley, he looked long and carefully, and he saw sympathy and worry in the younger man's eyes. His hand gripped Ettley's shoulder. Then he picked up a paper from the table, a paper with blue-pencilled paragraphs, and handed it silently to Ettley.

"I saw this a couple of days ago," Ettley said, glancing quickly over the account of the arrest and trial in Czecho-slovakia of prominent Communists. "Well, they are getting what they earned, I suppose." Traitors, he was thinking, traitors and deviationists.

"Are they?" Orpen took back the newspaper and laid it carefully on the table. He seemed to have forgotten about it, for his voice became more normal and there was a smile on his lips as he changed the subject. "Scott, do you remember a man called Jack who was here recently?"

"Why, yes!" Scott Ettley was surprised. It was less than a month ago when Jack had paid his last visit to Orpen's room just before flying back to Europe. He had talked a good deal about his experiences during the war in organising Communist cells in the French underground. That was the night, Ettley remembered, he had phoned Rona at her sister's—the night that Paul Haydn had been up there and had brought Rona home—the night that had started Rona's betrayal. "Yes, I remember that night well," he said. Then, forcing himself away from thoughts of Rona, he added, "Did Jack get safely back to France?"

"He got safely back. Not to France. He was only assigned to France during the war."

"I thought he was French." There was amazement, a touch of disbelief in Scott Ettley's voice. A touch of correction, too, Orpen noted with amusement. Young men always knew so much.

239

"He isn't French. That was only his cover."

"Efficient."

"Yes. What did you think of him, by the way?"

"He seemed all right to me. Very much all right."

Orpen nodded. Then he said, "He's probably the best friend I've ever had. I used to work in close contact with him when I was visiting Europe. I've talked with him a lot. A good man, a sound man."

"Plenty of guts," Ettley said, remembering Jack's story of the German occupation. "He's been a fighter for a long time. Didn't he serve in Spain?"

"He's served longer than that. He began with Lenin in Switzerland in 1916."

"It must be something to be known that way," Ettley said half-admiringly, half-enviously. Yes, that was something to be proud of. . . .

"Yes," Orpen said quietly. Then he suddenly pointed to one of the names of the Communists on trial in Czechoslovakia. "There he is!"

Ettley stared at him as if Orpen had suddenly turned insane.

"There he is!" Orpen repeated. "Now they say he was in Nazi pay. Now they say he's an American spy. That's Jack— a man who devoted thirty-four years of his life to the Party, five of them in prison, eighteen months of them in a German concentration camp—a man who helped make Czechoslovakia a Communist state."

"He is a Czech?" That was all Ettley could say at first. He read the charges against Jack again. "I can't believe it," he said slowly. "Why, it's only three or four weeks since he was right here in this room." Talking and arguing with all the zest of a man half his age. Then Ettley began to see what must be wrong. He looked up suddenly at Orpen. "This can't be pleasant for you," he said sympathetically. "But surely you won't be blamed for having been deceived by Jack? We all were. Spies can infiltrate the most careful organisation. We know that."

"You think *that* is what is worrying me?" There was almost contempt in Orpen's voice.

"Well, what then?" Scott asked. It was the only possible explanation. But Orpen was taking it all too seriously. After all, his own record was faultless; he had done his share of fighting and suffering. Then Scott, speaking now consolingly, said, "And I suppose our present visitor from Czechoslovakia is here to find out what information Jack extracted from us? But Jack didn't do too much damage, did he? He did most of the talking, it seems to me."

"You think Jack is a traitor?"

"It's pretty obvious, isn't it?"

Orpen smiled. "Let me put you right about one thing," he suggested. "Then the rest will seem clearer."

"And what have I got wrong?"

"Our present visitor from Czechoslovakia, called Comrade Peter, whom you met for five minutes or so, is not a Czech."

"No?" And I spent longer with Comrade Peter, wherever he comes from, than just five minutes, Scott thought angrily.

"No. He only visited that country recently. He's making a tour of inspection. First it was Hungary, then Bulgaria, then Poland, then Czechoslovakia. He leaves a trail of accusations and trials."

"You are hinting he's tracking down disloyalty and inefficiency?"

"Or men who have fought for Communism in their country and think they ought to be allowed to run it when they succeed."

"What could he hope to do over here?" Ettley was incredulous.

"Mark the men who might be future deviationists. They will never get very far in their political careers, it doesn't matter how loyal or efficient they are as Communists." Orpen's voice suddenly dropped and became desperate in its intensity. "Don't you see, Scott? Once we are in power, those of us who want to be free of foreign controls are going to find ourselves in the dock like Jack, labelled as traitors."

Scott Ettley said worriedly, "You're ill, Orpen; you don't know what you are saying."

"So you don't think that you, some day, could be Jack? It couldn't happen here?" Orpen began to laugh. "My God!" he said, almost hysterically. Then he took a deep breath. "Don't look at me that way, Ettley. I'm no traitor. I've worked for the Party. And I'm loyal to it. But will we get our Party when we are in power?"

241

"But America is different. It's bigger, farther away. We make our own decisions."

Orpen sat down wearily. "Not one important decision is ever made by us. Not one. *I* know that."

Ettley stared at him unbelievingly. Then he said, hesitatingly, accusingly, "Well, you need the help and the experience of those who led the way in revolution. That's only logical. You've accepted that for years. And then one little newspaper report comes along and you talk like a——" Ettley couldn't say the word. He flushed, shrugged his shoulders as if to excuse himself.

But Orpen said it for him. "A traitor?" He shook his head slowly. "This did not happen to me overnight, Scott. It's been a battle of months, and I've been forcing myself to avoid the issue. First, the Hungarian purge, and then the Bulgarian arrests. . . . I knew some of those men, too. I persuaded myself they had made a fool out of me. But now, there's Jack. I know him too well. I can't accept this!" He struck a blow at the newspaper with his clenched fist. "If anyone is making a fool of me, of you, of all the rest of us, it is Comrade Peter and the men who give him orders. We work and fight and suffer for the revolution. But they will win it."

Scott Ettley didn't speak. The flush had left his cheeks. His face was pale, his eyes were troubled. Then he found the explanation he had been seeking. Peter had discovered some fundamental errors in Orpen's work—the scandal attached to Thelma's apartment, for instance; Peter wouldn't approve of important meetings having been held in such a place—and Orpen was being disciplined. Orpen saw demotion ahead of him. And his years of work, his pride in having been a martyr were making him bitter. Bitter and dangerous.

Orpen was saying, "Open your eyes, Ettley! Who helped you get as far as you have? You don't think you did it under your own steam, do you?"

"I owe you a certain amount," Ettley said stiffly. "But I don't owe you everything. Let's get that straight!"

"Yes, let's get that straight. It's true. You don't owe me everything; you owe it most of all to your father."

"What?" Ettley's lips were tight with anger.

Orpen's voice became patient. "Scott, I'm telling you this
242

so that you will *listen* to me. Call it shock treatment if you like. But it's the truth. You owe everything to your father. If he hadn't been the owner of a newspaper, would I ever have been instructed to develop you so thoroughly, so carefully? If your father had been a plumber or a druggist, where would you be to-day? Attending mass meetings, handing out leaflets, carrying a picket sign, being given little odd jobs to do. Would you ever, in ten years, have met Comrade Peter? In twenty years? No. You can thank your father for your usefulness to us."

There was a pause. "Where is the meeting to-night?" Scott Ettley asked in a tight, cold voice.

Nicholas Orpen looked at him. "Now is the time to see what will happen to you," he warned. "Now is the time to leave. With little to worry you," he added unhappily.

"Leave the Party?"

"Until it's safe from foreign control. Until then, we are only betraying it."

"You're not sick. You're crazy!"

"No," Orpen said wearily, almost hopelessly. "I'm only seeing things in their future shape. Scott, have I ever given you bad advice?"

Scott looked down at him, and moved forward from the mantelpiece where he had been standing. "Yes," he said quietly.

"Ah," Orpen said, thinking of Rona too. "But that wasn't bad advice, Scott." Then he rose. And in a quiet grave voice he gave Ettley the address of the house where the meeting was to take place. It was on the west side, this time.

Scott Ettley picked up his hat, looked round the disordered room and then turned to the grey-haired man who stood watching him so quietly. Something in the troubled eyes touched him. He found himself saying, "Shall I see you at the meeting?"

Nicholas Orpen shook his head slowly.

"What are you going to do?"

There was a hesitation, a gesture of helplessness from Orpen. "I don't know," he said hopelessly. "I don't know."

In the street, the warehouse doors were beginning to close. The last trucks had pulled away. A mechanic stood at the

243

bleak black entrance of the deserted garage, pointing out a direction to a quiet inoffensive man in a neat dark suit. The man offered the mechanic a cigarette, gave him his thanks and, keeping a wary eye alert for the baseball that the kids were throwing over his head, set out at a leisurely steady pace after Scott Ettley.

The mechanic picked up the ball which had rolled near his feet, and threw it back to the boys. He felt pretty good. In the three days he had been working there, that was the first visitor Orpen had allowed to enter his room. And McMann, all dressed up as the new superintendent, tinkering with an electric outlet in the hall of Orpen's house, would be feeling pretty good too. As soon as McMann had signalled that the fair-haired, well-dressed stranger was a visitor for Orpen, the phone call had been made from the garage. And a reinforcement, suitably dressed, had arrived to leave his car and be ready to follow. Now, it was up to the quiet man.

The mechanic threw away the cigarette and admired the makings of a fine sunset this evening—a cleared sky, a nice grouping of high clouds behind the midtown office buildings. He didn't even seem to glance at the house that interested him as he turned back into the huge cavern of the garage. But from where he worked, he could keep his eye on the one necessary patch of street. That was lucky, he thought. In another half hour I'd have been off duty. If that fellow with the fair hair had come an hour later, then the night watchman would have been the guy who had the excitement of making a phone call. It didn't sound so very much, and it might mean nothing at all. But anyone who visited Orpen was liable to be interesting. That was a cheering thought with which to end a long day.

CHAPTER TWENTY

After leaving Orpen, Scott Ettley returned to his own apartment. He walked quickly, urgently, but the route he followed was as random and bewildered as his own mind. Orpen couldn't mean what he had said. It couldn't be true. Orpen had only been testing him, surely. Orpen was ill, crazy. . . . But what if Orpen did mean it? There, Ettley's thoughts stopped. Beyond that question, they could not reach out.

In his apartment, he changed his clothes, discarding his smart double-breasted grey suit for an inconspicuous brown tweed jacket, old flannels, a grey shirt and a plain brown tie. He was now driven by a cold excitement that steadied his nerves, made him feel alert and capable. As he dressed, he worked out a plan for reaching the west side in good time for the meeting. This was not a night on which to be late.

And then he set out. He walked towards Lexington, stopping at a drugstore for a quick sandwich and a cup of coffee. In spite of himself, he began thinking about Orpen again. So I owe everything to my father, he told himself. But do I? We'll see about that. His worry over Orpen changed to bitterness and anger. We'll see about that, he thought again, as he paid his cheque. He left the drugstore in a grim mood.

He walked half a block, his nondescript brown felt hat pulled well down over his brow. He lit a cigarette, and dropped the matches. As he bent to pick them up, he could look back along the street. There seemed to be just the usual crowd drawn out of doors by a hint of good weather on a spring evening. Certainly there was no one immediately behind him who could possibly be following him. Still, it was necessary to be careful. He was on his own to-night. From now on, he was definitely on his own. Yes, he admitted frankly then, Orpen had indeed meant what he said.

Did the Committee know about Orpen? Did Comrade Peter? Or was Ettley the first with this news? It was vital, of that there could be no doubt. Orpen must have held a key post in the Party. Jack proved that. Jack had been one of the leaders in Czechoslovakia, and it wasn't likely that Orpen

245

had worked so closely with him without being on the same high level. In that case, Ettley's report would be urgent.

Suddenly, Ettley's excitement left him. He was filled with a sense of shame, a sense of fear, as if Orpen were facing him, reading his thoughts.

No, he decided, I've no report on Orpen to make. That isn't my job. If Orpen is finished, then he is finished. I won't help in that.

A bus came lumbering down Lexington. He boarded it, counting out his small change. The door wheezed shut behind him, and then opened again with a resigned sigh as a man left on the sidewalk knocked sharply on its window. "You'll kill yourself yet," the driver warned the latecomer, who was red in the face, breathing heavily. "What's all the rush?" The bus started forward, the driver's bitter eye on the traffic lights which were about to change to red. The man, lurching suddenly with the abrupt start, let his money drop. He bent to pick it up, and all that Ettley noticed before he took a seat in the rear of the bus was a neat grey hat searching for a dime on the floor. "Rush, rush, rush, that's all people think of," the driver informed his load of passengers while he changed a dime with one hand, steered with the other, and watched the traffic ahead to gauge the lights he might be able to jump.

It was a quick ride. Ettley left the bus at Grand Central, and took a southbound subway to Fourteenth Street. There, he came above ground again and turned west along the broad sidewalk, making his way through the groups of window-shoppers eyeing the masses of cheap clothes so colourfully displayed under bright lights. He wasn't sure if he'd take a bus or a subway northwards again. But a bus was waiting at its terminus, with a crowd of people elbowing their way on board, and that decided him. He joined the crowd, and stepped on to the bus in the middle of a talkative group of men and women. Other people followed. By the time he had found a seat, the bus was full. This pleased him; safety in numbers, he thought. And he was pleased, too, when the bus travelled quickly through streets now practically deserted. For at this hour, there were no truckers from the garment district, no delivery vans, no crowds of jaywalkers forcing their way against the stream of traffic.

At Forty-second Street, he left the bus along with several other people, stepping off into a crowd that swallowed them up. He felt safe enough, as safe as he ever felt on this kind of trip. Better stop thinking about Orpen, though, he warned himself for the third time. Concentrate on yourself. He walked quickly, weaving his way under an awning of glaring lights through a crowded block of wandering pleasure-seekers. Times Square, with all its noise and movement and brilliance, was a good place to lose yourself. Then, satisfied with his care and adroitness, he slipped into a subway entrance and took the first express train uptown. When he left it, at Ninety-sixth Street, he had only a few blocks to walk southwards before he turned in the direction of Central Park. Thinking of the long journey, he congratulated himself on its speed and efficiency.

Before he turned east from upper Broadway, leaving behind the brightly lit movie houses and cafeterias, leaving the open-necked shirts and the mink stoles, leaving sidewalks where the older people sat at the doors of small shops and the voices spoke in foreign tongues, he halted at a delicatessen. Seemingly, he was admiring its rich display of lox and bagel, the golden plaited loaves, the bounteous bowls of potato salad and cole-slaw, the pyramids of cans and jars, the food boxes for abroad (You pay, We send, They get), the abundance of caviar and sour cream. But all his attention was focused on the quick glance he suddenly threw over his shoulder. Satisfied, he went on his way toward Amsterdam Avenue, where the names above the bars were now Irish, and small stores had Spanish signs advertising cheap travel from Puerto Rico.

The street he sought was a residential one where workers lived. Their cars, parked closely along the curb, shielded the sidewalks and discouraged tentative traffic on the street's narrowed width. Here, the tempo of city life had slowed down. Three boys played desultory baseball near one corner, two pretty Negro girls were setting out for a movie, a few children hopped and skipped and shared roller skates in front of their houses, one or two women sat at their doorsteps and watched the kids or gossiped, two or three men were passing by. It was a placid enough street, where most people were indoors watching television. A quiet street, a safe street.

The light was beginning to fade. The sun had set behind the Hudson River. And there was even a stiff breeze starting up from the west, bringing a breath of cool air.

Scott Ettley was glad of that. Whether it was the crowds through which he had travelled so quickly, or the hot glaring lights of Broadway, or the constant rush of traffic and noise through which he had passed, he felt uncomfortably warm. He mopped his face with his handkerchief, opened his jacket to let his sodden shirt dry. He halted at a closed laundry just after he had crossed Amsterdam Avenue. He still had a few minutes to wait, not enough time to walk around the block. In the laundry's sheltered doorway, he lit a cigarette. His hand, he noticed, was steady. Steadier than his thoughts. He forced them into a cold logical pattern. He would be businesslike, correct; he need not mention Orpen. That's not my job, he reminded himself again.

He threw away his unsmoked cigarette. Then as he buttoned his jacket over the damp shirt, he noted once more the number on the shop door. The address he wanted must lie in the middle of this block. He glanced at his watch and began walking, not looking at the houses, paying as little attention to the few people on the street as they paid to him. Then, in spite of his decision to keep unconcerned and calm, he felt his pulse quicken as he saw the house.

Like the others in this part of the street, it was a four-storied brownstone house with a row of steep steps leading over the basement area to the first floor. It was the first floor he wanted—a doctor's office, not distinguished by any name plate fixed permanently at the door, but with only a white card stuck in the window between the rain-streaked pane and its drawn shade.

It was exactly eight o'clock as Ettley walked quickly up the steps, stood in the deep entrance, and knocked on the ornamented glass pane of the door. He had been expected, for the door opened quietly and he was admitted into the dark hall. It was Martin, Thelma's "butler," who had opened the door. Now, without speaking, Martin led him into the first-floor apartment. The room they entered lay to the front of the house. Its windows were carefully shaded, its lights were crudely bright. Martin—or rather Bill, Bill's the name, Scott Ettley reminded himself—turned to face him.

248

He was looking very different from either the obsequious butler he had been last Sunday, or the genial conspirator of Monday night. Here was a third Bill, frowning, angry, nervous. Here was a man who was worried and suspicious. "So you did come," he said slowly.

Scott Ettley nodded. Obviously, he thought.

"He actually told you the time and place?"

Scott said, "Yes." And from these questions, and the way they had been put, he realised not only that Orpen's disaffection was already known, but that he himself was doubted by Bill and the others. And the whole picture changed, shifted its focus. He had hoped, in those last few minutes, that he could cut himself off from Orpen completely by forgetting him. But he couldn't. Nicholas Orpen's importance made his own silence impossible. There were—as Orpen himself would say—only two choices. He could choose either Orpen, or the Party. He might as well have spared himself all the arguments, all the worries which had accompanied him on the long journey here. No arguments were necessary. There was only the choice, and complete obedience to that choice.

Bill talked in a whispering voice, with quick glances over his shoulder at a closed door behind him. It was apparent that the meeting, in the room behind that door, was already in progress. And from Bill's narrow eyes, drawn with worry, it was equally apparent that the meeting was a serious one.

Were they discussing Orpen? Was he as important as that? Ettley felt the perspiration break over his forehead again.

Bill was repeating his question. "Did you see him?"

"Yes."

"He talked to you?"

Scott Ettley hesitated for a moment. Then he nodded.

"He won't come here to-night?" Bill's white face looked searchingly at Scott Ettley. Then he tightened his lips. "That means he is serious. He ought to have been here two hours ago. This is the third meeting in the last two days that he has refused. We've sent someone to see him; he pretends he isn't there. We've telephoned; he picks up the receiver quietly, he listens, but there's no answer." Bill shook his head slowly, uncomprehendingly. "This is a terrible thing," he said.

Ettley said, "I can't believe he is serious." But his voice lacked conviction.

"Comrade Peter will want a more definite answer than that." Bill's head turned again toward the closed door. Then, almost pathetically, he added, "But I can't believe it either. This is a terrible thing. Terrible. . . . Does he realise what"—again the head turned toward the door—"what may happen?"

Scott Ettley, who couldn't follow Bill's meaning, only looked blankly at the white face.

"There's too much of this," Bill said. "Too much. Doesn't he see that it must be stopped?"

Again the exact meaning escaped Ettley. Bill was afraid; that was all the meaning he could find. He's getting too old, Ettley thought. He's too old for any important job. "When did this trouble start anyway?" he asked. He nodded towards the other room.

Bill lowered his voice still more. "It's been going on. Hidden. But on Monday night, just after you left Thelma's, there was a bitter argument. On Tuesday,"—he looked at the door as if Comrade Peter's face was there, watching him—"on Tuesday there was an open disagreement on matters of policy." He pursed his lips, and once more he shook his head slowly. "Then there were other difficulties, too. Charles' death . . . and Thelma hysterical . . . and her apartment filled with insurance men investigating the windows—they've been all over the place, into every room . . . and reporters . . . and God knows what. Luckily, I got Comrade Peter out in time. But he doesn't place much confidence in Orpen's organising powers any more. Well—that's what happens when you trust a woman like Thelma and let Charles run all over the place."

Ettley said nothing at first. As far as he remembered, Orpen had objected to Charles' being in the apartment on Monday. It had been Bill's own negligence that had assumed Charles was as drunk as he pretended to be. But now Bill was saving himself. He, too, was making his choice. Then, on impulse, Ettley said, "That was Orpen's only defeat."

"One mistake can be enough if the timing is wrong." Bill looked at him shrewdly, waiting for further information. No doubt he knew more than Ettley about Orpen's successes. But he was interested now in finding out how indiscreet Orpen might have been with the younger man.

Ettley looked ignorant.

"And he's been making several mistakes recently," Bill went on. "There was Blackworth at *Trend*. There was Fremming in Hollywood, and Merlin in Chicago. Yes, they've all been fired from their jobs in the last month."

But there were others who hadn't been fired, Ettley thought. What about Wainway in Hollywood? Hadn't he just persuaded one of the major studios to let him make a picture on the Harlem slums? The story and its angle had been hand-picked by Orpen. And distribution of the film had already been guaranteed in Europe and Asia. Or what about Kensley? He had asked for a year's leave of absence from his Seattle job to write a book on the Korean problem. He had got the leave of absence and a grant, too, from an institute that subsidised deserving authors. The publisher had been picked by Orpen, just as the book's subject and title had been. Already it was being talked about as "the definitive account of Korea." Yes, there were plenty of successes still to be chalked up to Orpen's account.

Ettley couldn't resist saying, "How's Kensley's book coming along?"

"It will be published early in June," Bill said. Then he smiled. "But what made you think that was Orpen's idea?"

"Wasn't it? It seemed probable."

"Orpen only passed on the idea," Bill said. He looked at the closed door behind him and dropped his voice. "Comrade Peter wouldn't call it an idea, anyway. He'd call it a directive," he added, and the amusement left his face. He glanced at his watch and frowned, and his eyes were worried again. "Soon, now," he said almost to himself. He sat down on the dented arm of a battered mohair couch.

Isn't Bill allowed into the meeting? Ettley wondered. Has he been disciplined too? Here he is, playing office boy, keeping an eye on me, waiting to be summoned in his turn. Comrade Peter is a tough master. Yet that's what we need, we need toughness and discipline and strength; we don't want men who are corrupted. Then he glanced with a touch of contempt at Bill. He's gone fat and soft. His job was too easy. He was too sure of himself.

"What's your own news—good?" Bill asked suddenly.

Ettley nodded. On Monday, he would have reported it proudly. But to-night, he would keep it and tell it at the proper time, to the proper people.

Bill looked at him. His lips tightened. He said nothing more.

Ettley paced around the boxlike room. A cheap coloured print of the "Rape of the Sabine Women" hung on the yellowed plaster wall. At the windows, draggled lace curtains with holes adding to their openwork were stretched tightly over the dark green shades. Three naked bulbs clustered against the centre of the greyed ceiling. The mohair couch, its chequered pattern lost with years and grime, lay against one wall. Opposite, two high ill-assorted chairs were lined up like soldiers on parade. A small square of dingy rug lay apologetically in the middle of the room, making it still smaller. Any patient who came in to wait here for the doctor with the unpronounceable name on the window-card would feel twice as ill before he entered the consulting-room next door. Or did any doctor practice here? Looking at the film of dust on the cheap brown furniture, at the grimy floor, Ettley decided that no real doctor worked here or he would pass on more germs than he routed.

The connecting door half-opened. A man, tall, red-faced, dressed in a rough tweed jacket and grey flannel trousers, stood there, blocking any view of the dimly lit consulting-room behind him. He beckoned to Scott Ettley. Bill had risen to his feet, expectantly, but there was no signal for him.

Ettley looked back for a brief moment as he followed the stranger into the other room. Bill had settled back on the arm of the couch again. There was resignation on his face. There was also fear, now undisguised.

In the inner room, furnished in a miserable way to imitate a doctor's office, three men waited. A desk had been pulled out from the wall to serve as a table. Its single lamp seemed to give more light in the direction of an empty chair than it did to the rest of the room. The red-faced man who had acted as messenger took his place silently beside the others. Four faces, grave and watchful, turned toward Ettley. "Sit down," the red-faced man said, and gestured to the empty chair.

Ettley waited for Comrade Peter to speak. And when he did, it was obvious that he was in control. The pretences of Monday had been discarded. Now, his voice came cold and clear from the shadowed side of the warm room. As he questioned he smoked continuously, holding his cigarette in his curious way, his eyes half-closed, his head tilted back as he waited for the answers.

Ettley kept them businesslike, factual. He talked only about himself, about his father's reactions, about his future with the *Clarion*. Never again, he thought determinedly, would the criticism of "sentimental nonsense" have to be flung at him. He had learned a lot since his last meeting with this man called Peter. Now, as he gave exact answers to the brief searching questions, he began to feel his confidence returning. He could even notice a chart of a skeleton hanging near Comrade Peter's shoulder and the decrepit examining table on which hats and coats had been thrown. And he could sense that the men who listened so carefully were pleased with his report. The sudden note of approval in the grave voice of the man called Peter was the highest praise of all. Ettley, as he listened to his further instructions and repeated them carefully, had never felt so sure, so capable, so completely in control of his emotions. It was an intoxicating moment—this moment of alertness, of understanding and confidence.

And it was then that Peter, lighting another long cigarette, suddenly asked about Orpen. When had Ettley last seen Orpen? And why? And how?

There could be no change in Ettley's way of answering, no change which wouldn't be noted by the four quiet faces watching him so intently. And without any hesitation, any alteration in voice or expression, he answered. It was, he told himself, all a part of this efficient examination. Even when he was asked to give a full report on his meeting to-day with Orpen, he kept the same cold objectivity and repeated Orpen's words accurately. For this was a moment when all private emotions must be forgotten. Orpen was not to be judged as a friend in this room; here, he was only being judged as the renegade. Too much was at stake.

"And that was the last remark he made?" prompted the red-faced man, glancing at Peter as if he were speaking for him.

"Yes," Scott Ettley said. "When I asked him what he was going to do, he replied 'I don't know.' That was all he said. And I left."

The four men looked at each other, and then they seemed to avoid looking at each other. At that split moment, some decision—perhaps already argued—was made.

Peter cleared his throat. That would be all, Ettley was told. His instructions were clear? He would destroy all evidence of his Party membership? He would only use his new contact in the gravest emergencies?

Yes. Everything was clear.

Then, as he opened the door, there was a quick interchange of sentences, something about Orpen; but it was spoken too low for Ettley to hear. "Wait in the outside room," a voice called after him. And the man who had brought him into the consulting-room rose to follow him to the door. This time, the man's signal was for Bill.

"We've a decision to make," the man was saying to Bill as he closed the door behind them.

Scott Ettley, wondering what it was, feeling a nervousness which surprised him, knew one definite thing at least. Whatever this decision was, Bill would certainly agree with it. His vote, if a vote was taken, would be cast on Comrade Peter's side. Bill had learned a few things himself since Monday night, and he had learned them principally in this dismal room while he waited. But what had made him so afraid?

Waiting in his turn, Ettley's nervousness increased. Had he said something that was wrong, done something wrong? No, he thought as he went over his reports, first about the reactions of his father, about his job on the *Clarion*, then about Orpen, no, there was nothing there that was weak or inefficient. Nothing. There had only been one difficult moment, when Scott had had to explain to Comrade Peter that he couldn't possibly step into any job of major im-

254

portance in the *Clarion* even if his father did own it, that he had to begin in a position that was credible and work his way up toward the top. But he had explained as tactfully as he could. The others in the room had helped Scott by saying yes, that was the way things were worked. "In a capitalist bourgeois democracy?" Peter had asked angrily, scornfully. But in a moment, as he eyed the embarrassed look on their faces, he had said, "Very well, very well," with a rough good humour, and he had gestured to Scott to continue. And afterward, he had been approving. So that awkward moment had been forgotten.

But what else, then?

Ettley wished he could raise a window, let some fresh air into this room. He wished he could walk out of that door, out into the cool dark street. What was keeping him here? He had been given his instructions.

When the door opened at last, it was Bill who entered. Decision had returned to his movements, but his eyes were still tight with worry. Perhaps it was his own fear, hidden now, that made his voice harsh, uncompromising.

"You have a job to do," he said.

Ettley said, "I've been given my instructions."

"Here are additional instructions," Bill said, and the furrow between his eyebrows deepened. "You are to phone Orpen. Tell him you did not come here to-night. Tell him you've been trying to think it out, tell him you don't know what to do. Ask him to meet you, to talk to you."

"What if he won't come?"

"You must see that he does. If you are upset enough, he will come." Suddenly the voice lost its sharp edge. "You are someone he is very fond of. You know that?"

Ettley nodded. Too fond, he thought bitterly.

Bill said, "So we depend on you. Can we?"

Ettley stared at the grim white face. He nodded.

"Good. Telephone Orpen to-night. At midnight. Tell him you are calling from a drugstore on Lexington near Fifty-ninth Street. Tell him you'll wait for him at that corner, at the northwest corner."

"Then what?"

"The entrance to the I.R.T. subway will be just beside you. Take him down there to get a train to Grand Central. Tell

255

him you are leaving New York. Tell him you need his advice."

"Yes?"

"That's all." The voice was harsh again. "You've no more to do. Others will take over, then."

Scott Ettley moistened his lips. His eyes held more fear in them, now, than Bill's did. And he turned to stare at the closed door.

Bill said, looking at his watch, "It is now eight forty-seven. At twelve, you make the telephone call. I'll be waiting near Orpen's house. After he leaves, I'll enter. I'll make sure that he has no valuable information lying around."

"But what if Orpen won't meet me?" There was almost hope in Ettley's voice.

"Make sure he does." Bill's hand grasped Ettley's arm, steadying him. "What is Orpen's next move? He will betray us all. In his bitterness, he will betray us. He knows so much that—Ettley, listen to me!" His voice was low, urgent. "Do we matter? Does any one of us matter?"

"No," Scott said. "No. But he won't betray the Party. He's still loyal. He may break with us, but he won't betray what he knows."

"Loyal? After what he told you this evening? After what you told them, in there?" He jerked his head toward the other room. "We have to act at once. At once, before he can attract any publicity and safeguard himself. Any delay, and he may start giving out information. Any delay, and he may start infecting others with his doubts and heresies. If you can't see the danger he is creating for us, then he has already infected you. Has he?"

"No." Scott Ettley dragged his arm away from the other man's grip. "No," he said roughly.

"You and I must prove our loyalty. Don't you see?" Then Bill turned to look at the closed door once more. He said warningly, "This is the decision of Comrade Peter, backed by the unanimous vote of the Committee. They are now waiting for me to return. A delay means an argument with you. An argument means divided loyalty and doubts."

Ettley picked up his hat and began to leave the room. Bill followed him, speaking hurriedly and insistently. He was talking as though persuading himself. "Others have done what he is planning to do. And they've driven us under-

256

ground. Yet Orpen could do more damage than they did to us. He knows more than they did. We can take no chances. A traitor in thought becomes a traitor in action."

They entered the dimly lit hall. Bill's hand held Scott Ettley's arm, and they stood together motionless. From a room far upstairs, came the crying of a child. Then silence. Bill nodded, satisfied, and moved quickly toward the front door. "You know what you have to do," Bill whispered. "A phone call. That's all."

"Yes," Scott Ettley said, and it seemed to be another man who was speaking. He heard the door close quietly behind him. The dark, empty street lay ahead of him. A telephone call. A meeting between two friends. That was all.

And if he didn't obey Peter's order?—His connection with the Party would be severed. His future was over. And he would be exposed. His father, his friends would be allowed to find out why he had wanted to join the *Clarion*. There were other things, too, that they could learn about him. According to their standards, he had been a liar, a cheat, a traitor. But he didn't belong to their standards. He didn't belong to their world. There was no future with them.

He pulled his hat farther down over his brow, and began walking toward Amsterdam Avenue. His decision returned, wavered, returned. He had given his answer. He had said yes obediently. Obedience was all that mattered. Obedience was everything. Obedience and discipline.

The man in the neat dark suit pushed his grey felt hat back off his forehead. He ran a thumbnail across his brow, and went on telephoning.

"Sure," he was saying, "he's well trained. He's worth following. Honest guys don't go doubling on their tracks. He gave me quite a chase. From the garage, I followed him back to his own apartment—at least, he changed his clothes there. Then he ate at a drugstore on Lexington, took a bus to Grand Central, subway to Fourteenth, moved westward on foot, came back uptown by bus, Forty-second Street, subway to upper Broadway. Walked south, then east by Amsterdam. Waited in the doorway of a laundry until a minute before eight o'clock. At eight, he went into a house—no waiting, then—expected, I'd say. Here's the address . . . worth watching. That was my first headache. We had travelled through the city so fast that I couldn't ask for extra help. And when he went into that house, I was stuck. Couldn't leave to phone. All I could do was wait until he came out again. At eight fifty-three, he left and walked toward Amsterdam. He wasn't paying attention to anything then. He went into a bar near the corner of the avenue. O'Flannigan's. He talked to no one. He lowered three Scotches. Sure, three. He sat there for about twelve minutes. He kept looking at his watch. He ordered another drink, but he didn't touch it, just sat looking at it. I moved to the phone, keeping an eye on him. Then suddenly he threw some money down on the bar, and walked out of the door right into a taxi that had pulled up for a red light. There wasn't another cab in sight. That's how I lost him. At fourteen after nine. Well, here's the taxi's number, anyway. . . . And the address of his apartment. . . . And his description. . . . Got that? Yes, better read it back."

As he listened, he pushed his hat farther back on his head and then pulled it over his brow. "Yeah, that's it," he said at last. "That's it," he said, wearily.

CHAPTER TWENTY-ONE

Ten o'clock. Rona pushed aside the books and drafting paper on her desk. Work was impossible to-night; she was restless and unsettled. She rose impatiently and then hesitated, looking round the living-room. I've been too happy here, she thought: that makes it all the lonelier now.

She began clearing away the books, folding the newspapers, emtying the ash trays. She switched on the small radio and found a Chopin programme. Then she went over to the windows, pulling the curtains aside to let the cool breeze blow into the room. She stood there and looked at the night. Across the street, the windows were lit and disarmingly open to view. The man who favoured red suspenders was working at his desk. Next door, in a blue and yellow bathroom, a thin little blonde dressed in scant pink brassiere and panties was rinsing out some stockings. In the room below, a woman slumped in a comfortable arm-chair and dangled a bare foot in a bright green sandal.

All right, Rona admitted, you're unhappy. Because you're lonely. Because you're afraid of all the Friday evenings stretching ahead of you with this quiet ten o'clock emptiness. But there's got to be an end to it. No one can help you out of this, except yourself. You have a life to live, and you are the only person who can live it. You are what you make yourself. Each decision, each action you choose to follow makes you or unmakes you. Each time you say "yes" or "no," you make yourself—you, the real you that is buried deep inside.

It is as easy as that, Rona Metford. As easy as that, and as difficult.

She turned away from the window, and she caught a glimpse of her white face in the mirror above the fireplace. "Don't look so damned sorry for yourself, either!" she said aloud. She stared at her reflection for a few moments, and then she had to smile. She began to laugh. People were always so ridiculous when they admired themselves as tragic characters. Sure, we're all tragic, she told herself. And all sort of comic, too. She felt the better for her sudden laughter. The intensity of the last minutes vanished, and the sense of being alone was not so terrifying.

Next week, she thought, I'll start seeing people again. I'll be able to face them better if I just give myself a few more days. But now, there was an hour to put in before she'd even feel like drifting to bed. She'd read a chapter of Flaubert. He always made a good escort.

She switched on the reading-lamp beside the couch, opened a fresh pack of cigarettes, picked up *Salammbo* and settled a cushion comfortably behind her shoulders. For a long moment, the book lay unopened on her knees. She was looking at the night sky again. From here, it was framed neatly by the rectangle of the window opposite her. All she could see now was the black flat roof of the house across the street, its private lives hidden under the sharp shadow of its water tower. Behind the bold silhouette, were the solid and slender and further masses of higher buildings, climbing into the darkness.

Their lighted windows, small at this distance, seemed to hang in the sky in orderly rows as bright as the stars and as steadfast. They were real, yet they had all the unreality of beauty like a carefully decorated Christmas tree. They were part of the city, these lights, and they were aloof from the city. At their feet, the steady surge of sound ebbed and flowed; but they reached into the quietness of the cool sky and became as remote, untouchable.

She had only begun to read when the doorbell rang. Rona ignored it at first. Someone's made a mistake, she thought irritably, turning another page and concentrating determinedly on the vivid detail of Flaubert's story.

But the bell rang again. And again.

She laid the book aside, and switched off the radio. There was an urgency in the bell that quickened her movements. She went swiftly into the hall and released the lock of the street door. Then she half-opened her apartment door, and waited. She felt an unexpected nervousness. The footsteps on the stairs, mounting toward her, were hurried and heavy. A man's footsteps. She pushed the door until it was only a few inches open, and she hooked the chain that was attached to the wall on to its latch above the handle. Then she stood, hesitating, wondering, puzzled. She was half-ashamed of her admission of fear, half-annoyed at her stupidity in opening the street door at all.

The footsteps reached her landing. The door was thrust open, but it held on the chain. Scott's voice said, "Rona!— Rona!"

She stared at the straining chain. Then slowly, telling herself it was folly to start what had ended, slowly she said, "Just a moment."

"Rona! Please!"

She opened the door, and he pushed his way inside the hall, turning to face her, his hand on the wall to steady himself. His face was white and haggard, his eyes deep in their sockets and larger. He had loosened his tie. He dropped his hat on the telephone table, and he didn't even notice it when it slipped to the floor. Then he closed his eyes, the wildly staring eyes, perhaps to shut out the look of amazement on

Rona's face. He rubbed his forehead for a moment, and when his hand dropped to his side he had regained his control. He lifted his hand again, this time to smooth his hair. Then he gave a smile as he tightened the knot of his tie back into position. "I was afraid you weren't going to let me in," he said.

His voice was almost normal. Almost. He frowned, controlling his face. Then he looked around him with something of bewilderment, as if he were asking himself why he had come here.

But his words were a lie, Rona knew. His fear, whatever caused it, was a real fear. It was with him now. His words were only an excuse for his appearance, a cover to hide his embarrassment. Why had he come here? The hope which had risen in her heart as she had heard his urgent voice turned to cold disappointment. Her cheeks flushed, her step forward was halted, her impulsive embrace died before it could live, her words were stifled.

Instead, she heard her voice—troubled and practical—saying, "What's wrong, Scott?"

What's wrong? That was the question he had asked of Orpen. Only five hours ago he had asked that question, and now its echo came to mock him.

"Nothing is wrong," he said angrily. He pushed himself away from the wall and stood more erect. He looked at the door. "Oh, God!" His voice broke down. He turned away abruptly and walked into the living-room.

Rona's amazement gave way to alarm. She followed him slowly, giving him time to regain himself.

He had sat down on the couch. He had picked up *Salammbô* and was idly turnng over its pages. He seemed normal once more.

He looked up to see her standing hesitating in the doorway. "Haven't read this since I was a kid," he said. "Do you still like this kind of stuff?"

Rona took her cue from him. I always seem to take my cue from Scott, she thought wryly. That's the only way to deal with Scott—on his own terms. She came into the room, picked up the pack of cigarettes, offered him one and handed him a matchbox. She said, "Yes, I enjoy it. It's good escape."

"Escape?" His voice was bitter, amused. Escape in reading about Carthage described by a French realist in a romantic mood?

"Well, let's say it's my way of keeping a balance," Rona said quietly.

"Have you a drink?" he asked suddenly. "It's hot to-night. And I've been walking. I took a taxi first, and then I walked God knows where. Round and round this block, I guess. I saw your lighted window. You were standing there. I went away. Then I found myself back at your door. And I rang the bell."

She looked at him worriedly.

"I know," he said angrily, "I know. I've had a couple of drinks. Another won't do any harm."

She left the room, then, to get the ice and soda water. "I've only got some blended whisky," she said when she returned, keeping her voice calm and detached, her face smiling. The polite hostess. Ridiculous, she thought. . . . She felt sudden tears in her eyes, stinging them hotly. She was watching Scott, and she was watching a stranger. A stranger she knew so well that she could read each gesture, each expression, each tone of voice. She could read them all, and she could understand none of them.

"Thanks," he said taking the glass, drinking quickly. "I needed that. My nerves are all shot to hell." Then he looked up at her. "Rona," he said gently. It was the first time he had used her name since he had entered the apartment. He said it almost pityingly. "We've made a mess of things, haven't we?"

She nodded.

His face tightened. He looked away from her, down at the book which he had dropped on the coffee table. He placed his empty glass beside it. "Escape . . ." he said. "So that's how you keep your balance, Rona." A smile flickered over his face. He looked around the room. "Neat, peaceful, orderly. A well-arranged life. Everything that doesn't fit is discarded. Everything that spoils it is thrown out. Like cigarette stubs. Torn-up letters. Old magazines. Is that all I am, Rona?—Something that doesn't fit any more, something to be thrown out of your life?"

She didn't answer at first.' At last she said, "Did you come here to—to make me still more unhappy?"

"Why do you keep looking at me like that?" he countered.

"I'm trying to find out why you came to see me."

He stared back at her. "God knows," he said wearily. "Isn't it enough if I'm still in love with you?"

"Yes," she said slowly. "That would have been enough."

"You don't believe I am?"

"I don't know, any more. I don't know."

I don't know. . . . Words repeated less than two hours ago, repeated honestly, repeated damningly. But how could I guess, Ettley was thinking, how could I guess they were so damning? People said, "I don't know," and that was the end of questioning. But no one could say, "I don't know," to Comrade Peter. Only the positive could live. The negative mind was the enemy, the potential traitor.

"You don't know," he repeated softly. "But you go on living."

She turned her head and looked out of the window, if only to avoid watching his face. He needs me, she was thinking, or he wouldn't have come here.

"Still admiring the view?" he asked. He went forward to the window. He stood for a moment looking out on the city. "Every time I've come here, you've looked at that pyramid of cement as if it were made of diamonds. That's what it is, a pyramid of diamonds, a cenotaph built on men's blood and men's hopes." He turned away and came back to the couch. "Yes," he was saying, "it is easy to be well balanced if you look at the pretty things and ignore the cruelty beside them. All you allow yourself to see is the stars in the sky, Rona. That's the way. Keep your eyes fixed on the stars and you can escape." He pointed suddenly to the lighted windows outside. "But do you think of what they hide? Beyond those lights are filthy slums, ugliness, and squalor. Below them, are garbage cans and sewers. Do you remember that, too?" He shook his head, "You don't, Rona. You don't."

She looked at him curiously. "What's wrong with you, Scott?"

"Yes," he said, "that's all you can say. . . . I tell you about injustice and all you can say is 'What's wrong with you?' That's what's wrong with all of you, Rona,"

"All of me?" She was trying to smile, trying to make a small joke.

But he didn't smile. He was looking at her almost accusingly.

"What am I supposed to symbolise? All the evils of civilisation?" she asked, still trying to keep her voice light. "Oh, Scott—this is fantastic. You look out of a window and see a prosperous city and you are plunged in gloom. Then you talk as if people like me had no imagination, no sympathy at all. As if we didn't realise that those roofs covered a lot of differences—people who are miserable, people who are carefree, people who are hungry as well as people who are overfed, people who are planning holidays and parties, people who are planning theft and murder."

He stared at her. His face was expressionless. He sat motionless. Suddenly, he buried his head in his hands.

"Scott!" She rose and came over to him. She knelt beside him, taking his hands, trying to pull them gently down from his face. "Scott, what's wrong? Tell me. Perhaps that is all you need—to tell someone. You didn't come up here to argue with me, did you? Or read me a lesson?"

"No," he said, raising his head at last. He looked round the peaceful room, the secure little room, and then his eyes rested on Rona. "I came here to—to argue with myself. I trust you, Rona. You are the only person I can trust." He touched her shoulder, and slowly his grip tightened until his fingers sank to the bone and she flinched with pain. Then, suddenly, he let go. He rose, pushing her away from him. He walked over to the window. He pulled the curtains roughly together.

"Scott," she asked imploringly, "what is wrong?"

"Don't ask questions, don't ask any questions," he said sharply. "You must trust me, Rona, as I trust you."

She said nothing.

He was watching the expression on her face. "I've only done what is right," he said slowly.

"Then . . ." She looked at him helplessly.

"Then I have nothing to worry about?" He was angry again, angry with his own weakness. "Where's that glass?" he asked, and found it, and poured himself another drink.

"It's all right," he said bitterly, "I am not drunk." He walked over to the fireplace. His stride was steady enough, but his hand shook a little and he placed the glass on the mantelpiece almost too carefully.

He had stood there so often, Rona was thinking, even as he was standing now. Unconsciously, he had fallen into the same old attitude, his head bowed, one elbow resting on the mantelpiece, one hand smoothing his hair. But his face held an expression she had never seen before. He had the look of a man trying to escape, of a man seeing no escape. Oh, Scott, she said to herself, what is happening to you? But she kept silent. Her lips trembled. For the second time that night, her eyes were stung by hot tears. Scott Ettley looked up at that moment, looked at her face. She turned her head quickly away, but not quickly enough.

"Rona!" he said impulsively, and he took a step forward. For a moment his face softened, his eyes were filled with compassion and anguish. Then he checked himself. "No," he said. "No!" He stood there, quite still, as if the effort to master himself had left him lifeless.

I should never have come here, he was thinking. It was madness to come. And why did I? To get strength, to find reassurance. But I've only weakened myself. All I want to say is, "Rona, leave everything, come away with me, to-night, to-morrow we'll go. To Mexico, Canada. There's Brazil, there's the whole of America. We'll begin again. We'll escape." But there's no escape. Escape is weakness, escape is a delusion haunted by fears.

He said, "Do you still love me, Rona?" He waited for the answer, hoping for it, steeling himself against it. The moment of delusion and weakness was over. He could thrust his hand into the flame and watch it burn.

But the answer did not come. Instead, she said unhappily, "It isn't easy to break old loyalties."

"Loyalties . . ." he said slowly. "Is that all you feel for me?" Then his voice quickened and grew bitter. "And when would you break them? To-night? To-morrow? But you would call that treachery, wouldn't you?"

"Treachery?" She was startled.

"Wouldn't you?" he insisted.

"Treachery is a pretty strong word, Scott. It depends on—well, on what inspires your loyalties."

"My loyalties?"

"I was using the word 'your' in a general way," she said patiently. "*Anyone*'s loyalties, Scott." I can't bear this, she thought. I can't sit here and watch Scott kill our love, adding pain on pain. Yet I have to wait, I have to let him talk in this savage bitter way. He needs help. I can't turn him away.

She glanced at the clock and his eyes followed hers. It was almost half-past ten. He looked down at his wrist watch.

"No," she said gently, "the clock isn't slow. It's always on time."

"On time," he repeated. He wasn't speaking to her. Then he said quickly, urgently, "Go on, Rona."

"Go on?"

"When is treachery? When isn't it?"

"But Scott——"

"Go on!"

She hesitated, trying to remember what she had been saying. "Well," she began, "I suppose you can shift from some loyalties without betraying them. I mean, if you—if someone finds that he has been loyal to a delusion, then I wouldn't call it treachery when he sees his mistake and admits it. If he stayed loyal to something that was false, knowing it was false, then he would only start betraying himself."

Scott Ettley shook his head, as if that wasn't the answer he had wanted. He walked slowly across the room and poured himself another drink. Rona watched him anxiously.

"Scott," she began, but again he drank quickly and then stared down at the empty glass in his hand.

"Scott, let's have a walk. It's cooler outside. This room gets so——"

"But what if this man betrays something that is good?" Scott demanded. He turned to face her, and he brushed against a small table almost upsetting it. His voice had thickened. He spoke harshly. "What if—what if he betrays something good?" He laid the empty glass down on the desk, as if he had decided to drink no more. He walked away from it. "Rona, you aren't answering me."

"But I don't know what this man has betrayed," she said. "What is it? Friendship or—or love? Or his country?"

"Is that all you see in life, is that all?" He spoke contemptuously. He began to laugh.

266

She said angrily, "The only answers I can give are very simple. I know that. But does that make them false?"

He didn't seem to hear her words. He was saying, "To-night—to-night a man was condemned. As a traitor. He is a traitor. I know him. He has been my friend. Yet he is a traitor."

She was suddenly afraid. She couldn't explain why. She said, "Condemned? But, Scott, we don't execute traitors. Certainly not in peacetime. We don't even send them to the salt mines."

He stared at her for a moment. Then he looked at the clock again. Twenty-five minutes to eleven. Too little time to think, too much time to wait. But why had they chosen him? So that there would be no turning back, ever? Didn't they trust him? He was loyal, he had given them every proof. But this one last proof was too much to ask, too much. Didn't they see that? Yes, they did. That was why they had demanded it. That was why he must give it. The impossible proof was the final proof. By this, he would be measured. By this, he could measure himself.

He said, "To betray a traitor is not treachery. Is it, Rona? And if he dies, then no one is to blame."

She was watching him uneasily. She was trying to control her rising fears. "Has this man been tried and found guilty?"

"Yes. He is guilty." That, at least, was clear and becoming clearer.

"Is he already dead?" she asked suddenly. "And you are tormenting yourself by thinking you might have helped him as a friend? Is it Charles, Scott? But Charles wasn't a traitor. Please believe me, Scott. . . . Charles wasn't a traitor."

"Charles?" he asked, coming slowly back from his long journey. "Charles?"

"I sometimes wonder if they killed him. In a sense, they did."

"Who are 'they'?" He took a step forward, watching her face.

"I don't know," she said in sudden panic.

"No," he said slowly, "it isn't Charles I'm talking about."

He turned and walked toward the door. "I can't think straight. I was a fool to come here. I've only upset you." Then he halted, still as uncertain in his movements as in his thoughts. "That walk you mentioned," he said. "Are you coming?" Our last walk together, he thought, my last piece of sentimental nonsense.

She watched the pain and hopelessness in his face. He can't go alone, she thought, not like this. "Yes," she said. "I'll come if you want me to. But have you time? It's nearly a quarter of eleven." She rose and went into the bedroom.

"Time? Why shouldn't I have time?" He had followed her. He was standing at the door, looking around the green and white bedroom as if he were remembering. Kill the memories, he told himself. Memories are bad for you, Ettley; kill them and be free. He looked at the girl combing her dark soft hair before the mirror. Her arms were slender and white. Was she remembering, too?

She was saying, "I thought you must have an appointment to-night." Then she saw his face in the mirror. "You kept looking so anxiously at the clock," she explained, sensing that she had made some mistake. As she watched him, her fear grew. Fear for him. Not fear for herself.

"I haven't got any appointment," he said, his voice rising abruptly. Then just as abruptly he turned away and walked towards the front door.

She listened to his footsteps in the hall. Something is so far wrong, she thought, that I can't even begin to understand it.

In the hall, the door opened and closed.

She picked up her coat and her purse. She ran after him. As she shut the door, the telephone rang. She paid no attention. "Scott," she called, "wait!"

Outside the house, he braced himself. "This is better," he said, looking at the dark silent street, feeling the cool night air on his brow. He paused for a few moments and gripped the railing. He breathed deeply. "That's better," he said. He began walking, not too steadily. Behind him he heard running footsteps.

He halted as she caught up with him.

"You aren't running away from me to-night," he said. "Where's your temper, Rona? Where's your pride?" Then he walked on, without waiting for an answer, plunging along the dark street as if he saw nothing ahead of him. She followed him.

"Why did you come?" he asked truculently, his pace quickening.

"I thought you needed help," she said simply.

"Oh, so this is your night for pity."

"Please, Scott!"

"You thought you would walk me round a couple of blocks and sober me up? And that would solve everything?" he asked mockingly.

"I don't think that would solve anything."

The quiet answer seemed to pacify him. He said something which she couldn't hear, perhaps wasn't intended to hear. His pace increased so that she had to hurry to keep up with him. She hadn't had time yet to put on her coat.

They crossed Lexington and then Park. At Madison, the lights were against them, and he turned impatiently to walk up the avenue. He stared straight ahead of him, his eyes fixed on nothing. He paid no attention to the bright shop windows, or to the people who passed by. Yet he was walking purposefully, as if he knew where he was going. They crossed Fifty-ninth Street, still following Madison Avenue, still hurrying blindly northward along blocks that were now quieter, darker.

"This is better," he said again, as they neared Sixty-fifth Street. His head had cleared; he was in control of himself once more. "You'll catch cold," he told her, stopping abruptly, helping her to put on her coat. Then they were walking on, once more. But the furious pace had slackened. The direction seemed less decided, too. At Sixty-seventh Street, he hesitated and then crossed the avenue. There, he hesitated again. Rona glanced at him, and he was quick to notice. "You can stop worrying," he said, "I'm all right now." A smile flickered over his grim, unhappy face. He began walking westward.

"Scott," Rona said impulsively, "why don't you go home and get some sleep? To-morrow, you could see Jon Tyson. Or is your father in town? He could help you."

"No," he said harshly. "And I don't need help."

"What about Nicholas Orpen?" she asked. It was an admission of her defeat.

"Orpen," he repeated blankly. For a moment he halted. "What made you say Orpen?"

269

"He's your friend."

"What made you say Orpen?"

"Perhaps he could help you. That's all I meant."

"But you hate Orpen."

"I've distrusted him. He's a twisted man. I was always afraid of what he could do to you. Perhaps I was jealous of him." She tried to smile. It was a complete failure, disguising nothing.

"You hate him and yet you'd send me to ask his advice. No, Rona. Tell me the truth."

"After all," she said wearily, "you always defended him when I criticised him. So I suppose there's some good in him, even if I can't see it."

They had come to Fifth Avenue, and it was she who stopped now. They stood on the broad sidewalk under the lighted windows of a large apartment house. Across the avenue, there was only the darkness of Central Park, trees massed in heavy shadows, paths lighted by lamps that seemed overpowered by its enormous secrecy.

"I'm tired, Scott." She glanced down the avenue, stretched before her like a brilliant empty stage waiting for the play to begin, and then back at the quiet street which had brought them here. It was already asleep. A few parked cars. A man, who walked slowly. A speeding taxi. That was all. This part of the city seemed strangely lonely at night as if the silence of the Park reached out beyond its walls. "Which way? Down Fifth?" she asked.

But Scott didn't move. He was watching her face. "What did I say in your apartment?" he asked quietly.

"Nothing. Nothing I could understand."

"What did I say about Orpen?"

"Nothing."

He mastered his anger. He took her arm, grasping it firmly, leading her across Fifth Avenue. "We can talk here," he said, and he made toward the entrance to the Park.

"It's silly to walk there at night." She tried to draw him back from the entrance. "We can talk just as well out on the avenue."

"Afraid?" he asked. "What are you afraid of? Thieves in the shadows?"

"Scott, it must be after eleven o'clock. We'd better——"

"Isn't this one of your favourite places?" he asked bitterly. "You think it's so perfect because it's pretty to look at! You don't trust it, do you? In spite of all your fine words, you don't trust it." Then he stared over his shoulder, looking across the avenue, back along Sixty-seventh Street. His hand tightened on her arm. "Is that man following us?" His eyes narrowed.

She turned to look. The man she had noticed a few moments ago was almost at the corner opposite them now. "He's only searching for an address," she said, watching his movements.

"He was outside your house when I rang your bell. He passed me as I waited," Scott said quickly. "That was an hour ago."

"You're imagining things. Why should anyone follow us?"

"Quick, this way!"

"Scott, are you in some danger?" That would explain everything. Everything.

For his answer, he hurried her down the steps into the Park. "This way," he said, urging her on.

"Let's keep to the lighted paths, Scott."

"This way!" Scott said, looking back over his shoulder as they started to climb a hill. "Yes, there he is—entering the Park now." He pulled her roughly behind a group of rocks. Trees shadowed them. A thicket of bushes half-encircled them. She stumbled on the uneven ground as they ran. The lighted path was shut from view. Here, there was only darkness.

Scott let go of her arm. She couldn't see his face clearly. It, too, was lost in the shadows. "What did I say about Orpen?" he asked in a cold hard voice.

She stared through the darkness. "That man who was following us—you lied. He wasn't following us. You lied to get me here."

"I've *got* to talk to you. Listen to me! What did I tell you to-night in your apartment?"

"And I'm getting good and mad," she said bitterly. She moved away, but her heel twisted on a loose stone and a thorn branch tore her leg. She stopped. "Scott Ettley, you brought me here. Now take me out of it. I can't even see properly."

271

"I want to know what I said to you to-night. For God's sake, tell me!"

"Don't you remember, or is this more play-acting?"

"I must have told you something," he said grimly. "I've got to know."

"You talked of treachery. Of a man condemned to death." Her eyes were not yet accustomed to the blackness around her. She made a careful step, and then another. The ground was rough and treacherous; her foot slipped on an outcrop of rock. "Oh, let's get out of here!"

He didn't move. "To death?" he asked.

"I can't remember exactly. You said 'condemned,' I know. . . . But doesn't that mean death?"

He still didn't move. An animal rustled in the bushes behind her. The trees stirred in the night breeze.

And then she knew. She said slowly, "Is Orpen the traitor?"

She waited, but he didn't speak. "A traitor to what?" she asked fearfully. She was remembering Scott's words in her living-room. Suddenly, sense came out of them. A sense that was nonsense. It's the darkness, she thought, this blackness that blots us out. I'm afraid. I'm afraid of everything. She turned to run.

An arm caught her neck, choking her. A knee twisted her body to the ground, forcing her over on her back. "Scott!" she tried to scream, but the hand that fell over her mouth wasn't Scott's. She struggled violently. A strange rough voice said, "She's a wildcat," and someone behind her laughed. "More fight than he has," the laughing voice said.

She let herself fall limp. Then she bit the hand that held her lips, bit savagely and screamed as it fell away from her mouth for a brief moment. The man cursed and tightened his grip on her throat. Someone had seized her arms, pinning them back to the ground. There was a weight on her legs that she couldn't shift. The smell of sweet hair oil and rancid sweat suffocated her.

And then, suddenly, there was a shot. Shots repeated, echoing, splitting the shadows. A cry of warning. The weight was lifted from her body. The hands had left her. Feet were running. Shouts. A whistle blew, piercing, shrill.

She lay in the darkness, crying. Then she sat up slowly.

Someone helped her. A man said kindly, "You're all right now. You're safe. Take it easy. Easy. That's it."

"Sick—I feel sick," she said. The smell of hair oil and sweat, the groping hands . . .

"Take it easy," the man's voice said gently. And then, later, "Now, here's your coat." He tried to fasten the torn coat round her bare shoulders. "You're all right now," he said again. He waited until she had covered herself, and then he switched on a flashlight, turning the beam away from her.

"Scott . . ." she said. "Scott?"

"He's all right, too," the voice said, but there was a subtle change in it. Slowly, painfully, she looked up. Scott was sitting near her, motionless, his head bowed, his face covered by his hands.

Then she looked at the stranger who knelt beside her. His grey hat was pushed to the back of his head, his dark-browed face was watching her anxiously.

A clatter of feet came over the rocks, and a man in filthy tattered clothes appeared, carrying a heavy flashlight and Rona's handbag.

"Don't worry. He's a disguised cop," the man beside her said. "He's the one who fired the shot."

"We got one. The other two we'll get later," the Park policeman said. "They dropped this." He held up the handbag, smiling reassuringly. "Guess they didn't have enough time to take anything." He turned the light he carried on Scott Ettley. "Next time you want some necking stay where it's safe, will you?"

"Yes," the man beside Rona said. "If she hadn't screamed, we'd never have reached her."

Scott Ettley raised his head and stared at him. "So you were following me?" he said.

"I wasn't following you a goddamned bit," the man said. He glanced at Rona, and helped her to rise. "Okay?" he asked her, steadying her.

She nodded.

"That's the way," the man said encouragingly. Goddammit, he thought, I nearly mucked up this assignment. Keep an eye on her, they said. So I did. Three days and nothing happens. And then this boy-friend comes along and prac-

.tically ends her career for her. What would that have looked like on my report?

Scott Ettley rose slowly. "Rona," he said.

She only looked at him.

"Are you all right, Rona?"

She began to laugh. And then, just as suddenly, she fell silent. "Yes," she said at last. "I'm all right. Are you disappointed?"

The two men beside her exchanged glances. Hysterical, they seemed to say.

"Are you disappointed, Scott? Isn't this what you wanted?" She turned away from him. "Please take me home," she said to the strangers.

Scott Ettley moved over to stop her. "Rona . . ."

"What he can't have he destroys," she said, looking at him and yet talking of him as if he weren't there.

"Look, Bud, let us handle this," the policeman said quietly to Ettley. "I guess you aren't too popular around here at the moment." Not even hurt, he thought as he watched the young man's white face, not even a scratch on him that shows. What the hell had he been doing? You couldn't blame this girl for the bitterness of her words. "We'll get to the station and you can give us a description of your wallet. I don't suppose you could identify the men?"

"Easy now," the man with the grey hat was saying. His arm was round Rona, helping her toward the path. The policeman in the tramp's clothes hurried ahead to shine the flashlight on the ground before her feet. "I've sent a patrol car," he said. "We'll get you home soon, miss. See, there it is down at the gate."

Then he turned to make sure that the young man was following. But there was no one behind them. He swung his lamp back over the hillside. There was nothing to see except the dark stretches of the Park, now silent, innocent.

CHAPTER TWENTY-TWO

That Friday evening was a quiet one at the Tysons', for the end of the term was approaching, and Jon's students were putting in a few last despairing hours at their lecture notes. Paul Haydn was the only visitor to arrive. He came at nine o'clock as he had promised, and tried to hide his disappointment when he discovered that Rona wasn't going to be there.

"She had some work to finish," Peggy explained.

"Did you tell her I was coming up to see you?" Paul asked with a smile.

"Of course not," Peggy said, but she didn't lie expertly. She looked round for help. There was none—Jon had gone through to the kitchen to struggle with the ice tray. She watched Haydn's face for a moment. Then she said, "Paul, did you ever think that Scott Ettley might blame you for the end of his engagement to Rona?"

"I'm flattered." He looked at Peggy with amused disbelief. "But Scott always has to blame something. I've never yet heard him blame himself. And Rona wouldn't want to encourage any suspicion he has about you."

"In case we had a fight on Fifth Avenue?" Paul asked.

"Well, Scott can be very hot-tempered."

"He's a cold fish to me."

"You're prejudiced, I'm afraid."

"Sure, I'm prejudiced." And this is one prejudice I'm not going to lose, either. He said suddenly: "Do you like Ettley?"

"This isn't a good time to ask me that. At the moment, I'd like to shake him until his teeth rattled."

"He has a fine set of teeth to rattle," Paul said. "Or to have knocked down his throat."

Peggy began to laugh. "You and Jon agree, then. I've never seen Jon so mad as he has been this last week." She paused, and the smile left her face. "But perhaps this will all blow over, perhaps this will all come out right in the end." She studied the rug at her feet. She reached down and picked up a forlorn alphabet block that was hiding at the edge of the couch.

275

Paul said, "You mean they may still get married?" He hadn't thought of that. Yet it could happen. If Ettley had any good sense, it would happen. He searched gloomily for a cigarette and seemed to be concentrating on lighting it.

"I don't know," Peggy said frankly. "After all, you don't love a man for almost three years of your life and then slip away from him in one week. I suppose you keep thinking that it's all wrong for three years of your life to mean nothing at all. And so you keep hoping that everything can be changed back to the way it was when you were happy."

"But can people change back?"

Peggy didn't answer. She was listening intently, her head tilted slightly, her brow worried. Then, reassured, she said, "Sorry—I thought that was Bobby calling. What did you say, Paul?"

"I wondered if people could change back." He marvelled at the way a woman could worry on two different planes at the same time while she carried on a conversation at a third level.

"No, I suppose they can't," she admitted. "Not unless they can unthink all the thoughts they've had, or undo all the actions they've taken."

"Or untie all the knots in your oratory, honey," Jon said, carrying a tray of drinks into the room. "What's this all about anyway?"

"Scott Ettley, mostly," Peggy said.

"Oh!" Jon looked around for a place where he might set the tray. "How do you like Peggy's new dress, Paul? She put it on when she heard you were coming here to-night."

"Now, Jon," Peggy said, embarrassed, rising to clear a space on the coffee table. "We've always got so much stuff lying around here," she added, almost to herself.

"Sorry, I forgot," Jon said, rescuing his books and periodicals to carry them to his desk. "But what's a table for, anyway, if it isn't to dump things on?"

"It's a very smart dress," Paul said tactfully. "Green suits you."

"It used to," said Peggy, "but one of the depressing things to-night was that I've decided I look awful in green now." And I worked so hard on this damned dress, she thought.

276

Nine dollars and seventy-five cents for the material. Nearly ten whole dollars.

"Well," Paul said, looking round the quiet room, stretching himself comfortably in his chair, and trying to look as undepressed as possible, "this is a cosy place. I envy you both. And you're wrong about green, Peggy. You look good in it." He raised his glass.

Jon acknowledged. "Here's tae us! Wha's like us? Gey few. And they're a' deid." Then he grinned. "Haven't thought of that in years. I learned it from a Scotsman who once tried to teach me philosophy. Moral philosophy, naturally. Do you remember old Abernethie, Paul?"

"Sure," Paul said. He turned to Peggy. "Old Abernethie used to come into the classroom, look around us all, throw down his lecture notes on the desk, blow aside his whiskers and say, 'Good morning, fellow-sufferers!' And how right he was; we knew little about life, then. But translate for us, Jon. He never gave me the benefit of any toasts. I wasn't one of his star pupils."

"Here's to us. Who's like us? Very few. And they are all dead," Jon said. He reflected on the fact that translation, as always, lowered the blood pressure of the original.

Peggy said, "Cheerful little jingle. It's almost enough to sober up a man."

"That may have been the idea. The Scots invented whisky, but they are strong on moral precepts too," Jon said. "Now cheer up, Peggy. You can stop worrying about your dress, or about Bobby, or . . ." He didn't finish.

They all avoided looking at each other, thinking of Rona.

Paul said quickly, "What's wrong with Bobby?"

"Nothing," Peggy said. "That's the trouble. I wish I knew what was wrong with him."

"The doctor says he seems to be all right," Jon said, but he was worrying too, now.

"To-day, he's been so listless," Peggy went on. "I took the children out to the playground this afternoon, and Bobby had his new gun with him—the one you sent, Paul—and do you know, he didn't even play with it. He just sat on the bench beside me and let the other boys use it. I ask you!"

"By the way," Jon said, changing the subject determinedly, "I was talking to Milton Leitner to-day. I told him you were coming to see us to-night, so he may drop in on us this evening if he gets ahead of his work. He's been having an amusing time with that chap in your office, the one who works in advertising and spouts politics at parties."

"Murray?"

"Yes. Murray's been doing some heavy arguing with Milton, and Milton has been stringing him along just to see how far he would go. But this week, a great change has come over Murray. He's scared stiff about something, Milton says. Something to do with the death of that fellow who jumped out of a window. Rumours are starting, of course. A reporter—he's a friend of Milton's—got some information about the 'goings-on' in that household from one of the maids, but he couldn't print it. Libel, I suppose."

" 'The greater the truth, the greater the libel.' " Paul quoted.

Peggy said, "Rona seemed very upset about the man who jumped out of the window."

"About Charles?"

"Yes. Why was Rona upset, Paul? She only saw him once, didn't she?"

"He was a pathetic kind of figure."

"Tragic. An incurable drunk, wasn't he?"

"No," Paul said. "I don't think he was that."

Jon was watching him. "I don't suppose the true story will ever come out," he said, giving Peggy a warning signal to stop questioning.

"If it does," Paul answered, "it won't seem to bear any relationship to Charles. The poor guy won't even get that credit."

So that's the kind of story it is, Jon thought. He was interested, but he began a conversation about summer plans and other problems that troubled no one too seriously. Peggy needs a holiday, he was thinking as he listened to her talking to Paul. She's worrying too much about everything. We'll scrape along somehow, this year, even if I don't earn any money by teaching in summer school. And I'll finish that book of mine, and that will ease things a little. A book meant promotion, promotion meant more money; and that meant more chance to keep next summer free too from teaching, more chance to start writing another book. It's a spiral; either you go up, or you slip down.

"What's wrong?" Peggy asked suddenly, interrupting her remarks to Paul.

Jon looked up. "I was just thinking you don't grumble as much as you should," he said frankly.

Peggy gave her husband a warm smile. And watching them, Paul suddenly felt as if he were shut out of the room. Peggy may have sensed that, for she said to him, "I had a fit of grumbling this evening just before you arrived. When I tried on this dress and looked at myself in it—oh, well, why bring that moment up again? Anyway, I was thoroughly stupid and bad-tempered." She rose and went over to Jon as she spoke, and she gave him a quick, tight hug. "I'm sorry, too," she said softly, and retreated hastily to the door as the bell rang. "Probably Milton," she called back cheerfully.

Jon looked after her and then around the room. "Sometimes I think I chose the wrong profession," he said gloomily.

Paul looked at him in surprise. "You're pretty good at your job, I hear." And heaven only knew that we needed good teachers, now more than ever.

"Except when it comes to finding the cash to pay the bills," Jon said angrily. "Sometimes I think I'll give up the struggle, and go into business. Or perhaps teachers should be monastic: a cell and a cowled robe—that's just about all they can afford these days." Then his face and voice softened as he added, "But I couldn't teach well if I hadn't Peggy to keep me human." He rose and turned to the door, for Milton Leitner, followed by Joseph Locastro and Peggy, was coming into the room.

Paul noted the way the two students greeted Jon, the warm smile he gave them. He began to wonder why a man should be penalised for doing an essential job. If the best brains were to leave teaching to the stupid and ill-trained, what would happen to the Milton Leitners and the Joe Locastros? That thought gave him the beginning of an idea for a series of articles: the economic exploitation of the teacher by his students, their parents, and the good citizens who liked to talk of culture but hated to pay for it. That would just about hit every man jack of us, he thought. Then he pigeon-holed the idea for to-morrow's brooding and rose to shake hands with the two young men.

"We only came in to say hello," Milton Leitner said. "We're hitting the books to-night. Exams are breaking out all over." He handed a couple of heavy looking volumes over to Jon. "These have been hit, I'm glad to say. Thought I'd better return them before they got lost in the shambles I call a room at the moment."

"And Joe came to give us some news," Peggy said, her eyes smiling as she watched her husband to see his reactions. "He's—no, you tell it, Joe!"

"I've got that part-time job," Joe said, unable to control the grin of delight that was spreading over his thin aquiline face. "I can work it in with my classes next semester. So we are all set." He turned to Paul and explained. "I'm getting married this summer. I think you met Edith here, didn't you?"

"And Edith——" prompted Peggy.

"Edith is leaving Vassar but she'll finish her degree in New York. She's got a part-time job, too, in an advertising office. We'll manage."

"Good for you," Jon said, and shook his head warningly once more. "And good for Edith. But I never thought you'd get around Edith's people."

"Oh, they turned out to be human," Joe said cheerfully. "But they are still a bit dazed, though."

"Then that's your first bond in common," Milton Leitner assured him. And then as Joe began telling Peggy about a room he had found to rent, this afternoon, and Peggy was promising to go round and see it and report back whether it was a reasonable bargain and practical for housekeeping, Milton drew nearer to Paul.

"There must be something to this love business," Milton said. "In spite of the divorce rate, people keep on trying." His fine eyes watched Paul thoughtfully. "You wouldn't think, to look at Joe, that he's taking on enough work and worry to paralyse him for five years, would you?"

"Looking at Joe, I think I'd risk that. He's a good propagandist."

"Better than I am in my line," Milton admitted wryly. "Bob Cash—remember he was up here that last evening we met?—he's fallen hard for Thelma's little parties and all the bright lights he met there." He made a quiet gesture toward the other end of the room, and together, he and Paul drifted in that direction leaving Jon and Peggy listening to Joe.

"I've been doing a little research," Milton said, dropping his voice, "and I've found out several things. At one time, Scott Ettley did make a habit of cultivating Jon Tyson's students. Murray was next in the assembly line. Through him, they were taken to Nicholas Orpen who looked them over. If they made the grade, then they were in for a whirl of discussion groups and parties like the kind Thelma gave. After that first meeting with Orpen, they didn't see any more of him for quite a while. Not until they had been promoted to a series of meetings and intense discussions. And then, if they passed with top marks, they suddenly found themselves invited back to Orpen's place for small meetings that were big stuff. Scott Ettley reappeared in their lives, then, I hear. He was cagey—just like Orpen; they never mentioned Party membership. That was left to men like Murray. And that's as much as I could find out. The students who refused Murray's approach didn't get any further, and those who accepted aren't talking, naturally. But it's fantastic, isn't it? The amount of trouble some guys take to convert a few pliable young men."

Paul looked at him in amazement. "How the hell did you find all that out?"

"I began with the names of the fellows who had been coming up here on Friday nights for the last three years. I talked around with some of them—those who had just gone along out of curiosity, and then picked up their heels and ran when they found what they were getting into. It was they who gave me the pattern of the whole set-up. One thing, though,"—Leitner's heavily marked eyebrows straightened into a frown—"Ettley seems to have dropped out of the picture recently. Bob Cash and I were the two last contacts he made here, and that's about six months ago. Does that mean he has broken with the Communist Party?"

Paul Haydn didn't answer that. Perhaps, he thought. Or perhaps Ettley has got deeper in. "Have you told Tyson about this?" he asked quietly.

Milton Leitner looked at him unhappily. "How could I? I was kind of hoping that you'd drop him a word. Someone must. There's Rona to think of, too."

Paul said nothing, but his worry grew.

Then Joe, saying a cheery good-bye to Peggy and Jon, called over to Leitner. "Milt! We'd better shove off. We've still a couple of hours to put in on the books to-night."

"You're an optimist," Milton Leitner said. He began moving to the door.

Peggy said to him, "I never did get around to asking you about the summer. Have you taken the job in Cheyenne?"

Milton nodded. "Sure," he said, "I'll be able to give Bobby all the lowdown on broncho busting when I get back."

"I'll see you out," Jon said, leading the way toward the hall. The good nights were made, good luck was wished. And as Milton Leitner left the room, he turned for a brief moment to exchange a glance with Paul.

Peggy noticed it. "You like him?" she asked Paul. "So does Jon. Jon says he'll go far. And Joe will, too. That's why Jon is so pleased that he isn't giving up college, after all. It would have been a waste." She emptied an ash tray and straightened a cushion thoughtfully. "Joe was telling me that the reason he was determined to get married now is that he doesn't trust what's going to happen in the world. He thinks his generation had better get the happiness they can while they still can have it." Her voice became strained. "What has made them so much older than we were at their age?"

"Because we were too young to learn anything from the first world war, and they've grown up during the second one. That makes the difference, I suppose. Telling didn't teach us very much, did it?" Paul hesitated, then he said:

> "To think that two and two are four
> And neither five nor three,
> The heart of man has long been sore,
> And long 'tis like to be."

"What's this?" Jon asked, returning to the room. "Are you quoting poetry to my wife the minute my back is turned?" He grinned and put an affectionate arm around Peggy's waist. "But why choose Housman in one of his remorseful moods?"

"I was having an attack of gloom," Paul said, trying to smile. "I had to work it off on someone."

Peggy, still following her own thoughts, said sadly, "Yes, we were the five-and-three generation, weren't we?"

"And the bill was a steep one," Jon said. He looked at Paul Haydn again, wondering what was troubling him. "Well, let's sit down and be comfortable," he suggested. "Where's your glass, Paul?"

"I'll have to leave," Paul said. "But . . ." he hesitated, frowned. "I heard a piece of news about Scott Ettley," he went on. "Of course it may only be a rumour, a piece of gossip, but it's certainly—well, unexpected."

"You mean about his new job?" Peggy asked.

"What's that?" Paul looked at her quickly.

"He's going to join his father's newspaper. I suppose he will be editor some day, if he's good enough. Very nice, too."

"He will be good enough. He'll make sure of that," Paul said so bitterly that Jon and Peggy exchanged glances. "And we are all so damned helpless," he went on angrily. "What can we do? Go to William Ettley and tell him? He wouldn't believe us. And I wouldn't want to be the one to tell him, anyway."

"Tell him *what*?" Peggy asked.

Paul's lips tightened. His grey eyes seemed to darken with worry. "Perhaps we had all better sit down," he said. "Jon, here's a piece of news that Milton Leitner passed on to me. If it's true, it affects us all. In different ways. But I think we ought to——"

At that moment, a long piercing cry of pain drew them back on their feet. Then, just as suddenly, it was over, and there was nothing but silence, a grim warning silence filled with threats.

"My God!" Paul said. "What was that?"

"Bobby! It's Bobby!" Peggy cried, and she ran into the dark hall with Jon. Paul began to follow, but he halted outside the bedroom door. Barbara had wakened, and she was wailing with fear. But from Bobby, there was now only a small moan and then silence.

Jon rushed back into the hall and began telephoning for the doctor.

"Thank God he was at home," he said to Paul after his call was over. He stood beside the telephone for a moment.

"We'd better get hold of Rona," he said. He picked up the phone again.

"I'll do that," Paul said, taking the receiver. "You get Barbara quiet. What's wrong, Jon?"

Jon shook his head, unable to reply. He saw Bobby, stretched out so rigidly on his bed, his face small and thin and white with pain, his frightened eyes asking for help. He shook his head and went back to the bedroom.

Paul dialled Rona's number. There was no answer. He glanced at his watch. It was a quarter of eleven. Had she gone to bed early? He waited patiently, listening to the monotonous ringing of the bell. Then at last he came away.

He stood hesitatingly at the bedroom door, his grey eyes troubled as he looked at the still quiet figure of Bobby, and then at the haggard faces of Peggy and Jon. Jon was standing beside the bed. Peggy was sitting with Barbara in her arms. Only Barbara's questions broke the silence.

The doorbell rang, and Jon pushed past him to answer it.

"I'll look after Barbara," Paul said. He took a good grip of the fat soft waist and carried her into the living-room. Behind him, Paul heard the doctor's quiet businesslike voice as he hurried up the long hall with Jon.

Barbara raised her sleepy head, took a surprised look around the lighted living-room, decided this was an adventure not to be missed, and became suddenly awake. She sat up on Paul's knee and opened her large blue eyes very wide. "Tell me a story," she commanded.

"About what?"

"Tell me," she said. She smiled happily.

Paul smiled back, watching the tufts of golden hair pressed upward at the back of the small round head. "All right," he said. "And then you'll go back to sleep?"

She nodded, and folded her short fingers with a story-for-a-good-girl pose.

"Well," began Paul, "there was once a hippopotamus who lived in the Zoo." Shocking original writer you are, he thought. He listened to the doctor's voice telephoning the hospital. Emergency. Immediate operation.

"What Zoo?" asked Barbara.

"Central Park Zoo." No time for an ambulance. The doctor was bringing the boy in his car.

284

"What then?" Barbara yawned and mastered herself. She looked at him expectantly, apparently still more wide awake in spite of the yawn. In the hall, there was now silence.

"One fine day," Paul began obediently, "the hippopotamus was lying in the sun. And——"

"What was its name?"

"Rosebud. You approve? Good. All right; Rosebud was lying in the sun, flat on her side, her ankles delicately crossed for she had gone to a very good school, and her eyes closed."

"She was asleep." Barbara sounded disappointed. Nothing exciting ever happened when you were asleep.

"Oh, no! She was wide awake."

"Why her eyes closed?"

"She was tired of the view. Every time she opened her eyes she saw the same old scenery. She said to herself, 'What I need is a vacation. And besides, my bathtub is really much too small. I want a place where I can make a bit of a splash.'"

Barbara nodded understandingly.

"Right then and there, she decided to get away from it all."

"Itall?" Barbara repeated. Her brow creased. "What's itall?"

Paul looked blankly at the questioning blue eyes. "My dear young lady, we've reached an impasse, I fear. Well, let's say she wanted to get away from medicine and rainy days and early bedtime and rice pudding without currants in it. That do?"

Barbara considered that, and decided it would do. "Then what?" she asked again, insisting on the story-line.

"You'll be a whale of an editor some day," Paul told her. "Well, then she went to her friend the elephant and borrowed his trunk to pack her clothes. And she put on her new hat. The one with cherries on it. And a blue bow. And she was all ready."

Jon, behind him, said tensely, "We're leaving for St. Luke's. The doctor thinks it's a ruptured appendix. Is Rona coming here?"

"I'll stay until she does," Paul said.

"I'm having a story," Barbara announced happily, her eyes fixed on Paul.

285

"Good girl," Jon said and bent to kiss the back of her head. He left as silently as he had entered.

"Rosebud took a bus to Penn Station," Paul went on quickly.

Barbara looked doubtful. "A bus?" She glanced round suddenly. "Where's Daddy?"

"It was a *big* bus. A *very* big bus." Paul traced its size with his arms and recaptured her attention.

"A *very* big bus," she echoed, waving her arms too, smiling again.

"And so she arrived at the railroad station. She went into a big hall, all gleaming and polished, but she couldn't see a train, not anywhere. She went up to a kind man and asked where the trains lived. He said, 'Madam'—that's the way he always talked to lady hippopotamuses—'Madam, you go downstairs and there you will find a train all ready and waiting.' Rosebud nodded her head politely, and the cherries on her hat nodded too."

"And the blue bow," Barbara said, unclasping and then again clasping her hands. She looked at the blue ribbon on her dressing-gown approvingly.

"That's the colour exactly," Paul agreed. "So she started to look for the stairs to get down to the trains. She looked and she looked, but all the stairs had their gateways closed. And then, right over there in that corner, she saw an escalator."

Barbara frowned heavily and repressed another yawn. "Esslator?" she asked, puzzled.

Paul began trying to describe an escalator in words of one syllable.

"What then?" Barbara asked suddenly, tired of mechanical details. Her eyes tried to close and she forced them open.

Then what? "Well, Rosebud stepped on the escalator. And it groaned and wheezed. It wheezed and groaned. And then it gave a big sigh—like this!—and it stopped. Rosebud said, 'Dear me! What a nuisance. These things never work when you want them to.' She tried to walk down, but she couldn't. She tried to back up, but she couldn't. She was stuck, right between the waiting-room and the trains in Pennsylvania Station."

He looked down for a smile of approval. Barbara's eyes

were closing. "The hippopotamus was stuck," he repeated gently. But Barbara was suddenly asleep.

So much for my story, he thought. It's a good job I make my money in non-fiction. He waited for a few moments, and then rose quietly to carry her back to her cot.

He paused for a moment to look at the empty bed where Bobby had lain. Then, with a last glance at the sleeping Barbara blanketed to her chin, he went back to the telephone. There was no answer from Rona's apartment.

Almost midnight. There was still no report from Jon at the hospital, there was still no answer from Rona to any of his calls.

Paul Haydn walked through the apartment again, paced around the living-room, looked out at the darkened buildings across the street, and then went back to the telephone. This time he called the hospital. The cool, antiseptic voice told him that she had no information available. Yes, she would call him when she found out. Yes, she would give Dr. Tyson his message: all was well at home, Barbara was asleep. Yes, she would call him at once if there was any change. Yes, yes. . . .

He put down the receiver. "Yes, yes, yes," he said savagely. Then he calmed down. He wondered how many worried voices she had to answer each day. Pain and anguish and sorrow had become routine to her. Would she call him, would she even have time to find out how Bobby was?

The telephone answered him. He raced back down the long hall. Yes, the same cool voice told him, the news was as good as it could be so far. The operation was over, the boy was beginning to come out of the anæsthetic, his parents were with him.

"How good is all that?" he asked.

"As good as can be expected," the quiet voice said.

"It's serious? There's little hope?"

"It is much more hopeful now."

"But how's the boy?" he asked angrily. The doorbell rang insistently behind him. He tried to ignore it, to concentrate on the next words.

"He's resting comfortably," she said in a final way.

"Oh . . ." A goddamned lie . . . Bobby resting comfortably when he was retching out of the anæsthetic, his raw wound stitched round a tube draining away the poison. Then Haydn recovered himself. He said, "Thank you. Thank you for calling me so quickly." He had almost forgotten that. "Thanks a lot," he added gratefully.

"You're welcome," the nurse said, startled into sudden warmth and sympathy. "Don't worry, now." And then, as if alarmed at this breach of etiquette, she hung up the receiver abruptly.

Paul Haydn went to the door. The bell was ringing for the third time. Behind him, from Barbara's room, came a wail. That goddamned bell, he thought irritably and opened the door.

Outside, there was Rona. Rona, and a policeman, and a thin-faced, dark-haired man.

"You the brother-in-law?" the policeman asked.

"No, he's out," Paul said, startled. "Rona——"

"This all right, miss?" the thin-faced man asked.

Rona nodded. She stepped into the apartment.

"Rona," Paul said again.

She turned her face away, her hand over her neck, and drew aside as if to avoid touching him. She walked down the long hall without looking back. Then suddenly she stopped, as if she had just heard Barbara crying, and she went into the bedroom.

"She's had a bit of a shock. Attacked in Central Park. But she's all right," the policeman said in a low voice. "We'll come back later to get any particulars she can give. It didn' seem a good idea to ask anything except the routine ques tions to-night. The man who was with her was no help at all He beat it."

"You'd—you'd better come in and tell me," Paul said "Her sister and brother-in-law are at the hospital. There' been trouble here, too." And briefly he told them what ha happened.

The thin-faced man, who had been backing unobtrusively towards the elevator as soon as Rona had entered the apart ment, suddenly turned round. You're in a tough spot, h seemed to say. A crying child, a woman who might ge

288

hysterical at any moment. She had been far too quiet at the police station, far too quiet during the ride here.

The policeman felt the same way. He half-turned to look at his companion.

"And who are you?" Paul asked, looking at the unobtrusive clothes and the grey felt hat. Then he remembered the man he had seen in Benny's.

"Oh," said the policeman brusquely, "he was just passing by when it happened." He had suddenly become the professional.

"Will you come in? Both of you? I guess I need help as well as information now." He was still watching the man who had just happened to pass by. "A good job you were there. I wonder what happened to that smart FBI fellow who was supposed to be keeping an eye on Miss Metford? I guess he wasn't so smart."

The man looked at him. "I guess not," he said. He paused and added, "Well, if I can be of any help to you . . ." and he stepped over the threshold.

There was silence now from Barbara's room. Rona was still in there.

"What do we do?" Paul asked, hesitating.

"Leave her with the kid," the policeman suggested. He looked at his watch with a frown.

"Get her to go to sleep, I suppose," the quiet man said. The three men looked at each other.

"Well," the policeman said in a resigned voice, "if I delivered a baby last week, I guess I can handle this." He pushed the bedroom door open and looked round it cautiously. Then slowly and quietly he stepped back into the hall, closing the door gently. "She's taken both our advice," he said to the man who had come with his. "She's asleep on the bed beside the kid's cot." He smiled with relief. "Now," he said to Paul, "all we have to do is to tell you what happened, as far as we can piece it together."

They went into the living-room.

"Who was the man?" Paul asked, his face set, his eyes expressionless. "Who was the man with Miss Metford?"

The policeman opened his notebook. "Scott Ettley," he said. "That's the name she gave us."

"A tall man, young, well-built, good shoulders, fair hair,

regular features, eyes blue or grey—light colour, anyway," the quiet stranger said.

"Yes," Paul Haydn said slowly, his face suddenly white, his lips tight, "yes, that's Scott Ettley." He took a deep breath. "Go on," he said to the men watching him.

They left shortly, for what they could tell him was brief, brief but vivid in its cold lack of explanations. The policeman's unemotional voice gave the bald facts. Their bareness made his account all the more hideous to imagine into reality. "Don't worry," the policeman said, as they went down the hall toward the front door, "we'll get them all. We've got one of them. And another was hit by the park detective's bullet; there was blood on the grass. We'll get all three of them. Catch one thug and you catch the rest. Cowards. That's what all these muggers are. As yellow as they come. We'll get them," he added sympathetically, reassuringly, as he stepped into the elevator, followed by the man with the quiet face and watchful eyes.

"Yes," Paul said. But he was thinking of Scott Ettley. He closed the door and switched off the lights.

He looked into the bedroom and he stood in the darkness looking down at Rona. She was asleep, deeply asleep, so still that she might have been dead. He slipped the shoes gently from her feet. He covered her with a light summer blanket, and backed slowly out of the room. As he half-closed the door, leaving it open enough so that he could easily hear any sounds, he remembered he hadn't noticed Barbara. But she was all right, obviously, or there would have been a general uproar. Barbara was the kind of girl who let you know when she wasn't happy.

He switched off the lights in the living-room too, except for the reading lamp beside his arm-chair. He lay back, his eyes closed, remembering word for word the simple factual report which the policeman had made. Scott Ettley, he thought, I'll break his goddamned neck. . . . Then he remembered another quotation that old Abernethie liked to use when he was lecturing about certain famous men. "He's a clever chiel and nane the waur of a hanging," Abernethie would quote, relishing the grim realism of dialect. Yes, Ettley was a clever guy and none the worse for a hanging.

CHAPTER TWENTY-THREE

In the morning, around six o'clock, just as the pale weak sun filtered through the curtains and woke Paul Haydn in the Tysons' living-room, Jon returned. He stood at the door, looking at Paul, at Paul's wrinkled clothes, at the ash trays near him filled with cigarette stubs, but it seemed as if he registered nothing.

Paul rubbed the cramp out of a leg muscle and asked, "Bobby's all right?"

Jon didn't answer. His white face looked at Paul blankly. He said, "He's still alive." His voice broke.

"How's Peggy?" Paul asked quickly.

Jon regained control of himself. "She's—she's pretty wonderful," he said. He looked round the room again, at his desk with its pile of exam papers to be graded. Yesterday afternoon, he had begun to work on them. But yesterday was a thousand miles away. . . . "I came for some things," he said, trying to remember. "Clothes for Peggy . . . my own stuff . . . we'll work out some kind of routine between us so that there will always be one of us with him . . ." Again he paused, and a shadow crossed his face. "We sat outside his door last night. We weren't allowed inside. We'll get a cot moved into his room to-night. Peggy's going to stay with him. If Rona will look after Barbara, then I can divide my time between the hospital and here. And college. How's Barbara?"

He didn't wait for an answer, but opened the hall closet and brought out a suitcase. Then he went into his bedroom. He came back with a fistful of handkerchiefs and a nightdress. "A toothbrush," he said to himself, and hurried into the bathroom.

Then he came back and packed the articles he had gathered. "It isn't enough," he said, staring down at the empty spaces in the suitcase.

"What about slippers? A dressing-gown?" Paul suggested.

"Yes, that's it. And stockings. Peggy ripped one of her stockings." But he didn't move; he still stared down at the suitcase. "She wanted something for Bobby. . . ." He couldn't remember. "God," he said, "how can a kid bear so much pain? At least, he's alive. He has a chance. That's what the doctors say. And they're telling the truth, Paul. They told us, when they wheeled him into the operating-room, they told us they could promise nothing. They were frank then. Now they say he has a chance. We can believe them, can't we?"

"Yes," Paul said. "Yes. Look, Jon. I'm going to cook up some coffee for us. You take a quick shower and a shave. Then you can get back to the hospital and let Peggy have time out for her breakfast. Is that an idea?"

Jon nodded. He left the suitcase lying open on the floor. He moved towards the bathroom. He kept talking as if words were a release. "That's the way it happens with young children. There's no real warning. Just the sudden attack. Even then, you don't know what is wrong. The pain even isn't on the right side to tell you what it could be. If the doctor hadn't come round here at once, last night—if he hadn't lived near us—if Peggy and I had been out—if we . . . Oh, God!"

"But you got Bobby to the hospital. And he has a good chance," Paul said quietly. "No good torturing yourself with 'ifs,' Jon." He thought of himself during those last hours since Rona had arrived here. I ought to have given myself some of that advice, he told himself grimly.

"Barbara all right?" Jon asked again. "Rona's with her?" He looked as if he might enter their room to see for himself.

"Let them sleep," Paul said quickly. "Have that shower and shave, first." He went through to the kitchen, and began rummaging around to find where Peggy kept the coffee and the percolator. Eggs. Bread. A toaster. Butter. What was he going to tell Jon about Rona, about Scott Ettley? How little, how much? It depended on the punishment Jon could take. He had to know, and the sooner the safer. Not only for Rona's sake, but for his own.

It wasn't long before Jon came through to the kitchen. He had changed his wrinkled shirt and suit. His manner was different, too, as if the cold shower had put new energy into him. He said quickly, "I went into Barbara's room to see if she was all right. Rona—she's still in her street clothes. They're torn. There's a purple bruise at her throat." He took a deep breath. "What's wrong now?" he asked. I might have
292

guessed something was wrong, he thought, when I found Paul still here half-asleep in an arm-chair. Only, I was thinking of Bobby; I was thinking only of Bobby. "What's wrong?" he repeated.

"Easy, Jon, easy. Nothing is wrong now."

"You'd better tell me what *was* wrong," Jon said, his face white and taut.

"Here's some coffee. Drink it. And I'll tell you what I know." Paul watched Jon's face as he talked, keeping his voice unworried, his eyes reassuring. He chose his phrases carefully, giving only the brief details as he had learned from the policeman. He hid his own emotions as well as he could.

When he ended, Jon said, "And she's been asleep like this ever since?"

"Yes. It's probably the best treatment her nerves could have. I thought of phoning for a nurse. But the less fuss we make about this, the better. At least, that's what I thought Rona would want."

Jon nodded. Then his mouth tightened. "And Ettley disappeared? He didn't put up much of a fight and then he ran away—is that what I'm to gather? But why? I've never known him to be a coward. Has he gone crazy?"

"I don't think he's a coward," Paul said. "I don't think he's crazy, either."

Jon shook his head. "No sane man would have behaved that way."

"If he took Rona to that dark section of the Park, he did it for a reason. If he disappeared as soon as the officer mentioned a visit to the police station, he had a reason. We might not like his reasons if we learned them. We may never be able to understand them because we belong to a different world. But the fact remains he had his own reasons. They exist. And I, for one, want to find them out."

"I must say you are taking this more coolly than I'd expect," Jon said, his anger returning. "I'd like to break his jaw."

"Last night, I was all set to break his neck. But I've had some time for thinking. I know what has got to be done. I'm going to find out Ettley's reasons, I'm going to end his usefulness to the men who taught him his reasons. Yes, I'm going to find out all about Comrade Ettley."

293

"Let's keep the bitter jokes out of this," Jon said. "I'm too damned tired to be able to smile."

"I'm not cracking any jokes," Paul said. "I'm as serious as you are."

Jon stared at him. "Ettley?—I don't believe it . . . Ettley a Communist? You're crazy, Paul."

"Then so is Milton Leitner."

"Ah . . ." Jon said. He was remembering Milton's visit last night, the hushed conversation at the other end of the room, the worry on Milton Leitner's face as he left, the worry on Paul's as he had started to tell Peggy and Jon a piece of news. So Milton Leitner had brought that news. "Is there evidence, or is it just suspicion?" he asked. His voice was quiet again, quiet and controlled.

"That is the first thing I have to find out," Paul Haydn said, and poured another cup of coffee. "I go on from there, depending on what I find."

"But how are you going to do it?"

Paul passed over some toast and dished the fried eggs. "Let's get something solid on our stomachs," he suggested.

"Paul—how are you going to find out the truth? That will be a whole-time job."

"What if it is?"

"You mean you'll resign from *Trend*? But, Paul, you can't give up your career. You've just started it again."

"How many of us would have any careers worth following, if Ettley and his crowd won control?" Paul asked. He smiled grimly as he added, "Besides, once Ettley's friends discover what I'm going to do, they'll start such a campaign against me that I won't be left with much of a reputation, far less a career."

"You make them sound powerful."

"They can be powerful, all right. They are as powerful as we make them."

"Yes," Jon said bitterly. "They take our good will and turn it as a weapon against us." He was thinking of the news that Milton Leitner had brought. He was thinking of all its implications: Ettley making friends with his students, the seemingly casual introduction to Murray, the invitations, the easy path to Nicholas Orpen. . . . "But I can't believe it," he said almost to himself. "Ettley?" He looked at Paul, and then he added, "That was just my vanity. It is pretty hard to admit that you've been a bad judge of a man. If this is true, then I certainly have been one of the trusting fools who have helped them."

"So was I, if that's any comfort," Paul said. He was thinking of the way he had at first refused to listen to Roger Brownlee. Even later, he had only believed grudgingly. He had made a very unwilling recruit, cursing his own conscience for refusing to leave him in peace. But now—I'll see Roger at once, he thought. He'll be able to give me some advice, he'll put me in touch with men who know more about this kind of work than I do. Thank God I've had some training, though. Those years against the Nazis are going to come in useful now.

"I've gone numb," Jon said. "I can't even think what I must do about Ettley." But his voice was calm.

"I've told you I'm taking action," said Paul. He was watching Jon. The counter-shock treatment was working, slowly and cruelly. But it was working.

"I've been to blame for a lot," Jon argued. "Those who are to blame ought to pay the bill." He had said that often enough—each man must judge his own debts and make his own atonement. "Yes, I've been to blame," he repeated, his eyes narrowing, his white lips tight.

"Not you."

"If Bob Cash goes the same way as Ettley——" Jon began.

Paul said sharply, "Get rid of that idea. Let's pin the blame where it belongs. Ettley betrayed your friendship, he betrayed his father, he betrayed his girl. All in the name of Obedience to the Party, disguised in a flurry of double-talk about democracy and idealism. He hasn't stopped to think that each step takes him deeper into the gutter, that the filth of the gutter will cling to him, and that no double-talk will ever clean him of that. He hasn't stopped to think that his own corruption will corrupt the power he wants to have."

There was a pause. Then Jon said, "What if he ever does stop to think?"

"That's his problem," Paul answered bitterly.

"I wouldn't envy him that one." Then Jon remembered his

own. He glanced at the clock. "A quarter of seven . . . what's wrong with Barbara this morning? She's usually awake with the crack of dawn."

As if to answer him, so that both men were forced to smile, Barbara's light voice came drifting down the long hall. "Bobby," she was saying, "Bobby's gone. Aunt Rona, where's Bobby? Aunt Rona, Aunt Rona!" Her chant became a despairing cry ending in tears. I'm abandoned, the frightened wail seemed to say, I'm all alone and no one loves me.

Jon started down the hall, but even as he reached the bedroom door, the crying ceased. Rona was speaking. She was speaking hoarsely, in a strained voice, but the words were calm and gentle. Barbara began to laugh. "Funny voice," she said. "Do it again."

Jon turned to look at Paul who had followed him. "No?" he asked, nodding toward the bedroom door, trying to put off the moment of seeing Rona, of telling her about Bobby.

"Leave it to Barbara for a few minutes," Paul said. "What about finishing your packing first?"

They retreated into the living-room. Then they looked at each other. "All right," Paul said helplessly. "Let's admit it."

He began gathering the blue-covered test papers which Jon had been grading yesterday afternoon. "You want these along?" he asked crisply. He was trying to forget Rona's voice.

"Might as well," Jon said, equally brisk. "The results have to be posted by Monday." He brought the suitcase over to the desk. "Here, shove them in." He began picking out the other books he would take with him. As he worked, he was beginning to realise what kind of night Paul Haydn had put in. Paul's in love with Rona and I never even thought of it until these last moments, he told himself angrily; that's how selfish your own troubles can make you. Last night must have been as much hell for Paul as it was for us. But he was alone. And I had Peggy.

Paul looked up to find Jon watching him. "Yes?" he asked.

"I was thinking that Peggy had better come back here and take charge. Or perhaps we could get Moira Burleigh from upstairs to help us out."

"There's no need," Rona said from the doorway. "I'll look after Barbara. I'm—I'm all right." The two men turned quickly

o look at her. She was wearing one of Peggy's housecoats,
nd she had loosely twisted a silk scarf round her neck. Her
ace was white, but it was calm. She held Barbara in her
rms. "Don't worry about my voice," she said, "it sounds
vorse than it hurts."

"Funny woice," Barbara said approvingly.

Rona came into the room. "Where's Bobby? What's happened?" She didn't look at Paul, not even when Barbara
stretched out an arm to him and said, "What happened?—
what happened to the potamus?"

Rona, with her eyes fixed on Jon, kept that same un-
naturally calm look on her face. "I came in late last night,"
she said. "I was tired. I fell asleep. I was so stupid with
tiredness that I didn't notice I lay down on Bobby's bed.
It was empty. That was all I noticed. But why—where is
he?"

"He's in hospital," Jon said gently. "Appendicitis."

"Bad?"

"It was. He has a chance now, though."

"Oh, Jon!" Rona set Barbara down while she stared at him
unbelievingly.

He said quickly, watching her face, "I must get back to
the hospital right away." He pointed to the suitcase. "Help
me, Rona, will you? What would Peggy need?"

Rona looked at the suitcase, and she almost smiled. "More
than that," she said.

Jon picked up the case, and carried it toward the bedroom.
Rona went with him. She still did not look at Paul. Together, she and Jon finished the packing. When they returned
to the living-room, it was empty.

"Barbara!" Jon raised his voice.

"Here I am!" Barbara called back from the kitchen. She
sounded cheerful enough.

She was sitting in her high chair, a napkin tucked round
her neck, her face buried in a large glass of milk. She blew
gently into the glass and admiringly watched the bubbles
rise.

"Where's Paul?" Rona asked. The hall door closed quietly
to answer her. She looked at Jon.

"He's gone," Barbara announced, "to help the potamus.
It got stuck." She blew too hard and the milk splashed over

with a delicious noise. She looked up and laughed. Then her face became sad. "Poor potamus," she said dutifully. She heaved a remarkable sigh.

Jon kissed the top of her head. "Well, I can tell Peggy that everything is going on here just as usual," he said, looking down at the milky table. "I'll get our doctor to come up and prescribe for your throat," he told Rona. He put out his hand and touched her arm for a moment. "Good girl," he said.

Rona bent her head suddenly. Then she searched for a towel. She was wiping Barbara's milk-splashed face when Jon left as inconspicuously as possible. Yes, she was promising Barbara, Aunt Rona would take her for a walk. To Penn Station? Why to the station?

"Because," Barbara said, giving a good imitation of a toothless Mona Lisa. "Just because." Then she looked round. "Where's Daddy?" She listened to the silent apartment. The corners of her mouth went down. "Daddy!" The tears dropped into the milk.

It took Rona a full ten minutes before Barbara's smiles returned and her face cleared up as sweetly as a sky in April. But even then, Rona was given no time to think at all about herself. Barbara saw to that.

CHAPTER TWENTY-FOUR

Peggy phoned at nine o'clock.

"Rona," she began breathlessly, speaking in the way she did when she felt she had a hundred things to mention, "Rona, how's Barbara? Did she eat enough breakfast? You'll find her play clothes on the left of the bedroom closet . . . and it's chilly this morning, so you'd better put a cardigan on top of——"

"Yes, Peggy," Rona said with a smile. The cardigan was already covering the plump short arm that was struggling to take the receiver from Rona. "Just a minute, honey," she said to Barbara, "you can talk to Mummy afterward. If you keep still!" Barbara nodded, and put her head close to Rona's so that she could listen anyway.

"The cardigans are in the bottom drawer of the bureau."

"Fine," said Rona. "And what about Bobby?"

"He's half-asleep, half-awake. I've left Jon sitting by his door. Perhaps, later this afternoon, we'll get into the room. Rona—are you taking cold?"

"No. I have a strained throat. But Bobby—then he *is* getting better?"

"I keep telling myself that. The doctors won't say anything definite. Oh, Rona!——"

"Now, cheer up, Peggy. The worst is over."

Peggy blew her nose.

"What's that?" Barbara asked, starting back.

Peggy said, not too distinctly, "I hope so."

Rona decided this was the moment for Barbara to do her share. And as she held the phone at the right distance from Barbara's mouth while Barbara shouted her answers (the louder, the clearer, was Barbara's idea of telephoning), Rona had time to realise that Peggy had been told nothing about last night's incident in the Park. And for that she was thankful. If Peggy had known, she would have come back here and stayed while she worried about Bobby in the hospital. And then, Rona told herself, I would have time to think . . . and I don't want to think at all. I'm afraid to think about Scott. I'm more afraid to think about him than even to remember last night. . . . Stop that, Rona, stop!

"Barbara, it's my turn," she said almost desperately, and took back the receiver. "Yes, Peggy," she said quickly, "now what do you want me to do? No, don't leave the hospital for a moment until you are sure about Bobby." For a few more minutes Peggy talked about Barbara's routine and meals. The matter-of-fact conversation did them both good. The small details of living absorbed the shock of its cruel moments.

It's odd, Rona was thinking as she went back to the problems of housekeeping and of coping with Barbara, it's odd how you can feel so isolated by some hideous experience, and then find you still are only a very small part of the giant world that goes on and on. And so you have to go on too. You may lose your lover but you have to eat breakfast, if not to-day, then to-morrow. Your nephew may be dying, but you've got to cook a rice pudding in a double boiler and add the egg and sugar afterwards for your niece. You may think yourself a tragic figure, but you've got to go out shopping to the A. & P., and deal with a dozen oranges, and half a pound of butter, and a bunch of celery.

"Aunt Rona," asked Barbara, "why you crying?"

Just after ten o'clock, the Tysons' doctor arrived—a kindly, elderly man who examined Rona's throat, and then Barbara's as a tactful gesture to keep her happy. He prescribed what he could. "It will take time," he said, smiling cheerfully. "Don't worry. It's an ugly-looking bruise, and your throat must be painful, but it isn't serious. You may not think it, but you've been a lucky young lady, a very lucky young lady. Now, don't talk very much, and keep your voice low if you have to talk. And don't worry." Probably the reassurance in his voice was as much help as anything. And certainly the way in which he phoned the drugstore, and got them to promise to send round lotions and gargles and lozenges, was an extra touch of kindness. He needs sleep, Rona thought as she looked at the heavy shadows under the tired eyes. He's been awake all night, he's been with Bobby, and yet he calls a drugstore to save me the trouble. There are good people, kind people, too. I've got to keep thinking of them. I've got to remember them. There are people who help. Not only people who destroy.

And then he was gone, and Rona tried to finish the next round of household chores, while Barbara began examining all the throats of her dolls and asked for bandages to tie around their necks. "Poor Rona," she kept saying, as she attended to the dolls. "Poor Rona." But the dolls were abandoned as soon as the package from the drugstore arrived. That had to be opened and critically examined, and Barbara had to taste a lozenge to make sure they were good. They were too good, seemingly, for Rona was trying to find somewhere to hide the box when the telephone bell rang.

Eleven o'clock almost, Rona noted. She hurried to the telephone, still carrying the box of lozenges in her hand as the safest place possible. She was beginning to re-form her ideas of Peggy's capabilities. When did Peggy ever find time to do anything at all?

It was a strange voice speaking on the telephone, a woman's voice. "This is Moira Burleigh," she said. "I'm calling from upstairs." There was a pause. "Is that Peggy's sister?"

"Yes," Rona said, still puzzled.

"We met you one Friday at Peggy's, remember?"

Rona remembered. Moira Burleigh who hated Orpen, Moira Burleigh who had known Scott when he was a boy at Staunton. "Yes," she said.

"I've just heard the news. How terrible! I've been calling the hospital but you don't get much change out of them, do you? Poor Peggy! What a dreadful thing to happen! And it's so dangerous, isn't it? But why didn't you come upstairs and get hold of us? We'd have rallied round. You don't need help? You are sure? Well, in case you do, just call me. I'm going to be here all morning and most of this afternoon. Why don't you send Barbara up here for lunch? My brats have to eat anyway. It might take Barbara's mind off things. You know. And you could have time to read a book in peace, or put your feet up, or something. I know what it's like with children. You sound all worn out already."

Rona, glancing down at Barbara who was waiting with an angelic smile for another lozenge, replied that things seemed under control for the moment. "There's the doorbell," she added quickly, and truthfully. "Sorry." And she put down the receiver thankfully, and yet with a touch of embarrassment for feeling grateful that the doorbell had chosen this moment to ring.

It was strange how quickly news, especially bad news, travelled. How had Mrs. Burleigh heard about Bobby? From the superintendent? Had she also heard how Rona had arrived last night? Then she was suddenly angry with herself for such suspicion: Moira Burleigh had only phoned out of kindness, not curiosity. Yes, she told herself angrily, you had better start learning to trust people again. There are plenty of people to be trusted.

She opened the door. On the landing outside were two strange men.

She tightened her grip on the door, half-closing it, looking over her shoulder despairingly as if Jon might appear to help her—or Paul. But there was only Barbara, backing away, suddenly very small and helpless.

"Miss Metford?" one of the men asked. He had light hair, blue eyes. Like Scott. He was about Scott's age, Scott's height. Even his quiet clothes were like Scott's.

"Yes," she said, trying to close the door still more and yet feeling she had scarcely the strength to do that.

"I'm sorry to trouble you, Miss Metford. But this is an emergency."

"Bobby?" she asked, fearfully, hesitating.

"No." The stranger pulled an identification card from his pocket. "May we talk to you for a few minutes?"

She looked at the card. "But how do I know that you are——" She stared down at the card. She couldn't finish the sentence.

The two men exchanged glances. The fair-haired one said, "Well, that's a reasonable doubt. Why don't you call headquarters and check on our visit to you? We'll wait here until you've found out."

She closed the door, leaning against it. Then she opened it again.

The two men were lighting cigarettes. The fair-haired one was pacing slowly around, his hat pushed back on his head. The other was saying, "Well, you can't blame her. She had a bit of a——" He stopped in embarrassment and turned to face Rona. "That was a quick call," he said, trying to make a joke of it.

Rona said, "If you were thieves you could easily have pushed your way in here, in the first place." She tried to smile, too. But she was thinking, they know about me. They know. Her hand fumbled with the scarf at her throat. "Come in," she said.

"This is urgent, or we wouldn't trouble you," the fair-haired agent said. "It won't take long."

Something in his voice disturbed Rona. But she said nothing and led them to the living-room.

"Quite a hospital you've got here," the man said with a smile, as he noticed the bandaged dolls each occupying an arm-chair. He looked round and then laid his hat on the coffee table. The other hesitated, too. They were both so obviously ill at ease, so obviously trying to be tactful, that again Rona was warned. What else can hurt me now? What else?

"Who's that?" asked Barbara, beginning to regain her composure.

"I'm Fred," the other agent said to Barbara, speaking for the first time. "I'm Barbara," she answered. The two men exchanged a quick glance, and then Fred walked slowly over to the desk. He put his hat down and lifted a battered doll. "What's her name?" And he drew Barbara away from the couch where Rona sat.

"She'll be all right," the fair-haired man said to Rona reassuringly as he pulled a chair nearer the couch. "Fred's got a couple of kids of his own." Rona glanced worriedly across the room but Barbara, now perched on top of a telephone book and a couple of cushions, was being installed at the desk chair while Fred found a large pad of paper and sharpened a blue pencil obligingly.

The man beside Rona lowered his voice. "We are sorry we have to trouble you this morning. But we thought you might be able to help us. Do you feel fit enough to answer some questions?"

Rona stared at him. She nodded. But wasn't it the police who usually took charge of robberies and assaults? Yet these men were supposed to be from the FBI. She looked down at her hands and found she was still holding the box of lozenges. She studied its trademark.

He was saying, "You were accompanied last night by a man called Scott Ettley? That was what you told the police?"

She nodded again.

"You've known him a long time?"

"Three years, almost."

"You are engaged to him?"

"I was." She looked up. He was watching her.

"Did you know anything of Ettley's politics?"

"No," she said hesitatingly. Not until last night, she thought, and I may have been crazy. That moment of suspicion in the dark shadows of Central Park—that moment of fear when she had faced Scott and asked "Is Orpen the traitor? . . . A traitor to what?"—No, that was a moment to forget if she could.

"You knew his friends."

"Most of them."

"What were they like?"

She shook her head helplessly. "Just people like me."

"Did you know of any friends he had in the Communist Party?"

"Not definitely. Except . . ." Orpen, of course. Orpen was a Communist. *A traitor to what?* Yes, Scott had been identifying himself with Orpen's politics. She stared down again at the box in her hand. "Is Scott Ettley a Communist?" she asked.

"You don't sound too surprised at the idea, Miss Metford," he suggested, and waited patiently. If we knew the definite answer to that question, he was thinking, we wouldn't have needed to come here this morning. "You didn't know of any Communist friends except——?" Again he waited.

She flushed. "There was one, Nicholas Orpen. But that was only an old friendship from college days."

"Are you sure of that, Miss Metford? He was merely an old college friend?"

She put her hand to her throat. "I don't know," she said.

"When did you first begin to suspect Scott Ettley?"

The flush mounted in her cheeks. "I didn't say I suspected him."

"I'm sorry. I had the feeling that you did." He still watched her face. Then he said quietly, "The Communists cause a lot of real trouble for a lot of people, but it's strange how people don't want to cause trouble for Communists."

There was a pause. Rona said, "I'm not shielding anyone. I just don't know. I don't *know.*"

"That's fair enough," he agreed. "We don't want vague ideas. We want facts. Last night Scott Ettley came to see you just after ten o'clock. He stayed about three-quarters of an hour."

She looked at him in surprise. "Yes," she said.

"Did he tell you anything that might be of importance to us?"

"No. There was nothing definite."

"He mentioned no names?"

"No. He was—he was arguing with himself. He talked wildly. I couldn't understand." I was the one who mentioned names, she thought. Orpen . . . *is Orpen the traitor?*

"Why did you go out with him and walk into Central Park?"

304

"I was trying to help him."

"He was in trouble?"

"I thought he was."

"Did he say he was intending to leave the Communist Party? Did he express any fears for his own safety?"

"No. He was—he was just arguing with himself."

"Was he upset by the broken engagement?"

"He—he had been," she admitted. "He didn't speak of it last night." Only indirectly, only for a moment. He seemed to have forgotten all the wild threats he had made earlier in the week. As if he had come to accept the idea that she was no longer his. . . . Or had he ever accepted it?

"Did he know about the documents which you had received earlier this week?"

"From Charles?" She was startled. "No," she said. I was the one who spoke about Charles, she remembered. And immediately after I mentioned him, Scott started to leave. He left, and asked me to go with him. . . .

She shivered. That couldn't be true. Scott had acted on impulse when he went for that walk. I was still safe then. And yet, from that time, the pressure had mounted. Until then, Scott had been arguing with himself, as if he had been trying to persuade himself. Afterward, he had become afraid of what he might have said. And when I spoke of Orpen, he was doubly afraid. We went into the Park. . . .

"Did Ettley ever talk about killing——" the detective began.

"Oh!" she cried out, hurting her throat.

The man waited, watching, saying nothing, his face expressionless.

"So that's why you are here," Rona said. "Orpen has been killed." She spoke as if she had expected it.

"Nicholas Orpen?" Then that is something we have found out, the agent thought. He rose to his feet, and gave Fred a nod.

Rona looked at him in sudden panic. "Scott had nothing to do with that," she said. "I know." As far as I can know, she thought unhappily. She was remembering Scott's face— at the end—when she spoke to him so bitterly. She saw again the look in Scott's eyes, watching her contempt. And into his eyes had come contempt, too, and hatred. But not for her. "Rona," he had said pitifully, as if asking her help

305

for the last time, as if seeing himself as clearly as she was seeing him.

The agent picked up his hat. "Orpen is still alive," he said. He hesitated, and then he decided not to break the news. It would be broadcast over every radio this evening. Scott Ettley was the son of William Ettley, after all. Yes, that would be the simplest way for her to learn. The easiest way for himself, certainly. Yet he still hesitated. It would be a cruel way to learn, too.

He frowned down at the hat in his hand. With an effort, he said, "I'm afraid we have bad news for you." He looked up at her, but she didn't help him. He had to say it. "Scott Ettley was found dead, early this morning. He was killed by a subway train. I'm sorry, Miss Metford, But the news will be published in the evening papers, perhaps even in the early afternoon editions. So . . ." He looked at her and waited.

"Yes," she said, "it was better that you should tell me." She didn't rise. She sat so still that she seemed scarcely to breathe.

"Good-bye, Miss Metford. Good-bye, Barbara."

Barbara waved a starfish hand.

The front door closed firmly. The hall was silent again. Rona looked up to see Barbara's face watching her, half-puzzled, half-frightened. She took a deep breath and got up from the couch. Her movements were stiff, unnatural. "It's all right," she heard herself saying, "it's all right, Barbara." And as proof of that, she opened the box of lozenges which she still clutched tightly in her hand. "It's all right," she repeated, trying to put aside her thoughts of Scott and his father. But it wasn't all right. Her emotions were suddenly blotted out by a blinding anger: Orpen, she was thinking, Orpen. . . .

The two agents went downstairs in silence. As Fred unlocked the door of their parked car, he said, "That was a tough half hour, Tom."

"Yeah. But she took it well."

"Did she tell the whole truth?"

"As far as she could, I think," said Tom. "Pity we had to see her, though."

Fred nodded. They both got into the car. In its privacy,
306

he added, "And we still don't know whether it was suicide or a political murder. All that trouble for nothing." He glanced up at the windows of the apartment which they had just left.

"Not altogether," Tom said. "Orpen's in danger; we found that out. And there's only one reason why a man like Orpen should be in danger: he's breaking with the Party and he's ready to talk. Better stop at the first drugstore you see, Fred. I'd like to put in a call."

Fred started the car, and they began travelling westward. "Funny thing," Fred was saying, "yesterday afternoon we had never even heard of Scott Ettley. Then at five o'clock when he visited Orpen he walked right into the picture. And he insisted on staying in the picture, getting us more and more interested, until he was wiped off completely. What bothers me is the fact that we found so little on him. Where did he keep his Party card? Not even in his room—I thought we might have found it there this morning."

"Probably been told to destroy it," Tom said gloomily. "Which makes him still more interesting."

"Gone underground?"

"Looks more and more like it. I've a hunch the girl thought so too."

"One thing I can say about Scott Ettley. As a Communist who got mixed up with a bunch of suspicious characters, he's got the shortest file on our records."

"We can forget him now. Orpen's the man to watch. And the men who came out of that west side address last night after Ettley left it. Nice quiet little bunch, judging from their descriptions."

Fred grinned. "Sure," he was saying as they turned down Broadway and headed for the nearest drugstore where Tom could phone, "sure, they are always quiet and respectable guys these days. And all with names as Anglo-Saxon as Tom Jones even if they are straight from Bessarabia or Odessa. Funny thing that whenever they pick a false name it's always something like Brown or Clark or James. You'd think they despised Russians and Germans and Rumanians, the way they become Ye Olde Tea Shoppe. Now my name's Fred Bercowitz, and Bercowitz I stay even if it's a helluva trouble spelling it out for a store clerk. But if I were a Commie, I'd be Fred Berry or Frank Burns." He shook his head. "Bour-geois snobberies. . . . Who do they think they're kidding?"

"If they didn't kid themselves, where would they be?" Tom asked.

CHAPTER TWENTY-FIVE

On Saturday morning, Roger Brownlee's office was officially closed, giving him time to attend to his "extra-curricular" work as he called it. The outer office, where two typists usually sat, was silent. "No clatter of knitting needles to disturb us this morning," Brownlee had said when Paul Haydn arrived at midday. "Now, what's the trouble?" And he listened to Paul's story, and Paul's decision.

"That's all very well," Brownlee said. "Except that you won't need to worry much about Scott Ettley now. I've just had the information that he's dead. Sure—that's official." And briefly he gave the police report of Ettley's death.

"Was it suicide—or murder?" Haydn asked.

"Atonement or punishment?" Brownlee shrugged his shoulders. And at that moment the telephone bell rang.

Paul rose from the arm-chair, looking round the simply furnished room, and walked over to the window to study the courtyard outside. Scott Ettley was dead. Paul couldn't quite believe it. It seemed almost as unreal as carnations dyed emerald green, as snow in August. Yet these happened too.

Then he became aware that the telephone call was over. He turned to see Brownlee watching him with a frown.

Brownlee said, "What's worrying you now? He's dead, isn't he?"

"It's strange . . ." began Paul Haydn, and then stopped. "The hour before he died must have been pure hell."

Brownlee nodded. "Nothing worse than that kind of hell, the hell you realise you've created for yourself."

Paul Haydn said, "And Orpen—what will he think now?"

"As he is told to think. And that doesn't allow room for any personal guilt."

"How can he evade it? He began all this, back at Monroe

College, when he first worked on Ettley. Sure, I know that Ettley must have had something in him that responded to Orpen's talk—some lack of moral sense that let him accept lies and trickery as normal action. There must have been a willingness in him to believe Orpen, or he wouldn't have fallen for his line. Plenty of other young men came under Orpen's influence and weren't won over. So Ettley did follow the path he wanted to walk. But last night, it became steeper than he imagined. He jumped off. Where was Orpen? From what we know now, they've been working close together."

"We aren't the only ones who are interested in Orpen," Roger Brownlee said quietly. "That phone call was from Rona Metford. She wanted Orpen's address."

"Rona?" And Brownlee had given her the address. Paul had heard that much of Brownlee's answers on the phone.

"She was insistent," Brownlee said. Then he added quietly, "She knows that Scott Ettley is dead."

"She's going to Orpen's?"

"She didn't say."

"She's going to Orpen's," Paul said. He stared at the desk.

"It's well guarded, inside as well as out," Brownlee reminded him. "And Rona, although you may not know it, still has her own escort."

"You'd let her go to see that man?" Paul burst out angrily. "You'd——"

"Easy, Paul, easy. As I've been told, no one has been allowed by Orpen to enter his apartment in these last three days—except Ettley yesterday afternoon. He's kept himself out of touch, completely. He's afraid, obviously. Something is wrong. Something is very far wrong for Comrade Orpen. Rona might be the one person he'd see. If she brought him the news of Ettley's death, he might even talk to her. That might be the mood he's in."

"I don't like it," Paul said. "She's been through enough."

"Yes, she's suffered enough, I agree. But she isn't the one taking the punishment this time, Paul. She's going to hand out a little punishment, for a change."

"She'll only get hurt." Paul started toward the door. "You were crazy to give her that address."

"She was hard to refuse. She's angry, Paul."

"Rona?"

Brownlee nodded. Then he said quickly, "Where are you going?"

"Where do you think? To protect Orpen?" Paul closed the door with exaggerated care. He always did that, Brownlee remembered, when he was at his angriest.

Brownlee made one telephone call, suggesting politely that the watchers around Orpen's house be alerted. That, he was told, had just been done; a new angle to the Orpen situation had been reported. Then he tidied his desk, putting back into the safe the papers on which he had been working, and locked everything methodically. He left the office twenty minutes later than Paul. There was time enough, he thought. It would take Rona Metford at least three-quarters of an hour to travel from the Tysons' apartment to Orpen's street. This was a tricky situation. Yet the best way to deal with it might be the spontaneous idea, the natural action. He had proved that before in equally difficult problems—the solution was begun from the moment you accepted the spontaneous idea and made use of it. That was one reason why he had given Rona the address she asked for. And the other reason? Simply that Rona would have found the address somehow, perhaps from Milton Leitner or another student who had visited there. And, then, Brownlee would not have known when she was going to visit Orpen. That would have been really troublesome.

But Brownlee had misjudged one fact. Rona had not telephoned him from the Tysons' apartment uptown.

After the two agents had left her, Rona ended all indecision by borrowing a dress from Peggy's closet and taking Barbara to the apartment upstairs. There, she left Barbara safely with the slightly surprised but welcoming Burleighs. ("Delighted to Rally Around," Moira Burleigh had said, that being her phrase of the month, and she rushed to the kitchen to set another apple baking and shape up another hamburger, while the two small Burleighs and Barbara invaded the living-room with high soprano shrieks, quite ignoring Frank Burleigh at his desk, his pen poised as he searched for the *mot juste* to end another chapter. He gave up the unequal struggle and was last seen heading for the bathroom, manuscript and pen in hand.)

Rona took a taxi downtown, leaving it at Lexington and Fiftieth, entered the first cigar store she saw, and went straight to the telephone directory. But it gave her no help. Orpen's address was unlisted. His apartment was in this district, she knew. Scott had once said it wasn't too far from her own, and she had come here quickly, so determined and sure of finding Orpen. For a moment she hesitated, then she refused to be defeated. Perhaps Paul could help, he might know Orpen's address. Or Roger Brownlee would be better still. Paul would want to deal with Orpen himself. But Paul didn't know all the facts. He couldn't deal with Orpen.

As for me, Rona thought, I've only my suspicions and guesses—not enough to tell Paul or Brownlee or those two men who came to question me this morning. But Orpen won't know they are only suspicions. He may tell the truth, thinking that I know it. All's fair against Orpen.

She was in this mood when she telephoned Roger Brownlee. She remembered, as she dialled his number, that it was Saturday and his office could be closed. What would she do then? She must see Orpen before he had heard of Scott's death. That was important, she knew. But her sudden attack of worry, that nervous sickness, ended as the telephone's signal stopped and she heard Roger Brownlee's voice.

It's only a few blocks away, she thought, coming out into the bright May sunshine again. She hesitated on the sidewalk. I'll walk slowly and arrange my thoughts, she decided. God knows they need arranging at this moment. And I can't face Orpen unless I know what I mean to say. She turned eastwards, and then, reaching Third Avenue, she walked south. The street was busy, warm and friendly. People were relaxing; it was Saturday, another week of work was over, the sun was up and the sky was blue. She skirted a group of playing children, avoided the baby carriages heaped with the weekend groceries, listened to the words and the snatches of talk, watched the faces and the gestures and the carefree confidence.

This is not the real world, Scott would have said, echoing Orpen. This is as false as a dream, a myth, a pretence, a surface lie. A snare and delusion, Orpen would say. These people are the enslaved masses, the prisoners of the capitalist system, the victims of exploitation; this is not the real world.

311

Yet no one walked here as if he were afraid; no one looked over his shoulder before he spoke; no one felt the cold fear that now attacked Rona herself as she thought of Orpen's world. No, Rona thought, his is the dream, the nightmare world. This is the real. Real, because its faults are human faults. But Orpen's faults, and the faults of all men who believe as he does, are inhuman. That's the difference, I have only to take one step inside his world and I can feel its cold shadows, as black and cold as the iron shadows under which I'm passing now. She crossed Third Avenue quickly, stepping once more on to a pavement filled with window-shoppers, housewives carrying groceries, children playing, men in overalls returning from work.

"Rona!" a voice called, and a hand caught her arm. Rona stared blankly at the girl, in black slacks and expensive suède sandals and a slickly tailored white linen jacket, who was holding back a red setter at the end of a bright green leash. It was Mary Fyne, her pretty face smoothly powdered, her lips a deep coral to match her nails, a smile in her green eyes, her head tilted to show her excellent neck and the charming fall of her smooth red hair. She was giving all her attention to Rona, but the black flickering eyelashes were quite aware of the admiring stares from the men and the disapproving looks from the women who passed by. She pulled the dog closer with a sharp jerk on the leash. "Meet Hasdrubal!" She pointed to the setter with pride. "One of my beaux gave him to me last week, and all I do now is water and air the brute. It's a bit of a bore. But he looks kind of cute, doesn't he?"

She eyed Rona carefully. That dress didn't fit properly, and why choose navy to wear with black shoes and a black handbag? Rona's taste was slipping. She had even forgotten her gloves. Her shoes needed polishing. Mary Fyne smiled generously and decided to stand awhile and talk. She pointed one foot, ballerina style. "What *have* you been doing with yourself? I never see you nowadays. How's Scott? Oh—I forgot! I was so sorry to hear you'd ended your engagement, I really was." She gave Rona's face a sidewise glance. "Too bad. They say poor Scott is quite broken up about it."

Rona's silence seemed to irritate her. She leashed in the setter still more, her lips tightening. "Careful!" She sharply

312

warned away a small boy who had come too near. "He's kind of cute, but he likes to bite. Just a playful nip," she explained to Rona. "By the way, do you ever see Paul Haydn?"

"He works at *Trend*, too," Rona reminded her.

"My dear, *what* a cold you have! I wondered why you were throttled with a scarf on a hot day like this. Better rush home and gargle. And take my advice about Paul Haydn—don't waste your time on him." You've wasted enough time on Scott Ettley, the green eyes said. Then she laughed, throwing back her head just enough to show the excellent line of her jaw. "I shouldn't be surprised if Haydn's a bit of a queen," she added lightly, with just a hint of venom in the smooth voice. "No doubt he picked it up in Germany." The leash tightened suddenly. "Good-bye," she called over her shoulder as the setter suddenly lunged toward a hydrant. "Hasdrubal just adores Third Avenue. Such interesting smells!"

Rona walked on. Two more blocks to go. And the thoughts she had been trying to arrange had mixed themselves up again. Mary Fyne will blame Scott's suicide on the broken engagement, she suddenly realised. And so will most people. Scott's father? Yes, probably he, too. And Paul, what would he think when he heard? . . . And if I were to tell any of them that this was Scott's last revolt, a revolt against himself, who would believe me? Scott, she thought sadly, Scott has tied me to him. Will I ever cut myself free?

She felt sick, cold, and tired. She hesitated at the corner of Orpen's street, and stood suddenly irresolute.

Even if no one else will ever know the truth about Scott, she thought, I want to know. I must know. Then I can try to forget. Without knowing, there is no forgetting. I'll be tied to worries and doubts. No peace of heart, no freedom of mind . . . ever. She began walking toward the row of houses that faced the grimy wall of garage and warehouse.

Three children raced each other on roller skates. Two women with shopping bags on their arms talked about the price of meat. A young girl in a wide drooping skirt kept guard beside a baby sleeping in its carriage, while she watched three workmen beginning emergency repairs in the street. A mechanic leaned against the doorway of the garage and smoked a cigarette and watched them, too. At this hour

313

of the day, the lines of parked cars had thinned; a scattered trail of pedestrians, intent on their own business, followed the sidewalks. An automobile came slowly through the street, skirted the nose of a truck backed up against a loading stage in the warehouse, and swerved round the patch of roadway lined off with red flags where a pneumatic drill was driving its first bite into the pavement.

Rona flinched at the sudden clatter of the drill. She looked up. A workman grinned and gave a nod of his head. It was all so natural an incident, something that had happened so often to her before, that she welcomed it. She smiled back, almost gratefully. She felt as if she had stepped from the coldness of an icy hall into a room where a fire burned cheerfully. Then she halted, looking now at the number on the glass pane above the nearest doorway. She glanced along the street, noticed its mild bustle and everyday noises for the first time, and—as if reassured—she ran up the flight of stone steps. She hesitated again when she couldn't find the name she was looking for.

The workmen seemed to pay no attention to the girl in the navy dress who was standing at the doorway above them. One was concentrating on the vibrating drill, another was answering the questions of the small girls who had skated up to watch, the third was directing operations in general. Yet they were all noting the facts. Girl in blue dress, white scarf at throat—dark hair, even features, large eyes, pleasant smile—medium height, about 120 pounds, high-heeled shoes, excellent legs, walks well. And who was this guy following her? Quiet suit, grey felt hat, dark face. He had been keeping some distance from the girl, but now he quickened his pace as she ran up the steps. He stopped at the garage, though, to ask a question of the mechanic. Is he one of ours? the man with the drill wondered. Or is he another of that crowd? The workman straightened his back—a good excuse to glance along the street at a placid white-haired man who was half-hidden behind the loading truck, and then at a middle-aged woman who was sitting in the sunshine on a camp stool, placed near the warehouse wall, while she rocked a baby carriage gently and looked at the street scene with patient boredom. I wonder if they've guessed as much about us as we've guessed about them? the workman wondered.

Orpen's a popular guy this morning. That's one clear fact, anyway.

The girl in the navy dress had pressed one of the bells at last—the superintendent's bell, for a man in overalls and a dirty shirt opened the door. For a moment or two, the pneumatic drill was silent as a new spot for its attack was carefully chosen. The girl's question was too low to be heard. The superintendent nodded; he stepped aside and let the girl enter the house. He didn't close the door for a few moments. He came out and stood, as if enjoying this excuse for some fresh air. He lit a cigarette as he turned back to the house. So the girl had gone up to visit Orpen.

The men at work studied the roadway. The man in the quiet suit and grey felt hat had come to collect his car from the garage, for he followed the mechanic through the wide doorway, and halted just within its deep-shadowed cave. Farther along the street the white-haired man sat on a hydrant, his back against the warehouse wall, and lighted a pipe while he watched the loading of a truck with a critical eye. Beyond him, the sitting woman smoothed a light cover over the sleeping baby.

The man working the drill had a thought that amused him. There was Orpen, sitting quietly in his room, refusing to answer either telephone calls or any doorbells. Down here, in this ordinary little street scene, were two groups of people, both watching and waiting, both interested in the man upstairs who probably didn't even know that they were there. And now the girl in the blue dress was climbing the stairs to his door. What group did she belong to? To them or to us? Or to neither? If she belonged to them . . .

The same thought had struck one of his companions. He moved close to the drill and said, "Better lay off that, it's too noisy. We'll hear nothing." He was worried.

The man laid down the drill and picked up a shovel. He pointed to the cracked surface of the road and said, "I guess the superintendent knew that Orpen wouldn't let her in unless he trusted her."

The third man nodded, examining the pavement. "The bastard is probably safe enough." But how do you protect a man who won't even let you get in touch with him, far less accept an invitation to escape safely with escort arranged? The only way, he thought gloomily, to get hold of Nicholas Orpen will be to arrest him. But on what charges? He must have broken enough laws, but without legal proof we can't act. The workman reached for a pick-axe, spat on his hands, and then threw a quick glance along the street at the white-haired man near the truck, at the woman who gently rocked the baby carriage. All they can do is wait, too, he thought with relief. They probably can't pull any stunt as long as we are here—too many people around for any quiet kidnapping.

Then at that moment, the woman rose and stretched herself. She shook down the wrinkles in her cotton dress, folded the camp stool and hung it over the handle of the baby carriage. She looked at her watch and shook her head, as if she had sat too long in the sunshine and her husband's dinner would be overcooked. Then she began pushing the carriage, bending over it slightly as she talked to the baby, walking quickly toward the East River.

Perhaps she's genuine enough, thought the workman as he swung the pick-axe high above his head. Either she's genuine enough, or else it's a good act. Or perhaps I'm just too damned suspicious. He brought the pick-axe down on a crack in the pavement. And then he realised that the girl in the blue dress had not come out of the house. The woman, stumping quickly eastwards, had noted that too. No, he thought, you can't be too suspicious on this kind of job.

"She hasn't come down," he said to the man working beside him.

"Then she's the only person in New York he seems to trust."

He raised his voice. "Look out, Joe. Car coming!"

The man who had entered the garage was bringing his car out slowly. He drove it carefully past the excavation, leaning well out the window as he watched its fenders.

"Okay, boys," he said. And it wasn't a question. The car slowed down still more as he avoided a red flag. "They may play rough now," the quiet voice said. And the car moved on.

"Time for chow," the pick man said, downing his axe. They opened their lunch boxes, sitting on the debris they had created. And in between grumbling loudly and good-naturedly (time and a half was good pay, after all) at Saturday afternoons that were ruined, they had a laconic conference. The girl in the blue dress was a friend of Orpen's. The girl in the blue dress had been recognised by the woman with the baby carriage (or by the white-haired man who could have signalled the woman). The girl in the blue dress had been okayed by the agent in the car. Just where did that place the girl in the blue dress?

A man, tall, well-dressed in a casual way, had been waiting at the corner of the street near Third Avenue. Now he turned away impatiently, and came along toward the little group of men at lunch. He had dark hair greying at the temples, grey eyes that had a quick direct look, a good brow, a strong jaw, and a well-cut mouth. But he was too worried to even pretend to smile as he stopped and asked, "Has a girl come along this way? Did she go into this house just behind me?"

"A girl?" One of the workmen took another mouthful of sandwich and looked at the others. "Several girls went past here."

"Dark-haired? Pretty?"

"What was she wearing?"

"God knows," Paul Haydn said. What had Rona worn this morning? He could only remember the face that had avoided his eyes. Either she got here before I could stop her, he thought, or she's had an accident.

"No use getting worried," one of the workmen advised him. "You know what dames are. Probably gone shopping."

Paul Haydn hesitated. Then he mounted the steps and rang the superintendent's bell. The superintendent opened the door slowly; and before he answered he looked past Paul's shoulder into the street. Just for a moment, just long enough to get a careful signal. He shook his head in reply to Paul. He couldn't say.

"Well, I'll try upstairs," Paul said. "Where's Orpen's place?" He was already inside the hall. The superintendent shrugged his shoulders and lighted a cigarette as he gave him directions. Then he followed Paul up the stairway.

"Careful kind of guy, aren't you?" Paul asked angrily, looking at the dirty shirt and the stubble of beard on the man's chin. He was just the type who wouldn't notice Rona's arrival—probably he had been having a short beer in the
317

bar round the corner—and now was making up for his carelessness by officiousness.

"Sure," the superintendent said, looking at Paul's suit, "I'm a careful guy."

Paul turned and went on upstairs. As he neared Orpen's landing, he halted again. "This right?" he asked sarcastically, pointing to the only door there was.

"Sure," the man said. He halted, too, half a flight down. He waited expectantly.

Paul approached the door. He could hear no voices. He looked over his shoulder at the waiting superintendent. He had begun to feel he had been too quick to lose his temper with the man. He pushed the bell, half-angrily, half-defiantly.

There was on answer, no movement from the room.

He rang again. Then he knocked heavily. "Rona!" he called. He knocked again. "Rona!"

There was no answer, only the silence of an empty room.

He turned away from the door and looked at the superintendent expecting to see a look of open triumph. But it seemed as if the man was still listening.

"You were right," Paul said. "There's no one there, no one at all."

The superintendent said nothing. He was looking at Paul now, and there was a change in his expression. For a moment he hesitated, his eyes thoughtful. He decided to take the chance. "Look," he began, "seems to me as if——"

But Paul had hurried past him and was already half-way downstairs. "Where's a phone I can use? In the hall?" he called back.

As Rona had climbed the stairs to Orpen's apartment, her nervousness increased. Everything depended on her first phrases. If they were wrong, she would never get beyond Orpen's door.

She rang the bell and waited. There was only silence. Then from inside the room came a slight rustle suddenly stilled. He's hiding, she thought. He is in danger, then. And he knows it. Her doubts and hesitations began to recede. She knocked gently, and she spoke. "This is Rona Metford. I have an urgent message. From Scott Ettley."

She waited. "This is Rona Metford," she said again to the

318

man listening on the other side of the door. "This is urgent. About Scott." Suddenly, she had the feeling that she was being observed. How, she couldn't tell; she could see no obvious spy-hole. The door opened slightly.

"You came alone?" Orpen asked.

"Yes."

The door opened still more, just enough to let her slide through into the room, and it closed quickly behind her. Orpen locked it and bolted it.

She looked round the disordered room. Orpen had been writing. A steel box filled with papers stood open on his desk and sheets of typescript were scattered beside it. On the table were scraps of food—a piece of cheese, a hunk of stale bread, a half-emptied can of baked beans, a battered coffee pot, a dirty cup and plate. The hearth was littered with the thin black curling leaves of burned paper. The ash trays hadn't been emptied for days. They were overflowing with crushed cigarette stubs stained with dried lip marks. The windows were closed. The air was stale with pipe smoke, with the clinging smells of cheese and sardines and beer and coffee.

"Yes?" Orpen's quiet voice asked behind her.

She turned to face him.

He touched his unshaven chin, drew the opened neck of his shirt together. "I haven't been feeling too well in these last few days," he said, watching her eyes. "But you needn't look so horrified. I'm not as ill as I look. What's the message you bring?" He moved quickly over to the desk, jammed some of the papers into the steel box and snapped it shut.

"Don't worry," Rona said. "I'm not a spy."

He turned to look at her sharply. Then a smile flickered over his grey-white face. "What's the message from Scott?"

Rona sat down on an arm-chair. She said, "You are in danger."

"I am?" His mock concern hid his own feelings. He took off his glasses and wiped them.

She went on, in the same quiet voice, "Scott said you had been condemned. As a traitor." He was watching her face, but she stared back at him as impassively as she could.

"You expect me to take that seriously?" He made a good pretence of amusement. He gave his glasses a final polish and put them on again.

She shrugged her shoulders. "It seems ridiculous to me, or to anyone who isn't a Communist. But then, we don't live in your world." She looked down at the ashes on the hearth. "Scott took it seriously," she said. "And so will Thelma and Murray and your other comrades." She looked up at him quickly. She had struck deep. All the pretended scorn had gone from his face. He was tight-lipped, tense. His shadowed eyes, ringed with lack of sleep, stared out of a white mask.

"Where did Scott learn this?" he asked at last. At the meeting last night? Yes, it must have been there. Last night the decision had been made: Peter's decision. That explained the watchers down in the street this morning. . . .

Orpen walked over to the window. He stood there, hidden by the curtain, looking down at the warehouse wall. He had thought they had been sent as a warning, like the telephone calls he had treated with silence, like the visitors who had gone away from his door without seeing him. But now he knew they weren't watching down there in order to frighten him into obedience. They were more than a warning. How many of them? But did that matter? All that mattered was the fact that they were there. Comrade Peter had won.

"Scott didn't tell me where he learned it," Rona was saying. She was suddenly thankful for her hoarse voice, it couldn't give away her tensed emotions. "Scott only told me the message."

Scott, he was thinking, Scott had known the house would be watched and he had sent the girl. So Scott is on my side. Scott is one ally. But why hadn't he phoned? I would have spoken to him. In an emergency like this, he could have risked a call. Scott knew how to disguise a message and make it seem harmless. Or was Scott too afraid to risk that? Scott was playing safe. As all my friends will play safe, Orpen thought bitterly.

He left the window. He walked aimlessly as if he couldn't decide what to do next. He stopped at the desk, looking down at the box and the few remaining sheets of paper containing the lists of names that he had made. List after list of men who were in secret control, in absolute power—the policy makers of the American Communist Party. And the answer was always the same. The Americans on that list were few, their power was limited. They were tolerated as Orpen had been tolerated. The real power was in the hands of the Russians. Orders came from Moscow.

Yes, he had always known that; but he had never expected the grip to tighten, to grow more absolute as it had done in those last months. By using the foreigners for all these years, he had led himself to this defeat. By thinking to benefit from them, he had surrendered himself to them completely. And the Party—defeated and surrendered too? The Russians or the Party: that was the choice. That was what he had admitted at last, and he still hadn't found the answer. He had been condemned as a traitor before he could find the answer. The Russians, the Party. How was it possible to dissociate them, to refuse one and keep the other? And who would help him?

Orpen picked up the last of the lists that he had written. He had made them and burned them and made them again, as if to convince himself that there might be some hope for his revolt. But the answer was always the same. The real power was in the hands of the Russians or of those foreigners who had lived for years in Russia so that they were almost accepted as "reliable." He wasn't the only one who had felt this, but the others were wiser than he had been. They accepted the inevitable and forced themselves to rejoice over it. Cynics? What other choice was there, except to give up the Party too? And without beliefs, how did a man live? Without beliefs, and nothing to take their place? Nothing and nothingness. A man became a sleeping eating drinking animal, one of the unthinking mass to be controlled. Without beliefs, there was no power.

He crumpled the sheet of names and threw it back on the desk. I've been a fool, an impulsive fool with emotions out of control—the emotions I have always denied myself and warned others against. As I used to warn Scott. . . .

He remembered the girl, then, who sat so silently behind him. He swung around to face her. "Tell Scott to do nothing rash. Tell Scott I was wrong. I will admit my guilt." Yes, he thought, I shall confess openly that I've been wrong in questioning the recent policies of Comrade Peter. That is all they know against me; that is all they need to know. "Well," he said sharply, "why don't you leave? You gave me the message, and I've given you the reply."

But she sat very still, her eyes watching him curiously. "It's too late," she said, "too late to send any message through Scott."

Too late. . . . Then Scott Ettley had told the Committee about him. Last night, Ettley had gone to the meeting, last night Ettley had informed. "No," he said sharply. He put a hand to his eyes, half-covering his face. You can't even think clearly, he told himself, you can't even think, far less plan. "It's too late?" He repeated her words as if he refused to believe them.

Then suddenly, he looked up at Rona, his eyes narrowing, his voice cold and alert. "How do you know it's too late?" He crossed the room quickly and stood before her. "How do you know anything about me or Scott or the Party?"

Rona didn't answer. Here is the truth, she thought wearily. Now all the hideous suspicions are bitter facts.

Orpen's anger was sudden and terrible. "You weakened him. You destroyed him." Then he restrained himself, forcing his voice down to a quietness that was still more threatening. "He told you everything, didn't he?"

She shook her head.

"And did he also tell you the penalty he may expect?"

Rona said slowly, quietly, as if she were talking of someone she scarcely knew, "He's dead."

Orpen stared at her, unbelieving.

"He came to see me last night," Rona went on. "He was upset. And afraid. Then—he left me. I heard, this morning, that he had killed himself. He jumped in front of a subway train."

Was she lying? Was this the trap she had come to set? Orpen's eyes searched her face. Then, suddenly, he knew she was speaking the truth.

"Why?" he asked at last. "Why did he do this?" The lines on his face were taut. He turned abruptly away. He went over to a chair, but he remained standing, his hands grasping its back as if he needed the support more than he would admit. "Why?" he asked again.

"That is what his father will ask. That's what I've been asking. But perhaps your answer will be nearer the truth than ours." She looked at her hands and saw the faint white mark of the ring she used to wear. "He lived your kind of life," she said. "He was beginning to think like you, to act like you." She looked up at him suddenly, challenging him to deny it. "Have you never felt as Scott must have felt last night?"

His grasp on the chair tightened. "No," he said bitterly. Ettley the informer. . . . Have you never informed, Orpen? You didn't call it informing then, you called it duty to the Party. You called it the extermination of traitors and saboteurs. Have you never felt as Scott must have felt last night?—"No," Orpen repeated, thrusting the chair away from him so that it fell against the table, "you don't trap me, as you trapped Ettley."

"Trap you?" she asked, her eyes widening.

"Who sent you here? Ettley is dead. Who sent you?"

"No one." Did Orpen live in a world of commands, as well as of fears and suspicion?

He looked at her searchingly. Then he moved quickly to the window, standing well behind the curtain, moving it gently so that he could watch the street.

"You see," Rona said, rising and coming over to him, "you can't even look out of the window like a normal man. You hide, you are afraid. You can't walk down a street without looking over your shoulder as if your own shadow would rise up and denounce you. And it isn't my world that terrifies you. You aren't half as afraid of my world as you are of your own. Why do you live in it?" She stepped in front of the window.

Orpen caught her wrist sharply and pulled her roughly back to the centre of the room.

"Let me go," she said angrily.

The grip on her wrist tightened. Last night the grip had tightened.

"Who sent you here?" Orpen asked.

"No one," she said. "People don't always have to be told what to do. Let me go!"

"And no one else knows what Ettley told you?"

The grip on her wrist warned her. She kept silent.

He pressed the advantage. "You are the only one who knows about Ettley," he said.

She shook her head slowly, watching him.

"Who else?" he asked mockingly.

"The police . . . the police are interested. And the FBI."

He laughed. "They are?" Then, just as suddenly his mood changed again and he said bitterly, "You are lying. Scott might have told you, but he would tell them nothing."

"They know," she said.

He let go her wrist. "Sit down," he commanded. He stood in front of her, his hands on his hips, his eyes watching her face intently. "Did Scott go to the police? Or to the FBI?"

She shook her head again.

"Did you go to the FBI?"

She hesitated.

He noticed it. "I beg your pardon," he said with his old biting sarcasm, "did you go to the FBI *and* the police? I mustn't forget the double threat." He shook his head and smiled. "That was too good a try, Miss Metford. One of them might have been believable. But two were a little too much."

Rona said wearily, "Have it your own way." Whatever I say, this man only interprets according to his own reasoning. I had to be ordered to come here, I am trying to trap him, I argue with hidden threats, I lie. . . . Must he always doubt the truth?

"If you went to the FBI," Orpen said with evident enjoyment, "do you know what they are doing now? They are checking on you, not on Scott. They are checking first on you to see if you are reliable before they act. And if you gave them only a lot of wild suspicions, how can they take action? They need facts."

"So they aren't the tyrants your propaganda makes them out to be?"

His lips tightened. "And you had no real facts to give them—just an emotional outburst from Scott Ettley. Even if they ever could prove he was a Communist, that would mean nothing. It isn't illegal to belong to the Communist Party." That idea seemed to amuse him, for he smiled and added, "You have talked contemptuously of my world, Miss Metford. But at least we aren't the fools that inhabit yours."

He looked over at the telephone on his desk. "What did

ou say to the FBI about me?" he asked. "If you did go
o them, that is."

"I didn't go to them. They came to see me," she said.
He was very still. Then slowly, he looked back at her.

"They came to see me this morning about Scott," she
vent on. "They seemed to know that he was a Communist.
think they've been following him. He was afraid of that,
ast night."

Orpen's face was rigid. Then he moved quickly over to
he telephone. I have to risk it, he thought. This phone may
e tapped, I may be under observation, but I have to risk it.
The others must be warned. But he still hesitated, his hand
on the telephone.

"Did the FBI know he was dead?"

"It was they who told me."

He said slowly, "You are cleverer than I thought, Miss
Metford. You know how to hit and when to hit. Am I supposed to be so alarmed and confused that you can persuade
me to go to the FBI? Is that why you came here—to persuade me?"

"I had hoped you would go," she said frankly, "but not for
those reasons."

"For what reasons, then?" He looked at her in amazement.
"Did you really believe I was a traitor?"

"I believed you might still have a conscience."

"Ah," he said bitingly, "I thought you'd bring in conscience,
somehow. You've the usual bourgeois weakness for lofty
moral sentiment."

He lifted the telephone and dialled. He was still watching
her with amusement. Then, as he waited for the answer, he
became the expressionless man again, the white-faced mask
with the quiet, commanding voice. He identified the speaker
at the other end of the wire carefully. "Jim? Ed speaking. I
can't leave here at the moment, and I've run out of cigarettes.
Bring some over, and we can have a talk. Thanks."

He replaced the receiver. "Disappointed?" he asked. "Well,
you'll probably hear more when Jim gets to the nearest
cigar store and phones me in safety from there. But I doubt if
you'll understand any better than you did that time."

Rona had risen to her feet,

"Leaving?" he asked with a smile.

"If you'll unlock the door with the key you put in your pocket."

"You take your defeat well," he said. "You can go back and tell your friends in the FBI that this little attempt failed badly. I'm highly flattered that you thought I was so important."

Rona took a step toward the door, but he barred the way.

"Not yet," Orpen said. "I have some questions to ask you, Miss Metford. Sit down."

The telephone rang.

"Jim was quick," he said. At least, he thought with some satisfaction, they still paid attention to him. He lifted the receiver and answered, his voice confident. "Jim? Ed speaking. Sorry I couldn't see you this week. Don't worry, it was nothing serious—just a touch of grippe. I'm all right now. I want to see you soon. This evening? Good. I have a lot to tell you. And make it a party—invite Peter and the rest of the boys. I feel like a party. . . . No, I've seen no one this week. No one. Except Mac. Did he say I was ill?—Seriously ill? He did? I thought that was the trouble. Well, you can't trust what Mac says . . . I said you can't trust what Mac says. Don't worry about my health. And tell the others I don't have to be looked after like an invalid. By the way, Mac isn't in such good shape himself. No hope. The doctors have been with him. Yes, it's serious. . . . He called the doctors last night, I understand." Orpen glanced over at Rona. "His girl brought me the news. I'm convinced she's right. That has been one of my worries this week, frankly. Thought you'd like to know at once. See you later."

Orpen stood for a few moments looking down at the phone. Well, he had given them the warning that Scott Ettley was now a danger to them. It might have been an exaggeration to say that Ettley had gone to the FBI last night. But Ettley was dead, and his evidence was silenced. And if I produce counter-evidence, Orpen thought, if I can show he was a traitor, that his lies were an attempt to mislead the Committee, to attack me, to endanger our work?—Yes, that is my case. Ettley's death strengthens it.

He left the desk and came forward to where Rona was still standing. "Sit down," he said quietly.

Rona looked at him with horror. She retreated a step. "I brought you news of Scott's death," she said, "and you've used it to—to——"

"To blacken Ettley and whitewash myself? But you are wrong, Miss Metford. Ettley was the traitor, not I." He paused. He was listening, suddenly alert, to the sound of men's voices on the staircase. A man's footsteps were coming this way.

Rona said, "Your friends? They didn't believe you after all. You are still 'ill' to them, Orpen."

He turned on her, clamping his hand across her mouth, seizing her arm and twisting it behind her back. He looked desperately at the box on his desk, at the last list he had written and not yet destroyed. "Still!" he whispered, tightening his grip on her body, pressing her arm higher against her spine.

She tried to move her feet, to make even the smallest sound, but the pain silenced her. Last night the grip had tightened, last night. . . . The terror and nausea surged back. Even as the doorbell rang, as she heard a voice—a voice that sounded like Paul's, a voice calling "Rona!"—she sagged toward the floor. The voice, faint and fading into the black silence that fell over and around her, was gone. The pain was gone. The room stretched out endlessly; the door drew back and farther back, receding into the distance, smaller and still smaller until it vanished.

Orpen tightened his hold. Was her faint a pretence? He daren't risk anything. He stood, holding the dead weight against his body, his hand still muffling her mouth.

In a little while, the knocking at the door stopped and the footsteps retreated. ". . . no one there at all," a man's voice said. The footsteps were hurrying, growing fainter, becoming only a distant clatter.

Orpen moved then, dragging the girl to an arm-chair. Let her revive slowly, he thought; the more slowly, the safer it will be. He crossed quickly over to the door and stood there listening. But the footsteps had gone.

He lit a pipe, his hands trembling, his annoyance growing as he watched their fear. I have never used violence in my life, he thought. I'm unnerved, that's all. Ettley's treachery, my danger, the danger to the Party—they've all unnerved me. He looked down at Rona. And this girl, too, he thought, the way she has of talking, the way she twists my words. . . . I have never used violence in my life, he repeated, trying to calm himself. But he thought of what the girl would say if she heard him. She would say, "You have known of violence committed, you have seen comrades disappear and never asked questions, you have abandoned Jack and silenced the doubts over his death, you have——" Stop this, he told himself, stop this!

He stared down at the girl. Yes, he could begin to see how she had weakened Ettley. It was she who had killed Ettley. He stared down at the white face, at the soft dark hair.

She opened her eyes, her lips parted, she put a hand to her throat. Slowly, she tried to sit up. She looked around helplessly, then she looked at him.

Silently, he brought her a glass of water. His movements were decided once more, his face was calm. He drew a chair up to face her. "Now," he said quietly, almost gently, "tell me what Scott told you. All of it." He reached toward the small table at her elbow and picked up a battered pack of cigarettes. He offered her one, saying with a pleasant smile that he didn't smoke cigarettes himself and that these were remainders from a party last week. Rona refused the slightly bent, crumpled cigarette. She felt sick, but she didn't give that as an excuse. He must not know how the touch of his hand on her arm, the feeling of his fingers on her flesh could make her so afraid—afraid beyond all reason, beyond all control.

She looked at the window. "Please," she said. "There's no air in the room. I can't breathe."

He rose. He hesitated. Then he opened the door into the small darkened room which lay at the back of the house. Here, a suitcase lay on the floor beside the disordered bed, and clothes and books and papers were heaped around it. He stepped carefully over the litter. (I'll have to clear this up, now, he was thinking. He could even smile grimly at the evidence of flight scattered around him.) He reached the windows and opened the heavy shutters. Then he unlocked the window quickly, and lowered its upper half a few inches. He drew back against the folded shutters and

oked down into the courtyard with its high wall. The
uperintendent's dog was there, a large brute that guarded
he fire escape as if Orpen had trained it himself. Orpen's
mile deepened.

He came back into the living-room. The girl was sitting
s he had left her. All the fight in her is gone, he thought,
ll her resistance. He said, with great good humour, glancing
ack at the opened window, "That will have to do meanwhile. However, this state of siege will soon be over. In
act, it is over. For whoever came to the door was not inter-
sted in me. Only in you, Miss Metford. And he wasn't
ven sure if you were here. So no one knows that you are
ere. Isn't that right?"

He sat down on the chair facing her, drawing it nearer.
Now, before I leave for my meeting, tell me about Scott
ttley. I must know. You understand?" His voice was kindly,
eassuring. There was a small smile on the thin lips. But
he grey eyes behind the glasses were cold and hard.

CHAPTER TWENTY-SIX

Paul Haydn ran down the narrow stairs from Orpen's apartment. Behind him, quick enough, but paying more attention
to torn linoleum and sloping treads, was the superintendent.
The noise they made brought a woman on to the third-
floor landing, with a pot of potatoes still in her hand. "What
d'you think you are?" she yelled after them, leaning over
the shaking handrail. "House-wreckers?" And having registered her protest, and underlined it with a sharply banged
door, she retired to mash the potatoes.

In the hall, Paul paid no attention to the superintendent,
but went straight to the phone that hung on the wall. He
found a nickel and dialled the Tysons' number. As he expected, there was no answer. Rona was gone. Perhaps she
was delayed, he thought, perhaps she's only now on her way
here. He tried to imagine where she would have left Barbara
for safety, but that question beat him completely. Well,
he thought, I'll get hold of Roger Brownlee. He can check
up with his friends at the FBI and find out where Rona is

—after all, they are supposed to be keeping an eye on he

"Have you change?" he asked the superintendent, holdin
out the loose money he had found in his pocket—a fift
cent piece and a clutter of pennies.

The man shook his head. "I know!" he said, suddenl
helpful, and opened the front door eagerly. "Hey, there!
he called to the workmen. "Any of you guys got a nicke
or a dime? We're stuck, here."

One of the workmen rose quickly and came over to th
house. "Sure," he said. He ran up the steps, fumbling in hi
pocket.

"Thanks," Paul Haydn said. "This is kind of important."
He nodded gratefully to the red-haired young man in work
stained jeans and white cotton undershirt, and turned onc
more to the phone.

The man hesitated in the doorway, his back to the brigh
street now settled into midday silence. He caught a brie
sign from the superintendent. Then he said, "Any water t
drink around here?" The easy grin on his round, good
natured face had gone. His eyes asked a different question

"Sure," the superintendent said quickly. "Help yourself."
He pointed to a door at the back of the hall. "I'll find you a
spare bottle," he said, following the workman. The two mer
disappeared down the basement steps.

The sunlight streamed over the threshold, picking out the
cracks on the yellowed wall, the streaks of dust on the dingy
linoleum. Paul waited, the receiver at his ear, listening to
the repeated signal that told him Brownlee's office was as
empty as this narrow hall. He stood there, listening long
after he knew it was hopeless, his eyes dark with worry, his
jaw clenched. Then he hooked the receiver on to its box. But
he still stood there, staring at the cracked plaster and the
dust-streaked floor.

"You know," the superintendent said as he returned to the
hall, "Orpen's up there, all right." He glanced at the red-
haired workman who stood at his elbow. "I heard him
moving around this morning when I was up on the top
floor fixing the light."

"Why the hell didn't you tell me before?" Paul asked
angrily.

"Wouldn't have done you much good," the superintendent

aid. "He's playing possum. The minute he hears someone, he's silent as death. Guess he wants to pretend he's visiting his aunt in the country."

Paul Haydn frowned. A thoughtful look came over his face,

"Having trouble with bill collectors?" he suggested, but he obviously didn't believe what he said.

The superintendent looked Haydn up and down. "Yeah," he said. "That's about it, I guess."

"You know," Paul said, "it might be an idea to call a cop and see what's wrong upstairs. Orpen could be ill." He smiled grimly. "We might even have to hammer our way in. What about borrowing a pick-axe?" he asked the workman, who seemed to enjoy spending the last ten minutes of his lunchtime just standing around listening.

The red-haired man stared at him and then looked at the superintendent.

"Forget it," Paul said. "At the moment I've other things to think about than a man who doesn't answer his doorbell." He looked angrily out into the street.

"I've been wondering about that girl," the red-haired man said. "Was she wearing a blue dress?"

Paul looked at the man helplessly. "I couldn't say." Rona didn't wear much blue, he remembered.

"Did she——" began the workman, but light footsteps at the door interrupted him. He turned quickly around. He saw a white-haired man, thin, medium height, alert face, coming into the house.

"Something wrong, Paul?" the newcomer was saying.

Haydn straightened up. "You're damned well right," he said angrily to Roger Brownlee. "Rona isn't here."

"That's odd," Brownlee said. "I saw the agent who is keeping an eye on her sitting in a car parked along the street. He wouldn't be sitting there so calmly if she weren't here." He glanced at the superintendent and the red-haired man in work clothes. "I'll call the FBI. They've slipped up." He looked again at the superintendent. "Paul, you run out and talk to the man in the grey Plymouth. I think he's the same guy you met last night."

Paul glanced up the staircase behind him. "I'd rather start talking to Orpen," he said grimly.

331

"We've got to be sure I'm right," Brownlee said.

Then the superintendent took a step forward. "What's your problem?" he asked. His voice had lost its drawl. "Perhaps it's our problem, too."

The red-haired workman said, "A dark-haired girl in a blue dress went upstairs over half an hour ago. That right?" He looked at the superintendent for confirmation.

Paul took a step forward.

Brownlee caught Paul's arm and held it back. "Steady, Paul. He didn't know who you were."

The superintendent nodded. "Had to make sure you weren't using the girl as an excuse to get to Orpen." He looked at Brownlee with more annoyance than he did at Paul Haydn. "We didn't slip up," he said. "So far, Orpen is still here. And that's more than he would have been if we hadn't been around this morning." He thought of the ambulance and the white-uniformed attendants who had tried to persuade him that Orpen had phoned for them urgently. When he had begun checking the hospital, they had suddenly left. "Hey, where are you going?" he asked Paul.

"Up," Paul said, from the staircase. "Or do you still think that I'm out to murder Orpen?"

"The fire escape in back might come in handy," the superintendent said slowly. "That door of his isn't so easy."

Paul halted half-way up the first flight of stairs, and retraced his steps. "At the back of the house?" He was already past them, heading for the door in the hall that led to the basement. "Does this get me to the courtyard?"

"Yes. And tell the man you see down there that Frank sent you. He'll get you past the dog."

Brownlee raised an eyebrow. "Comrade Orpen would be much impressed. Is he as important as all this?"

The superintendent ignored that. The remark about "slipping up" still rankled. He was watching the basement door close behind Paul Haydn. "Yes, that's our best bet," he said. "He'll go up and break in and perhaps have that fight he's looking for. We'll call a cop and get the whole top floor arrested for disorderly conduct. Louie," he turned to the man with red hair, "call a cop!"

"Okay," Louie said. He gave a grin as he left; the cop would be as mad as hell when he found what they had

332

cooked up. At the doorway, he stepped aside to let a white-aproned grocery clerk carry a large box into the hall.

"That's a lot of groceries you have there, Bud," the superintendent said, eyeing the newcomer. Youngish—about twenty-two, slightly built but wiry, grey eyes, fair hair, long chin, sharp nose, uneven eyebrows, narrow face, full-lobed ears.

"Just another load," the man said, balancing his foot on the bottom of the steep flight of stairs. Old army wash pants, the superintendent noted, a faded blue shirt with rolled-up sleeves, apron soiled, an automatic pencil clipped to the shirt's breast pocket, good brown shoes, a wrist watch.

"Where's it going?" A loaf of bread, a bunch of celery, leafy carrots, a box of eggs, and more underneath.

The man shifted his grip on the box. He looked at the superintendent and then at Brownlee. "Orpen's," he said. He sounded bored with his job.

"Know where that is?" The superintendent's voice was casual, his eyes careful.

The man transferred a wad of gum from one thin cheek to another before he answered. "No," he said. "Where's it?"

"Top floor."

"Just my luck." He looked up the well of the staircase as he spoke, shaking his head wryly. He started climbing.

"You can leave it here," the superintendent called. "I'll take it up."

"Got to deliver. Personally. Rules of the store."

"Leave it here!"

"And lose my job?" The man didn't stop. The superintendent and Brownlee exchanged glances. Then they ran after him. The superintendent caught his arm. "Hey!" the man said, puzzled, angry. "Can't a guy do his job?"

"Who ordered this stuff?" the superintendent asked, looking into the box. He opened the box of eggs. They were eggs, all right. He left the celery, the bunch of carrots. The bread was soft to his grip, concealing nothing. Underneath, there were only groceries too.

"Hey, what's the idea?" The man's face showed sudden truculence.

"Who ordered this?" the superintendent repeated.

"He did." The man jerked his thumb upstairs. "He just phoned. Urgent."

"Wait here! I can check on that." The superintendent hurried downstairs toward the basement.

So Orpen's telephone wire is being tapped, Brownlee thought. And he smiled, for he liked to see a job being well done.

"What's so funny?" the man demanded. He looked after the superintendent worriedly.

"You'd better wait here," Brownlee said quietly. "What's all the hurry for, anyway?"

"I've other deliveries to make. We're shorthanded to-day." But there was a nervous drop in the man's eyes. He frowned at the watch on his wrist. "Half-past one already," he said angrily, and he seemed to hesitate as if he were making up his mind. He looked over the bannisters, down toward the basement door. He's nervous, Brownlee thought; he's lied to the superintendent.

"Okay, okay," the man said unexpectedly. "You deliver it." He dumped the box on the step below him and started to move downstairs.

But Brownlee blocked his path. "Yes, we'll go down together and talk to the superintendent, shall we?"

The man stopped, backing away, staring down at Brownlee. And then, at that moment, a door opened above them on the third-floor landing and a woman came out screaming. She waved a dish towel frantically as she leaned over the railing. "Get a cop!" she yelled. "There's a man on the fire escape. He's breaking into the top floor—get a cop!"

The man's stare deepened as he listened. For a second he stood motionless, and then, his face tightening, he turned and raced upstairs. Brownlee started after him. Far below there was a shout. Doors opened. Voices exclaimed and questioned. A babel of sound soared up through the house.

Brownlee kept on. The blood pounded in his ears, a searing band tightened round his chest, his shoes were soled with lead, his thigh muscles strained painfully. Yet he kept on. And he was gaining. Three steps, just over an arm's length, separated him now from the running man. But there, just ahead, was Orpen's landing. The man stumbled slithering on to it, his hand fumbling in his pocket for the pencil. He pulled it free and twisted it sharply. He threw it at Orpen's door even as Brownlee made a desperate lunge for

334

his arm. The twisted pencil lay at the edge of the sill, seemingly simple and innocent.

Brownlee stared at it. An incendiary pencil. Its action had started. From the moment it had been twisted, from the moment the thin dividing wall inside its body had been snapped, the action had started. And nothing could stop it. Nothing. The two substances it contained were no longer separated: they were mixing, flowing together, forming a third force, inevitable and deadly. He made an instinctive movement to pick it up, even as he knew it was hopeless. The third force was working; its power was already born in the first little jet of white flame, no bigger than a pilot light under a gas burner, that now pointed its warning. In a minute now, perhaps even in a few seconds . . . The man beside him was staring, too, his breath coming in heavy gulps. Suddenly, he twisted away from Brownlee and darted for the staircase.

He won't get far, Brownlee thought grimly. But now, the warning is the important thing; that has to be clear. He left the landing, too, leaning over the rail as he went downstairs. Below him, the superintendent and a couple of aroused tenants grapple with the escaping man. "Get back there! Fire!" Brownlee yelled. "Fire!" And as the superintendent looked up toward him, startled, he gathered all the breath he had left in his lungs to shout, "It's an incendiary pencil."

The superintendent's face went tense. He knew what they had to deal with, for he was translating Brownlee's warning for the others. "Everyone downstairs, everyone downstairs, at once!" And even if he had no time to explain that the pencil's flame could not be extinguished, that they had to wait until it had died and only a normal fire was left to fight, the urgency in his voice was unmistakable. "Later!" he yelled at a tenant who had grabbed a pail of sand. "Not now. No use. Get downstairs!" Still holding a firm grip on the man he had caught, he herded the tenants downstairs, trying to count them as they came out of the apartments.

Brownlee halted on the third floor. The woman with the dish towel had stepped back into her room. She was saying, "Fire? Fire?" in a bewildered way. "But there's nothing burning!"

"Come on," Brownlee said, following her, catching her arm.

335

She looked at her apartment, looked at its neatness and care and work. "Oh, no!" she cried.

Brownlee urged her away. "We'll save it," he said as he pulled her toward the staircase. "But first, we must get downstairs." She went unwillingly, looking at him, still carrying the dish towel.

"What's that?" she asked, clutching him. From the landing on the top floor came a deep steady hiss. Brownlee quickened their steps. Suddenly, the woman screamed and covered her eyes with the towel.

A strange light, bleak and white, hung over the well of the staircase. And then, with a rushing noise the gush of flames broke loose, violent jetting spreading flames.

Paul Haydn reached the third floor.

Down in the courtyard, the dog and man were now hidden by the shade of the ailanthus tree. The dog had lost sight of him as he climbed the fire escape. Paul could still hear an uneasy whine, but the man who had taken Paul past the dog must have said something to reassure it again, for the whine stopped and the bark was checked. And now down there below him was only silence, and the leafy spray of ailanthus leaves blotting out the sad grey earth of the walled yard. The grimy frame of the fire escape shook at each movement and it seemed to cling more closely to the house wall. From the apartments inside this soot-stained box of stone came a hodge-podge of sound—the clatter of dishes, a man's voice laughing, "Chattanooga Choo-Choo" competing with Mozart, a girl arguing bitterly with an older woman, an announcer warming up for a baseball game, an imitation Southern voice singing that if she'd have known you were coming she'd have baked a cake. The windows he passed belonged to bedrooms, some frilled and gaily painted, some untidied and dreary, but they all seemed empty. Until the third floor.

There, as he moved quietly and quickly toward the last flight of skeleton stairs, he saw a movement. But the peeling, weather-bleached frame of Orpen's window lay ahead of him, coming step by careful step nearer him. He reached it, stood for a moment to gather his breath. He noticed, first with dismay, that the window was crisscrossed with wooden spars dividing it into small panes of glass; then with a surge of relief, that the upper half of the window was a few inches open from the top. He tried to raise its lower half, but it was screwed firmly in place. Then, suddenly, from the floor below him, a woman screamed.

The upper half of the window screeched like an echo as he wrenched it down. He swung himself up and over, and then dropped to the floor of the bedroom.

The door ahead of him lay open. But neither Rona nor Orpen was paying any attention to him. His neat entrance had gone completely unnoticed. Orpen was on his feet, facing Rona, his hands brushing his face and shoulders free of cigarette stubs and grey ashes. On the floor beside him lay a large empty ash tray. Rona was standing behind the table, a coffee pot raised in her right hand. "You've no right to keep me here, you've no right to make me answer. You've no right," she kept repeating, "you've no right. . . ."

Orpen, taking off his glasses to wipe them, said angrily, "You might have broken them. . . . Put down that coffee pot. You look ridiculous. And I'll decide my own rights for myself." Then his attention was caught by the sounds of footsteps running upstairs and of voices calling from far below. He took a step toward the door, listening, still watching Rona. "That's an old trick," he said. "Am I supposed to look behind me to see what you pretend to see? Put down that coffee pot!"

Paul Haydn stepped into the living-room. "Yes," he said, "you can put it down now, Rona." He went over to her and stood beside her.

"He had no right," she said. "He had no right!"

"None at all," Paul said gently, "none at all." He was watching Orpen.

And Orpen, watching Paul Haydn, was still listening to the sounds outside. The running footsteps were reaching the last flight of stairs.

"You needn't watch us," Paul said quietly. "We aren't your friends." As he kept his voice low, he could feel Rona relax beside him. Her near hysteria was passing. That's the main thing now, he thought. And he gave up his first impulse to smash Orpen's glasses properly. Not that Orpen was worth fighting, a white-faced little runt with tight pale lips and blinking eyes and thin grey hair—a frightened little clerk

337

who had never been promoted and was afraid for his pension. You'd better stop that, Paul told himself, or you'll begin to feel he's a human being, someone you could be sorry for.

A look of indecision crossed Orpen's face. Outside, the heavy footsteps stumbled.

Paul Haydn took Rona's arm and drew her away from the door. She flinched for a moment, and then looked up at him as if to excuse her foolishness. But he was listening to Roger Brownlee's voice shouting on the landing outside: "Get back there! Fire! Fire!" And then the words, "It's an incendiary pencil."

Paul glanced at Orpen. He knew what that meant, for he had run to the desk and was gathering up the steel box as he jammed a crumpled sheet of paper into his pocket. He started pulling out books from a deep shelf, sweeping them on to the floor with one hand. But whatever he had to do required both hands. He laid the steel box down, and then—just as suddenly—picked it up, turning to face Paul Haydn as he held the box tightly against his chest.

Paul Haydn looked at him contemptuously. "We aren't thieves," he said. Then his voice changed as he turned to Rona. "This way." He drew her toward the bedroom and the fire escape.

She was puzzled by his haste, but she went with him. "A pencil?" she asked in wonder, listening to a sudden hiss that came from the other side of the door.

"Surest way of starting a fire."

Rona halted for a moment. She looked back at Orpen. But she said nothing. Orpen, standing with the box still clutched in his arms, turned his eyes away. Then, as the hissing became a rushing sound, the sound of a torrent unleashed from a dam, he stared at the door unbelievingly, hopelessly.

Paul Haydn pushed a bureau under the bedroom window. "Come on, Rona," he said, lifting her on to its top. He climbed up beside her and helped her through the upper half of the window. He glanced back at Orpen. "Make up your mind!" he yelled.

But Orpen didn't move. He was still standing in the middle of the room, his face now calm, expressionless.

Paul looked at Rona. She was waiting on the narrow platform of the fire escape, shrinking back against the wall of the house as she stared down through the skeleton steps and the thin iron struts. He hauled himself through the window, and stood beside her.

"I'm scared," she said, shutting her eyes for a moment, steadying herself against the railing. "It shakes," she said, "Paul, it shakes!"

"I'll go first. Don't look down. I'll count the steps for you. Here's my hand."

She slipped off her high-heeled shoes. "No good twisting an ankle," she said, now keeping her voice equally calm. She put out her hand and grasped his.

There were men down in the yard. And Brownlee.

"Where's Orpen?" Brownlee asked.

"Making up his mind. We'll have to go back and pull him out."

"Damn his eyes," Brownlee said, and started on his way up the fire escape.

"Hey you, come back here!" a voice shouted from the courtyard, but Brownlee climbed on. From the street, came the clanging of fire engines. And now other men were mounting the fire escape, carrying axes.

In the street, the ladders were up and hoses were playing on the fourth floor and roof.

The superintendent, blackened and red-eyed, said wearily, "We held it back with extinguishers and sand and a stirrup pump. It didn't get downstairs. But the top landing is a mess and the firemen are worried about the roof. These old houses are dry—they go up quickly." He looked at the tenants grouped in a worried huddle beyond the fire engines. "No one hurt, thank God. They got enough warning. But there's been a lot of damage. Who's going to pay for it?" He cursed Orpen silently. Then he looked at Rona. "We'll follow Orpen when he comes down," he said to Paul. "We've got men out back and in front. Pity we hadn't the goods on him so that we could have arrested him this morning. *And* picked up some of his papers. There must be some valuable stuff up there." He looked at the fourth floor again and his mouth tightened.

Paul said, "I'm taking Miss Metford to her sister's. Tell Brownlee when you see him. I hope to God he's all right."

"He can take care of himself."

"Who started the fire, anyway?"

"We got *him*," the superintendent said grimly. "He's just another stooge. He lost his head. That fire was useless the moment we got suspicious of him."

"Pretty drastic measure to make sure of Orpen," Paul said. "There are other ways."

"It's my guess they wanted to destroy something he has got stored away in his room. After all, he could always walk down that fire escape. But there's something up there that they don't want to fall into our hands." He turned to Rona. "I wouldn't be surprised to learn that the moment you went up there this morning, and stayed—well, that was when they decided they could take no more chances." He half-smiled as he looked at the girl with the wide dark eyes. And I'm talking too much, too, he thought suddenly. There's nothing like a fire and a fright to loosen up one's tongue. "Did Orpen say much?" he asked more casually.

Rona shook her head.

"Later," Paul said quickly to the superintendent. "Later." He gave the man a nod, as much as to say *You know where to find us*. He made way for Rona through the curious crowd that had gathered so quickly and spontaneously.

"Oh, it isn't much," one woman said, disappointed. "Look, they're winding up the hoses."

"Some men are still on the roof," her companion said hopefully. "They've got their axes. Ever seen the way they start swinging those axes when they think anything is smouldering? My God, they do as much damage as the fire. Last fall, September, no, it was October, my aunt's kitchen caught fire. No, I'm a liar, it was September. . . ."

They heard Brownlee calling "Paul!" as they neared Third Avenue. They turned to see him running along the street toward them, his suit stained and torn at the knee, his hair dishevelled, his excited face streaked with sweat and smoke. He caught up with them, looked at Rona and clapped his hand on Paul's shoulder. He regained his breath painfully. "Paul——" he began, then as he looked at Rona he hesitated. He controlled his excitement. "I'll phone you at the Tysons'?" he asked Paul. "That's where you are taking her now?"

Paul nodded, watching Roger Brownlee carefully.

Rona was watching him, too. She said quietly, "Orpen is dead."

Brownlee stared at her. Then he nodded.

Rona turned away and began walking to the corner. Once, she glanced over her shoulder at the house with its broken windows and blackened roof. "It was the telephone call," she said. "He was so sure. So sure they'd believe his lie. He almost believed it, himself. When they didn't, he admitted his guilt. . . . To them. Not to us."

Paul Haydn didn't even try to make sense of what she was saying. He must make her think of something else.

"Barbara," he said suddenly, "we'll go and collect Barbara."

"Barbara? Oh, yes . . . " Then she said, half to herself, "There's always a Barbara, isn't there?" Her pace quickened.

He hailed a taxi on Third Avenue. The streets were alive with traffic. People dressed in fresh bright clothes filled the sidewalk.

"And Bobby . . ." Rona was saying. "We must call the hospital." She was entering her own world again.

"Yes, we'll do that," Paul said reassuringly. "By the way, did you get a doctor for that throat of yours? What did he say?"

Rona almost smiled. "I wasn't to talk much," she said.

"Okay, I'll do the talking for the rest of to-day," he said. He smiled, too. But as he lit a cigarette, his hands were unsteady, and he found he couldn't talk. All he could do was to sit silently beside Rona in the taxi, to pretend not to be watching her face.

As they approached the street where Rona's apartment lay, she looked at him. "I'll need some clothes," she said. "I can't go on borrowing Peggy's."

He redirected the cab driver. "Shall I wait down here?" he asked her, as the taxi drew up at her door. "Or shall I come up and telephone the hospital while you pack?"

"Yes," she said. "I don't want to go up alone." She looked at the steps and hesitated. She thought, this is the first memory I destroy, this is the first piece of self-pity to be discarded. She went up the front steps, opened the door, and started climbing the stairs. Last night, she began to think in spite of herself, last night . . . But Paul's voice was behind her, making small jokes, asking questions, forcing her to listen to him, drawing her thoughts away from everything except the present.

Even his voice, telephoning in the hall, reassured her. She snapped the lock of the small suitcase quickly, made certain that she had packed everything she needed, and then went to join him in the hall. I'll sub-let this apartment, she was thinking, I never want to sleep here again.

"It's good news?" she asked Paul, seeing the relief on his face, the real smile in his eyes.

"Yes," he said. "The worst is over, now." He took the suitcase.

She stood for a moment, looking at the hall. It's all over, she was thinking, the worst and the best. All over. Then under the shadow of the hall table, she saw something. She picked it up. It was Scott's hat. This was where he had dropped it last night. . . .

"Will it ever be over?" she cried suddenly, her face tense, her body stiff with fear. She threw the hat away, and turned and ran into the kitchen. She began to cry, at first quietly and then with a deep terrifying sobbing.

Paul dropped the suitcase. He followed her, and halted at the door. I may lose her forever, he thought. If I do what I want to do, I may lose her forever. He remembered the fear in her arm as he had held it in Orpen's room, the way she had taken her hand so quickly from his as they reached the foot of the fire escape, the refusal of all physical help, all physical touch.

I may lose her forever, he thought again. But he stepped forward and took her in his arms. He felt the warmth of her slender body, saw the soft dark hair and the white brow, the curve of the smooth cheek. He stood, holding her, until the sobs had quieted. And even when she had stopped crying, they stood together in silence.

At last, she drew back. She looked up at him, then. She saw the worry in his eyes, the drawn lines at the side of his mouth. He turned away abruptly and went into the hall. He stood waiting for her at the door, the suitcase in his hand. He avoided her eyes. And when he spoke, his voice was studiedly impersonal.

342

You're a fool, he was thinking, a fool to be afraid you might lose her. You never had her to lose.

By the time the long ride to the Tysons' apartment was over, he believed that. But he had control of his emotions again, and he could force a smile and even make a joke or two.

I'll wait at the apartment, he decided, until Jon arrives to take charge. And then I'll fade out. But this time—and he was thinking of that morning—this time, I'll stay out.

CHAPTER TWENTY-SEVEN

"It will take about six weeks," Jon was saying to Roger Brownlee and Paul Haydn. "Then Bobby will be up and around. If all goes well," he added. But it's got to go well, it's got to. . . . At least, Bobby now had a chance. Last night, he hadn't even that. Only twenty hours ago—Jon glanced at the clock disbelievingly. And then he became aware again of his visitors. "Sorry," he said, "I've been talking ever since you got here. I guess I'm sort of lightheaded." He smiled apologetically and brought over the drinks he had poured. "God!" he said suddenly. "A disaster hits like a cyclone, doesn't it?" And when you get through it, you can't quite believe that this was really you, in a certain place, at a certain time. He looked at the clock again and shook his head.

"I won't stay long," Brownlee said. "I only——"

"No, no. It wasn't that," Jon said quickly. "I'm just trying to figure out what happened to twenty hours of my life. But there's no answer to that, is there?"

"Except that you got through them," said Brownlee. He glanced at Paul Haydn, who was silent. Ever since Brownlee had arrived, Paul had scarcely spoken. "I hope I didn't trouble you by coming up here, but I decided against phoning my news to Paul. I thought I'd better see him to tell him what happened this afternoon. And frankly," he admitted, looking at Paul, "I wanted to find out how Rona was. I've got a lot of guilt about her. She ran into more trouble than any one of us could have guessed."

"Rona seems much better than I expected," Jon said. "In

fact, I'm a bit amazed. But women are . . ." Again he shook his head helplessly. He was thinking of Peggy.

"Yes," Brownlee agreed. "I remember a Frenchman telling me during the war—he had been connected with the Resistance in occupied France—that the biggest surprise to him in the whole campaign had been the women. They could take more punishment than men. He'd send a girl on a dangerous mission—they did a lot of night courier jobs—and she'd run into trouble, nothing too serious but just enough to fray a man's nerves into making a false move, and she'd not only get through her brush with the Gestapo, but next morning she'd be standing in her kitchen, trying to cook a dinner and blaming the Boches for the scarcity of vegetables."

Paul Haydn said, half-angrily, "It isn't as easy as that." If the Frenchman had been in love with the girl, he wouldn't have talked so glibly about her.

"The Frenchman didn't say it was easy," Brownlee said, watching Haydn. "He only admitted he wouldn't have been in a state of mind to remember what went into a soup pot."

Jon looked in the direction of the hall. "Listen!" he said gently. Barbara was having supper in the kitchen. She was laughing, that long series of rippling gurgles which drew a smile even at this distance to the faces of the men in the living-room. "Rona's cooking seems kind of comic," Jon said.

"She's going to stay here meanwhile?" Brownlee asked. "What are your plans for the summer?"

"I've decided to take that job at summer school, after all." Doctors' fees, hospital bills—insurance was never enough, somehow. "Peggy can take the children to the country as we arranged. That will be the best thing for Bobby. It might be a good thing for Rona too. But then, there's her job at *Trend*. . . . It all depends on what she decides to do. She's welcome to stay with us as long as she wants. In fact, we need her."

"That sounds like a solution," Brownlee said. One solution, he thought, as he looked at Paul Haydn. "What's worrying you, Paul?" he asked frankly.

"Is she still in any danger? From Orpen's friends?"

That isn't the only thing that's worrying you, Brownlee thought. He answered evenly, "She might have been. But Orpen's dead. And anything he told her won't be important
344

now. We know more than he had time to tell her. And they know that we know."

There was a pause. Jon was looking startled, as if he hadn't realised that there might still be danger for Rona.

Paul stared gloomily at a faded rose on the carpet.

"Judge for yourself, Paul," Brownlee said. "Here's the story I came to tell you. Perhaps it will stop you worrying. When I left you and Rona, I pounded my way up the fire escape. It took a little time, for I'm no good at heights, and it was a rickety kind of staircase. Normally, I wouldn't have climbed it for a fifty-dollar bet." He lit a cigarette and his face became serious, although there was still a touch of humour in his voice. "I reached the window, and scrambled in with some difficulty, and ruined a perfectly good suit. But Orpen didn't seem to be appreciative of my efforts. He ignored me completely. He was rushing between the two rooms, selecting papers and books, thrusting them into a suitcase. I must say the humour of the situation struck me—here were his friends trying to smoke him out, and there was I, one of the people who hate his guts, trying to persuade him to get down that fire escape. The door was beginning to kindle, and little leaps of flame were running along the cracks. In a few minutes, the whole door would go up in a sheet of fire. But he didn't see the funny side, at all. He didn't even see that, if I had come to steal his damned suitcase, I could have knocked him on the head and made off with it down the fire escape. True, I was interested in the suitcase. But I was much more interested in Comrade Orpen himself. He was worth fifty suitcases. Perhaps he knew that."

Then Brownlee's voice became grim. "The smoke was increasing. Just as I thought I'd really have to hit him on the head and carry him out, the firemen came up the escape and started hacking away at the window frame. One of them shouted to us to come out. I obeyed, because you just don't argue with a fireman when he has a job to do. But Orpen was trying to open a safe he had hidden at the back of a bookshelf. So a couple of men jumped into the room and grabbed him and forced him back toward the fire escape, just as the door disappeared and the flames entered his room. Orpen was shoved out on the fire escape beside me. I started climbing down. Orpen was yelling, 'The suitcase, the suit-
345

case.' One of the firemen, perhaps to humour him, perhaps to get him down without any trouble, said 'Okay, fellow. Here she comes,' and he threw it through the window at Orpen's feet."

Brownlee paused. "I was looking back at Orpen. I saw the suitcase land and snap open. Orpen bent to close it, but he moved too quickly and he fell against it. The suitcase toppled on the edge of the fire escape and everything began to spill out of it. Something heavy—a steel box, I think—smashed down a few steps and then bounced between the railings into the courtyard. And the loose things scattered around at his feet, and hundreds of sheets of paper floated around and then blew over the tree in the yard. I began to laugh. Yes, I was laughing. And at that moment, he straightened up, still holding the lid of the suitcase so that it dangled from his hands. He looked at me. Then he looked at the city. He dropped the suitcase. And then he swung himself over the rail, and he let go, and he fell."

There was a pause.

Then Paul said, "Did he know who you were?"

Brownlee shook his head. "No. I could have been—anybody."

"Was that his reason?" Jon asked.

Brownlee said, "I don't know. I've thought of ten reasons. By to-morrow, I'll have thought of another five. Yet there's one reason I keep coming back to. It's the only one that makes any sense when I start thinking myself into Orpen's character, Orpen's beliefs. Then, I see his death as a confession. A confession of heresy, a confession of treachery to the Party."

Paul leaned forward. "That's almost what Rona said. She called his death an admission of guilt. To them. Not to us."

"What else did she say?" Brownlee asked quickly.

"Not very much. To be quite frank, I was trying to get her mind away from Orpen. She did mention a telephone call, though. She seemed to think it was important."

Brownlee nodded as if he had already learned about that. For a moment or two, he sat quite silent. Then he said, "Rona was right. Orpen was trying to justify himself by that call, but his friends didn't believe him. Their reply was to put their plan into operation right away. The attempt to burn his room and destroy his records was a very plain answer."

"A cold-blooded answer," said Jon. He was thinking of his pupil Robert Cash, who would never believe this story. Cash was a romantic beginner in Communism, still seeing it in its most idealistic stage. Even Scott Ettley had been only half a Communist compared to the professional like Orpen. But Orpen had travelled the full road. He not only understood but accepted its final logic. "Yet Orpen must have thought of escape. The suitcase—his attempt to gather his documents together. . . . Why didn't he go on down that stairway, search for all the papers that had been scattered, and then disappear as he had plann——" Jon broke off. "But of course," he added, "where could he go? What could he do? He rejected our world, and his world had condemned him. Is that it?" He looked at Brownlee for confirmation.

"Partly. But only partly. You are forgetting that Orpen was the complete Communist: he was a fully initiated member of a fanatical primitive religion. Recently, he had obviously committed some heresy. Whatever it was, it must have been something that the Party feared so much that it had to be rooted out at once and destroyed. Orpen was in the last stage of his revolt—perhaps it even had become only a protest against the sentence passed on him—when he packed that suitcase and thought of escape. But as he stood on that narrow iron platform with the empty suitcase dangling from his hand and watched his escape fail so ludicrously, his revolt was over. And with the end of his revolt, he returned to complete obedience. The Party was everything and he was nothing. He was guilty; even the suitcase which he now dropped at his feet was a witness against him. His escape and rebellion would have weakened the Party, just as his death would strengthen its discipline. So he admitted his guilt, fully, calmly, obediently. And he not only accepted the sentence that had been passed on him, but he went out to meet it. He executed himself."

Again there was silence in the room.

"And what was in that suitcase?" Jon asked at last.

"It gave the FBI a fine paper-chase."

"You don't know if there was anything valuable after all?"

"We won't be told," Brownlee said with a smile. "Nor will we be told what the safe contained."

"Then the room wasn't burned out?"

"Only badly damaged. The firemen pumped a lot of water into it."

"That's going to be disappointing for Orpen's friends," Paul said thoughtfully.

"Yes. The police stopped one man trying a little too hard to get up to see the remains. He said he was a reporter. Another tried to climb the fire escape with a camera. I shouldn't be surprised if a lawyer has appeared on the scene by this time, claiming to represent Orpen's estate and wanting all his private papers intact."

"Then there *is* something valuable in the safe," Jon said.

"Looks like it."

Paul said, "One day we'll see the results when we pick up the morning paper and read about some new exposure of the enemy working underground—a sabotage plan discovered, a propaganda ring shown up, a carefully staged riot prevented, an attempt to creat a 'revolutionary situation' beaten. And we'll make a guess or two that we saw the beginning of that. It's about all we'll ever know."

"That's about all," Roger Brownlee agreed. "But the evil that men do lives after them. . . . Orpen isn't dead yet, to a lot of people." He rose, and held out his hand. "You at least can forget him," he said to Jon.

"I'll see you to the door," Jon said.

"I must go too," Paul said.

Jon looked at him. "No, you don't. I've got some things I want to talk to you about."

But Haydn followed them into the hall.

"Did you hear of Paul's idea about giving up his job?" Jon asked. "He says he's going to leave *Trend*. Isn't that drastic? I'm against it."

Roger Brownlee halted at the kitchen door. "Yes, he told me to-day." He looked at Barbara in her high chair, and Rona sitting opposite her. "Hello, you two! How's that egg custard, Barbara?" Ghastly, he thought, as he looked at the yellow goo in the rose-painted dish. But then he wasn't an egg custard or milk pudding addict. Barbara seemed to be thriving on it, though. She turned her round pink face to

mile at him as she took another spoonful. She aimed for her
mouth but the spoon jabbed against her cheek. "Keep your
eye on it," he advised her. "It goes in the front door. I've
tried for years, but the ear is no good at all."

"Funny man?" Barbara asked Rona, and let her jawline be
wiped free of custard.

Rona looked at the men grouped in the doorway. "Yes,"
he said, and she began to smile.

"That's Barbara's polite way of trying to evade the fact
that she didn't understand one word you said," Jon explained.
Then he grinned as he added, "She must like the look of your
face, though, or she wouldn't have been polite."

Brownlee said, "The only women who like the look of my
face are always under two years old." He was watching Rona
as he spoke. "Good-bye," he said, giving them both a warm
smile as he turned away.

"Frankly, Paul," he said, stopping in the hall to continue
Jon's discussion, "I don't think you should give up your job,
yet. I don't know—and I hope I'm wrong—but I've a hunch
that a lot of us may have to give up our jobs soon enough."
Then he moved towards the door. "After all, you've been
doing useful work at *Trend*, and we need loyal editors. No
good letting the Blackworths and Murrays have a clear field.
That's how your boss Weidler sees it, I'm sure. I know you
were pretty upset this morning and wanted some action,
but . . ." His voice faded.

Rona, watching Barbara finish the custard and try to scrape
the rose off the plate, heard the distant good-bye's being made.
Suddenly, she rose and went to the kitchen door. "Paul,"
she called. "How does the story end?"

Paul came back. "The story?"

"The hippopotamus with the hat and the cherries and the
bow?"

"Blue bow," Barbara prompted.

"She's been asking me all morning to finish it. And I can't."

Paul said awkwardly, "I guess I—I don't know the end. I
got stuck, too."

Behind them, Barbara said, "Tell me a story, tell me a
story." She tried to struggle down from the high chair.

Jon returned. "Come on, Paul, let's have another drink. I
349

need one. You go ahead and pour it, while I call Peggy. And invent an end to that story, or we'll never get this bundle to bed." He lifted Barbara before she could fall, and carried her toward the telephone.

Rona said, "What did Roger Brownlee mean?" She looked at the table, lifted Barbara's plate and then set it down again. "Did he mean you were going away? Again?" She couldn't bring herself to say the word *war*. Instead, she said, "Does he think there will be—trouble?"

Paul said, "He's a pessimistic kind of optimist."

But no fool, she thought, no fool. She looked up at Paul. "Oh, no, Paul. Oh, no!"

"Time to worry about that when we come to it—if we come," he said gently.

"Yes," she said. She met his eyes. And she smiled for him. The tears in her eyes were for him too. She held out both her hands. "Oh, Paul!" she said.

Helen MacInnes

Born in Scotland, Helen MacInnes has lived in the United States since 1937. Her first book, *Above Suspicion*, was an immediate success and launched her on a spectacular writing career that has made her an international favourite.

'She is the queen of spy-writers.' *Sunday Express*

'She can hang up her cloak and dagger right there with Eric Ambler and Graham Greene.' *Newsweek*

Agent in Place

The Snare of the Hunter

Assignment in Brittany

North from Rome

The Salzburg Connection

The Venetian Affair

The Unconquerable

Neither Five Nor Three

Pray for a Brave Heart

Decision at Delphi

The Double Image

and My True Love

Message from Málaga

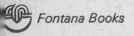 *Fontana Books*

Fontana Paperbacks

Fontana is a leading paperback publisher of fiction and non-fiction, with authors ranging from Alistair MacLean, Agatha Christie and Desmond Bagley to Solzhenitsyn and Pasternak, from Gerald Durrell and Joy Adamson to the famous Modern Masters series.

In addition to a wide-ranging collection of internationally popular writers of fiction, Fontana also has an outstanding reputation for history, natural history, military history, psychology, psychiatry, politics, economics, religion and the social sciences.

All Fontana books are available at your bookshop or newsagent; or can be ordered direct. Just fill in the form and list the titles you want.

FONTANA BOOKS, Cash Sales Department, G.P.O. Box 29, Douglas, Isle of Man, British Isles. Please send purchase price, plus 8p per book. Customers outside the U.K. send purchase price, plus 10p per book. Cheque, postal or money order. No currency.

NAME (Block letters)

ADDRESS